PRAISE FOR JOY AVERY

"Talented author Joy Avery regales her readers with a well-written story and a plot twist that validate her place among the great storytellers of romance."

—Brenda Larnell, RomanceinColor.com

"There are few things more exciting than a Joy Avery book; it is sensuous, exciting, and a veritable utopia of beautiful prose."

—Stephanie Perkins, Book Junkie Reviews

"When I read a book by Joy Avery, whether it's a novella or a longer story, I'm always captivated by the way she writes her characters. Their personalities jump off the pages, and I feel as if I'm right there in the story with them. You can always count on her to take your imagination to another level and [write] a romance that makes you want to believe in true love."

—Shannan Harper, *Harper's Court Literary Blog*

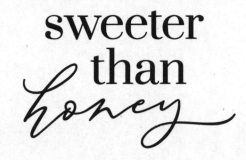

sweeter than honey

OTHER TITLES BY JOY AVERY

Honey Hill

Something So Sweet

Indigo Falls

His Until Sunrise (Book 1)

His Ultimate Desire (Book 2)

The Lassiter Sisters

Never (Book 1)

Maybe (Book 2)

Always (Book 3)

The Cardinal House

Soaring on Love (Book 1)

Campaign for His Heart (Book 2)

The Sweet Taste of Seduction (Book 3)

Written with Love (Book 4)

Additional Titles

In the Market for Love

Smoke in the Citi

Cupid's Error

One Delicate Night

A Gentleman's Agreement

The Night Before Christian

Another Man's Treasure

Hollidae Fling

Collaborations

A Bid on Forever (Distinguished Gentlemen)

Sugar Coated Love (Carnivale Chronicles)

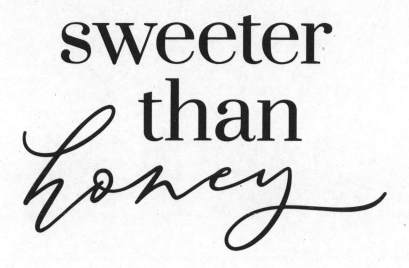

sweeter than honey

Honey Hill

JOY AVERY

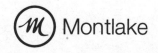

Montlake

Text copyright © 2022 by Joy Avery
All rights reserved.

Published by Montlake, Seattle

www.apub.com

Amazon, the Amazon logo, and Montlake are trademarks of Amazon.com, Inc., or its affiliates.

ISBN-13: 9781662500848
ISBN-10: 166250084X

Cover design by Hang Le

Printed in the United States of America

sweeter
than
honey

CHAPTER 1

Rylee Harris died a quick and rather painful death.

Well . . . she didn't technically die, but the second her friend, hairstylist, and now honeypot slayer snatched the wax strip from between her thighs, Rylee was sure she'd been close enough to death to claim it.

"Stop!" Rylee's voice vibrated the lavender-colored walls inside the small room when Happi Daniel's eager fingers gripped the corner of the second strip. Clamping her trembling legs shut and trapping Happi's hand just in case the woman got a notion to yank, she said, "No more." A tear escaped the corner of her eye. "I'm done!"

Happi's gaze met Rylee's. "I've only completed one side. Do you really want to walk around with one bald and one hairy coochie lip?" Happi asked.

Rylee would have laughed had she not been experiencing such discomfort. "Yes. I'll shave when I get home."

"Come on, Ry. Another quick yank, and you'll be done."

Rylee glared across the room at her snickering best friend, Lunden Pierce, soon-to-be Cannon. As usual, not a single auburn hair stood out of place on Lunden's head, her makeup was applied flawlessly, and her brown skin glowed. In addition to being the holder of all Rylee's secrets—well, the majority of them—Lunden led their lovely small

North Carolina town as mayor. Honey Hill, where friends were family and family was everything.

How had she allowed the woman to talk her into this? Especially when Rylee had no one waiting at home for her to showcase a freshly plucked vagina to. But even when she was married, she'd never done this. And with 1,000 percent certainty, she'd never do it again.

"This is your fault," Rylee growled.

Lunden's brown eyes widened. "My fault? How's it my fault? You're the one who decided you wanted to do this after reading about it on Ms. Estella's blog. I simply agreed to come for support."

Ms. Estella ran the town's nighttime-attire shop, with a not-so-secret room in the back where you could score anything from role-playing costumes to crotchless panties, of which, after this, Rylee just might need a pair. The sixty-something, Harley-driving, leather-wearing grandmother also penned a blog called *The Untamed Kitten*. Her recent post was what had gotten Rylee into this predicament.

Exhilarating, my ass. Ms. Estella and that damn blog. Always urging people to try new things. Rylee made a note to leave a comment. Anonymously, of course.

"Well, what you should have done was talk me out of it. You know how impulsive I can be sometimes." She had adoption papers for an elephant in Africa, a humpback whale in Maui, and a loggerhead sea turtle named Wet Willy to prove it. Oh, and how could she forget the time she'd paid $200 to name a bald eagle? Impulsive.

"Let's finish this," Happi said. "Another twenty seconds, and you're done. Just relax. Take a deep breath. Imagine you're on a tropical island, sipping your favorite drink."

That was easier said than done. Placing a death grip on the white sheet draped across her lap, she reclined back. "D-don't tell me when you're going to do it; just do it," Rylee said in an unsteady voice.

"Okay," Happi said.

Rylee's legs relaxed as she did as Happi advised.

Inhale, exhale.

Inhale, exhale.

Rylee could see the turquoise-blue beach water, hear the ocean waves crashing against the rocks, smell the flower-scented air, feel the pink sand between her toes, taste the sweetness from the fruity concoction the ultrasexy, handsome bartender delivered to her, wearing nothing but a fig leaf.

But not just any ole bartender. Where would be the fun in that? Plus, there were no limitations in regard to fantasies, so like an Olympian of fantasizing, she went for gold.

In her head, she saw just one man. Sheriff Canten Barnes. Butterflies fluttered in her stomach just from thinking about Honey Hill's top cop, her brother's best friend, and the man she couldn't get out of her system, despite how hard she'd tried.

Rylee's attraction to Canten held an intensity she hadn't experienced in a long, long while. Something she didn't want to feel, because even though her husband, Lucas, had died nearly five years ago, the magnetism toward Canten felt like betrayal. And not only that, but she'd vowed to never fall for another man whose profession placed him in harm's way.

Granted, their town couldn't quite be considered a cesspool of crime. Unless, of course, you considered the occasional trespassing alpaca, nut-tossing albino squirrel, or jaywalking peacock.

Snatch.

Rylee wanted to scream, but the muscles in her throat seized. A rainbow of colors exploded in front of her eyes, and she was sure she would pass out. Earlier, Happi had stated she recommended four sessions total, something about getting the hair down there in the same growth cycle. All Rylee wanted to know was, Who in their right mind would ever subject themselves to such torture a second, third, and fourth time? Definitely not her.

"See, that wasn't so bad, was it?" Happi asked. "Now you're as smooth as a baby's bottom."

Finally finding her voice, Rylee croaked out, "I will never ever again in life make another hasty decision."

Yet somehow, the statement didn't ring true for any of them, because they all laughed. Lunden's cell phone rang, calming them.

"Excuse me, ladies. This is my honey calling. I'm probably going to talk dirty to him, so I'll be excusing myself now."

Once Lunden left the room, a smile on her face bright enough to eclipse the sun, Happi said, "Now, that is the look of a woman in true love. Seeing how happy Quade makes her almost makes me want to reconsider my stance on romance and relationships."

After reconnecting with her childhood sweetheart, Quade Cannon, a little over a year ago, Lunden had gotten a second chance at love. Ask anyone in town, and they would all make the same claim: the two were meant for each other. Rylee's heart smiled anytime she saw them together, along with Lunden's son, Zachary—Rylee's godson—who Quade treated just like his own. Soon, Rylee would stand as Lunden's maid of honor, and she couldn't have been happier.

"One day, maybe you'll tell us why you have such a disdain toward love," Rylee said.

Sadness cloaked Happi's face. "One day."

Apparently, she'd gone through something traumatic or at least life altering enough to decide to shun relationships. Happi had been in Honey Hill several years and, as far as Rylee knew, hadn't gotten serious with anyone in all that time, which was sad, because Rylee had the perfect man for her. Her brother, Sebastian. He, too, seemed determined to grow old alone. In her opinion, they would be perfect together. And Rylee was sure her notorious matchmaking mother—who regarded both her children still being single as an atrocity—would agree.

"So what's up with you and the sheriff?" Happi said.

The question snatched Rylee from her thoughts. "W-what do you mean?"

"I heard through the grapevine a while back that you were sweet on the sheriff," Happi said. "But I didn't believe it—"

"Thank you, because I'm not," Rylee said, sounding a bit too defensive.

"—until I saw the two of you together the other day," Happi continued. "*Whew.* There's some serious chemistry there. He's into you, too, you know. You can tell by the way he looks at you."

The way he looks at me? How does he look at me? "You're being ridiculous," Rylee said with a wobbly smile. But out of curiosity—which had already killed one cat—she asked, "What do you mean? How does he look at me?"

"Like he's mesmerized by your presence."

Happi spritzed her with something minty and quite refreshing. As nice as it sounded—that she actually wielded the power to mesmerize a man, especially one as commanding as Canten—Rylee applied little credit to what Happi had said. Instead, she offered, "Canten and I are just good friends."

"I think I've heard that line before." Happi popped her forehead with her palm. "Oh, wait, I *know* I've heard it before. When Lunden said the same thing about Quade. Now look at them. About to be husband and wife."

For someone who held such negative views about relationships, Happi seemed determined to push others toward them. "That's different," Rylee said.

"Well, you better hurry up and make your move. I also heard through the grapevine that Katrina Sweeney is prowling for him again like the little prairie dog she is."

Rylee wondered if this all-knowing grapevine happened to be one that grew in Happi's aunts' flower shop. Bonita and Harriet Chambers.

Sixty-something, sassy, and shameless, and they never missed an opportunity to meddle, which held true for most of the town's elders.

Rylee had also heard rumors about the waitress at the Honey Hill Diner and Canten. But as far as Rylee could tell, they were just friends. Admittedly, there had been several times she'd been tempted to query her brother, Sebastian. Just out of curiosity, of course. She'd resisted because what—or who—Canten did was none of her business.

Besides, who could blame Katrina? The man was brave, intelligent, and one hell of a looker. But above all else, Canten was kind to everyone he met and oftentimes went out of his way to help others. He was also caring, especially when it came to the town and its sometimes-intolerable residents. And while he looked daunting and fierce, deep down he was a huge teddy bear.

"You're beaming, which can only mean one thing. You're thinking about the sheriff," Happi sang like a teasing schoolgirl.

So what if she was? It didn't mean a thing.

"When are you two going to stop pretending you're not into each other."

"No one's pretending anything." Besides, if Canten were into her, he would have made a move already, right? And even if he did, she wasn't ready to trust love again.

Canten loved Honey Hill, but some of its residents got on his nerves.

The last thing he should have been doing was running down Main Street in the middle of May on what felt like a thousand-degree day, trying to catch an inebriated Elmo Bishop—the town lush—who'd somehow thought taking a joyride in his granddaughter's princess-themed Power Wheels Jeep had been a good idea.

"You can't catch me, copper," Elmo said, sounding like a gangster-movie wise guy, buzzing past one of Canten's deputies.

Weren't those things only supposed to go around five miles per hour? With the way this kiddie vehicle moved, no doubt Elmo had souped it up. The man was an A-plus mechanic when he wasn't swimming in the bottom of a whiskey bottle. Canten stopped running, rested his hands on his hips, released a heavy sigh, and shook his head. At sixty-something, the man was too old to be acting out like this.

Canten squinted as the battery-powered car whizzed by. Was that a wig on the roll bar? *Please don't tell me the man was involved in a hit-and-run and someone is unconscious somewhere, missing a hairpiece.* He groaned at the possibility.

Canten sensed a shift in the atmosphere and glanced over his shoulder to see Lunden, the mayor of their fine town, alongside Rylee—Honey Hill's baker extraordinaire, his best friend's little sister, and the woman he never had to actually see to know she was near. Somehow, his body just knew.

While Rylee was only a couple of years younger than him, labeling her as his best friend's little sister kept things in clear perspective. In his head, if he continued reminding himself of this, it would keep him from focusing on the sexy, beautiful, kindhearted woman she—

"Watch out, Sheriff!" came from somewhere. "He's coming in hot."

Canten whipped his head around. *Oh shit.* There was nothing he could do but brace for impact.

In his drunken stupor, Elmo apparently mistook Canten for a parking space, because the man barreled into him, knocking him to the ground. The asphalt broke Canten's fall, and the Jeep came to a rest atop Canten, pinning him underneath. Luckily, the pavement beneath him hadn't broken anything else as far as he could tell.

"Uh-oh. Sheriff, you all right down there?" Elmo asked, peering down at him with spooked, bloodshot eyes. "Didn't mean to tap you. Doggone brake pedal switched sides with the gas pedal. Am I going to jail? Now, Sheriff, you know I don't do well in jail."

When Elmo belched, Canten prayed the man wouldn't spew on him. He bit back a string of cusses. Several of his deputies detained Elmo and lifted the battery-powered car off Canten. A pain shot through his knee, and he closed his eyes as if doing so would somehow alleviate the ache. It didn't.

When he opened his eyes again, Rylee had materialized like a gorgeous angel. Suddenly, the discomfort he'd experienced moments ago no longer existed. People gathered around him, hurling questions of concern, but he and Rylee became the only two in the sea of others.

Concern filled her soft brown eyes as she lowered to her knees beside him, inched a hand under his head, and formed a barrier between it and the scorching road.

"Are you okay?" she asked.

I am now. But he didn't dare let the declaration slip past his lips. Mesmerized, all he could do was stare at her. Had he told her how much he liked her hair? The short, curly style hadn't changed, but the color had. From a shocking blonde to a light-brown color that complemented her flawless almond-brown skin nicely. He suspected she'd be just as beautiful if her locks were a pumpkin orange. Some women simply had a natural beauty. Rylee was one of them.

She bit at the corner of her kissable bottom lip, and his heart skipped a beat. At thirty-eight, he was probably too old to have a crush on someone, but he was fairly certain he had an innocent schoolboy one on Rylee. But their connection would never be anything more than platonic.

For one, she was his best friend's little sister. Two, he cherished the friendship he and Rylee had cultivated. Lastly, he wasn't totally available. Rylee deserved someone who could give himself 100 percent. That wasn't him. He carried way too much baggage.

Admittedly, he hadn't been this drawn to a woman since Jayla. He banished the thought of his dead wife, one of the main reasons he was stuck in this torturous limbo state of wanting Rylee but not allowing himself to have her.

Shaking himself out of the trance, Canten said, "Yeah, I think so." What he didn't feel today, he would surely feel tomorrow.

"You probably should have moved out of the way," she said, chuckling softly.

"Yeah, you're probably right, but I was a little distracted." He didn't offer the fact his focus had been diverted by her; however, something in her gentle, almost hesitant smile told him she suspected she had been the reason why.

He made a move to get up because Rylee's hand had to be on fire. His back certainly was.

"Are you sure you should move? You should probably get checked out first," Rylee said.

He loved the way she always displayed so much concern for others. Whether it was delivering cupcakes to the sheriff's department for his staff, volunteering at Honey Hill's literacy program, or preparing special sugar-free treats for his father. That kind of selflessness was an endearing quality in any woman. No wonder he'd fallen so effortlessly for her. But he desperately needed to shake her from his system.

Sirens blared in the distance, and he groaned. That would certainly draw the remainder of the town that hadn't already congregated around them. "I'm good." He motioned to get up again.

"Such a stubborn ass," she said. "Well, will you at least let me help you?"

While he was wholly capable of getting up on his own, he couldn't resist the opportunity to be this close to her a little while longer. For him, Rylee was like a limited-edition, expensive bottle of the finest cognac. You placed it on the shelf to admire daily but would never dare open it to taste, because in the back of your mind, you knew you wouldn't be able to stop drinking after just one glass. Then you'd be left with nothing. *The story of my life.*

Canten allowed Rylee to drape his arm around her neck and help him to his feet. Knowing Honey Hill as he did, their interaction would definitely spark a few rumors, but he didn't care. As long as he knew the truth, that was all that mattered. And the truth was Rylee wasn't and never would be his. Something about that troubled him more than it should have because she would eventually be someone's.

Rylee groaned as she came to her full height. Alarm set in. "You okay? Did I hurt you?" He'd intentionally supported most of his own weight. Not that he was a huge guy, but he didn't dare risk knocking an inch of Rylee's well-put-together frame out of place.

"Let's just say you're not the only one who's experienced a traumatic episode today," she said. "And I'll leave it at that."

Since she'd punctuated the comment with finality, he didn't ask any questions. However, he was curious about what clearly taxing episode she'd gone through. "The way you groaned"—and a beautiful noise it had been—"it sounds like I should be helping you instead."

"You gonna scoop me up and carry me in front of all these people?"

"I am here to protect and to serve."

She grinned and patted his chest. "I'll see you later, Sheriff."

A second later she walked off.

Sliding on his mirrored sunglasses, Canten pretended to listen to the individuals recounting their version of the events. What he was actually doing was watching Rylee walk away. Her steps were a little slow and cautious as if she'd spent several hours in the gym doing squats. In preparation for Lunden and Quade's upcoming nuptials, possibly? Regardless of the reason, he didn't imagine her body could get any more appealing. That round behind, those shapely thighs, and those long runway-model legs would be a beacon for any man. And he loathed the thought of another being drawn to her flame in the same manner as he.

Rylee glanced over her shoulder as if to see if he was watching her walk away. Even with the sunglasses, he had a feeling she knew his eyes were planted on her, because her stride became more uniform and sexier. *Flirt.*

His gaze slid past Rylee and landed on Katrina Sweeney, standing next to her cousin and town troublemaker Hilary Jamison. The smile melted from his face. He regretted the day he'd offered Katrina a ride home from the diner during a rainstorm. It had been the one time they'd ever been spotted together, yet somehow, rumors of the two of them being a thing had surfaced from the innocent gesture. *No good deed goes unpunished.*

Hilary whispered something to Katrina, and they strolled off. After seeing him and Rylee together, maybe the townsfolk would link him to her. That particular tattle he didn't have an issue with.

Today, something had felt a little different between him and Rylee. Rylee's fret over him had come off as that of a concerned lover, not just a friend. Hell, maybe he'd imagined it. He had hit the ground pretty hard. Either way, he was grateful for her being in his life. Rylee's presence reminded him that he wasn't completely dead inside. He needed that because, often, he felt like nothing more than a shell.

After fielding numerous questions about his well-being, Canten moved away from the crowd and headed back to the department for some much-needed peace and to pop a couple of ibuprofen. While he was still in decent shape, his body wasn't as resilient as it had been in his twenties.

"*Sher-reef. Sher-reef Cun-tone,* might I have a sliver of your time?"

Canten pressed his lids together. That butchering of his name and that deep southern drawl could only come from one person. Herbert Jamison, the town's self-appointed monarch. There was no doubt in Canten's mind that this conversation would send him spiraling down a rabbit hole. He turned. "Mr. Her . . ." His words dried up at the appearance of the short, stout man, who looked as if he'd skinned a hot-pink leopard and fashioned the flesh into a too-tight, too-short pair of pants and a vest that threatened to put someone's eye out if Mr.

Herbert inhaled too deeply. Erring on the side of caution, Canten took a step to the side. "What can I do for you, Mr. Herbert?"

"Elmo is a town nuisance who should be locked up for endangering the lives of others. It's still drunk driving regardless of the vehicle. He nearly ran down Ms. Cortez outside the bread shop. Made her so mad she threw her good wig at him."

Ah. That explains the dangling hairpiece. What a relief.

Mr. Herbert continued, "And he did mow you down. Had you sprawled out on the ground like a saint at Sunday service. Not to mention the drunkard almost scuffed up my click-clacks."

Canten pushed his brows together. Knowing he would regret it, he asked, "Your click-clacks?"

Mr. Herbert jutted out his foot and showcased a black platform patent-leather-and-suede tasseled loafer. "Nice, right? Come by the shop and pick you up a pair. I'll give you a real good deal."

Mr. Herbert's idea of a real good deal was marking the item up by twice what it was worth, then offering a so-called discount. In all his years, Canten had never visited another store that offered a 2 percent–off sale. "I . . . um . . . don't think I could wear them as well as you do," Canten said.

"You're probably right. It takes a classic man to pull this look off." Mr. Herbert scanned Canten from head to toe. "You're more the modern type." He waved his hand through the air. "But anyway. Back to the matter at hand."

Mr. Herbert rested his hands on his waist, and sure enough, a button popped like a kernel of corn, whizzing past Canten. Mr. Herbert didn't acknowledge the wardrobe malfunction, and neither did Canten. But it was all he could do to hold back his laughter.

Already exhausted with the conversation, Canten said, "You can rest assured the situation is being handled, Mr. Herbert. And I want to thank you for your concern for the citizens of Honey Hill. I, personally, am extremely grateful to have you keeping an eye on things. You're an asset to the community. A true pillar." One thing Canten had learned about Mr. Herbert . . . the man loved praise.

Mr. Herbert's chubby brown cheeks swelled as he rocked back on his heels and beamed with pride. "Why, thank you very much." He tugged at his vest, which had risen a little too high. His voice rose in volume when he added, "I'm glad *someone* appreciates my efforts." Perhaps for the benefit of the passersby.

A second later, he cinched his lapels, held his head high with confidence, and moseyed back into his menswear shop with the grace of a king returning to his throne.

When Canten's cell phone vibrated in his pocket, it startled him. Sebastian's name flashed across the screen. Making the call active, he said, "What's up, man?"

"Damn, bro. You okay? I heard you got run over by a big-ass Jeep and was pinned underneath for like ten minutes and passed out."

It did not at all surprise Canten that an incident that had occurred less than twenty minutes ago had made it to his best friend, who was three towns over on a home-improvement job. Nor did it shock him that the details had become skewed. "It was a Power Wheels Jeep. But yeah, man, I'm good. And I didn't pass out."

There was a brief silence over the line before Sebastian burst into a laugh. "A Power Wheels Jeep? How the hell did you get run over by a Power Wheels Jeep? The top speed on those things is like three miles per hour."

More like five, but that was neither here nor there. To save face, Canten said, "Elmo must have put a Mustang engine in that thing or something. It was going at least sixty-five." A slight embellishment, but when you'd been run down by a battery-powered kiddie car, the story needed enhancing.

"Why didn't you get out of the way?" Sebastian asked.

Of course Canten couldn't say, *I wasn't paying attention because I was ogling your sister,* so instead, he went with, "I was making sure all the onlookers were safe."

"Huh," was all Sebastian said.

While it had been innocent, Canten waited for the man to mention something about how Rylee had come to his aid. He was sure whoever had told him about the incident hadn't left that part out. But Sebastian didn't bring it up.

"Well, as long as you're good," Sebastian said. "I'll holler at you later. Try to avoid any more speeding Power Wheels."

A second later, the line went dead.

"Sheriff?" crackled over Canten's radio. "Sheriff, you there?"

Canten keyed the radio attached to a loop on the shoulder of his shirt. "Go ahead."

"Um, Sheriff, you better hurry back. Ms. Cortez is here, and she's threatening to flatten Mr. Elmo in her dough sheeter if he doesn't replace her good wig."

Canten released a heavy sigh as he massaged his now-throbbing temple. *What a Monday.* Where was Rylee with her soothing presence when he needed her?

CHAPTER 2

Rylee couldn't have been more relieved when she slid into a booth at Finger Leafing Goode, the town's newest establishment, dedicated to serving fresh salads with ingredients sourced from local farmers. To most folks' surprise, the buffet-style restaurant with its green, orange, and yellow decor had been the buzz since its opening two months ago. Judging by the number of people in attendance, Honey Hill was no longer just a meat-and-potato town.

She'd desperately wanted to order a Ziploc bag of ice to plant at her crotch. Not only did it ache, it itched. Like a thousand fire ants were attacking her. Was this her punishment for intentionally trying to make Katrina Sweeney jealous? In her defense . . . *ha!* Who was she kidding? She had no defense.

Lunden stabbed a forkful of lettuce and brought it to her mouth. "We definitely have to talk about what just happened."

Ignoring her discomfort the best she could, Rylee said, "It was crazy, right? I don't think I've ever witnessed a Power Wheels move so fast. It's a miracle Canten didn't break something when he plummeted to the ground. *Hard.* Twenty dollars he didn't even lock up Mr. Elmo." That was the kind of person Canten was. He played hard, but it was all a front. *A gentle giant.* The thought made her smile.

"You know that's not what I'm talking about," Lunden said around a mouthful of veggies.

Rylee had figured as much. She'd just hoped to divert this conversation away from herself and Canten and their . . . unique, for lack of a better word, connection.

"You could barely walk when you hobbled out of Happi's shop, but you sprinted over to Canten like you saw gold at the end of a rainbow."

Rylee's lips parted to dispute Lunden's claim, but there was no use. Lunden knew her better than anyone in this town. Her actions had simply been yet another display of her impulsiveness. "When he went down, raw panic I can't explain thrashed through me. My first instinct was to go to him." Apparently, adrenaline had kicked in and had numbed her down there, because she'd felt nothing as she'd dashed toward him. Unfortunately, the feeling had come back, times two. She needed to sit in an ice water bath. "In hindsight, that probably wasn't a good idea. Especially with the way this town talks."

"That's what we do when it comes to people we care about. We rush right in," Lunden said.

Yeah, fools rush in too.

Lunden continued, "Who cares what anyone has to say? It's none of their business."

"You're right." Rylee absently picked at her salad as she thought about what Happi had said at the shop. She recalled the way Canten had stared at her when he'd opened his eyes. Maybe she did mesmerize him. Or more likely, he'd been suffering a concussion and had been confused at the moment. Either way, she liked being admired that way, with tender eyes that seemed to see only her.

"I always know when you're thinking about him. You get this amazing glow," Lunden said.

Smashing back to reality, Rylee said, "I do not," fighting the smile threatening to break through. Inwardly, she admitted that maybe, just maybe, Lunden might be right. Whenever she thought about Canten, a feeling of euphoria washed over her. On occasion, she allowed herself not to feel guilty over it.

"You've admitted to me how you feel about Canten. Why won't you tell him you're crazy about him?" Lunden asked, her tone gentle.

Rylee's gaze lowered briefly. Once it settled on Lunden again, she said, "Lucas," in a voice so tiny she barely heard herself, as if saying his name too loudly would stir him in his grave.

When Lunden placed her fork down, pushed her plate away, interlocked her fingers, and rested her chin against them, Rylee knew they were about to enter into a deep conversation. One she wasn't sure she was up for right now.

"I know you have qualms about Canten's job, Ry, and its potential to put him in harm's way, but let's face it: Honey Hill is not exactly a crime-stricken community. You don't have to worry about his safety. Well, as long as there are no Power Wheels nearby."

They shared a laugh.

While Canten's job did concern her, because there was always that possibility, that wasn't it this time. "That's not it," Rylee said.

"Then what is it?"

Rylee swallowed hard, emotion welling inside her. "I'm the reason Lucas went back to Afghanistan." Her voice cracked, and a tear slid down her cheek when she said, "I'm the reason he's dead."

Did she deserve to be out here living her best life with Canten while Lucas lay in his grave, one she'd put him in? The thought brought forth more tears. Rylee swiped them away, hopefully before anyone could see.

"Oh my God, Ry, have you been living with that all of this time? Is that what you believe? That Lucas's death was somehow your fault?"

Rylee nodded, her words trapped in her throat by emotion.

Lunden reached across the table and squeezed Rylee's hand. "Listen to me. Extremists were responsible for what happened to Lucas. You are *not* responsible. You are not responsible," she repeated. "And I refuse to allow you to torture yourself because you think you are."

"But if it hadn't been for me, he would have never gone back," Rylee said.

For the next several minutes, Rylee told Lunden the story of how Lucas had ended up on another tour in Afghanistan. It was her pastry-school debt that had been drowning them. Her frequent talk of one day owning her own bakery. Her constant whining about money and financial freedom. There was so much more she could have told Lunden but didn't. The constant arguments. The days they'd gone without speaking, months without lovemaking. So much more. A tear escaped her eye.

"It was Lucas's decision, Ry."

"But I didn't stop him. A good wife would have stopped him."

"Were you ever given the opportunity? Hadn't he already committed before ever even telling you he'd done so?"

Well, there was that. Lucas had claimed to have done it for the money, but Rylee often wondered if he'd actually done it to get away from her. Their marriage had been in trouble, but she'd loved Lucas and had hoped, prayed, things would get better. They hadn't. Though Lucas had never admitted it, the truth of the matter was he hadn't been happy for a while. Honestly, neither had she. Somewhere along the way, they'd lost each other. But she'd been willing to stick it out for as long as it took to find their way back to each other. They hadn't been given enough time.

"You were right, Lu, I am crazy about Canten. He's a *good* man. But he deserves a better version of me than I have to offer right now. Right now, our friendship has to be enough. Maybe one day I'll feel free enough to allow myself to love him and hope that he wants to love me back."

"He'd be a fool not to," Lunden said.

Rylee batted her eyes. "Okay, can we *please* talk about something else? Like your bachelorette party."

Lunden jabbed a finger at her. "Do not let Happi talk you into anything crazy. I just want to spend an evening with my girls, sip wine, eat delicious food, and laugh."

"I can't promise you anything," Rylee said. "It's—" She stopped abruptly when Canten entered with his father. The second their eyes met, butterflies fluttered in her stomach. Usually, seeing him made her all giddy. This time it didn't. It only fueled the guilt she already felt, draining her rather than energizing her. He said something to his father, then headed in their direction.

Shit.

"Ladies," he said on approach.

Plastering a smile on her face, Rylee glanced up at him. Instantly, the gleam he'd worn vanished, and fine lines crawled across his forehead. Of course he would home in on the fact she'd been crying.

"You okay?" he asked.

"Yes. We're just having some girl talk." To redirect the conversation, she said, "You look refreshed. Getting plowed down by a Power Wheels make you hungry?"

By the serious expression on his face, it hadn't worked. His curious eyes moved to Lunden, who slid her gaze away and massaged the crook of her neck. With his focus firmly on Rylee again, he said, "Are you sure you're okay?"

"Yes, Sheriff." This time she offered him an authentic smile. "Now go. You're keeping your father waiting. Tell Senior I'll come over and say hi before I leave."

Canten gave a single nod and moved away. Her attention remained on him until he took a seat at a table located on the opposite side of the room. When he glanced in her direction, she turned away as if she'd been caught doing something she shouldn't have been doing. In a way she guessed she had been.

"What?" Rylee asked, noticing the way Lunden scrutinized her.

Lunden chuckled. "You can fight it all you want, but you two are inevitable," she said. "Take it from me—the universe will always get its way."

Rylee disagreed.

※

Canten listened as his father talked about his day so far at the barbershop. The man always had stories to tell. And had he told most of them to an outsider, they would have sworn Honey Hill was filled with crazies. Well, they wouldn't have been too far off base. They definitely had their share of loonies. Like drunk men who drove their granddaughters' Power Wheels through downtown.

In hindsight, instead of locking Elmo up long enough for Ms. Cortez to cool down, he should have allowed the woman to flatten him. Then Elmo would be feeling some of the discomfort he was experiencing now. A long, hot soak was in his near future.

"Son, you sure you're all right? You took quite the fall earlier. You look a little out of it. Did you hit your head?"

"I'm good," he said, sending an inconspicuous glance in Rylee's direction. *Just concerned.* As sheriff, showing interest in the residents of Honey Hill was part of the job. So when one of them appeared troubled, he was duty bound to help.

"She sure is a pretty thing, ain't she?"

Playing clueless, Canten said, "Who?"

"The only baker in town you can't seem to keep your eyes off of. She sure was awfully concerned about you when you hit the ground."

Canten had wondered when his father would bring that up. "That's what a friend does. Show concern."

"Mmm-hmm," Senior hummed.

To shift the conversation, Canten said, "Rylee's eyes were red like she'd been crying. I'm just concerned. As a friend," he added.

20

Worry lines crawled across Senior's forehead. "Did you ask her what was wrong?"

Canten wasn't the only one with a soft spot for Rylee. When his father had been diagnosed with type 2 diabetes, Rylee had started carrying a line of diabetic-friendly treats at her shop. Going a step further, she occasionally popped into the barbershop with his favorite red-velvet cuppies—mini cupcakes that were so delicious that, unless told, you wouldn't know they were sugar-free.

"She said nothing, but there's something." His gut and law enforcement training told him as much. If their conversation had really been emotional girl talk, wouldn't Lunden have been in tears too?

"Well, if you're so concerned about her, why don't you go over there and demand she tell you what's going on? Course, you're liable to come back with a lump on your noggin from demanding anything from a Honey Hill woman. They can be fiery."

Didn't he know it. And stubborn as hell. "If she says she's fine, she's fine," Canten said, tossing a cursory glance in her direction just in time to see her heading toward the bathroom.

"Why don't you tell her, son?"

Canten returned his attention to his father. "Tell her what?"

"How you feel about her. A blind man can see the attraction between you two. Y'all could help each other."

Canten assumed his father was alluding to the fact they'd both lost spouses to violence.

"You're single. She's single. She doesn't seem to date. You definitely don't date. It's kind of like you're waiting on each other," Senior said.

"Give it a rest, old man."

Of course his dad didn't listen. "Is it because of Jayla?"

Canten's eyes left his father, his appetite suddenly gone.

"Son, I get that you still feel honor bound to your late wife. That's commendable. But life is passing you by. You deserve to be happy. It kills me to see you denying yourself that happiness. Kinda seems like you're punishing yourself. You're not guilty for her death."

"Then who is, Pop?"

"The damn lowlife coward who pulled the trigger."

"If it hadn't been for me pushing her to . . ." His words dried up. A second later, he closed his eyes, took a deep breath, and blew out the anger swelling inside him. One decision, his decision, had led to her death. What he hadn't told his father, told anyone, including Sebastian, was that not only had he lost Jayla that night, but he'd lost their unborn child. For that, he could never forgive himself. And he could never accept this happiness his father felt he deserved.

"Blame is a heavy burden to bear, son. Even for a strong man like you."

Needing to end this conversation, he pointed to his father's bowl. "Eat your salad. You're talking crazy; I think your blood sugar is falling."

Obviously, his father took the hint, because his worried expression softened, and he looked like his normal carefree self again.

Senior barked a laugh. "Well, my blood sugar's not going to rise eating this rabbit food. When you said you were taking me for something filling, I thought you meant a rib eye and a baked potato." He forked at his lettuce. "Not plate decoration. This thing doesn't even have meat."

"What are you talking about? You have bacon *and* grilled chicken. And with your elevated blood pressure, old man, you should consider the bacon a bonus because you shouldn't be eating it."

"I've been eating bacon for as long as I've had teeth. And thanks to these fancy dentures, I still have teeth, so I'm gonna keep eating bacon," Senior said.

To lighten the mood even more, Canten said, "I thought you wanted to be around for your grandkids. Give 'em their first haircuts. Share all your wisdom."

Senior chuckled. "No offense, son, but at the rate you're going, I'll be too old to hold the clippers and too senile to recall any wisdom." Senior's brows knit. "Unless there's something you want to tell me."

Canten flashed his palm. "No one's pregnant."

Senior blew out an exasperated breath. "Are you even having sex, son?"

"Pop!" Canten scanned their surroundings to make sure no one had lent an ear to their conversation.

"Well, are you? I need to know if I should stop eating bacon."

Canten huffed. "Yes. I'm having sex. Plenty of sex. Backward, forward, side to side." If only that were true. Unfortunately, his sex life was as dry as the banana bread Ms. Jasper had brought to the church picnic last weekend.

"Wow, that sounds exhausting," came from behind him. "No wonder you eat so much. From the sounds of it, you need all the energy you can get."

Canten instantly recognized the voice as belonging to Rylee. He scowled at his smirking father, who'd undoubtedly seen Rylee approaching.

Rylee rustled a playful hand over his head. "It's good to know you take the *serve* part of your job seriously. I hope you take the *protect* part just as seriously."

Senior burst into laughter. "That's a good one, Rylee." He laughed some more.

Canten didn't embarrass easily, but his cheeks were a little warm. "You two should take this act on the road."

Rylee and his father chatted for a little while before she excused herself. He fought it, but his eyes had a mind of their own and followed her all the way back to her table.

Turning back to his father, Canten chuckled when he saw him digging through his salad. "What are you doing?"

"Picking out the pig. Something tells me I should stop eating bacon."

"Very funny."

Canten's and Rylee's eyes met through the oversize restaurant window. When she smiled, he smiled back. They had some serious chemistry going on. That was undeniable. He was glad Rylee had never acted on it, because he had no idea how to tell her they couldn't happen. At least, not without making things weird between them. Not without ruining a friendship he cherished.

CHAPTER 3

While Rylee wanted to repaint her bedroom, she just couldn't decide on a color. There were too many damn options. She stopped flipping through wall-paint sample cards when she thought she heard Canten pull into his driveway. Tossing the ring of colors aside, she peeped out the window. Yep, it was him, all right. She felt a little safer having Honey Hill's finest as a neighbor.

Instead of heading over now with the chicken Alfredo she'd prepared for him, she decided to let him get in and settled before bothering him. He eased out of his vehicle and hobbled to his door like an old man. Clearly, he was feeling the aftereffects of the spill he'd taken earlier. Maybe she should take him some pain reliever too.

The ringing phone drew her attention away from the window. Making the call active, she said, "Hey, Mom."

"Hi, dear. I'm not disturbing you, am I?"

"No, ma'am. Just looking out the window and admiring God's bountiful creations." And what a wonderful job he'd done with Canten Barnes. "Everything okay?"

"Yes, all is well. I've been busy today."

"Really? What all have you done," Rylee asked absently.

"Well, I organized the pantry, washed several loads of laundry, performed about ten minutes of yoga. Oh, and I've set you up on a blind date."

Rylee's brain had been on a five-second delay, but when her mother's words registered, she drew her attention from the window. Had her mother just said she'd set her up on a date? *How did I become a check mark on my mother's to-do list?* Typically, Sebastian was the target for these types of things. How had Rylee gotten a bull's-eye painted on her back? And how was the woman matchmaking from Florida? "You did what?"

"Before you overreact, just hear me out. He's a looker. Plus, you already know him. And he's been building up the nerve to ask you out."

I already know him? A flutter of excitement swirled in her stomach. Could her mother be talking about Canten? *Has he been building up the nerve to ask me out?* Her lips curled upward. "Who, Mom?"

"Leonard Jamison."

Rylee bolted to her feet. *Leonard Jamison!* Apparently, she'd been single for so long her mother assumed she no longer had standards. Of all the men her mother could have suggested for her . . . *Leonard Jamison. Really?* The man's ego was the size of Mars. Not to mention he was a Jamison. They were all a little cuckoo.

Pacing back and forth, Rylee kneaded at the tightness in her shoulder. "Mom—"

"He owns that nice car dealership, and I hear he's opening a second one soon."

Rylee didn't care if he opened a hundred new dealerships. "Mom—"

"And did I tell you he's building a house? I hear it's huge!"

Still not interested. "Mom—"

"And he doesn't have any kids."

With her patience paper thin, Rylee was determined to tell her mother to butt out of her love life, but what actually came out was, "Mother, I'm seeing Canten." The words flew past her lips so fast she hadn't even realized they were coming. It was like her mouth had been possessed by some evil spirit who clearly appreciated a good laugh.

Realizing the severity of what she'd just said, Rylee froze. *Oh God.* What had she been thinking? Ah, she knew. That she wanted no part of her mother's intrusive matchmaking scheme. *Leonard Jamison? Really, Mom.*

Rylee was about to double down on the comment until her mother squealed, causing Rylee to yank the phone from her ear. She couldn't afford to be deaf *and* dumb. Okay, she could still walk this back. All she had to do was start laughing hysterically, then tell her mother she'd only been joking. *Great idea.* Rylee drew in a deep breath and readied herself for the performance, but she stalled when she heard her mother . . . *sniffling?* "Mom, are you crying?"

"Yes." Her mother sniffled again.

"Why?"

"Because I'm just so happy. You've made me so, so happy."

Dear God. Her mother was crying. Actual boo-hoo tears. And she was to blame. What had she done? *You're a horrible daughter, Rylee Harris. And you're going to hell. And you're going to be forced to get a bikini waxing every single day.* She deserved it.

More sniffles.

Her mother spoke again. "I worried less about you before because I knew you had Lunden to lean on. But now that she's getting married, her priority will be her new husband. And with Sebastian away so much these days . . ." Her mother's words trailed off. "I'm just happy you have someone in your life."

Rylee's heart both swelled and sank. Swelled for the love her mother always showed her. Sank because she'd had no idea her mother had been so concerned about her well-being. "Mommy, you don't have to worry about me."

"A mother never stops worrying about her child."

Rylee tried to sound upbeat when she said, "But I'm fine."

"I know you are now, and I can worry less because you have Canten by your side. My prayers have been answered. Thank God, because I didn't want you to be with that nitwit Leonard Jamison."

Rylee stopped moving and eyed the phone as if she couldn't figure out how it had gotten into her hand. Placing it back to her ear, she said, "So why did you try to set me up with him?"

"Because I didn't want you to be alone far more."

Rylee pinched her lids closed. Dear God, what had she done to deserve this? *Told a big fat lie. What am I going to do?* Telling her mother the truth now would crush her.

With her tears dried up, her mother went on and on about how this news had made her day; how thrilled her father would be because he already loved Canten like a second son, anyway; how she couldn't be any more elated if she'd hit the lottery; and how she couldn't wait to tell everyone she knew that her daughter was dating the sheriff.

Rylee gasped. "*No!* Um, I mean, y-you can't tell anyone, Mom. Not a single soul. N-no one. Canten and I have chosen to keep things quiet until we ascertain where our relationship is going."

Why the hell was she burying herself even deeper in the hole of deception?

"Ascertain where your relationship is going?" Her mother laughed. "Goodness gracious, dear, you sound like one of those couples from a reality television show. They're all fake, you know. Just puppets paid to entertain."

Oh, if you only knew.

"Sweetie, you're dating the sheriff. You should be screaming it from the rafters. He's quite the catch."

That was the issue. She hadn't caught him. "Not a word, Mom, please."

Her mother sighed. "Very well. If that's how you want it, I promise not to tell anyone but your father. Your father and I don't keep secrets from each other."

"Of course you can tell Daddy. Just no one else." Overwhelmed, Rylee said, "Can I call you back, Mom? Someone's at the door." Clearly, she was a lie-churning machine today.

"Okay, dear. Love you. And I'm so happy for you and Canten. Give him my love, will you?"

"Love you too. Thank you, and I will. Remember, not a word."

Ending the call, Rylee collapsed down on the sofa and groaned. "What have I done?" When her parents came for Lunden and Quade's wedding in a couple of months, they would be expecting to see two happy couples. "This is bad. Really, really bad."

Wait. Maybe she could—no, Canten wouldn't go for that. Would he? If she asked nicely, maybe he would agree to pretend they were dating. Just until after the wedding. Pretending to be her significant other for two months wouldn't be so bad, would it? They were friends, after all, and friends helped each other out of jams all the time. She'd helped him off the ground earlier. That had to earn her some grace, right? *Ugh.* Who was she kidding? He would never go for such deception. Canten Barnes played it by the book.

Struck by genius, she bolted forward. "I got it." A week or two before her parents' arrival, she'd simply tell them she and Canten had decided to just be friends again. Give them an *it was me, not him* speech so they wouldn't hold any ill will toward him, and all would be fine. "Perfect!"

Rylee gnawed at her bottom lip. All she had to do was get Canten on board. At some point, she would have to mention to him what she'd done before her parents arrived. *He'll understand, right?* Especially when she explained the circumstances. She just had to figure out how to deliver the news without Canten thinking she was batshit crazy.

She ran a dozen scenarios in her head, none of them ending well. All the logistics made her head hurt. Luckily, she had a good month and a half to polish her plan. Actually, she had to have a plan first to polish it. The fact she had time made her feel a little better. For now, she pushed the lie to the back of her mind, retrieved the dish from the kitchen, and headed across the street.

A couple of minutes later, she stood on Canten's doorstep, thinking she probably should have called first. After a few raps with no answer, she assumed he'd fallen asleep or was avoiding visitors. But just as she turned to leave, the door crept open.

Canten flashed a wide smile, almost making her think he was happy to see her.

"Hey," he said, pulling a black T-shirt over his head.

The glimpse she caught of his midsection snatched her breath away. While she'd seen him shirtless before, this time the sight of his defined abs and trail of fine black hairs that disappeared beneath the waistband of the black underwear peeping out from the gray sweatpants he wore did something wicked to her body.

"Sorry, I almost missed you. I was in the shower," he said and held the screen door open. "Come in."

Rylee snapped from her trancelike stare. Oh, she would have loved to have been the soap that got to glide over his body. An image of him in a steam-filled room, water droplets cascading down his naked frame, made her dizzy. Pulling herself together, she said, "I want to bathe you." Her eyes widened. *Oh, sweet baby Jesus.* Had that really just slipped out? Obviously, she hadn't pulled herself tight enough. "Bother. I mean bother. I meant I don't want to *bother* you." *Dammit. Get it together.* "Of course I don't want to bathe you. That would be weird."

"You think?"

Didn't he? Before the prospect made her delirious with desire, she said, "Um, a little birdie told me you were having a rough day, so I figured I'd be neighborly and make you dinner." She pushed the dish toward him.

Accepting it, he said, "Get in here. I could use the company."

"Well, since you put it like that."

Rylee brushed past him, getting a whiff of his cologne and the smell of soap. *Mmm.* Was there anything better than a good-smelling man? Her eyes took in her surroundings. The wide-screen television attached to the wall was tuned to a music station playing soft jazz. The dark-gray curtains were drawn, and the room was dim as if he were trying to set a sensual mood.

"Are you expecting company?" she asked. "It's kinda romantic in here."

He chuckled. "Just trying to decompress from a hellacious day, where I got ran over by an elderly man driving a kid's battery-operated vehicle. But the night's looking up."

Rylee smiled softly, then followed him into the kitchen. For a bachelor, Canten kept his place immaculate. And it smelled amazing. She pushed her brows together. *And familiar.* "Is that one of Lunden's Power of Persuasion candles I smell?"

In addition to running their town, Lunden also owned a candle-making company. Her candles had recently been featured in several major magazines. The bold and daring scent palettes she created made her candles truly unique.

"Yeah. She brought it by the station today. Apparently, it is supposed to relax you after a trying day. I don't usually burn candles, but there was something oddly soothing about this one before I even lit it."

"I have one. Several, actually. It definitely works. After a long day at the bakery, I run a hot bath, light my candle, grab me a glass of wine, and unwind. Out of all her scents, this one is my favorite."

"That explains why it smelled so familiar," he said, placing the dish on the countertop. "Is this what I think it is?"

"After the day you've had, you don't think I'd bring you just any old thing, do you?"

"Damn, woman, I could kiss you right now. I'm addicted to your chicken Alfredo." He retrieved two plates from the cabinet, then silverware from the drawer. "I'm starving, and this smells amazing. You're joining me, right?"

Rylee was still stuck on the *kiss you* comment. She bet Canten's lips would feel like cotton against hers. *No! No, they wouldn't. They would feel like rough and painful sandpaper.* "Are you sure you want to share?"

"With anyone else, no. For you, I'll make an exception."

"Look at you being all gentlemanlike."

Rylee excused herself to wash her hands. On the way back from the bathroom, she noticed all the bedroom doors were open except one. In fact, she couldn't recall ever seeing that particular door ajar. Did the sheriff have a kinky room? She imagined opening the door and being greeted by handcuffs, ankle cuffs, nipple clamps, whips, feather teasers, blindfolds, rope, ball gags. A little turned on, she moved away.

When she returned to the kitchen, Canten had the table set. He'd even poured her a glass of wine. Just what she needed to calm her overactive libido. He'd poured himself what looked like cognac. Maybe she could get him drunk and then spring her news on him. Would agreeing under the influence be binding? She doubted it.

Like a true gentleman, he pulled out her chair. "Thank you," she said, easing down.

He was about to sit when his cell phone rang. "I have to take this. It's my pop."

"Absolutely," she said. While Canten took his dad's call, she fixed their plates.

"Hey, Pop. A little stiff. The hot shower helped. Actually, I'm good. Rylee's here. She was kind enough to bring me dinner. I think she feels sorry for me."

Rylee pinched together her thumb and index fingers and mouthed, "A little."

"Chicken Alfredo. Yep, my favorite." A second later, Canten's eyes left her, and he rubbed two fingers back and forth across his forehead, a sheepish grin on his face. "Bye, Pop. I'll call you later. Love you." He ended the call.

Hearing Canten say those words to his father made her swoon. She loved a man capable of embracing affection. "Everything okay?" she asked.

"Yeah. Yes. It's all good. He wants me to save him a plate," Canten said, joining her at the table.

"I love how close you two are. It reminds me of Sebastian with our dad."

"That's my main man. He can be a character sometimes, but he's always been a great father. Never missed a school function, was there at every football game. He's always been there when I needed him—and when I didn't know I needed him."

Rylee thought about her mother. "That's a parent's superpower, I guess. To know what we need before we do."

Canten held out his hand.

Resting her palm against his, she closed her eyes while he said grace. With the tingling sensation shooting up her arm, it was hard to focus on the words that seemed to be taking him forever to recite.

Finally, he said, "Amen. Let's eat."

As usual, they laughed a lot, talked a lot, and laughed a lot more. Rylee chatted about her childhood; Canten chatted about his. Lord only knew how he'd made it past the age of five in one piece with all his daredevil antics. They discussed music, television, even sports. When Canten talked about being in law enforcement, she could sense his passion. Until now, she hadn't known he'd followed in his grandfather's footsteps or that the man had once been sheriff of Honey Hill too.

"Why not become a barber like Senior?" Rylee asked.

Canten shrugged. "Since I can remember, all I ever wanted to be was a policeman. My grandfather had made it sound so cool. In Charlotte, my plan had been to make bureau commander. I was on my way." He sighed. "But things don't always work out how you want them to."

She could attest to that. Life had a way of tossing you curveballs. Some that you hit and some that hit you smack-dab in the forehead.

"And you? Was becoming a baker extraordinaire always your dream?"

"I'm not sure about the extraordinaire part, but yes. From the moment I received my first Easy-Bake Oven."

Canten brought another forkful of Alfredo to his mouth. "What's your favorite part about your job?"

That was an easy one. "Watching people enjoy something I've created. Don't laugh, but sometimes at the bakery, I stand back and observe as someone takes their first bite just to see their reaction. And when they pull whatever it is away from their mouth and display a *damn, that's good* face, right before wolfing it down in the next bite . . ." She shook her head. "It's priceless."

"You're passionate about what you do, and it shows." He pointed to his plate. "Prime example. I'm about to pop, but I can't stop eating. It's a good thing I don't have someone like you cooking for me every day. I'd be in trouble."

An image of her standing in his kitchen whipping up a meal for two filtered into her head. She forced it away. "Good trouble," she said.

Canten agreed with her.

"What's *your* favorite part about your job?" she asked.

"Actually, all of it. Never a dull moment," he said.

"I imagine your least favorite part is getting run down by drunken residents driving a Power Wheels."

Canten barked a laugh. "Something tells me it'll be a long time before I live that one down."

"Don't worry. Folks will be talking about something else before long. There's always something gossip worthy happening in Honey Hill."

Canten stared at Rylee and wondered what was roaming around in her head as she absently stared at her wineglass. The somber look on her face made him want to say something to pull her back to reality, but he also wanted to give her time to process whatever was on her mind.

Moments later, her eyes rose to meet his. "'In a Sentimental Mood,'" she said.

"I get into those sometimes myself," he said.

Rylee laughed gently. "Playing on the TV."

Canten eyed the screen. "*Ohhh.* My bad." He chuckled. "I thought you meant . . ." He brushed his words off. "Never mind. So you're a John Coltrane fan, huh?"

"Who isn't? He's one of the greatest saxophonists of all time. Did you know he was born in North Carolina?"

Music obviously excited her, because she appeared to be back to her boisterous self. "I did not," he said.

"I'm also a Louis Armstrong fan."

"'What a Wonderful World,'" they said in unison.

Rylee beamed. "I *love* that song."

"I know. When I'm outside and your windows are up, I hear you playing it on repeat." Because of her, he'd grown quite fond of the song himself.

"It puts me in my happy place. When Sebastian and I were young, we spent the summers with our grandparents. My father would call every single night and sing that song to me. Every single night," she repeated as if recalling it. "Even now, he'll sometimes call me and sing it."

"Daddy's girl."

"A hundred and ten percent," she admitted.

"How are Mom and Pop Charles? They'll be here for Lunden and Quade's wedding in a couple of months, right?"

"They're good. Loving Florida. And yes, they'll be here for the wedding."

Canten looked on in surprise when Rylee brought her glass to her lips and downed the contents in one gulp. Up until now, she'd only taken tiny sips. "Refill?" he asked.

She offered her glass. "Yes, please."

After topping her off, he watched her chug that one too. He couldn't recall ever seeing her go through glasses of wine with such urgency. "Thirsty?"

She gave a nervous laugh. "Yes. And it's good wine."

It should have been. It was her favorite. While he wasn't much of a wine drinker, he kept a bottle for when she visited. When he started to fill her glass again, she stopped him. Pushing his clean plate away, he said, "Thank you so much for dinner. You have to let me repay you somehow."

"No repayment necessary. That's what friends do, help each other in need," she said.

"Well, if there's ever anything you need, friend, just let me know."

With a hesitant expression on her face, she said, "Well, there is one thing I need."

As good as this meal was, she could ask him to repave her driveway, and he would do it. "Name it," he said.

"How's your stroke?"

Well, he hadn't expected that, but he answered, "Exceptional."

CHAPTER 4

Rylee liked the way Canten moved. His long, unhurried, steady strokes told her he knew exactly what he was doing. From the beginning, she could sense his dedication. Every second that ticked past brought them closer to the finish line. Selfishly, she didn't want their time together to end too soon, so she held back.

"You were right," she said. "You're really good at this."

"I told you not to underestimate me, woman. What room do you want me in next?"

The question caused a sensation all over her body. "Oh God, I don't think I can handle another round tonight. You're like an Energizer Bunny. I'm drained."

Canten chuckled, a sexy sound that danced around in her ears. "If memory serves me correctly, I told you to relax and let me do all the work."

"I wanted to be an active participant. Sorry it's taking me so long to finish. It's been a while since I've done this."

"Take your time. As long as you're satisfied, that's all that matters."

If they had been having sex, Rylee would have come right then and there. Instead of such a pleasurable pastime, they'd spent the past hour or so painting her master bedroom.

"So why the color green?" Canten asked.

"On one of Ms. Estella's blog posts, she had a reference to colors and what they symbolized. Green represented new beginnings and growth. Renewal and abundance. Some may associate it with envy or jealousy, but I like to focus on the positive aspects."

Canten eyed her. "Always the optimist," he said. A second later he refocused on the wall. "I love that about you."

While it would have been barely noticeable to anyone else, Rylee noticed the second Canten's body stiffened as if he hadn't meant to say—or regretted saying—the words aloud. Had it been the use of the word *love*? Did he fear she'd take it the wrong way? Surely he was allowed to love things about her. They were friends. Practically family. Though the dream she'd had about him the night before stood to refute the *practically family* claim.

Recalling the XXX-rated dream made the room heat up just a bit. It was the first time she'd ever had an orgasm without physically being touched. The intensity of the release had awakened her, the wave of pleasure still coursing through her body. If he could do that to her in a dream, what would happen if they actually had sex?

"So you read Ms. Estella's blog, huh?" Canten asked.

Regaining her composure, she said, "Occasionally."

Canten barked a laugh. "Did you read the comment on the bikini-waxing article? It was hilarious. I laughed for an hour straight."

Rylee whipped her head toward him. "So you like laughing at other people's pain, I see," she said dryly.

"Normally, no. But when the commenter said she went home and put a bag of frozen peas on her privates like they had a black eye, I howled."

It had been the most relief she'd gotten since the whole ordeal. "Howled, huh?"

He laughed more. "Yes. It must have been one hell of an experience, because she said she could hardly walk afterward. And that every time she'd moved it had felt like she'd been shooting fire from between her thighs."

"I would imagine that having hair *snatched* with brutal force from such a sensitive area of the body could cause a negative effect. Wouldn't you?"

"I guess."

When her secret suffering garnered even more amusement from him, Rylee was tempted to slap him with her paintbrush. A green streak across his handsome face . . . now *that* would have been funny.

"Why would anyone voluntarily have that done?" Canten asked. "It sounds brutal."

"It is," she said absently. When Canten stopped painting and eyed her, she added, "Or so I've heard. You know, I wouldn't be surprised if she did it for some man. Women are always doing the drastic to please men."

"I guess I'm old fashioned, because I don't think that would excite me."

This time Rylee stopped to stare.

He continued as if he didn't feel her eyes on him. "Funny story. When I read the part about her not being able to stand without groaning, I thought about you helping me up the other day and the way you—"

"It wasn't me," Rylee blurted, cutting him off.

"—groaned when you helped me up." His expression went from amused to curious and back to amused. "You're Cupcake36."

Easily broken under pressure should have been stamped on her forehead. She was definitely not the person you wanted to commit a crime with. Rylee jabbed her paintbrush in his direction. "You better not laugh, Canten Barnes. If you do, I'm going to paint you green."

Canten swallowed hard. "I would never gather amusement from your suffering."

His bottom lip trembled, and it looked as if he was doing all he could do to cage his hysterics.

Clearing his throat, he said, "It sounds like it was a very unpleasant experience for you." He rubbed a hand over his lips as if to hide a smile. "I'm just glad you survived to share your colorful story with the world.

It could save some lips—I mean lives." A second later a snicker broke through, followed by full-on, bent-at-the-core belly laughter.

"I warned you," Rylee said, nearing him, wielding the paintbrush. With a quick stroke, she used his black T-shirt as a canvas.

"I can't believe you did that," he said through continuing laughter.

"Well, if you can't believe that, you're definitely not going to believe this." In one swift swipe, the side of his head was green. When Canten looked at his paintbrush, then back at her, she had a feeling she would regret her actions. Her first instinct was to run, so she did. Unfortunately, she'd only taken half a step before one of Canten's strong arms had her hooked around the waist. "I'm sorry. I'm sorry," she said, her own amusement jumbling her words.

"Too late for that," he said, holding her back tightly against his chest.

Rylee could feel the wetness seep through her shirt. A second later, Canten nestled his head against hers, transferring some of the paint onto her face. She didn't put much effort into breaking free, because as messy as he was making her, it felt good to be in his arms.

Canten held the paintbrush out in front of them.

"What are you going to do with that?" she said. "Canten Barnes, you better not do what I think you're—" Before she could finish the sentence, he dragged the wet bristles down the front of her shirt.

"Now we match."

"I'm going to strangle you," she said, feigning another attempt at escape.

"Are you communicating threats against a law enforcement officer? You do know that's a serious crime."

"Remember that carrot cake I promised to make you for helping me?"

"Oh, now you're playing dirty," he said. "Let's say we call a truce."

Rylee waved her paintbrush. "Truce." Mostly because her body was in an absolute frenzy and she feared if Canten held on to her a second longer, she'd melt into a puddle at his feet.

Rylee retrieved a cloth. "Come here," she said. Once Canten stood dangerously close in front of her, she wiped at the side of his face. He stared at her as if he were attempting to read her thoughts. Oh, he couldn't handle the sinful things racing through her head. "That's a little better."

"Thank you," he said. He swiped his thumb across her cheek. "You had a little something-something on your face."

"Oh, so you're just going to ignore the entire side of my head, huh?" Before he could answer, she said, "Oh my God. I love this song." When she cranked the radio, Luther Ingram's "I'll Be Your Shelter" poured through the speakers. Using the paintbrush as a microphone, she pretended to perform. She sang a line about cloudy skies and having a friend that was true.

Canten moved to the rhythm of the song, seemingly enjoying the performance. When the song ended, he applauded like she'd been performing onstage. Playfully, she bowed and blew kisses as if the room were filled with admirers.

Lowering the volume, she said, "I love this station. They always play the best music."

"Yes, they do."

"Okay, random confession. When I'm in bed at night listening to their slow-jam dedication hour, I craft a story in my head about the one dedicating the song and the one receiving it based on the song. Weird, I know."

"Do they all end happily ever after like those romance novels you like so much?" Canten asked.

"Most do."

They dampened their brushes and continued painting. With their constant stopping and starting, they would be here all day. *No objections here.* She couldn't think of a better way to spend her Saturday.

"I apologize for laughing at you earlier," he said.

"Thank you." She flashed mock disdain.

"But you have to admit, it is a little comical."

Rylee jabbed her paintbrush at him as a warning. "Don't make me use this again."

He flashed a palm. "Okay, okay."

The room filled with comfortable silence but only for a second.

Never taking his eyes off the wall, Canten said, "What man were you doing it for?"

Pausing, Rylee eyed him with hitched brows. "What?"

Canten finally looked at her. "You said women are always doing the drastic to please men. What man in town were you trying to please?"

Did he really think she'd do something like that just to please some man who probably wouldn't have been worth the effort anyway? Clearly, he didn't know her as well as she'd thought. Deciding to have a little more fun with him, she said, "You wouldn't know him."

"I know a lot of people. What's his name?"

Rylee returned her focus to the wall. "He's not from around here."

"That's okay. I'll still be able to find him. You're like a little sister to me. I have to make sure you're safe."

Like a little sister to him? She didn't want him to view her as a sister. When he looked at her, she needed him to see a woman he wanted to pin against the wall and screw senseless. A little perturbed by the comment, she made up a name and tossed it at him. "Bartholomew."

"Bartholomew Jenkins over in Connard? He's married with like fifteen kids."

Damn. He really does know a lot of people. Swallowing hard, she said, "U-um . . . I-I mean . . ." *Say something!*

✵

Canten fought to keep a straight face as Rylee fumbled over her words. She really did suck under pressure. Deciding to put her out of her misery, he said, "You're full of it."

42

"Excuse me?"

He shook his head. "Do you actually think I believe you would do something like that for a man? Come on, Rylee. I know you." Obviously, better than she thought. "Plus, you don't lie very well. You do that stuttering thing. It's kind of cute."

"I do not," she said.

The teeny smile she attempted to hide revealed her guilt. She would be no good at poker.

Turning away from him, she said, "What would Katrina Sweeney say about you thinking it's kinda cute? Something tells me she wouldn't approve."

She smirked as if she'd won some undeclared war of words. This was clearly a diversion technique to take the heat off herself, because she'd never mentioned Katrina Sweeney's name to him before.

"Everyone has jokes this week, I see. If I were interested in dating, she would be the last woman I pursued."

"Why aren't you interested in dating?" she asked. "There are plenty of women in Honey Hill who would *love* to parade around town arm in arm with you. You should hear some of the things they say about you." Rylee fanned herself.

Canten wasn't sure if Rylee was serious or messing with him. Either way, now he was the one needing to take the heat off himself. "I'll answer your question if you answer mine," he said.

She eyed him a moment. "What's your question?"

"Why were you crying at Finger Leafing Goode the other day?"

The rapid change in her expression, from jovial to apprehensive, told him that had been the last question she'd expected.

"I-I told you already. Girl talk." She gave a shaky laugh. "You know how emotional I can be."

"I don't believe you." When her eyes lowered, he regretted sounding so brash. He placed a finger under her chin and tilted her head upward. "Hey, you know you can talk to me about anything, right?"

A delicate smile lit her face. "I know. I just don't want you to think—"

Before she could finish the thought, her cell phone chimed, alerting them someone had pulled into the driveway. Checking the camera feed on her phone, she gasped. "Oh no. No, no, no."

Canten pushed his brows together as concern set in. "Who is it?"

"My parents. Oh God, what are they doing here? This is bad. This is really bad."

He was confused over Rylee's reaction. She and her parents had always been so close. When they'd moved away a few years back, Rylee had cried like they were kids she was sending off to college, not adults going to Florida for retirement. What was so bad about their arrival?

"Do you want me to let them in?" he asked.

"No!"

His head jerked in surprise. "No?"

"I mean, yes. But in a second." She bit into her bottom lip and stared at him with desperate-looking eyes. "Canten, I have to tell you something. And *please, please, please* don't be mad. I didn't mean for it to happen, it just . . . did."

Well, this doesn't sound good.

Rylee wrung her hands as she paced back and forth in front of him. She babbled on and on, not making a great deal of sense. Something about being impulsive and jumping before she saw the ground and rarely landing on her feet. At one point, her breathing became so labored he thought she would have a panic attack. Something told him whatever she needed to tell him was going to be a doozy, if she ever got around to doing so. "Rylee," he said, cutting her off, "just tell me."

She stopped and faced him, a sheepish expression on her face. "Okay. Okay," she repeated. Pressing one hand against her stomach and the other to her forehead, she took a deep breath, exhaled, and said, "I, um, may have told my mother that, um, we're . . . dating."

He rubbed the back of his neck. Yep, a doozy.

CHAPTER 5

Rylee nearly gnawed her lip in half, waiting for Canten to say something. His neutral expression made him difficult to read. The man was good at masking. On rare occasions, she garnered glimpses of emotion she was sure he hadn't wanted her to see. This was definitely one of those times. The anticipation was killing her. *Say something!*

Finally, he did. "Wow, I didn't expect that." A second later, he added, "Out of curiosity, why would you tell your mother we're dating?"

A reasonable question. "*Leonard Jamison*," she said.

Rylee thought she saw Canten's jaw muscles flex. He was probably seething inside from the uncomfortable position she'd placed him in. In her defense, she'd never intended on him finding out this way.

Canten rocked back and forth on his heels. "Leonard Jamison? I don't understand."

Again, of all the men her mother could have suggested for her. *Leonard Jamison. Really?* Leonard Jamison happened to be the last man in Honey Hill Rylee would have invited into her life. A liar and a con artist. You'd think the smug bastard were a sheikh instead of a used-car salesman by the way he expected every woman in town to bow down to him. *Not this one.*

Continuing, she said, "When my mother tried to set me up with him, I told her I was already seeing someone. Your name accidentally flew out."

Canten's eyes narrowed on her as if he were trying to decipher how his name had *accidentally* flown out of her mouth.

Continuing to ramble—because she'd clearly lost all control of her common sense—she said, "I think it was because I had been watching you hobble into the house. Well, not *watching you*, watching you, like a stalker or anything." She gave a shaky laugh. "That would be weird. I had thought I heard your SUV, so I looked out the window. When my mother called, I was staring at you." *Shit.* "Well, not *staring at you*, staring at you. Again, weird. I was . . ." Exhausted, she let her words dry up. Sighing heavily, she said, "I had chicken Alfredo."

"Huh," Canten said again.

Were these good *huh*s or bad *huh*s? "I never expected my parents would come. But my mother's really excited we're dating." She stopped abruptly. "Well, not—"

"*Dating*, dating," Canten said, finishing her sentence.

She nodded. A thought crossed her mind. "Maybe she didn't believe me and has come to verify."

"Did you stutter?" Canten asked.

A hint of humor lingered in his voice. That had to be a good sign, right?

"No." Or had she? Noticing the look of skepticism Canten was giving her, she said, "Okay, maybe."

"Well, look at the bright side," he said.

Bright side? He saw a *bright side*? Was there a bright side when you were caught between a rock and a hard place? "Bright side?" she said dryly.

He shrugged. "Imagine if you'd said Bartholomew."

Rylee didn't want to laugh, because this wasn't a laughable situation; however, she did, right along with Canten. She loved how he could still amuse her when all she wanted to do was run and hide. "What a mess," she said more to herself. One of her own making. "This would have never happened if, for whatever reason, my mom didn't have in her head that I'm lonely and in need of affection." She hadn't actually meant to say that aloud.

"Are you?" Canten asked.

"N-no." Another look of skepticism. "Well . . . I mean, sometimes, I guess. But who doesn't get lonely occasionally? Stormy nights when rain's hitting the window, lightning's filling the night sky, thunder's booming." When she realized she'd drifted off into a daydream, she snapped back to reality. "It's completely normal," she said, a little too defensively.

"The only thing I feel during storms is angst," Canten said. Before she could ask why, he added, "I'll explain later. We have to deal with this right now." He scratched the side of his face. "Out of curiosity, Rylee, how exactly was this all supposed to play out? Prior to your parents showing up, I mean."

He had to ask. It was all supposed to be so simple. "I told my mother you and I were keeping our relationship quiet until we knew where things were headed. I swore her to secrecy. We all know one mention to any of her friends here, and the news would burn through town like a five-alarm blaze."

"Don't I know it," he said.

She continued, "I'd planned to allow my mother to believe we were dating. Then, a few weeks before they would arrive for the wedding, I would tell them we decided to just be friends. That way, when they arrived, we wouldn't have to pretend to be a couple. And to keep my mother from trying to set me up again, I had planned to tell her I needed time to heal." And her brilliant plan would have worked, had her parents not just pulled into her driveway.

"Sounds like you had it all worked out."

"Full disclosure: my plan never included you hearing any of this so soon." She gave a nervous chuckle. "Plot twist." Her so-called elaborate plan had made far more sense in her head at the time, but standing here, reciting her intentions to Canten, made her feel like the village idiot.

"So in your fictional version of our breakup, who would have broken up with whom?"

Rylee wasn't sure why that mattered, but she said, "I broke up with you. I didn't want to chance my parents viewing you as the bad guy."

"I hope you let me down easy."

Were they seriously having a real conversation about an imaginary breakup? "I gave you the *it's not you, it's me* speech. You seemed okay with it."

His brows arched, but he didn't comment. He studied her a long second. "Can I ask you one question?" he finally said.

"I already know what you're going to ask. Why not just tell my mother to butt out?"

He nodded. "Yes."

"You can't just tell Dorsetta Charles to butt out. It doesn't stick. Just ask Sebastian."

"I'm sure she just wants the best for you," he said. "My pop can be meddlesome too. However, he's never tried to set me up. I wouldn't put it past him, though."

The doorbell rang, and Rylee panicked. Shifting her weight from one foot to the other, she said, "Canten, I have no right to ask you this, and you can absolutely say no, and I promise there will be no hard feelings whatsoever. I get it if you don't want—"

"I'll do it."

"—to do it. And I know I'm putting you in an awkward position, and I probably shouldn't even—" *Wait. Did he just say he'll do it?* "Did you just say you'll do it?"

"Yes."

"Just like that?"

"Uh-huh."

"You don't want to think about it for a few more seconds?"

Canten laughed. "Why does it sound like you're trying to talk me into a no?"

Rylee flashed her palms. "I'm not. Trust me, I'm not. I just want you to be absolutely sure. This is a heavy lift."

"The both of us will benefit from this. As soon as word gets out we're 'dating'"—he made finger quotes—"no one will ever link me to Katrina again. A win-win for us both."

Rylee's eyes widened. "*No!* We can't tell anyone. It's just between you, me, and my parents. And maybe Lunden. She'll probably tell Quade. Oh, and we'll definitely have to tell Sebastian because we'll need him to play along. But other than that . . ." She shifted her weight nervously from one foot to the other. "We can fool my parents, but the whole town?"

A knot tightened in her stomach when Canten ran a hand over his head, an uncertain expression on his face. *Oh no, he's going to change his mind.* Why wouldn't he? With the Katrina component off the table—which clearly had been why he'd agreed in the first place—he no longer had anything to gain from agreeing to this.

"I don't like the idea of lying to your parents, Rylee."

"I understand. It's—"

"But . . . you need me. And I did say anything you needed. Though I think you might have used that one up when you asked me to help you paint. But you're in a bind, so I'm willing to help. That's what friends do, right?"

She nodded vigorously. "Yes. Yes, it is. Thank you, Canten. I could kiss you right now." And she did, pressing her lips to his in a motion so swift that the only way she knew they'd kissed was the fact her lips tingled. Wide eyed, she touched her lip, then said, "Oh God, I'm so sorry. I-I got carried away." Would he believe she had been going for his cheek?

Canten slid his hands into his pockets. "Um, don't sweat it. These things happen."

"How can I ever repay you, Canten?" She saw the wheels turning in his head. "Say it," she said.

"Maybe one or two home-cooked meals?" he said.

Rylee's brows knit. "Wait. That's it?" All he wanted was food? For what he was doing for her, he could have asked for a night of wild, hot sex, and she probably would have given it to him. She laughed to herself. Canten Barnes was way too much of a gentleman to make such a demand.

He shrugged. "I'm easy."

Yes, he was. Easy to look at. Easy to talk to. Easy to like. "I'll take you on a delicious culinary journey around the world. Each night we'll visit a different region."

"I'm not sure my waistline can handle every night." He jutted out his hand. "We should shake on it before you change your mind."

Was he serious? He stood a better chance of changing his. When she rested her palm against his, the pulse through her body was instant. God, she had to remind herself to stop touching this man. She definitely didn't need her brain scrambled right now. She needed it firing on all cylinders. *Pull it together, girl.*

"Deal," he said.

"Deal." To be on the safe side, she added, "Just so we're absolutely clear and on the same page, you do know I'm asking you to fake a relationship with me?"

"Yes. Stop stressing. It'll be a piece of cake. And if it's any consolation, I was president of my drama club in middle school. We've got this."

No. No, that wasn't any consolation at all. But what she said was, "I feel so much better knowing this."

The doorbell rang again, drawing their attention.

"Coming," she said, hopefully loud enough for them to hear. "I'm sure my parents will only be here a couple of days, which means you won't be shackled to me or this little white lie for too long."

Canten rubbed his stomach. "I'm just looking forward to traveling."

Rylee wasn't sure who was a bigger foodie, she or Canten. Headed out the room, she paused and turned to face a trailing Canten. Pinching her thumb and forefinger together, she said, "One more teeny-weeny little thingy I should probably mention. My mother will be watching us like a hawk."

Rylee gasped when Canten grabbed the hem of her shirt and tugged her to him. Mashed against his warm, hard chest, her pounding heart threatened to crack her rib cage. What was happening? The hot and sultry way he stared into her eyes caused the air to seize in her lungs. His lips hovered within inches of hers. And just when she thought he'd kiss her, he positioned his mouth close to her ear and spoke in a low, seductive whisper that sent a warm sensation straight to her core.

"In that case, I guess we'd better be convincing." He reared back to eye her again. "Now get the door, woman. We have a show to put on."

Rylee released the breath she'd been holding in a single puff, dizzy from all the sexually charged energy surging through her. Obviously, he'd retained a little something from drama club, because his performance had surely convinced her.

A single question bounced around in Canten's head as he followed Rylee to the front door. Actually, two. The first: Would his body ever stop humming from being so close to Rylee's mouth—twice—and fighting like hell not to ravish it? He was a walking, talking contradiction. One minute he wouldn't allow himself to want her; the next craving her was all he did.

The second question, and perhaps the most relevant at the moment: What the hell had he been thinking when he'd agreed to a fake relationship? With Rylee of all people. This was the woman he fantasized about more often than not.

Actually, he knew exactly what had helped prompt his decision. *Leonard Jamison.* The name made his jaw muscles tighten. The idea of the man pawing at Rylee churned his stomach. Canten had loathed him since that one summer he and Jayla had come to visit his father and Leonard had hit on Jayla, then pretended not to have known she was his wife. That had been almost seven years ago. Today, his grudge had been renewed.

Leonard Jamison? What had Mrs. Charles been thinking?

Canten wasn't sure who irked him more, Leonard or his grandfather Herbert. Just then, he heard the elder Jamison's voice in his head. *Sher-reef. Sher-reef Cun-tone.* Who couldn't pronounce *sheriff*? And where the hell had *Cuntone* come from? He settled on the two being an equal nuisance.

Rylee's words echoed in his head. *This little white lie.* It gave him a moment of pause as he remembered how a little white lie had altered his life. Lies, no matter how small, could have irreparable consequences. This he knew firsthand. *This situation is different,* he told himself. *No one will die.* A significant wave of despair raged inside him. *This situation is different.*

"Hey," Rylee said, snapping her fingers in front of Canten's face. "You're not having second thoughts, are you?"

Canten slammed back to reality. "No. Just getting into character."

Rylee pulled the door open and invited her parents inside. Mr. and Mrs. Charles had always treated Canten like a member of the family. And while he hated the idea of deceiving two of the kindest people he knew, he liked the fact he could help out his best friend's sister. *Little* sister.

Mrs. Charles looked patriotic in a striped red-and-white shirt and royal-blue capri pants. Mr. Charles wore coordinating colors. Had Mrs. Charles dressed him? Canten laughed to himself.

Mrs. Charles stood several inches shorter than Rylee, which meant Rylee had probably gotten her height from her dad, who towered over his wife. Mrs. Charles's almond-colored skin held no signs of a woman in her late sixties. Rylee had definitely inherited her beauty from her mother.

"Surprise!" her mother said. "Honey, what in the world? Why are you covered in green paint?"

Rylee shot a glance toward Canten. "We're painting my bedroom."

"It looks more like you two were painting each other." Mrs. Charles smirked. "Your father and I did that once. But we took our clothes off first." She winked. "You two should definitely try it. It's stimulating."

The woman's words didn't seem to faze Mr. Charles. Not a single line of concern creased his dark-brown skin. Apparently, after forty-some years of marriage, he'd grown accustomed to her oversharing.

"Mommy!" Rylee said.

Showing no regret, Mrs. Charles said, "What? We're all grown here." She blew Canten an air-kiss. "That will have to do for now. I'll get my hug later."

Canten playfully pretended to reach for her, making everyone laugh. He was as comfortable with them as he was with his own family.

"Hey, baby girl," Mr. Charles said, using the pet name he'd given his daughter, then kissed the side of her head that wasn't speckled green.

Rylee's face bloomed into a high-wattage smile. "Hi, Daddy."

Definitely a daddy's girl.

"Canten," Mr. Charles said, giving him a firm handshake. "I brought my poles. You game?"

"You know I never miss an opportunity to reel 'em in." Anytime the Charleses visited, Mr. Charles, Sebastian, Canten, and his father spent at least half a day mostly not catching fish. What few they did manage to hook were usually released back into the water. They were there for the fellowship more than the actual fishing. And man, did they always have a great time.

"Excuse me," Mr. Charles said. "It was a long drive. I need to step into the little boys' room."

Canten eyed Mr. Charles as he moved from the room. He grew concerned when the man swayed a little like he'd gotten dizzy before disappearing around the corner. Obviously, he'd been the only one to see it, because no one acknowledged it.

"What are you guys doing here?" Rylee asked her mother.

"Aren't you happy to see us?" Mrs. Charles said.

"Of course," Rylee said. "But had I known you were coming, I would have postponed painting."

"Look at you. Always thinking of others. You're one lucky man, Canten."

Slipping into character, Canten wrapped his arm around Rylee's neck, then kissed the top of her head. "Don't I know it."

Following suit, Rylee encased him in her arms and nestled in close. "I think we're both pretty darn lucky."

Their interaction—seamless, effortless—made it appear as if they'd done this a thousand times before. Clearly, he wasn't the only one capable of putting on a good performance. While he tried, he couldn't deny how good Rylee felt snuggled so close to him. In his head he might have viewed her as a little sister, but in his arms, she was a woman he could easily spend all night pleasing.

"Remember, Mom, not a word to anyone. We don't want to jinx this."

Mrs. Charles zipped her lips and tossed the key. "Your secret is safe with me."

"And Dad knows this, too, right?"

"Really, dear? Who is your father going to tell?" Mrs. Charles grinned. "A clandestine love affair. That's so romantic."

Canten swore he saw stars glitter in the woman's brown eyes. He hoped she was better at keeping a secret than she was at not meddling in her daughter's business.

"I'm sure Lunden won't mind putting you up at the inn for tonight. The paint smell won't be so potent tomorrow," Rylee said.

Mrs. Charles brushed Rylee's words off. "No need. Your father and I actually rented a lake house. A darling little bungalow with tons of windows and plenty of natural light. The master bedroom has an unobstructed view of the lake. It's so quiet. All you hear is nature. Very relaxing. We're practically the only house for miles. I can't wait for you two to see it. Oh, and since we rented it for the next three months, the owner included the use of his pontoon boat. It's sexy. Black and white with tons of leather."

Did she just say they'd rented the lake house for the next three months? Rylee went stiff against Canten. *Yep, that's exactly what she said.*

Welp, things had just gotten a whole lot more complicated. A day or two was one thing. Three months was something entirely different. What in the hell had he gotten himself into?

CHAPTER 6

Rylee was sure she hadn't heard her mother correctly because it had sounded like she'd said they'd rented a lake house for three months. *Three months.* When they came on an announced visit, they typically got homesick after three days. Now they were here for three months? Not only had they arrived two months earlier than expected, but they were on an extended stay. Which meant she and Canten would have to keep this sham going from now until August.

Pulling away from Canten, she said, "Mom, did you say *three* months?"

"Don't fret. We're not going to cramp your style. You two can carry on as usual."

Rylee tossed a nervous glance to Canten. If he was bothered by what her mother had just said, he didn't show it. "You and Daddy are usually trying to rush back home after a few days. Is everything okay in Florida?"

Something fast and faint flicked across her mother's face before her mother turned away and headed toward the kitchen. "Yes, dear. We needed some work done to the house and figured now was as good a time as any. The contractor said it would take several months. He estimated a completion time of early August. So we figured, why not come to Honey Hill much earlier than intended. We would have been here in a couple of months anyway for Lunden's wedding. I love July weddings. How is the planning coming along?"

Her mother gave a plausible explanation, but when she rambled like this, something was up. Instead of pressing her in front of Canten, she decided to wait until they were alone. "It's Lunden, Mom; the planning was done two weeks after the proposal."

Mrs. Charles laughed, but Rylee noted a lag in her usual boisterousness. *What the hell is up?* And should she be worried? Of course she should. Not just for what was going on with her mother but the fact her little white lie, speckled with gray, kept spiraling further out of control. When they'd pulled into her driveway, Rylee had assumed her parents would stay a few days, a week tops, then leave and return again in July for the wedding. Now it would be three months before they left. Three months before Canten could reclaim his freedom? Was it fair to ask him to alter his life for that length of time? She sighed. No, it wasn't. "Mom, we need to talk."

Before she could finish the thought, her father reentered the room. "I just spoke with Senior," he said.

Rylee's mouth fell open, but nothing came out. Her father had called Senior? Her uncertain gaze bounced to Canten just in time to see him run a hand over his head. Oh, this situation was getting worse and worse by the minute. *Oh, what a tangled web we weave, when first we practice to deceive.* She wasn't sure who'd originally penned the quote, but they'd hit the mark.

Relax, Rylee. Maybe you're getting all worked up for nothing. Maybe her father hadn't mentioned anything about her and Canten's quote-unquote relationship. Maybe he'd just been letting Senior know he was in town and scheduling a fishing trip. Maybe she was panicking for nothing.

"Don't worry, Canten, I smoothed everything over with your father. He was a little perturbed by the fact that you kept him in the dark about you and my baby girl's relationship. Understandably so. But I explained everything to him. He's okay now."

Well, so much for not panicking. Rylee couldn't breathe, which meant she didn't possess the ability to ask her father what exactly he'd said to Senior. At this point, she doubted it even mattered anyway. This rope of deception was in its infancy and already unraveling. "Mom, Dad, I have to tell you—"

"Senior's as excited by the news as I am," her father continued, cutting her off.

Dammit. Why wouldn't they allow her to come clean?

Mr. Charles clapped Canten on the shoulder, a proud smile on his face. "You're a good man, Sheriff. I know I have nothing to worry about. My baby girl is in great hands."

Canten eyed her. "Yes, she is, sir. You have absolutely nothing to worry about."

Even though they were a sham, Canten had delivered the words with so much conviction she almost believed him. *Damn, he's good.* Convinced they just might be able to pull this off after all, she yet again abandoned the idea of telling her parents the truth.

Mr. Charles continued, "You're probably going to want to give your father a call."

There was no need, because Canten's phone rang a millisecond later. No doubt who was on the opposite end.

Canten eyed his screen. "It's Pop. I better take this. I'll see everyone later," he said and headed for the door.

"Looking forward to it, son. Looking forward to it," Mr. Charles said.

"I'll walk you out," Rylee said, willing to wait as long as necessary for him to get off the line with his father, because they *urgently* needed to talk.

Outside, Canten made the call active. Rylee could hear Senior's voice but couldn't make out what was being said.

"Pop, let me call you right back," Canten said, kneading his temple.

When he ended the call, he didn't readily look at her. Instead, he studied the ground, massaging the back of his neck. She felt terrible for being the one to cause him such visible anguish.

"Three months," he finally said.

Seeing the distress it was causing him and not wanting him to be forced to lie to his father, she said, "Don't worry. As soon as I get back inside, I'm coming clean. I'm so sorry for putting you in this position,

Canten. It was unfair and a little selfish. If you need for me to talk to Senior, I will. This is all my fault."

Finally eyeing her, he said, "I'm kind of roped in now, Rylee." He inhaled and exhaled slowly. "Your parents seem really happy about us."

"They love you. Always have," she said.

"Which is why we have to go through with this. If you told them now that we just stood there and lied to their faces, they would be upset with you but they would loathe me. I don't want that."

Rylee hugged her arms around her body. "I messed things up big-time, didn't I?"

"Unintentionally," he said. "You couldn't have predicted this."

"Canten, I kinda think you should be yelling at me instead of trying to make me feel better."

"I don't like to yell. Plus, I know you would do the same for me if the shoe were on the other foot."

"Without question," she said. "You know that. I guess we're doing this."

"I guess we are. Now, laugh like I said something funny," he said.

Rylee pushed her brows together. "What?"

"Don't look, but your mother is watching us. Just laugh like I told the best joke in the world."

So she did.

"We can do this," he said.

Rylee wasn't sure if his affirmation was for her or himself, but she echoed his sentiment. "We can do this. Hug me goodbye."

Canten didn't hesitate. He wrapped his strong arms around her in the most genuine and soothing manner. Rotating her, he positioned his back toward the house. A second later he leaned forward and kissed her. From her mother's viewpoint, it probably looked as if he'd given the most spine-tingling kiss ever. In actuality, it had only been a lingering kiss to her cheek. Nevertheless, it energized her entire body.

Canten reared back, eyed her several long, heated seconds, released her, and left.

Back inside, Rylee prepared her parents a quick lunch. After eating, she ventured into the kitchen to clean. From the kitchen, she observed them in the living room. Her father watched reruns of his favorite TV series, *In the Heat of the Night*. Curled up next to him, wrapped in a throw, her mother read on the Kindle Rylee had gotten her for Christmas. Her mother was definitely where she'd gotten her love for reading.

Both her parents looked so content. A smile curled her lips as she watched her father absently caress his wife's arm, like he'd done it so many times before that it had become second nature. After all these years, the fact that her parents were still so much in love swelled her heart. She was so happy they were here. Even more elated by the fact she got them for three months. That gave her plenty of time to learn what her mother was keeping from her.

As if sensing Rylee's energy, her mother looked in her direction. "Everything okay, dear?"

"Yes, ma'am. Do you guys need anything?"

"I think I'd like a water, but I'll get it," Mrs. Charles said, hopping off the couch before Rylee could offer to get it.

After claiming a bottle from the fridge, her mother joined her at the sink. "Something's troubling you," she said. "What is it?"

"Mom, is there something going on? Earlier, when I asked about your visit, I got the feeling you weren't telling me something."

Mrs. Charles flipped one of Rylee's curls. "You worry too much, dear. If there were a reason to do so, I'd tell you. Everything is fine."

"Okay," Rylee said, with no other choice but to believe her.

"I should have known you and Canten would eventually end up together. He has always looked at you with such tenderness. You two have some seriously potent energy. And I can tell he really cares about you a lot."

Where was her mother getting all of this? To appease her mother, she said, "I care about him too." Actually, that hadn't been a lie, which was probably why it had rolled off her tongue so effortlessly.

"I know you do. I can see it when you look at him too. You two were friends first; now, you're lovers. You're starting on a strong foundation. I'm so happy for you both. Like I said, I worry about you. But my mind and heart are both at ease now."

In a skewed way of thinking, maybe what she and Canten were doing wasn't so wrong after all. Not if it gave her mother peace of mind. *But what happens when Canten and I call it quits?* She couldn't worry about that now. One catastrophe at a time.

"The sheriff must be a patient man."

"Why do you say that?" Rylee followed her mother's gaze across the room to the one photo of Rylee and Lucas still sitting on a shelf. *Shit.* With everything else unfolding, she hadn't even thought to remove it. Heck, she'd barely remembered it was there, partially obstructed by a large jar candle.

When Mrs. Charles rejoined her husband, Rylee started to stress again. Her mother was too damn observant. Could she and Canten really pull this off under this woman's keen and watchful eye?

Canten stared out his office window, recalling the conversation he'd had with his father over the weekend. When he'd left Rylee and her parents, he'd headed straight to his father's place. While he'd arrived with the intention of telling his father the same lie they'd told Rylee's parents, he hadn't been able to bring himself to do so. Of course, Senior disliked the idea of lying, but he'd reluctantly agreed to go along with it.

The twinkle that had sparkled in his father's eye told Canten the man had read too much into the situation. Canten recalled something his father had said. *You told me Rylee's motivation; what's yours?* He had no motivation beyond wanting to help out a friend in need. And that was exactly what he'd told Senior. The man's laughter still rang in his ears. *Good luck, son,* Senior had said. *You're going to need it.*

"Knock, knock," came from behind him.

Canten turned toward Deputy Christina Jacobs standing at the door. "What's up, Jacobs?"

"You have a visitor. Mrs. Douglas—"

Before Deputy Jacobs could finish her thought, Mrs. Douglas brushed past her. Honey Hill elders could be pushy that way.

"Sheriff, I must speak with you concerning an urgent matter," Mrs. Douglas said.

Rarely were Mrs. Douglas's matters urgent to anyone but her. The petite, dark-brown-skinned woman reminded him of his grandmother, right down to the headful of jet-black hair, dyed to mask the gray . . . and her age. Mrs. Douglas took full advantage of his open-door policy, visiting weekly with some new atrocity inflicted on her. He couldn't wait to hear what it was this time.

Last week, she'd claimed the speed gun one of his deputies had used had wiped her memory of the day. Somehow, she'd been able to recount the events leading up to her speeding ticket and argue the reasons why she didn't deserve it. Unfortunately, claiming the laser had caused a surge of adrenaline that had resulted in a foot spasm that had made her press harder on the accelerator hadn't been the best defense.

Canten gave Deputy Jacobs a nod, and the woman backed from the room, closing the door behind her. Outside the door, he swore he heard her snicker. Standing, he rounded the desk, pulled out a chair at the small conference table, and invited Mrs. Douglas to sit. "What can I do for you, Mrs. Douglas?"

"The noise, Sheriff. Every morning Milton Randal, the cantankerous old fool," she said with a look of distaste, "cranks up that jalopy of a truck of his and revs the engine over and over. And it backfires. Makes me think it's a drive-by. It's giving my chickens anxiety, which is causing them to lay teeny eggs. I want him arrested."

Canten covered his mouth with his hand to hide his smile. Clearing his throat, he said, "Unfortunately, cranking his vehicle is not an arrestable offense; however, I will speak with him."

Mrs. Douglas patted his leg. "Well, I guess that'll have to do." She smiled warmly. "Thank you, Sheriff. You're such a dear. It broke my heart when Herbert told me how his granddaughter had dumped you."

Canten's head jerked in surprise. *Dumped me? What the hell is Mrs. Douglas talking about?*

"Don't be sad. You may have dodged a bullet with that one. Not to speak ill of any of God's children, but all those Jamisons are a little touched, if you know what I mean."

Oh yes, he did. Evidenced by the fact Mr. Herbert had told Mrs. Douglas that Katrina had dumped him. He'd never been hers to dump.

She stood. "Like Tupac said, you gotta keep your head up. I'm sure you'll find a nice young lady soon. One who's willing to deal with your commitment issues. Don't worry, when the right one comes along, it'll feel as natural as the sun kissing your skin. Ta-ta."

Canten stared at the door. *Dumped? Commitment issues?* What in the hell had Katrina told her grandfather? Well, apparently, that she'd dumped him over his inability to commit. How did you dump an individual you weren't dating? He shook his head. *A bunch of psychos.*

The only seemingly sane one of the bunch appeared to be Grandma Jamison, but even she had her moments of questionable behavior. Like the time she'd plucked one of Presto's—a usually harmless peacock that roamed the town at will—feathers to make a quill.

The memory made him laugh. Apparently, Presto had figured if Mrs. Jamison could pluck him, he could do the same to her. Somehow, he'd snatched the wig right off her head, then fluttered down the street with Mrs. Jamison running behind. They never had found that wig.

Just a normal day in Honey Hill.

Moving back to his desk, Canten opened the bottom drawer and removed the correspondence he'd received from the Charlotte-Mecklenburg Police Department, informing him he'd made it to the second round of bureau commander interviews. Studying the letter, he massaged the back of his neck. He hadn't yet shared the news with his father that he might be leaving. But he knew his pop. While the man would hate to see him leave, he would encourage him to follow his heart. Maybe that was why Canten hadn't told him, because he was torn. Other than his father, there wasn't a thing keeping him in Honey Hill. *Universe, give me a sign.*

"You look like a man who could use something sweet."

The sound of Rylee's voice stilled him. *Is this . . . nah.* The universe definitely didn't work that fast. Stashing the letter back in the drawer to mull over later, he eyed her. Canten's lips parted, and his gaze fixed on her. *Damn.* The sleeveless black denim jumpsuit she wore hugged her in all the right places. Snapping out of it, he came out from behind his desk. "Please tell me there are cupcakes in that box."

"And an ice-cold chocolate milk," Rylee said.

Canten pumped his fist like a kid who'd collected his favorite baseball card. "I am so in need of this." The first bite into the lemon cupcake with a raspberry-compote center put him in sugar heaven. "Mmm. You do know how to make me smile, don't you? Sit. Have a cupcake with me."

"I can't. I'm on my way to a dress fitting. I wanted to drop off some goodies for you and the crew first."

A dress fitting. He envied the fabric that got to caress her skin. "You know you have my deputies spoiled, right?"

"Just them, huh?"

He admitted to nothing.

Rylee checked her watch. "I have to go." She pointed to the baker's box. "Don't eat the entire box. You're going to want to save your appetite."

"Don't worry about me. I have an insatiable appetite."

Rylee smirked. "Probably because of all that sex you're having." Giving him a wink, she disappeared through the door.

Watching her leave, he groaned. Just the damn mention of sex, especially by Rylee, and the sway of her hips stirred him below the waist. *One night.* That was all he needed.

CHAPTER 7

Parking in a space in front of the dress shop, Rylee mentally prepared herself before exiting her vehicle. Mrs. Cora Jane Ridley—known to the town as Lady Sunshine because of her merry disposition but mostly because the woman was always piping hot with gossip—had a way of extracting information. Rylee couldn't allow herself to overshare as she usually did. Thankfully, Lunden would be there to run interference.

And speaking of Lunden . . . Rylee didn't see Lunden's vehicle, so she just assumed she'd walked over from town hall. She chuckled to herself. No one in the state loved walking more than her best friend.

The second Rylee entered the shop, her cell phone vibrated. Fishing it from her purse, she read the text message from Lunden.

Lunden: Running late. There in 10.

Of all the times to run late, Lu. Rylee typed back, K, then made a beeline for the door. But before she could make her great escape, Lady Sunshine appeared from the back.

"I'm here, I'm here," Lady Sunshine said, dangling a bottle of champagne in the air. "Just had to grab this. Can't have a celebration without the bubbly."

Shit. You've got this. Rylee plastered on a smile, then turned to face her. "There you are."

Lady Sunshine was a hair over four feet with big brown, expressive eyes that told a story of kindness and compassion. Her waist-length, auburn-red dreads were pulled back into a braided ponytail. While she was the best dressmaker in several counties, possibly even the state, the woman was also a walking, talking gazette. If Lady Sunshine wasn't privy to the information, the news wasn't worth knowing. Their local newspaper, the *Honey Hill Herald*, blamed Lady Sunshine for its decline in readership. Rylee believed it. Some also swore the woman had a sixth sense and could tell you things before they even happened. *That part* Rylee didn't believe.

"Don't you look pretty," Lady Sunshine said.

Rylee eyed the denim jumpsuit she wore. "Thank you. I just left the sheriff's station." Her gaze shot up. "N-not that I wore this to see the sheriff. I, um, mean, I didn't go there to see the sheriff. Just to take him cupcakes. To take them all cupcakes," she added. *Change the subject.* "Lunden's running a couple of minutes late. She'll be here shortly."

"I'm sure the sheriff appreciated it," Lady Sunshine said. "The cupcakes, I mean."

Something about the sly look on her face told Rylee Lady Sunshine hadn't been referring to the cupcakes at all. "Wow, these are pretty," Rylee said, diverting her attention to the several maxi-style dresses hanging against the wall. One in particular drew her eye. It was pure white with spaghetti straps and large purple lotus flowers all over it. "Gorgeous," she mumbled to herself.

Lady Sunshine joined Rylee. "One of my favorites," she said. "The purple lotus flower represents self-awakening." Lady Sunshine removed the dress from the rack and held it up against Rylee. "Did you know lotus flowers can withstand thousands of years without water and still emerge like new?"

"No, I didn't know that," Rylee said.

Lady Sunshine continued to tease the material as if making sure it lay just right against Rylee's frame. "They grow in muddy waters, then bloom without a single speck of mud on them." Lady Sunshine's gaze met Rylee's. "Some people are like that, you know? Able to bloom under the most unfavorable conditions. The lotus flower's unwavering faith to continue living regardless of what it's gone through should be an inspiration to us all."

Why did Rylee get the feeling there had been a hidden message in Lady Sunshine's words?

"This dress is absolutely perfect for you," Lady Sunshine said.

Rylee smiled. "I believe it is."

The door chimed, and Lunden rushed in.

"Sorry I'm late." When Lunden hugged Rylee, she whispered, "Everything okay?"

Instead of revealing she'd nearly crashed and burned, Rylee said, "Yes."

Pulling away, Lunden said, "I got held up by Mr. Herbert."

"Oh Lord, what did he want this time?" Rylee asked.

"Apparently, he's pissed that Canten didn't arrest Mr. Elmo and wants me to make him do it."

Rylee and Lady Sunshine laughed.

Lady Sunshine shook her head. "That Herbert. Do you know that nut is going around town telling anyone who will listen that his granddaughter dumped the sheriff?"

"What?" Rylee and Lunden said in unison.

How could I not have heard this? All she needed was for this to make it to her mother's ears.

"Yep. He tried to come at me with that foolery, and I asked him how in the world could she dump a man she wasn't even dating?" Lady Sunshine popped the cork of the bottle. She poured a glass and passed it to Lunden. "He scoffed and marched off. He's the one who should be arrested. For slander."

"He got upset with you for telling the truth? How childish," Lunden said.

"That's not why he got upset." Lady Sunshine passed Rylee a glass. "He got upset when I told him the sheriff was destined for a lotus flower, not a ragweed."

Lunden laughed. Rylee didn't. Instead, she eyed the dress in her hand. Now she was sure Lady Sunshine was trying to tell her something. Rylee was sure her mother had spoken to her by now. Had her mother let something slip? *Mom.*

After they finished their champagne, Lady Sunshine escorted Lunden to the back. Alone, Rylee sent a text to her mother:

Rylee: Mom, did you say something to Lady Sunshine?
Several seconds ticked past before her mother responded.

Mom: No, dear, why do you ask?

Rylee: She's being cryptic. Like she knows something.

Mom: You know she's psychic. She probably does know something. You should ask her if she sees a wedding in your future.

Rylee: I'm sure she does. Lunden's. Talk later, Mom.

Rylee dropped her phone back into her bag. Admiring the lotus dress again, she smiled. The piece was perfect for when she and Canten planned to spend the day at the lake house with her parents. Her mother had their day all planned out, she was sure.

"What do you think?" Lunden said.

Rylee slapped her hand over her mouth, her eyes stinging with unshed tears. Allowing her hand to fall, she said, "You look absolutely amazing."

Lady Sunshine had outdone herself with this one. Instead of tradi-tional white, the gown was an elegant muted golden color, fashioned out of satin and decorated with lace appliqués and sparkle. A detachable train transformed it into a fitted mermaid-style gown.

"Quade's going to cry when those doors open and you're standing there." Rylee fanned her eyes. "Oh my God, I'm so, so happy for you."

"Thank you," Lunden said, batting her eyes. She eyed herself in the mirror. "I'm getting married, Ry."

"Yes, you are. And to an amazing man who loves you to pieces." And she couldn't have been happier for her friend.

"Ladies, I will be right back. I need to run to Jewel's for some more fabric," Lady Sunshine said.

When Lady Sunshine was out the door, Lunden eyed Rylee. "Are you ready for your big performance this weekend?"

She had no other choice but to be. "Pretending I'm infatuated with Canten is not going to be a problem. We're pretty good at this fake-relationship thing." However, trying to hide her true feelings for him would be the challenge.

Saturday morning, Rylee stood in front of the full-length mirror inside her bedroom and scrutinized herself from head to toe, falling in love with the lotus dress all over again. Lady Sunshine had magic sewing fingers.

Why was she so concerned about how she looked anyway? It wasn't like she and Canten were going on a real date. Spending the day at the lake with her parents was just part of the ruse. After the hellish week she'd had, this was a welcome escape.

On Monday, one of her ovens had died. Tuesday, instead of sugar being in the sugar bin, someone had accidentally filled it with salt. Luckily, she tasted every batch of batter before she placed it in the oven. But she'd lost a much-needed hour. Wednesday . . . actually, Wednesday had been okay. She'd placed a help wanted sign in the window that morning, and Ms. Jewel, one of the town elders, had found her the perfect candidate that afternoon. A young man fresh off the bus.

The women of Honey Hill had another man to paw over. Ezekiel Mosley. Thirty-six, unmarried, tall, dark, and handsome. The man was definitely going to be good for business. The only thing that might make him less attractive to some was the fact he'd been recently paroled. However, that hadn't mattered to her. Everyone deserved a second chance. Plus, Ms. Jewel had vouched for him, and if you couldn't trust Ms. Jewel, you couldn't trust anyone.

The doorbell rang, drawing her from her thoughts. "Come in," she yelled. Of course, she'd have to have the usual conversation with Canten. *Lock your door. Check your peephole.* The man was like a broken record. Moving toward the front of the house, she said, "I know, I know. Stop leaving the door—" She stopped abruptly and gasped. Leonard Jamison stood in her living room. "Leonard? What are you doing here?" The grin he flashed made him resemble a weasel. His gleaming white teeth stood in stark contrast to his dark-brown skin. She couldn't lie and say he was a bad-looking man, because he wasn't. He was just an asshole, which made him extremely ugly.

"What, no hello?"

"Leonard, what are you doing in my house?" she said.

"You invited me in."

Had I known it was you, I wouldn't have. And her mother really wanted to set her up with this creep? *Really, Mom?*

Leonard held up one of the *Honey Hill Is Home* tote bags Quade sold at his shop. "My grandmother asked me to drop this off to you."

Why did she get the feeling that wasn't the only reason he was here? She reached for the bag. The sooner she took it, hopefully, the sooner he left.

"It's heavy. I can place it where you want," he said.

"I'm sure I can handle it." When she took possession, she nearly dropped it, not having expected it to be this heavy. *What the hell is in here?* The clank of glass told her Mrs. Jamison had been canning again. The woman made the best preserves around. Rylee usually purchased the preserves at the market. Why was Mrs. Jamison sending them to her? She wasn't sure she trusted this home delivery by Leonard. "Tell your grandmother I said thank you very much."

That had been his cue to leave, but he didn't budge.

"Was there something else?" she said.

The way his eyes crept over her body made her uneasy. Thankfully, he'd left the front door open. Not that she thought he'd try anything, but you never truly knew what a person was capable of, especially one as unpredictable as a Jamison.

"You look really nice," he said. "Big date?"

Why was he all up in her business? "No. Just going out with a friend."

"Maybe I can take you for coffee sometime," he said.

"Um, no. I have plenty of coffee at the shop."

"Maybe I can swing by there and have a cup with you."

Clearly, he couldn't take a hint. Just to get him going, she said, "Sure. If I'm available, I'll have a cup of coffee with you." She didn't intend to ever be available.

When he finally left, Rylee took the tote into the kitchen, then moved to the door to close and lock it. She yelped when Canten stood there about to ring the bell. Resting her hand over her heart, she said, "You scared the hell out of me," stepping aside for him to enter.

"I'm sorry." His eyes raked over her body. "*Wow*," he said. "You look great."

Those eyes on her, she appreciated.

She smiled a little. "Thank you. So do you." And he smelled as good as he looked in the khaki cargo shorts and sage-green polo shirt. "Make yourself at home. I'll be right back."

He nodded.

"I, um, see you had a visitor," he called out.

Rejoining him, she said, "Yeah. Oddly, Mrs. Jamison sent him over with some preserves."

Canten laughed. "Sounds like a ploy to see you."

"I learned an important lesson today," she said. "One you've tried to teach me for months."

"Oh yeah? What's that?"

"Always lock the door."

※

Canten was lost in his thoughts as he drove to the Charleses' lake house rental. He recalled the pang of jealousy he'd felt, looking out his window to see Leonard Jamison's luxury vehicle parked in Rylee's driveway. *Delivering preserves, my ass.* Instead of rushing over, which had been his first instinct, he'd waited until the egotistical bastard had left. He wasn't in a pissing contest with the asshole. Besides, if he were—Canten glanced over at Rylee in the passenger seat—he would be winning.

"I hear Katrina Sweeney dumped you. Are you okay? I'm here for you if you need a shoulder to cry on."

Canten swerved. "What?" *Dammit.* How many people had Herbert told this lie to? "Who told you that?"

She smirked. "Lady Sunshine."

Lady Sunshine? Dammit. Well, if Lady Sunshine knew, half the town was sure to know by now too. He was surprised he hadn't gotten a call from his father.

"Don't worry," Rylee continued, "Lady Sunshine didn't believe him. Actually, she stood up for you."

When Rylee told him what Lady Sunshine had said to Mr. Herbert, he burst into laughter. "I owe Lady Sunshine a hug." Confused about something, he said, "What did the lotus-flower thing mean?"

Rylee's gaze slid out the window. "Who knows? It's Lady Sunshine. It could mean anything."

She had a point.

They arrived at her parents' place a little after eleven. The location was beautiful, nestled amid a forest of plush trees, with the sparkling lake as a backdrop. He could see why Mrs. Charles loved it here. This seemed like the perfect spot to come to escape your troubles. Nothing but the sounds of nature and not another house in sight for miles.

Inside, the bungalow was decorated in earth tones and blue hues. Plush brown sofas looked like they'd provide one heck of a napping spot. The open floor plan provided an unobstructed view of the large modern kitchen. Oversize windows allowed for a spectacular view of the lake. This place was both comfortable and cozy.

A short time after their arrival, they boarded a pontoon boat with Rylee's parents and headed onto the lake. Mrs. Charles had planned for them to enjoy lunch on the water. She'd packed an eye-popping selection of food: sandwiches made with her homemade pimento cheese, fresh-cut fruit and veggies, croissants filled with either ham and Swiss cheese or turkey and cheddar, chips, olives, and several more delicacies. While the food made Canten's mouth water and stomach growl, Mr. Charles seemed more interested in fishing than eating. Mrs. Charles nixed that real quick, letting Mr. Charles know food would come first.

"Who's hungry?" Mrs. Charles asked.

Canten's hand shot into the air.

Everyone laughed.

"Between you and Sebastian, I'm not sure who has the bigger appetite," Mrs. Charles said.

"Canten needs his energy. It takes a lot to protect and *serve*," Rylee said.

The sly expression on her face told him she was hinting toward the *plenty of sex* comment she'd overheard at Finger Leafing Goode. Their inside joke.

Rylee fixed him a hefty plate, then prepared her own. Mrs. Charles did the same for Mr. Charles. Compared to Canten's plate, Mr. Charles ate like a bird. No wonder he'd lost a little weight since the last time he'd seen him. Settling around the small table, they feasted.

"You two never told us how long you've been dating," Mrs. Charles said.

Rylee choked on a cracker. Giving her the same advice she'd given him once, he said, "Raise your arms." However, he didn't pound her on the back. While Rylee got herself together, he took it upon himself to answer the question. "A little shy of three months."

"And how did it happen?" her mother asked.

"You want to answer this one, buttercup?" Canten said. *Buttercup? Where in the hell did that come from?*

Rylee coughed several more times, then patted a hand on her chest. "You go ahead."

He wondered if she'd intentionally started another round of coughing just so she wouldn't have to respond to the question. In hindsight, they probably should have discussed these little details. Canten took Rylee's hand into his. "Well, one day I looked at her and no longer saw my best friend's little sister or the girl who was like a sister to me. I saw a strong, intelligent, kind woman whose inside beauty was just as ravishing as the outside."

"Aww," Mrs. Charles said.

"My baby girl is something special," Mr. Charles said.

Rylee's coughing dried up, and she regarded Canten with sentimental eyes, a neutral expression on her face.

"Go on, go on," Mrs. Charles said.

Canten kissed the back of Rylee's hand. "I wasn't sure how she saw me, so I didn't say or do anything that would make her uncomfortable. I just waited and watched."

"I was into you too," she said, her eyes never leaving his. "Just never knew how to say that."

Canten eyed Mr. and Mrs. Charles. "I wanted to be respectful of my friendship with Sebastian, so I asked him would he object to me asking her out. He said as long as I treated her right, he didn't have an issue." His gaze found Rylee again. "He knew I would."

While Canten played it cool on the outside, inside, his heart threatened to break through his chest. *Damn.* Obviously, he didn't have an issue lying to the Charleses after all.

Rylee flashed a delicate smile. "So did I," she said.

"How did you feel about Canten, dear?" Mrs. Charles asked.

Rylee's gaze settled on their joined hands. "Before he ever asked me out, I was sweet on the sheriff," she said. Her gaze rose. "His kindness. His humbleness. His willingness to help people when they need him most. Somewhere deep down, I think I'd always known our friendship would become more. But I don't think I could have ever imagined just how much more."

Damn. If they'd both been nominees in the best-actor category, he wasn't sure who would have earned the Oscar, because they'd both given outstanding performances.

Canten pulled his unwilling eyes from Rylee and focused on her parents. "Well, that's it in a nutshell."

Mrs. Charles swiped a tear from her cheek. "I think it's safe to tell anyone and everyone who will listen about your relationship. I think we all know where it's headed?"

"Not yet," Rylee said.

Mrs. Charles sighed heavily and rolled her eyes heavenward. *"But why?"* she whined like a toddler questioning a parent after being told they couldn't have ice cream.

Mr. Charles patted Mrs. Charles on the leg. "It's their decision, bunny. They'll let us know when they're ready." Mr. Charles eyed them. "Until then, we'll respect their decision."

"Thank you, Daddy."

After finishing his meal, Mr. Charles wasted no time pulling out the fishing rods. Canten was too full to even think straight, let alone hold a fishing pole. Rylee eagerly joined her father. It stunned Canten to see her willing and able to bait her own hook, not to mention doing it while wearing a dress. *She cooks, bakes, and fishes. A total package.*

Mrs. Charles eased down next to Canten and stared across the boat at her laughing husband and daughter. "Those two have always been so close," she said. "I'm so grateful I met a man who believed in being a great father, husband, provider. We were just kids when we fell in love. All these years later, I still love him with that same intensity. He's my whole world."

Canten eyed Mrs. Charles, who looked to be a thousand miles away.

Coming back to reality, she donned a wide smile and said, "My daughter is gorgeous, isn't she?"

Canten stared across at Rylee, her skin glowing under the rays of the sun. Something quivered inside him. Startling at first, then calming. What her daughter possessed was something far more than beauty, but he said, "Yes, she is."

"Those lotus flowers on her dress are fitting. She always finds a way to bloom."

Awareness jostled him. *Lotus flowers?* Canten scrutinized the purple flowers on her dress, recalling what Rylee had said Lady Sunshine had said to her. That he was destined for a lotus flower. It freaked him out a little.

As if knowing his eyes were on her, she glanced over her shoulder. With a tilt of her head, she invited him over. "Come fish with me," she said.

"You can mind my pole," Mr. Charles said.

Canten stood elbow to elbow with Rylee. She looked over her shoulder toward her parents, and so did he. They were cuddled up in a loving embrace. By the way Mrs. Charles giggled like a schoolgirl, Mr. Charles had whispered something sweet into her ear.

"Get a room," Rylee said.

Mr. and Mrs. Charles waved her off and remained focused on each other.

Rylee stared out at the water. "I bet it's gorgeous here at night. The light of the full moon glistening off the water. That would be so romantic."

Rylee appeared to be talking more to herself than to him, so he simply minded his line.

In little more than a whisper, she said, "Buttercup?"

How had he known that would come back and bite him in the ass? "Had to make it sound authentic, right?" He winked.

"What you said earlier . . . thank you for covering my ass. You're excellent under pressure. I freeze. Or more accurately, choke." She chuckled. "It's amazing how you were able to come up with all of that off the top of your head like that."

Canten wiggled his line. "They say the best lies are rooted in the truth."

Without looking at her, he knew Rylee's eyes were on him. Okay, maybe he should have kept that part to himself.

CHAPTER 8

Rylee and Canten said goodbye to her parents a little after ten that night. Rylee was exhausted, but she didn't want her night with Canten to end. Yes, she knew they were only pretending, but today had been fun. From lunch on the water to snapping several pictures of Canten and her father knocked out on the sofa. The lake, spending time with her parents, dinner on the deck with so much laughter her side still hurt—she'd enjoyed it all. Today had been . . . "Perfect," she mumbled to herself.

"You say something?" Canten asked, turning down the radio.

"No. I was just singing."

"I had a great time today," he said.

"So did I." She desperately wanted to ask him to elaborate on his comment from earlier, about the best lies being rooted in the truth, but she didn't. "I can't believe how many fish we caught. I see panfried trout fillets with herb-butter sauce in your future."

"Stop teasing me, woman," he said. "How the hell did you catch so many fish? Usually, when Pop Charles, Senior, Sebastian, and I go out, we catch about five between us."

She blew her breath on her fingers, then polished them against her dress. "Skills."

"Those fish were just drawn to you in that dress," he said.

"I look that good, huh?"

"Amazing."

She smiled. "You know, I could really go for something sweet right now. A fresh, gooey cinnamon roll with extra icing. Wanna swing by the bakery? It's late. No one will see us."

"Fresh cinnamon rolls . . . do you really have to ask?"

They laughed.

A short time later, they arrived on Main Street. Not a soul stirred. Entering the bakery, Rylee intentionally left the light off, except in the kitchen. She tied an apron around her waist, then passed one to Canten.

Fine lines crawled across his forehead. "This is nice." One brow arched. "What do you want me to do with it?"

She laughed. "Put it on, silly. You're going to help me make the cinnamon rolls."

"But—"

"*Op,*" she said, holding up her hand to foil his protest. "It'll be fun."

"Okay, but if I burn down your kitchen, don't be mad."

"I'm insured."

Rylee collected all the items from the rack they needed and arranged them on the metal prep table while Canten grabbed the things they would need from the refrigerator. After retrieving the countertop mixer she used for small-batch jobs, they started.

"Since the recipe calls for softened butter and this is hard as a rock . . ." She tapped the stick of butter on the table. "I'll show you my secret." She took a glass bowl, filled it with boiling water, and allowed it to sit for several minutes. After dumping the water, she placed the sticks of butter on a plate, then covered it with the heated bowl. "It'll be soft enough by the time we need it."

"That's a neat trick," he said.

To the mixer, they added warm milk, instant yeast, butter, sugar, a pinch of salt, and two room-temperature eggs. She'd cheated the process of bringing the eggs to room temp by placing them into a bowl of luke-warm water for several minutes.

"The key to making the perfect dough is not to add too much flour," Rylee said, scooping out a cup of flour, then leveling it with a butter knife. She allowed Canten to do the remaining three and a half cups.

"I've apprehended hardened criminals, but helping you make cinnamon rolls has me nervous as hell," he joked.

"You're doing great."

Once the dough was all mixed, they set it aside to rise and prepared the cinnamon-roll filling and icing.

Rylee scooped a small amount of icing and put the spoon to Canten's mouth. "Taste."

His eyes never left her as his kissable lips wrapped around the spoon. Her breath hitched at the far-too-sensual sight. When he pulled away and licked his bottom lip, her legs wobbled. Afraid she'd collapse to the floor, she rested a hip against the prep table.

"Scrumptious," she said, absently.

"Yes, it is. That maple flavoring gives it something extra."

"What?" The word came out in a moan, snapping her back to reality. "I mean, good. Great. I, um, I'm glad you like it." She pointed over her shoulder. "I should check the dough."

When the dough had doubled in size, Rylee sprinkled the table with flour and guided Canten as he rolled it into a rectangle. With each push of the rolling pin, his forearms flexed. How could something so simple be so damn arousing? His pronounced veins pushed against his flesh, which was lightly dusted with flour. The white was a beautiful contrast against his brown skin. *Look away.*

When Canten finished, she retrieved the filling they had prepared. "Some people like to just spread the butter onto the dough, then sprinkle on the brown sugar and cinnamon. I prefer mixing it all together first, making a paste. But either way you do it, the rolls will still be delicious."

An hour later, they sat on the kitchen floor, backs propped against the wall, enjoying the fruits of their labor. God, she laughed so much when they were together. His humor constantly surprised her because when he was in uniform, he was always so poker faced. Being one of the few who ever got to see this side of him made her feel . . . privileged? Was that the right word?

"These cinnamon rolls are giving me life," Canten said. "You did great."

"This was all you," she countered.

"You were a great teacher."

Even with credit due to him, he chose to give the spotlight to her. So modest. "It was a team effort."

Canten bumped her. "We work well together."

Yes, they did. Evidenced by their performance earlier. She popped a piece of the roll into her mouth. "We do, don't we? I wasn't sure I could pull it off. It's been a long time since I've dated. I'm well past rusty."

"When is the last time you've gone on an actual date?" he asked nonchalantly, biting into his treat.

"Several years?" She rolled her eyes heavenward. "And it was horrible. With a capital *H*."

"Should I ask?"

"Let's just say things went downhill fast. From the moment he picked me up, all he talked about was himself. When the waiter arrived for our orders, before I could tell the waiter what I wanted, my date had the audacity to order for me."

"What did you say?"

"I told him that sounded like a great suggestion, then ordered something else."

Canten barked a laugh. "He sounds like a narcissist, so I bet he didn't like that."

"No, he didn't. I wanted to order dessert, but because he'd been so rude to everyone, I was afraid to order it in fear of someone spitting in it."

"Sounds like an asshole."

"Top shelf. What about you? When was the last time you were on a date?"

"I haven't been on one in a long while." His eyes left her. "I guess you can say I'm a little rusty too."

"I wouldn't have known by your performance today. It was superb. We might have actually been a little too convincing with my parents, though. I could see that sparkle in my mother's eyes. By the time they return to Florida, she'll have us married with a houseful of babies. Don't worry. I would definitely not ask you to fake a marriage. That would totally be crossing the line." As a joke, she said, "I mean, unless you're willing."

"I think we should."

Rylee bit her tongue as she whipped her head toward him. Surely, her face showed every ounce of shock she felt. "What?"

"Gotcha."

She gave a shaky laugh. "Yes, you did."

"You must really be enjoying that cinnamon roll. You have icing all over your chin."

Reaching over, he used his thumb to remove it in a slow, arousing manner. His gentle touch set off a firestorm inside her. Heat rushed up her neck and warmed her face, her nipples beaded inside her bra, and her core hummed.

"There. All gone."

Their gazes held for a long heated moment. It could have been her imagination—or wishful thinking—but she swore Canten's mouth moved a half inch closer to hers. What she definitely *didn't* imagine was the moment when his dark, daunting gaze lowered to her mouth. Lucas popped into her head, rattling her. Flurries of guilt swirled inside her.

She shouldn't be here like this, wanting desperately for Canten to kiss her. But she did. And just when she thought she might get the opportunity to taste him, at least this one time, he turned away.

Eyeing his watch, he said, "*Wow.* Time really does fly when you're having fun. It's almost two in the morning. I should probably get you home."

That was probably for the best. "Yeah, it is kinda past my bedtime," she said, hoping to cut through some of the sexual tension in the room so she could breathe again.

Canten stood and offered his hand. When he pulled her to her feet, they stood toe to toe. For a millisecond, she contemplated backing him against the wall, pressing her lips to his, and kissing him until her mouth ached. Lacking that level of courage, she trailed him out the room instead, sparing them both from the consequences of another one of her ill-thought-out decisions.

Almost a week had passed since Canten had spent the day with Rylee and her parents. Yet he couldn't get the day out of his mind. What stuck with him the most from that day was the time he and Rylee had spent in her bakery. They'd had fun making cinnamon rolls, talking, and laughing until the wee hours of the morning.

Thinking about the fact he'd almost allowed himself to kiss her in a moment of foolishness both tantalized and tortured him. He'd almost lost control. He didn't lose control. Ever. The fact that she could throw him off his game so effortlessly made him vulnerable, unpredictable. That didn't sit well with him. In his line of work, such a deficiency could be deadly. Well, at least, back in Charlotte. But even here in Honey Hill, it could be, at the very least, dangerous. He had the memory of being sprawled out on Main Street to prove it. All the time he and Rylee would be spending together made the fact he was easily distracted around her even more perilous. *Shit. You have to get control of yourself.*

"You're distracted, son. Chess is a game of strategy. That strategy requires concentration and focus. Care to share what's on your mind?"

His father knew him too damn well. From the moment Canten had joined him at one of the several cement chess tables scattered throughout the square, his mind had been elsewhere. He shot a glance across the way to the bakery. "Just thinking about the logistics of the Founders' Day parade," he lied.

Senior chuckled. "Lying to me too, now, huh?"

Too damn well. Before Canten could respond to his father, Mr. Clem, one of his father's good friends, joined them.

"Mornin'," Mr. Clem said.

"Mornin'," Canten and Senior said in unison.

Mr. Clem was about five seven, brown skinned with a full head of gray hair.

"Clem, it's a hunnerd fifty in the shade. Why you wearing a long-sleeved shirt?" Senior asked.

Mr. Clem eased down next to Canten on the bench, probably hoping he would move so he could play his father. Those two constantly disagreed on who was the best chess player between them. Truthfully, it was Senior. His father was probably the best chess player in the county.

"I read one of Estella's blog posts the other day. It said black folk can get skin cancer too. It said we should be checking our skin monthly. A full-body exam. I had a hell of a time checking my buttocks."

For the next several minutes, Mr. Clem educated them on what to look for during a self-exam and how to reduce their skin-cancer risks: not lingering in the sun, wearing clothing that protected the skin from the sun, wearing sunscreen—SPF 30 or greater.

"That's something to think about," Senior said.

"Do more than think," Clem said. "Adhere." He tilted his head back and looked toward the sky. "Sitting under this shade tree is good. Less exposure to sun rays."

Canten found himself wondering about his ancestors and the grueling hours they'd spent out in the fields under the intense heat of the sun. Had any of them developed skin cancer? Sometimes, he found himself wondering about the oddest things. He glanced toward his horse tied to a nearby patience pole. When he rode Ellington, he wore sunscreen—most of the time. He needed to do a better job of applying it.

"Hey, hey, hey."

Canten looked behind him to see Sebastian headed toward them. His presence put a smile on Canten's face. He hadn't seen his best friend in close to a month. The man stayed on the move. The second Canten stood to greet Sebastian, Mr. Clem moved into his spot.

"I saw Ellington and knew you were here," Sebastian said.

"When'd you get back in town?" Canten asked, giving Sebastian a brotherly hug.

"About an hour ago," Sebastian said.

"How long you here for?"

Sebastian blew a heavy breath while running a hand over his head. "Not long. I'm headed to the bakery to see Rylee, then to the lake to spend some time with my parents, then I'm headed out again. Pop. Mr. Clem."

"Hey, son," Senior said to Sebastian. "Good to see you."

Mr. Clem didn't break his concentration from the game. "Hey, Sebastian," he said without looking up. "Heard you're out there doing big things. Proud of you, young brother."

"We all are," Senior said.

"Thanks," Sebastian said, a look of true appreciation on his face.

After his fiancée had ended their engagement two days before their wedding, Sebastian had spiraled out of control. Brawls at the local watering hole, countless bad decisions, and a bunch of selfish behavior.

Concerned about his friend, Canten had been forced to show him some tough love before he self-destructed. Locking him up and giving him a choice: spend time in jail or get his shit together. It had taken a minute, but Sebastian had finally gotten the message, focusing all his pent-up frustration on something positive and starting his own business. Nothing had changed between them.

"You heading to the bakery with me?" Sebastian asked.

"Mmm-hmm," Senior hummed.

Canten ignored his father.

"Bring me back a cuppie, son," Senior said.

"I'll take a bear claw," Mr. Clem added.

"I guess I am," Canten said. "Keep an eye on Ellington, please."

Making their way to the bakery, Canten and Sebastian played catch-up. Not much new had happened with either of them, except, of course, for the fact Canten was lying to Sebastian's parents by pretending to be his sister's love interest.

"Senior know about you and Rylee's . . . arrangement?" Sebastian asked.

"Yes," Canten said.

"Did you get a lecture?"

Canten chuckled. "No. Just the look. A lecture would have been better."

The moment reminded Canten of the time in his childhood when he'd accidentally broken his father's favorite mug. He'd wanted to drink coffee like his dad—after being told not to do so. The dark roast had been so hot and so nasty it had shocked his system, causing him to drop the ceramic drinkware Canten had given Senior for Father's Day. His father had always cherished any gift his son had given him.

Instead of fessing up to what he'd done, he'd attempted to glue the mug back together. That had been a bad idea because he'd ruined the kitchen table his mother loved and had glued his fingers to the mug.

His father had given him the exact same look of disappointment the night he'd told him about Rylee as he had that day Canten had broken the mug.

"The only reason I'm going along with this is because I love my sister. Plus, I know how relentless my mother can be when it comes to matchmaking."

Rylee had alluded to the fact he was usually the one in his mother's sights.

Sebastian continued, "I get a phone call every other day about some nice young lady in Honey Hill I should meet. It's exhausting, but I get it. She just wants to see us both happy. Sounds like you and Rylee's date with our parents turned out far better than the last date Rylee went on."

"You're talking about the narcissist who tried to tell her what she was going to eat."

Sebastian stopped and eyed him with a raised brow. "She told you about that?"

"Yes." Why did he seem so shocked?

Sebastian started moving again. "She must really trust you. It's a good thing she had a nosy neighbor." He made a fist. "Man, I still wish I could get my hands on that asshole. I would beat his head in for slipping my sister a roofie."

This time Canten stopped. "What!" Rylee clearly didn't trust him that much, because she *hadn't* told him that part of the story. "The bastard drugged her?" Canten's blood boiled. He needed more details.

"Yes. Her old neighbor back in Goldsboro saw them returning and noticed Rylee stumbling like she was drunk. She knew Rylee wasn't a heavy drinker, so she intervened. He tried to object, but when the neighbor threatened to call the police, he fled."

Canten couldn't label all the emotions building inside him, but anger was the most prevalent. "Did Rylee press charges? Was the SOB arrested? Charged? Jailed?" He needed answers, dammit.

Sebastian shook his head. "Rylee just wanted to forget it, put the whole situation out of her mind. She moved back to Honey Hill not long after that incident. I'm so glad she did."

Canten wiped away the perspiration on his forehead caused by his outrage. Sebastian wasn't the only one who'd like a few minutes with the man. Scratch that, the coward. Because no real man would need to drug a woman to get what he wanted. Thank God for the nosy neighbor. Canten knew how horrible that situation could have turned out.

Sebastian spoke, tearing into Canten's overwhelming thoughts. "Don't mention to Rylee I told you any of that, okay?"

"No, no. I won't," Canten said, still disturbed by what he'd just learned. How defenseless Rylee must have felt. A fierce need to protect her swelled inside of him.

"Back to you and my sister. I sure hope you two know what you're doing. My mother has senses like a bloodhound. She can sniff out deception," Sebastian said.

Allowing himself a reprieve from what he'd just learned, he said, "You have nothing to worry about."

Sebastian hadn't seen him and Rylee in action. They were seamless in their performance. If Canten hadn't known better, he would have been convinced he and Rylee were an actual couple. While he might have doubted before whether they could pull this off, he no longer harbored any uncertainty. They were surprisingly good at being a couple. He felt as connected to her as he had to Jayla. Maybe even more so. And it pained him to admit that. Especially when everything between him and Jayla had been real and nothing between him and Rylee was.

"Just remember," Sebastian said, "*when* the shit hits the fan, I had absolutely no knowledge of anything."

"Don't worry," Canten said, "no one is going to find out."

He was sure of it.

CHAPTER 9

Her chakras were out of balance.

That was the only explanation Rylee had that would explain the day she was having. And she had cramps. Monster, monster cramps. Like a T. rex had decided to perch in her uterus and claw away. What was worse, she had no pain reliever. Not in her purse. Not in the medicine cabinet. Not in the entire bakery. Why? Because clearly the universe hated her.

Sadie—Sweet Sadie, as Rylee called her—popped her head into the kitchen. The woman was Rylee's jack-of-all-trades. Whatever needed to be done, she could trust Sadie to do it. Except bake. The poor girl could barely boil water.

"How much longer on the bread pudding?" Sadie asked.

"It'll be ready soon," she said.

Ugh. She needed Ezekiel, but he'd taken the day off to take care of some business. While he'd only been there a short time, he'd definitely proved himself. He was almost as good at baking as she was. Almost. He still had a few things to learn.

Using her shoulder, Rylee brushed sweat off her brow. "Why the hell is it so hot in here?" Abandoning the piping bag she'd been using to pipe *Happy Birthday* on her signature and popular white vanilla bean–almond cake, she moved to the thermostat. "No way it's sixty-five degrees in here." She tapped it as if doing so would alter the reading. "I just had this thing serviced."

Needing to focus on one task at a time, she made a mental note to contact the HVAC company. *Again.* Too bad Sebastian had left town already. He would have definitely gotten the system running like new. The memory of his surprise visit put a smile on her face. Her excitement had grown when she'd realized Canten was with him. Canten had hugged her extra tight. Like he'd missed her. Had he?

A timer sounded, reminding her she had no time to daydream. Removing a batch of chocolate chip cookies, she placed them on a rack to cool. One thing off her massive to-do list. Only 1,576 more to go. She eyed the wall clock. *Eleven o'clock. Great!* Kelsey, her part-time kitchen assistant, would be there in an hour. However, with the way her day was going, Kelsey would likely call in sick.

Remembering the macarons she needed to personalize, she placed them in the Glowforge laser cutter, sent the file to the software, then pressed the flashing magic button. "Seamless," she said. This workhorse never disappointed her.

Returning to the prep table, she stopped abruptly. Had she fed the sourdough starter today? She was pretty sure she had. *Oh God, these cramps have my brain on freaking autopilot.*

Sadie stuck her head in again.

"No brownies yet," Rylee said.

"You have a visitor."

Visitor? "Who?" she asked. A part of her wanted Sadie to say the sheriff, but Canten would have found his own way back.

"Leonard something."

Rylee tossed her head back and sighed heavily. "Tell him . . ." She sighed again. "Tell him I'm swamped and can't come out right now. Give him a coffee on the house." *Hopefully, that will get him out of here.*

"'Kay."

Not ten seconds had passed when Sadie appeared again. She was starting to not be so sweet. *What now?*

"He wants to know if he can make it a large specialty coffee."

Are you kidding me? "Fine," Rylee said.

Rylee stared at the entrance, waiting for the door to swing open again. She breathed a sigh of relief when it didn't. A beat later, her face contorted into a ball, sniffing several times. "What's that—" *Shit, the bread pudding.* She raced to the oven and yanked the door open. A puff of rancid smoke greeted her. The dessert was burned to a crisp. Could her day get any worse?

Canten relaxed on the sofa, flicking through television stations. He rarely knew what to do on days off. The sound of sirens drew his attention. That never was a good sign. Retrieving his radio, he keyed up the station because when you were the sheriff, you never really clocked out from the job. "Dispatch, come in."

"Howdy, Sheriff," Deputy Gunter said, his deep southern drawl unmistakable.

"I hear sirens. What's going on?"

"There was a small fire at the bakery. EMS and HHFD are on the scene."

Canten froze midstride. *Did he say the bakery?* "Did you say the bakery?" he asked for clarity.

"Yes, sir."

Canten's heart pounded against his rib cage. He clipped the handheld radio to his belt, slid into his shoes, snatched up his keys, and bounded out the door. Sirens blaring, he made it to Main Street in record time. A crowd of onlookers had gathered outside Pastries on Main. He muscled his way through.

Relief washed over him the second his eyes landed on Rylee, talking to one of the several firemen present. *She's okay. Thank God, she's okay.* The urge to rush to her and wrap her in his protective arms overwhelmed him, but he resisted. How would that have looked? The fact he could see with his own eyes that she was okay had to be enough.

Canten chatted with the fire chief, who informed him the fire had been caused by a laser Rylee had been using to personalize macarons and that she'd put the fire out herself before the sprinkler system had activated. One of her staff had called 9-1-1. Minimal damage, except to the laser, which was a total loss. No injuries, thank God. But Rylee was pretty shaken up.

Canten's eyes locked on her. Even from here he could see how visibly shaken she was. "Thanks, Justin," he said, giving the man a firm handshake before making his way to Rylee.

"Hey," he said.

"Hey," she said, her voice trembling.

By her red-rimmed eyes, he knew she'd been crying.

"Are you okay?"

"Yes."

Her shuddering body told a different story. He ached to hold her, comfort her.

"I wasn't paying attention," she said. "I knew better. I had so much going on. The cake, brownies, bread pudding. I was so distracted." Tears spilled from her eyes. "I'm sorry," she said, swiping at her eyes.

"Don't cry," he said, pulling her into his arms and not giving a damn what it looked like. Though he suspected it looked like what it was. One friend comforting another. Who was he kidding? Someone would definitely run with this. He held her at arm's length. "Don't beat yourself up. What's done is done. It could have been so much worse."

When she nodded, he stupidly pulled her back into his arms.

"I thought you were off today," she said, her warm breath tickling his neck.

"Is the sheriff ever truly off?" he said, instead of admitting he'd rushed over after learning there had been a fire at her shop. "So I hear you were a badass and put out the fire yourself."

Before she could respond, her parents rushed into the shop, their eyes wide with fear. Understandable. Canten reluctantly released her as Mr. and Mrs. Charles hurried toward them. Mrs. Charles wrapped Rylee in her arms, and Mr. Charles wrapped his arms around them both.

"Are you all right, baby girl?" her father asked, while her mother simply clenched her daughter tightly, probably too relieved to talk.

"I'm fine, Daddy, but Mommy is about to suffocate me."

"All right, bunny, all right. She's fine. Don't suffocate the child," Mr. Charles said, peeling his wife off.

A second later, Mrs. Charles's arms encased Canten. "Thank you for being here. Thank you for making sure my baby was okay."

"Always," Canten said, staring at Rylee. "She'll always be safe when I'm around."

"She's so lucky to have you."

"Mom!" Rylee said in an urgent whisper.

Mrs. Charles released Canten and eyed Rylee. "Dear, your father has something to tell you. To tell you both, actually."

Canten wasn't sure he liked the sound of that. Were they about to get a lecture for hiding their "relationship"? He already knew Mrs. Charles wanted to shout it to the world.

"Go ahead, my love," Mrs. Charles said, running a hand up and down her husband's back.

Mr. Charles scratched the back of his ear several times. "Well, on the way here, I exceeded the speed limit a bit and was stopped by one of your deputies."

That was it? He'd gotten a speeding ticket? Probably Deputy Martin. The rookie loved passing out tickets like he was trying to meet some nonexistent quota. They didn't practice that kind of policing in Honey Hill. "If you got a ticket, I'll take care of it," Canten said.

"Well, that's not exactly it," Mr. Charles said, scratching at his ear again.

"*Daddy*," Rylee dragged out. "What did you do, Daddy?"

"Baby girl, Canten . . . tensions were running high. I was desperate to get here, get to you. Your mother was in tears. And you know how much I hate seeing her cry." He eyed his wife with loving eyes.

Canten wasn't sure what would follow. Had Mr. Charles left the scene of an accident?

Mr. Charles continued, "In my lack of diligence, I told the young deputy I needed to get to the bakery and that if he didn't let us go right then, I would call the sheriff, whom you were dating."

Rylee gasped.

Canten couldn't find the words to respond. What was that old adage about secrets? Ah, he remembered. *The only way a secret survives is if only two people know it and one of them is dead.* Or something like that.

Rylee groaned, resting one hand on her forehead and the other against her stomach. "*Daddy*, you didn't."

"I'm sorry, baby girl. I wasn't thinking. It just slipped out."

The man looked truly remorseful. Canten was sure his actions hadn't been intentional.

Mrs. Charles soothed her husband. "You didn't mean to do it. Emotions were running high."

"I know you didn't mean to, Daddy," Rylee said, giving him a hug.

Canten had a thought. "Excuse me a second," he said. Moving away for privacy, he made a call to Deputy Martin. "Martin, it's Canten."

"Oh, hey, Sheriff. What's—"

Canten cut him off before he could finish the sentence. "Martin, did you stop Rylee's parents earlier."

There was a brief beat of silence on the line.

"Um, y-yes, sir. I'm sorry. Had I known it was them—"

"Rylee's father told you something. Something I need you to keep to yourself."

"About you and Rylee, sir?"

"Yes."

"Okay, you got it, Sheriff."

Whew. They'd dodged that bullet.

"I won't tell anyone else, sir," Martin said.

Anyone else? "Who have you told?" Canten asked.

"Only Mr. Clem. When Rylee's father peeled off, he nearly ran him off the road. He wanted to know what was going on."

He'd told Mr. Clem? The man gossiped worse than some women. Canten eyed Rylee, who stared back at him. She said something to her parents, then moved toward him. "Thanks, Martin," he said and ended the call.

"Is everything okay?" she said, her tone uncertain.

"Well . . . that depends," he said.

"On what?"

"On whether or not you think we'll be able to fool the entire town?" Because by now, half of it knew they were "dating."

Rylee circled the heel of her hand against her forehead. Her eyes glistened with unshed tears. "I can't take one more thing today," she said, her voice cracking. "What are we going to do?" She shrugged. "I got us into this mess, but I don't know what to do."

"Nothing," Canten said. "We do nothing. Instead of two people, we'll just be performing for a few more people. It'll be okay, Rylee." He wasn't 100 percent sure he believed that, but it seemed to make her feel better. Since their secret was out, he didn't hesitate to hug her to his chest again and give her the comfort she clearly needed. "It'll be okay," he repeated. "I promise."

But could he really make such an assurance?

CHAPTER 10

Rylee couldn't enjoy a peaceful lunch with Lunden without someone coming up to their patio table to comment on the town's hottest new duo. Their words, not hers. She hated being the center of attention, but ever since it had gotten out a few days ago she and Canten were an *item*, they had become like a celebrity couple.

Maybe Canten deserved such fanfare; he'd had countless women wanting to hold this position she played. Her only suitor had been Leonard Jamison. At least one good thing would come out of the town knowing: her Leonard problem was solved. He'd have to set his sights on someone else because she was off the market. Actually, *off* to *the market* would have been a more accurate representation of her current relationship status.

"Dang," Lunden said. "I thought Quade and I had caused a buzz when we started dating. You and Canten are causing an avalanche."

Yep, and she felt buried. "All of this was supposed to be so simple, Lu. It has turned into a fiasco." Rylee massaged her temple. "Now, when Canten and I 'break up'"—she made finger quotes—"I'm sure the rumors will say I got dumped by the sheriff. I'll get all these looks of pity and words of encouragement. *There are more fish in the sea. You're a pretty girl, you'll find someone else. Things like this happen.*" She cringed. "Katrina Sweeney and her crew will certainly get a kick out of it."

"Forget Katrina and her minions," Lunden said.

Rylee kneaded her temple a little harder. "It's all been so overwhelming. I'm so stressed. A part of me wants to come clean right now, but I don't want Canten to lose credibility. I'm more concerned for him than I am myself. He's a trusted town official. If folks found out he's been lying to them, regardless of the reason, some would distrust him."

"Unfortunately, he would probably be crucified," Lunden admitted. "What can I do to help?"

Rylee sighed. "Pin a note to my shirt that says *Do not fake a relationship*, then send me back in time."

Lunden laughed. "Okay, pretty sure that's not going to happen, so how *else* can I help?"

"Just listening to me complain about a situation I created for myself is enough." Rylee sipped from her glass of perfectly brewed, perfectly sweetened iced tea. The Capri House Restaurant always got tea brewing right. "I feel horrible that I've roped Canten into this."

"*Roped* seems like too harsh of a word. If Canten had wanted to say no, he would have. Believe me, that man has no problem speaking up for himself. I've seen him in action at our closed-door committee meetings."

"I guess." But it wasn't like she'd given him much wiggle room to do so.

"Have you ever considered the possibility Canten actually enjoys playing your love interest?" Lunden asked.

"Deep down, he's probably miserable. Just too much of a gentleman to say so."

"Well, the man I overheard talking to my soon-to-be husband didn't sound all that miserable to me. In fact, he sounded quite enthusiastic as he talked about the time he'd spent at the lake with you and your parents."

He shared that with Quade?

"He sounded quite impressed by the fact you could bait your own line," Lunden said. "And he went on and on about you."

Now Rylee understood where Zachary had gotten his eavesdropping from—his mother. Rylee smiled a little. She'd been baiting hooks and scaling fish since she was about ten. Watching her grandparents had made her an expert.

"Oh, and apparently, you're quite the teacher." Lunden flashed a confused look. "Something about you teaching him how to make cinnamon rolls at two o'clock in the morning."

He mentioned that too? "On the way back from the lake, we both wanted something sweet. I suggested cinnamon rolls." She smiled a little more. "We had fun," she said absently, recalling that night. "We baked and talked. Ate and laughed." She held back the part about nearly kissing. Mostly because she wasn't 100 percent sure they had. All the sexual tension wafting around the room had probably made her imagine the entire thing.

But there was no confusion in one thing. The way he'd studied her mouth. While she might be unsure about whether they'd almost kissed, she was certain he'd wanted to. More jarring, she'd wanted him to kiss her.

She hadn't simply pushed Lucas's memory aside. Not that easily. But she no longer capsized with guilt when her desire for Canten surfaced. It still rocked her a little, though.

"He's coming over tonight," Rylee said.

Lunden's brow hiked. "Really? You two spending a quiet evening in, huh?"

Rylee tossed a fry across the table. "No. Well, kinda. Just dinner, no freaky business."

A mischievous look spread over Lunden's face. "What if he kisses you?"

Rylee barked a laugh. "We're talking about Sheriff Canten Barnes. He wouldn't make such a move. I think he still sees me as Sebastian's little sister."

This time Lunden barked a laugh. "The way that man looks at you, the only thing he sees is Sebastian's little sister in his bed, underneath him, moaning his name."

Rylee would be the first to admit how much she liked the picture Lunden had painted. Bringing it to life in her head, she enjoyed the reel flicking through her mind even more. Too bad such a scene would never play out in real life. Something told her a night with the sheriff would be oh so sweet.

Canten arrived at Rylee's place a little after six. The second he hit the porch, he could smell the delicious aromas escaping from inside. His stomach growled with anticipation. He knew from experience that not only was Rylee a phenomenal baker, but she was also an excellent cook. Whatever she prepared behind that door would undoubtedly satisfy him.

When he rang the bell, Rylee yelled for him to come inside. *Jesus.* Hadn't he told this woman a hundred times about leaving the door unlocked and not checking to see who she was inviting inside? Honey Hill was no hotbed for crime, but it didn't hurt to be vigilant. Hadn't the whole Leonard Jamison episode taught her anything?

Ever since Sebastian had shared with him that Rylee had almost been date-raped, he'd been even more protective of her. Sometimes in the middle of the night when he couldn't sleep, he'd get out of bed, go into the living room, and peer out the blinds toward her place just to make sure everything looked okay.

"Don't say it," Rylee called out from the kitchen, beating him to the punch. "I literally unlocked the door two minutes before you arrived. Plus, I knew it was you."

"Yeah, right."

"Thankfully, my neighbor's the sheriff of this fine town. I feel safe just knowing he's near."

Maybe not for too much longer. He had a good feeling about the bureau commander job. But he wasn't ready to share any details. Joining her in the kitchen, he said, "I'm not always across the street. When my SUV is gone is likely when a criminal would strike."

"Now you're trying to scare me," Rylee said, an uneasy expression on her face.

Shit. "I'm not. Sorry." He sometimes forgot he wasn't in the big city any longer, where criminals lingered around every corner. To get her mind off the subject, he said, "Man, it smells amazing in here." His head jerked back when he saw the buffet of food. Baked salmon, kabobs—chicken and beef—hummus, pitas, grape leaves, antipasto salad, and several other delicious-looking items. It looked as if she were catering a small dinner party. Had she invited her parents?

"I hope you brought a huge appetite because I think I went a little overboard."

"From the looks of it, you went a lot overboard," he said. "Who else is joining us?"

"It's just the two of us," she said.

Canten barked a laugh. "Rylee, you prepared enough food to feed a starving football team."

Her eyes swept the room. "I did, didn't I? Well, whatever's left over, we can pack up and you can take to your crew at the station."

"You're really trying to put them to sleep." He rested his backside against the counter and watched Rylee make homemade tzatziki sauce. As always, not a hair was out of place. And even in the generic navy blue shirt, jeans, and brown sandals, she exemplified beauty. His inquisitive eyes trailed along her jawline and down to her neck. For a millisecond, he fantasized about placing delicate kisses on her soft skin. Snapping back to reality before he swelled below the waist, he said, "You look nice."

Eyeing him, she said, "So do you. We're coordinated. Blue looks nice on you."

He eyed the plaid blue-black-and-white short-sleeved button-down shirt he wore. "Thank you. Can I help with anything?"

"I got it."

"Come on, you have to let me do something." After all the work she'd clearly put in, he needed to pitch in somewhere.

"Do you really want to do something?" she asked.

"Yes."

"Fine. If you really want to do something, grab yourself a beer from the fridge, pop the top, then relax, lawman."

He chuckled, conceding defeat. "Do you want one?"

"No, I'm good."

Pushing off the counter, he grabbed a bottle from the fridge, then returned to the same spot. "I'm starving. There might not be any leftovers."

With her gloved hand, Rylee picked up a grape leaf. "Try this," she said, holding it to his mouth.

Canten bit into it. The mixture of seasoned meat and rice awakened his taste buds, and he gave a moan of satisfaction. Damn, this woman was an all-star in the kitchen.

"Good?"

Did she really have to ask? "Delicious," he said.

When she claimed the rest for herself, he protested. "Hey, that was mine."

Rylee passed him another. "I remember when I first convinced you to try a stuffed grape leaf. You were like a whiny five-year-old who didn't want to eat his veggies."

"And you said if I tried it and didn't like it, you'd bake me a lemon pound cake to get the taste out of my mouth."

"And you lied and said you didn't like it. After I'd baked that dog-gone cake, I caught you with a grape leaf in your mouth and another in your hand."

Canten burst into laughter. "Those damn grape leaves were phenomenal. But I really wanted that cake."

"All you had to do was ask," she said.

"That was the exact same thing you said back then."

"It still holds true."

A beat of silence played between them, each seemingly lost in their own thoughts. Canten flashed back to when he'd first moved back to Honey Hill. Takeout and TV dinners had been his go-to. Then Sebastian had invited him over to Rylee's one day for dinner. His taste buds had never been the same.

Jayla hadn't been much of a cook. They'd had a drawer full of takeout menus to support that claim. And while he'd tried, he hadn't been much better in the kitchen. Vegetables had never been his go-to food. Rylee had changed that. "I blame you for my new love for vegetables, along with the other foods I would have never tried had you not been the one preparing them," he said.

"Now you're just trying to swell my head."

"Have you considered adding a breakfast, lunch, and dinner menu? Or at the very least a breakfast menu. I have dreams about you and that sausage casserole."

"Really?" she asked with an arched brow. "Are they sinfully delicious?"

"Oh yeah," he said, bouncing his brows.

They both fell out laughing. If anyone overheard their flirtatious banter, they would probably believe they truly were a couple.

"Are you ready for Lunden and Quade's wedding?" Canten asked.

Rylee's face lit up. "Yes. I'm so excited. When Quade sees Lunden, he's going to bawl. She looks gorgeous in her gown. I'm so happy for those two and their second chance at love. They're like the perfect ending to a romance novel."

Canten, Sebastian, and Quade had grown pretty tight since Quade's arrival in Honey Hill. Canten had known Quade and Lunden would one day meet at the altar, because their chemistry was undeniable to anyone who'd spent any amount of time with them.

"I'm honored he asked me to be one of his groomsmen." He paused a second. "What about you? Are you going to make anyone cry when they see you?"

"Cry, no. Take a second look . . . hell yes."

He wholeheartedly believed it because he took second looks when she wore anything.

"I'm not so sure Quade asking you to be a groomsman was such a good idea," Rylee said.

Canten's brows furrowed. "Why?"

"You in a tux? You're going to start a ruckus. Half the women in town are going to be falling over themselves trying to get to you."

She was giving him far too much credit. For kicks, he said, "Will you be one of them?"

"Could be," she said. "Guess you'll just have to wait and see."

A beat of silence played between them.

Canten plucked an olive from the counter but didn't put it into his mouth. "Hey, so I was wondering if you wanted to go on a date?" he asked.

Rylee turned toward him, a perplexed expression on her face. "You want to take me on a date?"

He nodded, suddenly feeling like a shaky high schooler asking his crush to prom. "I mean, we don't have to. I just figured that since the town thinks we're dating, we should probably be seen together occasionally. In a more intimate setting." This entire thing had gone way better in his head. And why was he so damn nervous? It wasn't like it would be a real date. Just two actors playing parts.

Sure, they would probably hold hands. *All for show, of course.* Yes, they were likely to stare lovingly into each other's eyes. *Have to make the date believable.* Heck, they might even kiss. *A quick, simple touch of the lips. In performance art, it's all about the details.*

Canten finally popped the olive he'd been holding into his mouth. "What do you say?"

"On one condition," she said.

"What's that?"

"You let me order for myself."

"I will definitely do that," he said.

A short time later, Canten and Rylee sat on pillows around the coffee table in the living room and ate, talked, laughed, listened to music, and even enjoyed comfortable beats of silence. Though the quiet moments were few and far between and never lasted more than about twenty seconds. They'd always been able to talk about anything. Well, almost anything. One of the few subjects they hadn't had an in-depth conversation about was their late spouses.

Canten knew Rylee's late husband had been an army man who had been killed in action. The only thing Sebastian had said about the man was that he hadn't liked him much. Sebastian hadn't said why; Canten hadn't asked.

"Are folks stopping you in the streets like they're doing to me?" Rylee asked.

He chuckled. "Yes. I'm not sure I've ever gotten so much relationship advice. I took a few notes," he joked.

"How's Katrina Sweeney handling the news? Not well, I would imagine."

Canten thought he saw Rylee smile a little before she looked away. "I'm fairly certain I'm off her radar now, because she passed right by me today and didn't so much as look at me." A relief. This arrangement had its benefits.

"I didn't mean to mess things up between the two of you."

"There isn't, nor has there ever been, a 'two of us.' And now, thanks to you, I won't have to entertain any more rumors. You saved me," he said.

"We saved each other."

Canten raised his bottle. "We should toast to that." When Rylee's glass was in the air, he continued, "Here's to keeping the Katrinas and Leonards of the world from further pursuing us."

"I'll drink to that," Rylee said, clinking her glass against his bottle.

Before Canten knew it, the clock struck nine. Despite needing to get some rest for what he was sure would be another colorful day in Honey Hill, he was enjoying himself too much to leave. Rylee needed to get some rest too. She was usually at the bakery at four each morning. He knew this because he always made it a habit to drive by to check on her.

When Rylee excused herself, Canten watched her leave the room, the sway of her ass driving him insane. His gaze swept past the decorative shelf that sat in the corner of the living room, and he did a double take. The photo of Rylee and her late husband that usually sat there was gone. Before he could speculate, Rylee returned, drawing his full attention.

"I hope you saved room for dessert."

Canten rubbed his stomach. "I'm not sure I can hold another bite."

"You didn't save room for a Greek orange-honey cake with pistachios?"

"Oh, you're playing dirty now." He loved honey cake and pistachios, and she knew this. "Maybe a sliver."

Again, Rylee had outdone herself. He racked his brain for a time she had prepared a dish or dessert he hadn't liked. As far as he could recall, there hadn't been one. If he ate like this too often, his horse would gallop away when he saw him coming.

Rylee studied him a second. "I bet you cried when you saw your wife on your wedding day, didn't you?"

The question took Canten by surprise. "I . . . didn't. No." His gaze slid to his half-eaten piece of cake. An image of Jayla walking down the aisle filtered into his head. Smiling, he said, "But she was beautiful. I remember thinking, *Why in the hell would this woman want to spend her life with me?*"

"That's not hard to answer," Rylee said. "You are a dying breed of man. Honorable, generous, protective. There aren't many men like you left. You're a pretty good guy, Sheriff Barnes."

Canten studied Rylee, her words touching him. He'd had good role models, who'd shown him consistently what being a man looked like. He was thankful for this. Unfortunately, not all men got that exposure. "Thank you. What about your husband—did he cry?"

"If he'd seen me in a wedding dress, he probably would have."

"You didn't wear a wedding dress?" Why didn't this surprise him. She'd probably worn a sexy pantsuit that had had the jaw of every man in the venue dragging on the floor. He imagined her wedding having been an extravagant affair with mouthwatering food and a wedding cake that touched the ceiling.

Rylee's eyes turned sad. "Lucas and I were married at the courthouse in front of the justice of the peace. I wore a generic white dress."

Or maybe not. "Did you not want a wedding?"

"I'd dreamed of my wedding since I was five." She shrugged. "But I was marrying a military man, who could have been reassigned at any moment. I was willing to take a gamble on a wedding, but Lucas thought it best not to potentially waste all that money." Her half smile didn't linger.

How could a man giving his future wife the day of her dreams ever be considered a waste? That had to be a disappointment for a woman who'd dreamed about her wedding since she was a little girl. His heart ached for her and that lost moment. "Hey," he said, bumping her playfully. "I'm sure you were still a breathtaking bride."

"I was . . . generic, but thank you for trying to make me feel better."

Generic? Was she serious? "There has never been or ever will be anything generic about you, Rylee Harris. Whether you're in a flowing gown or a muumuu, you would still be the most exceptional woman in the room because you have something none of them could ever have."

"And what's that, Sheriff?"

"The privilege of being *you*. Which is magnificent, extraordinary, bold. Anything but generic."

"Thank you for saying that," she said in a tender voice. "For the record, if we were an actual couple, this would be the moment I pulled you into the bedroom to show you just how much I appreciated you saying that."

Canten wasn't sure if it was the heavy emotions swirling in the room, the alcohol flowing through his system, or the potent desire thrashing inside him that forced him to say, "Maybe this one time we pretend we *are* an actual couple, and we show each other how much we're both appreciated."

Rylee stared at him. Her lips parted slightly, and a dazed look spread across her face. A second later, she burst into laughter. "For a millisecond, I thought you were serious." She laughed some more. "I should clean the kitchen."

When she stood, Canten captured her hand, pulled her down to him, and in an uncharacteristically reckless move, showed her just how serious he was.

CHAPTER 11

Rylee's world moved in slow motion the second Canten pulled her close to him, placed a hand behind her neck, and kissed her senseless. Initially, she froze, stunned by his actions; however, it didn't take her long to thaw, because the kiss raised her temperature to a dangerous level. The swirling inferno inside her threatened to ignite them both.

Sweetness from the cake still lingered on his tongue, and she did her best to claim every hint. Making sure to not break their kiss, she maneuvered until she was straddling his lap. The bulge of his erection pressed against her throbbing core. God, she wanted him to the point of delirium. If he were to end this now, she'd die right here on the spot from sexual deprivation.

She'd imagined this moment a thousand times in her head, Canten claiming her mouth in an all-consuming kiss, but never had she actually believed it would happen. He'd always been so cautious with her. Sure, they'd done their fair share of flirting, but it had all been so innocent.

This was definitely not one of those times. This sexually charged moment dripped with sinful intent, and she welcomed every second of it. Her body, mind, and soul needed this. Consequences be damned. Tonight, she would pretend they were more, and she'd deal with the repercussions tomorrow.

Granted, it had been a long time since she'd kissed a man, but she couldn't recall Lucas ever capturing her mouth so completely. That pained her to admit. It was odd that she didn't experience a single iota of guilt, especially when usually simply fantasizing about Canten drowned her in it. Maybe she'd dwell on the reason why later, but right now, she chose to live in this blissful moment.

To Rylee's dismay, Canten's mouth left hers, but he didn't refrain from tantalizing her body. His soft lips peppered kisses along her jawline, down her neck, then back up to her ear. Kissing her lobe, he whispered gently, "Tell me to stop and I will. I've lost the willpower to do so on my own."

If he'd only known how damn arousing his words were. The fact that he wanted her so badly he couldn't pull away made her desire for him increase tenfold. While she knew tonight could potentially change things between them, there wasn't a chance in hell she'd give that order. "Why would I do that? I want this too bad."

As if her words supercharged him, he reclaimed her mouth, kissing her raw and hard. Their moans and groans mixed with Rachelle Ferrell's voice pouring from the radio. Rylee agreed with her: nothing had ever felt quite like this before.

They kissed for what felt like an eternity. Never had she imagined so much satisfaction could be derived from a mere lip-lock. But was it the action or the man performing it that enthralled her? Both, she settled on. How far was Canten willing to take this? The swell in his pants suggested all the way. She prayed that was the case.

※

A tiny voice of reason chirped in Canten's head, but Rylee had a hold on him, and nothing could save him now. And he wasn't sure he wanted to be. Every fiber in his being wanted her. On some level, even needed her. So no, he wouldn't deny himself the pleasure of being with her this one night. Despite the feeling that one time with her wouldn't come close to being enough for him, but it would have to be.

When Rylee broke her mouth from his, he panicked. Physically panicked. *What the hell?* Obviously, her lips had turned him into a junkie who desperately needed another fix. Determined to get one, he tried to kiss her again, but she pulled away. Couldn't she see he was going through withdrawal and fiending for another hit of her?

Cradling his face between her hands, she said, "Take me to the bedroom."

With no hesitation on his part, he stood with her still attached to him and moved down the hall, kissing her every step of the way. After he placed her on her feet, clothes flew in every direction. Obviously, they were both eager to finish what they'd started.

Rylee's naked body was a whole other level of arousing. It was everything he'd imagined and more. His hungry eyes gobbled up every inch of her, stopping to admire her wax treatment. Maybe he wasn't so old fashioned after all, because the lack of hair between her legs actually excited him. Of course, a fern could have been growing down there, and he suspected he'd be just as turned on.

Rylee's eyes took him in, too, her teeth biting into her lower lip as she stared at his erection. Scooping her into his arms, he carried her to the bed and placed her down on her back. Though he was full, a hunger grew inside of him that he knew only making love to Rylee could satisfy.

After wildly kissing her once more, he explored her skin with his mouth. Teasing one of her taut nipples with his tongue caused her to release a sweet sound that reverberated all through his body. He kissed, licked, nipped a slow trail down her torso until arriving at her treasure—or more like his. As he claimed his fortune, Rylee cried out in what he perceived as pleasure.

"*Canten*," drifted past her sweet lips.

It made him even more eager to please her. Every flick, suckle, twirl of his tongue caused her moans to grow deeper, louder, and more frequent. He had her in his clutches and refused to let go, not until she did.

Her essence, taste, response to him all drove him insane. *Rylee, Rylee, Rylee,* he said in his head. *Do you have any idea what you're doing to me?*

"Right there," she cried out. "Oh my God, right there."

A short time later, she came. Hard. Her body shook and jerked, and her arched back collapsed down onto the mattress. Reaching to the floor for his pants, he removed his wallet and pulled out the lone condom inside, thanking God he'd placed it there for a just-in-case moment. After tearing into the foil with his teeth, he sheathed his throbbing erection.

Spreading Rylee's still-trembling legs, he wasted no time filling her. *Shit.* He closed his eyes in an attempt to block out how good she felt to him, which only made things worse. With each thrust, he grew closer and closer to his breaking point.

Rylee moaned. "I'm . . . oh God . . ."

Her nails dug into the backs of his arms as her muscles contracted around him, making it difficult for him to hold on. But he did, until he couldn't a second longer. Moments later, he exploded with a guttural moan. The release put his system in a full-on tailspin. He saw shooting stars. Heard crashing waves. Felt sensations he hadn't experienced in a long time.

Once released from the intense grip, he collapsed onto his back and effortlessly pulled Rylee's limp body into his arms. She made herself at home in them, nestling snugly against him and draping her arm over his chest.

Maybe he should have gathered his clothing and gone home right then, but he wanted Rylee to know she wasn't just some cheap one-night thrill. He cared about her and her opinion of him. Plus, this hadn't been some random hookup even though he didn't plan to be with her in this way again. Their energy was too damn potent for him not to be sucked into a place he couldn't return from.

"You're quiet," he said. "What's on your mind?"

"I'm thinking that had I known you'd planned to seduce me, I would have worn matching undergarments."

Canten barked a laugh. *Seduced her?* Actually, the more he thought about it, he guessed he had. "Red and green matches. I kinda felt like I was getting an early Christmas present."

Rylee pinched his nipple.

"*Ouch*, woman."

He was grateful they'd instantly reverted back to their usual playful selves. If Rylee felt any awkwardness from what had just happened between them, she didn't show it.

Her fingers glided gently over his nipple, and his manhood twitched back to life. *Down, boy.*

"Do you want me to kiss it and make it better?" she asked.

Only if she wanted him to spread her legs and reclaim what was his for tonight. "That's probably not a good idea," he said. Though the clock hadn't struck midnight, so technically, their time together wasn't over.

"Things won't get weird between us, will they, Canten?"

He noted a hint of concern in her voice. "Do they feel weird now?" he asked. They certainly didn't for him.

Rylee smiled against his chest. "Things never feel weird between us. Not even now," she said.

"There you have it. We're just two people who needed each other tonight, Rylee. Tomorrow, everything goes back to normal." *Two people still needing each other but ignoring it.* But he kept that part to himself. "Agreed?"

"Agreed," she said.

A long beat of silence played between them, and for an instant, he thought she'd fallen asleep.

"I haven't been with another man since my husband died," Rylee said. "And I'm not even sure why I just told you that."

Probably because she knew he would understand. "I get it. I haven't been with anyone since my wife either. In full disclosure, I tried once. Nothing happened."

Rylee came up on her elbow. "You had limp dick?"

Canten laughed. "Do you have to make it sound so harsh? It was embarrassing enough back then."

"Sorry," she said, easing back down. "What happened?"

He thought back to that night. *Jayla's memory.* Of course, he didn't admit that aloud. "I just wasn't into it, I guess. She was so pissed. Even asked if I was gay, because apparently, no man had ever been able to resist her."

"Sounds like you chose a monster to sleep with."

"More like the monster chose me."

"This 'she' . . . anyone I know?"

Canten knew she'd wanted to ask if it had been Katrina Sweeney. "No. It was a long time ago. Before I moved back to Honey Hill. My first and last attempt at a one-night stand."

"This attempt worked for you," she said.

"*Ouch.* Don't cheapen our night together. This was more than a one-night stand," he said. By definition, maybe that was all this had been, but it hadn't felt that way to him. He felt Rylee smile against him again. Maybe it hadn't felt that way to her either.

"Well, if it's any consolation, there was absolutely nothing limp about you tonight. And just to make sure it wasn't a fluke"—she glided on top of him with the ease of cascading water—"maybe we should perform an additional test. For verification purposes, of course."

"I don't have—"

Rylee captured his words with an intoxicating kiss.

Hours later, Canten lay wide awake, staring at the light dancing on Rylee's ceiling. She was fast asleep in his arms, her warm naked body stretched out over his. Making love to her had both drained and energized him.

Back to normal? Who in the hell had he been kidding? *Normal*, at least for him, had officially left the station. The train was moving way too fast for him to jump off now. If she'd awakened right then and wanted more from him, he wouldn't have hesitated in giving it to her.

Would Rylee be unaffected by their changed dynamics? Would she be better at compartmentalizing than he was? Unless she brought it up, he would never mention this night, though he suspected it would linger in the air around them like shimmering fairy dust anytime they were in each other's company.

Dammit, Barnes. You brought this on yourself.

Their night together wasn't supposed to feel so . . . perfect. Wasn't supposed to imprint on him like this. Even now, when they had gone round after round, he still wanted more of her. He'd never felt about a woman the way he'd felt about Rylee, not even Jayla. This scared him because he needed to be able to let go of Rylee when the time came.

I should have stopped at one time. But no, he'd stupidly made love to her several more times. All of them without protection. Their need for each other had been so potent that when he'd told Rylee he'd only had that one condom, she'd welcomed him inside her without.

His only concern had been getting her pregnant, but she'd assured him she was on birth control, which had initially seemed odd since she'd stated she wasn't having sex. But after she'd explained it helped to regulate her cycles, all his worry had faded.

Being inside her without a barrier had felt amazing. He'd felt her on a cellular level, invading him, ravishing his body. One thing was for certain. If he wanted to keep his sanity, he could never be with her like this again.

CHAPTER 12

Tonight was their date night, but Rylee couldn't understand why Canten had driven to her parents' lake rental. Had he planned a double date with them, and they were there to pick them up? That was the only logical explanation. What other reason would they have for being here? And why hadn't her mother mentioned anything when she'd spoken to her earlier?

"Canten, what's going on?"

Canten didn't answer. Exiting, he rounded the front of the vehicle and opened her door. Offering his hand, he helped her down onto the gravel. Her heel caught, and she stumbled. Canten made sure she didn't fall by planting his hands on either side of her waist to steady her.

"Careful," he said.

Those few seconds he stared into her eyes caused Rylee's breath to hitch. Their night together came rushing back, causing all her sensitive parts to pulse to life. "Thank you," she said.

Rylee headed for the front door, but Canten redirected her steps.

"This way," he said.

"Where are we going?"

"You'll see."

The brilliant glow of the full moon guided their path to the side of the house. Rylee gasped. There were very few moments that left her speechless. Not only did this moment do just that, but it also left her breathless. Dozens of paper-bag lanterns lined a path all the way to the dock. In the distance, she could see the pontoon boat. The interior and exterior glowed a soft blue hue. The moon, so low in the sky, looked as if it were melting into the lake. The light bouncing off the water was magical. She'd been right. It was beautiful at night.

Canten extended his arm. "You're probably going to want to take my hand. The walk could prove difficult for you in those shoes, which are really spectacular, by the way."

Rylee's gaze dropped to the strappy three-inch sparkly gold stilettos she wore. Had she known they would be doing whatever it was they were doing, she would have opted for more sensible footwear. The shoes were sexy. And so was the black, off-one-shoulder shorts romper she'd paired them with. Both intentional.

Canten's outfit—a medium-gray button-down shirt, dark denim jeans, and black, comfortable-looking shoes—coordinated well with hers. They would have been a striking couple walking down the sidewalks of Main Street.

She intertwined her fingers with his. "Lead the way."

Several steps in, her heel sank into the earth. After her fourth time nearly falling, Canten stopped.

"I have an idea," he said. Without warning, he scooped her into his arms.

"*Whoa!*" She hadn't expected that. One arm instinctively wrapped around his neck, while the other hand rested on his shoulder. Looking into his daunting eyes, she said, "Are you sure about this? I'm not what you would call *light as a feather*." Though he didn't seem to be having any trouble at all.

"What are you talking about? I can barely tell you're in my arms."

She smiled a little. "Liar."

Rylee made note of just how close their mouths were. All she had to do was lean forward just a little, and her lips would be on his.

Ignoring the desire to kiss him, she said, "So did you invite all of Honey Hill?"

Lines of confusion creased his forehead, and he chuckled. "What?"

Their date was supposed to be for show, allowing the town to see them together as a happy couple. No one would see them here. "Who's going to see us here?"

"Your parents. I figured we'd kill two birds with one stone. Your parents would see us now. Later, we'll head into town and be seen. Multitasking," he said.

Sounded as if he had it all thought out. "You haven't told me what we're doing here?" she said.

"I recall you saying something about how beautiful you bet this place was at night. I just so happened to read that it would be a full moon, so I thought, why not have dinner on the lake."

"Dinner on the lake?" It sounded so romantic. But their visit here wasn't about romance. *It's about keeping up a facade,* she reminded herself.

"Yes. Your mother thought it was a fabulous idea when I called to ask if it would be okay for us to use the boat. I arranged for the Capri House to deliver our meals."

"You—"

"Before you protest, I ordered one of every meat option and several sides so you'd be able to choose for yourself what you want to eat."

What she'd been about to say was, *You're chock full of surprises,* but his thoughtfulness rendered her speechless.

"Your parents helped me set it up. I surprised them with a romantic dinner, which is probably why we haven't seen them."

"*Canten Barnes.* Why would you order every meat option? That had to be crazy expensive."

"Who needs retirement funds?" he said with a wink.

Him and those winks.

117

Canten placed her on her feet when they reached the dock. Instantly, she missed the warm, solid feel of his chest. Missed being in his arms. "Thank you for carrying me that entire way. Just for the record, I'm not responsible for any soreness you may experience tomorrow."

"Noted," he said. "But if there is any . . . it'll be well worth it."

He guided her onto the boat. If this had been a real date, Rylee would have given Canten his props for making it ultraromantic. "What is that?" she asked, pointing to something that resembled an oversize Styrofoam cooler.

"It's supposed to keep the food hot," he said.

"Ah."

"You ready?" he asked.

When she nodded, he started the engine and slowly headed out. Sitting in one of the two captain-style chairs, Rylee closed her eyes and allowed her head to recline back. She enjoyed the feel of the wind kissing her skin. Inhaling a lungful of the fresh air, she released it slowly. Canten turned on the radio, drowning out the hum of the boat and sounds of nature.

She swayed back and forth to the hypnotizing sound of Anthony Hamilton's voice as he pleaded for Charlene to come home. Opening her eyes, she eyed Canten. "I heard Charlene finally came back," she said.

He burst into laughter, and she laughed right along with him, realizing how ridiculous the comment had been.

"The way that brother is begging, I hope she did," he said.

An hour later, Rylee and Canten sat on the floor of the boat, backs propped against the bench-style seats, both sated and full. Numerous food containers sat scattered around them. Canten hadn't exaggerated about ordering every meat on the menu. Chicken prepared several different ways, steaks, pork chops, lamb chops, veal, salmon, and more. Rylee had taken delight in sampling it all. Now, she could barely move.

Dropping her head back on the cushion, she said, "Why did you let me eat so much?"

Canten chuckled. "I was afraid to intervene. I need all my fingers."

Rylee swatted him playfully. "I didn't want anything to go to waste." She eyed him. "What you did was extremely thoughtful. I would have been content with whatever you ordered, but I'm happy you gave me an option. This is absolutely the best fake date I've ever gone on. Thank you."

"You're welcome. It's getting late. We should probably get going if we want to make our rounds downtown."

"A few more minutes," she said. "It's so peaceful here."

"Are you chilly?" he asked.

"A little, but it's okay."

"I'll be right back." He stood, made his way to a storage compartment, and removed an oversize fleece throw. "I figured it would get a little cool. And I know you don't like to be cold, so I had your mother put this here."

He knew her so well. Canten eased down and covered them both. He sat so close to her that her body rested against his, causing the temperature to tick up several degrees. Before long, she'd be sweating.

"I hope you don't mind sharing," he said.

"Not at all." A second later, she rested her head on his shoulder. "It doesn't feel awkward."

"What, my shoulder?"

Rylee chuckled. "No, silly. Being here with you. After the other night . . . I wasn't sure. I didn't feel awkward then, but I thought tonight would be. I'm glad it's not. I'm glad we were able to go right back to normal. I would have hated if things had gotten weird between us, because I kinda like having you around. You're a good friend, Canten. A great friend, actually."

"Don't go getting all mushy on me," he said, wrapping his arm around her shoulder. "Of course we were able to go right back to normal. Like I said, we were just two people who needed each other. We both got what we needed that night."

Yes, they had. Now she needed and desperately *wanted* more.

✺

Canten wasn't sure how he'd choked those words out. Normal? He was still feeling the effects of their night together. That was far from any normal he knew. He wasn't sure what the hell she'd done to him that night, but somehow, Rylee had gotten inside him.

When they weren't together, he felt her. All the time. Coursing through him like endorphins. When they were, like now, cozy and comfortable, the grip she had on him tightened. There wasn't a damn thing he could do about it but ride out the ferocious storm of desire and pray he didn't capsize.

"I feared dating," Rylee said. "It wasn't that I didn't have invitations. I was just afraid to go. But now you have me wondering what I've been missing. Maybe after all of this I will try dating again."

Canten stiffened. The image of Rylee sitting across from another man, gazing longingly into his eyes, was like a gut punch from Tyson. *What the hell is wrong with you, man? She's not yours.* "Why were you afraid to date?"

The question obviously spooked Rylee, because she removed her head from his shoulder and sat forward. He instantly missed the weight of her against him. She stared out into the night. With her withdrawing the way she had, Canten was sure it had something to do with what Sebastian had told him. Was she replaying that horrible night in her head? If so, he hated himself for planting it there.

"What's wrong?" he asked, hoping she'd tell him, understanding if she didn't.

Rylee eyed him, a troubled look in her once-cheerful gaze. "I didn't tell you everything about my last date."

"Okay. You want to tell me now?"

Her eyes left his again. "I'm embarrassed."

Canten wanted desperately to tell her he knew everything. That she had no reason to be embarrassed. That she'd done nothing wrong.

But he couldn't betray Sebastian's trust. He reached forward, guided her back to him, and returned his arm around her shoulders. "Tell me when you're ready."

She relaxed against him. "I love that about you. You never force things. You let them happen organically. I think that's why I'm so comfortable with you. And I haven't been comfortable with a man in a long time. There's never any pressure when we're together."

Canten rubbed a hand up and down her arm. "I would never put you in a position to do anything you didn't want to do." Including sharing her secrets with him.

"I know. But that's exactly what he tried to do. My date. He put something in my drink."

Feigning surprise, he said, "He did what?"

"I knew better than to leave my drink unattended. My parents had drilled that into both my and Sebastian's heads. *Never leave your drink unattended, and never accept a drink from a stranger.*"

Canten continued to play clueless. While he truly didn't want to hear the circumstances a second time, he knew it would seem odd if he didn't ask. "What happened?"

"All I can remember is feeling drunk, which had been strange because I'd only had half a glass of wine. I had this neighbor who I used to always complain about because she was so doggone nosy. She watched my every move. Going and coming."

Canten knew for a fact nosy neighbors could be a blessing and a curse.

Rylee chuckled. "I called her Ms. 227, after the eighties sitcom, because of the way she stayed perched in the window like Helen Martin's character Ms. Pearl." Sobering, she said, "I was grateful for her inquisitiveness that night."

A wave of anger crashed inside him. He was with Sebastian. If he could just get his hands on the asshole.

"Ms. Beulah—that was my neighbor's name—said she knew something was wrong when he practically carried me toward the house, that she'd never seen me come home drunk before. Plus, I'd left in my own car and returned in his. He must have looked at my license to get my address."

"I'm sorry for what you went through." She was safe here with him.

"Don't apologize. It wasn't your fault," she said.

A beat of silence played between them.

"He came back," Rylee said. "Later that night. I've never told anyone that. Not Lunden, not Sebastian. No one but you."

Canten's body went still. A knot yanked tight in the pit of his stomach as he waited for her to say more, both afraid to hear it and needing to at the same time. He clenched his jaw but relaxed the muscles when it felt as if he would crack a tooth. "Wh—" He stopped abruptly to clear his throat, clogged with fear. "What happened to you, Rylee?"

It felt as if an eternity had passed before Rylee spoke. In actuality, only seconds had ticked by.

"Luckily, nothing. Ms. Beulah had slept on my sofa that night because she had a feeling he would return. And when he did—to the back door—she greeted him with a gun she kept in a *bra holster*. He fled."

Canten pinched his lids together and blew a sigh of relief, scrubbing his mind of all the things that could have happened.

"Ms. Beulah saved me from only God knows what."

"And the creep? What happened with him? Did you get the police involved?" According to Sebastian, she hadn't. And he wanted to address that but needed her to open the door.

"No," she said.

"Rylee, you—"

"I know what you're going to say. Yes, I should have gone to the police, but I just needed to forget that night. But then I thought about the fact he could be preying on someone else, so I contacted the online

122

dating service I'd used, but he'd deleted all traces of his profile, and there was nothing they could do beyond flagging his information. Which had probably been fake, they'd said."

Canten spared her the lecture. From the sound of it, the drugger creep had definitely been up to no good.

"And now that I've put a damper on the night, maybe we should head back," Rylee said.

"A few more minutes," he said, mimicking her words from earlier, not quite ready to share her with anyone else just yet and maybe not at all. "Maybe we should skip downtown tonight. We have plenty of time to parade ourselves around town. Who knows when we'll get a moon like this again?" He needed more time with her, wanted her to linger in the security of his arms a little longer.

"I was thinking the same thing," she said, nestling a little more snugly against him.

Relaxing on the lake, a spectacular full moon, the woman who made him feel alive in his arms . . . *the perfect ending to any night.*

CHAPTER 13

Sunday afternoon, Rylee stood in Lunden's kitchen, shucking corn and filling her BFF in on all the details of her evening with Canten. From all the smiling she'd done recalling every moment, her cheeks hurt.

"You fell asleep in his arms on the boat?" Lunden said.

Rylee nodded, her lips ticcing upward. "Yes. One minute I was enjoying the peacefulness of the lake, my head on Canten's shoulder; the next I'm being jolted awake by the sound of my ringing phone."

When her mother had realized the boat hadn't been docked and Canten's SUV had still been parked in the driveway, she'd gotten worried and phoned. Of course her mother's first thought had been that they'd fallen asleep after an intense night of lovemaking, like she and her father had. Rylee had protested with, *Way too much information, Mom,* then had cleared up the woman's misconceptions.

"And you two never made it downtown?" Lunden asked.

"Nope." Honestly, being in Canten's arms had been a much better use of her time than them prancing around town like two show dogs.

"Because you fell asleep in his arms," Lunden reemphasized. "After enjoying a romantic, moonlit dinner on the lake."

She got what Lunden was hinting at. "There was nothing romantic about it." When she saw the look on Lunden's face, she said, "Okay, it was romantic, but the night hadn't been about romance."

"Are you sure?"

"Yes," she said to debunk whatever whimsical fairy tale Lunden had crafted in her head.

"Did you want something to happen? Again," Lunden added with a smirk.

Rylee playfully rolled her eyes. "No."

Lunden tossed a piece of a turnip green at her. *"Rylee!"*

"Okay, yes. Yes, I did. But it can't. Not again." One night with Canten had her craving him like an illicit drug. What would another do to her system? "I think I need to stop spending so much time with him. But he feels so good to my soul, Lu. I'm confused as hell."

"It sounds like you feel good to his soul too. And I don't think you're confused. You know exactly what you want. I think you're just scared to open your heart again. I think you're carrying around unfounded guilt like a security blanket. I think you believe you don't deserve to be happy."

Rylee didn't dispute any of Lunden's claims. "When we were together last night, I actually imagined what it would feel like to truly be loved by him."

"So in your imagination, how did it feel?"

"Amazing."

"Instead of fighting it, why not just focus on enjoying the moment, focus on having fun. If it's not meant to lead anywhere, it won't. But if it is meant to lead somewhere, it will, because like I said—"

"The universe will always get its way," Rylee said, completing Lunden's mantra with an eye roll.

"Exactly. Now repeat after me: Let loose. Let go. Have fun," Lunden said.

Before Rylee could recite the words, Lunden's seven-year-old son—Rylee's godson, Zachary—charged through the door.

"Aunt Rylee!" He darted into the kitchen and flung his tiny arms around her. Staring up at her with happy eyes, he said, "I'm glad you're having dinner with me," claiming her for himself.

"Me too," she said, running a hand over his head. "Where have you been? I've missed you."

"I was at the grocery store with Quade." He waved her forward. "I have to tell you something," he said.

When she knelt to his level, he cupped his small hands around her ear.

He bounced up and down as he whispered, "I'm going to call Quade Dad when he marries my mom in July. I can't wait, because he's the best dad ever."

"I think you should call him Dad," she whispered back. "And I think it's going to make him very happy."

"Hey, I want to hear the secret too, Peanut," Lunden said in a whine.

Zachary smacked a hand on his forehead. "*Mom*. I'm a big kid now. Peanut is a little kid's name."

The kid was so much wiser than his seven—and a half, he would add—years.

"You'll always be my little Peanut," Lunden said.

Zachary tossed his arms into the air. In an exhausted tone, he said, "*I know, I know*," then walked over and hugged his mother. "Love you, Mom."

"I love you too."

Rylee's heart melted as she watched the interaction between those two. For a moment, she imagined herself as a mother. Her own mother had told her once that motherhood was the purest form of love.

Releasing Lunden, Zachary sprinted down the hallway toward his room. "I'll be back," he yelled.

"Where's Quade?" Lunden asked.

"Outside," Zachary called back.

Lunden moved to the window while Rylee positioned herself at the kitchen sink to wash the corn.

"Hey, Ry?" Lunden said.

"Uh-huh."

"Remember when I said the universe always gets its way?"

How could she not? The woman recited it more than her name. Rylee rolled her eyes heavenward. "Yes." Like before, she silently disagreed.

"And remember a few minutes ago, when you said you needed to stop spending so much time with Canten?"

Again, she said, "Yes."

Lunden chuckled. "Well, I don't think the universe agrees with that decision."

"And how would you know that? Did the universe send you a tele-pathic message?" Rylee laughed at her own wittiness.

"No, it didn't. It sent Canten instead."

Sent Canten instead? Rylee turned to query her friend just as Quade entered the house, followed by none other than the sheriff, looking more scrumptious than her tastiest dessert in a pair of black cargo shorts, a red polo, and black sneakers. Rylee ignored the flutter of but-terflies taking flight in her stomach.

Canten and Quade joined them in the kitchen.

"What's up, Rylee?" Quade said.

"Hey. Where'd you find this guy?" she said, accepting a hug from Canten. The interruption to her system lasted long after he released her.

"He was just outside, roaming around like a lost puppy. I decided to bring him home and feed him."

They all laughed.

So the universe isn't responsible after all. Of course, she'd known that already, but now Lunden did too.

After placing the bags of groceries down, Quade hugged Lunden from the back and kissed her neck. "Hey, baby. I missed you." He kissed her again.

"I missed you too," Lunden said, a massive schoolgirl grin on her face.

"These two literally have only been apart for like fifteen minutes," Rylee said to Canten. But that was love. And it wafted off Lunden and Quade in thick sheets. She couldn't help but smile anytime she saw them together. She loved second-chance-at-love romance novels, but she'd witnessed it play out in real life with these two.

"You two need some privacy?" Canten asked.

They shared another bout of laughter.

An hour later, they all gathered around the dinner table. Hands down, Lunden made the best smothered turkey wings in the country. In addition to the turkey wings, they'd prepared homemade dressing, fresh corn, cabbage, turnip greens, fried okra, and mac 'n' cheese.

"This is the best mac 'n' cheese ever," Zachary said. "Thanks, Aunt Rylee."

"Anything for you," Rylee said.

He shoveled another helping into his mouth. "When you and Sheriff Canten get married and have kids, they're going to be lucky just like I am."

Rylee choked on her corn while Canten gave a nervous laugh before taking a long sip from his glass. Lunden and Quade looked as if they were both trying to mask their amusement.

"Sheriff Canten, Senior said he hopes you have babies before he dies. But I told him if he dies first, I'll tell them all about him. That made him happy."

Canten brought his glass back to his mouth. Clearly, Zachary had him as uneasy as he had Rylee, because there wasn't a drop of liquid in the glass, yet he appeared to be swallowing.

Zachary continued, "Then Senior and Papa Charles started arguing about naming the baby. And then they both burst out laughing. And then Mr. Clem called them both the f-word."

"The f-word?" Lunden asked.

"Fools," Quade said.

Zachary nodded quickly. "Yeah."

"I think it might be Mr. Clem's favorite word," Quade said.

Rylee recalled her father saying he'd visited the barbershop. What he hadn't mentioned was the baby conversation. Obviously, Senior had been helping to add legitimacy to the sham because he knew her relationship with his son wasn't real. That was the only thing that could explain why he'd been having such a conversation with her father.

"I know how babies are made," Zachary said.

Lunden and Quade said, *"What!"* in unison.

Rylee couldn't help but chuckle at the alarmed look on their faces. Canten . . . well, he still looked dazed.

An anxious-looking Lunden placed her fork down, clearly stressed by the fact someone had told her seven-year-old about the birds and the bees. "Um, son, how do you think they're made?"

Every set of eyes was on Zachary.

Zachary forked more noodles into his mouth, chewed as if intentionally keeping them all in suspense, then said, "My friend Johnathan said the mom and dad have to go into the bedroom and lock the door." He looked at Lunden. "Like you and Quade do, Mom."

Rylee stifled her laughter when Lunden scowled at her.

Zachary continued, "Then the mom has to say to the dad, *Give it to me, big daddy.* Johnathan said after his parents did that, they told him he was going to be a big brother."

Canten burst out laughing. And not a gentle chuckle but a robust sound that had to have come from deep in his gut. This made Rylee laugh harder, causing tears to spill from her eyes. Quade and Lunden were both in stitches too. Poor Zachary eyed all the adults like they were insane.

"What's so funny?" he asked, shrugging his shoulders.

"Nothing," Lunden said, through laughter.

Once they all sobered, Rylee said, "Is that all Johnathan said?"

"Well, he said it doesn't always work, because his mom says *Give it to me, big daddy* a lot, but she doesn't have a baby every time. He's glad, because he says his baby sister cries all the time."

More laughter.

After Rylee helped Lunden clear the table and clean the kitchen, Lunden suggested they walk off some of the calories by heading downtown for ice cream, and then they would walk off *those* calories by walking back to her house. Apparently, it made sense to everyone, because they headed out the door.

"After you," Canten said, giving her one hell of a smile.

Let loose. Let go. Have fun.

Every time Canten thought about what Zachary had said at the dinner table about how babies were made, he couldn't help but laugh. Kids did say the darndest things. What he hadn't found amusing was the apparent conversation Senior had had with Mr. Charles.

While he should have gone straight to his father's place, he hadn't been able to pass up an opportunity for ice cream. At least, that was what he told himself. It sounded better than admitting he hadn't been able to resist spending more time with Rylee. Clearly, he was a glutton for punishment.

The first stop he planned to make after he walked Rylee back to Quade and Lunden's place would be to his father's house to clear some things up. *Marriage? Babies?* Why would his father have such a conversation with Mr. Charles? *Pop knows the deal.* There would be no marriage, no babies because in a few months, there would be no him and Rylee. Why was Senior giving the Charleses false hope?

Canten eyed Rylee walking ahead of him with Lunden. One good thing about wearing these sunglasses: he could stare at her without being too obvious. Longing swelled inside him when he recalled how he'd gripped her ass when she'd been on top of him. That night was still stamped in his brain.

The sway of her full hips had him hypnotized. His mother would have said those were childbearing hips. The sign of a woman meant to have a houseful of kids. He wasn't sure hips could reveal all of that, but Rylee's were perfect either way.

Did Rylee even want kids? *I bet she does.* How many? *Three. No, four. Possibly five. Probably no more than that.* And did she want boys? Girls? Either? *A combination of both, more than likely.* With her nurturing manner, he bet she'd make an excellent mother. Seeing her with Zachary, he had no doubt she'd be a natural at parenting.

Why hadn't she had kids of her own? Could it be she actually didn't want them? That was okay. There was nothing etched in stone that said a woman had to bear children. It was her choice. No one had the right to judge her on it. Especially a man. Maybe she'd been too busy building her business? Since it sounded as if her late husband had been away a lot, maybe she hadn't wanted to raise kids on her own.

"Man, I apologize if Zachary made you uncomfortable earlier," Quade said.

Canten slammed back to reality. "Don't sweat that. I can't figure out why Senior would even have a conversation like that with Mr. Charles. He knows the deal."

"Wishful thinking?" Quade said. "Maybe he hopes this thing will turn into something real for you and Rylee. Don't give your pop a hard time. I'm sure he just wants to see you happy."

Canten got a sneaky suspicion Senior and Quade had been discussing him.

"Do you think it will?" Quade asked. "Blossom into more for you and Rylee. You two *definitely* have some major chemistry."

Pinning his gaze to Rylee, he said, "Maybe in another life."

"I thought the same exact thing once. Best decision I ever made was to focus on the life I was living right then. Changed my entire world." Quade eyed him. "Live this life, man."

Live this life. That was easier said than done when this life had yielded so much tragedy and pain. Everyone could urge him to move on, but no one truly understood how difficult moving forward could be. Actually, he was sure one person understood. *Rylee.*

Maybe she was his key to moving forward; however, he wasn't ready to trust the journey. But that didn't stop him from wanting her in his bed again, because the only thing better than being beside Rylee was being inside her.

CHAPTER 14

There was a line inside Lickety Split's Ice Cream House, but there always was on a Sunday evening. When they finally entered the shop, Rylee spotted the mean-girl crew sitting at one of the tables. Hilary, Izzy, Katrina, and Ellie. Or HIKE, as Rylee called them, because that was exactly what you wanted them to do: take a hike.

If looks could kill, Rylee and Lunden would have been dead on Lickety Split's black-and-white checkerboard floor. Seeing them here with Canten and Quade had to touch a nerve for both Katrina and Hilary. Hilary had wanted Quade for herself when he'd first arrived in town. That hadn't worked out so well for her. And of course, everyone knew Katrina wanted Canten. Things didn't seem too promising for Katrina either. Katrina and Hilary were like two bottles of the water repellent Rain-X, except they repelled men.

Canten intertwined his fingers with Rylee's, the move feeling so natural she didn't flinch a muscle. When both Canten and Lunden spoke to HIKE, Rylee figured that as sheriff and mayor they had to play nice with the locals. That didn't mean she and Quade had to, because neither of them parted their lips.

Waiting in line, Canten stood behind Rylee and hooked one arm around her neck and kissed the back of her head. *Damn, he's good.* A second later, she found herself wondering if the show was for the general public or Katrina specifically.

The buzz of conversation, sounds of metal hitting metal, and boisterous laughter all faded when what sounded like two or three gunshots rang out. A dish fell to the floor, causing several people to take cover.

"Was that gunshots?" came from somewhere.

"Oh God, they're shooting," came from somewhere else.

Shooting? Someone's shooting? Rylee's heart nearly banged out of her chest.

Canten eyed her. With stern words, he said, "Don't leave this shop. Quade, take them to the back," he said.

"Wait, where are you—" Canten was out the door before she could finish her sentence. The next thing she felt was a hand gripping her arm and tugging her away.

Tucked inside the men's restroom with Lunden and Zachary—Quade standing guard outside the door—Rylee was nauseous with fear. She tried to hold it together, but her entire body trembled, and she was sure her legs would give out at any moment. Obviously, Zachary noticed how out of sorts she was, because he reached over and held her hand.

His voice trembled when he said, "It's okay, Aunt Rylee, Sheriff Canten will protect us."

But who would protect him? He'd sprinted toward the danger. No protection. No firearm. No backup. She washed a hand over his head. "Of course he will."

"And my dad's at the door. He's not going to let anything happen to us either."

Rylee smiled at Zachary calling Quade his dad. God, this kid was amazing. He was clearly frightened himself, yet here he was focusing his energy on trying to make her feel better.

Rylee wasn't sure how much time had passed when the bathroom door flung open—five, ten minutes, maybe—but it had felt like a lifetime. Quade moved inside, hugging Lunden and Zachary to him. While Lunden was much better at hiding her emotions than Rylee, Rylee could tell she'd been shaken by the incident too.

Where is—

Before the thought fully materialized, Canten appeared. The amount of relief she felt shocked her system. "You're okay," she said.

"Of course. It was just Milton Randal's truck backfiring," Canten said, closing the distance between them. Worry lines were etched across his forehead. He touched her arm. "You're trembling."

She forced an unsteady smile. "It's freezing in here," she lied. "You know how I hate the cold."

Canten flashed a look of skepticism, but he didn't challenge her.

"Let's get ice cream," she said, brushing past him.

Canten hadn't bought what Rylee had tried to sell in the bathroom for one second. Cold hadn't caused her to tremble; it had been fear. So why hadn't she simply admitted to that? Did she believe it made her look weak? Heck, everybody in the shop had probably experienced some degree of terror. He had but for different reasons.

The sounds of *gunfire* had briefly taken him back to a period in time he relived daily. Jayla's murder. But another moment had overpowered the flashback of that night. Making sure Rylee had been safe. Maybe the two went hand in hand. A need to protect Rylee because he hadn't been able to protect Jayla. Oddly, that didn't feel like the full version of the story, but it was the one he went with for now.

Rylee had been uncharacteristically quiet in line at Lickety Split's. Even now, as they walked back to Lunden and Quade's, she hadn't said more than two words to him. Was she just lost in her thoughts or upset with him about something?

"I'll let you lick mine if you let me lick yours," he said. While he'd been referring to her strawberry-cheesecake cone, his mind flew straight into the gutter.

She passed the cone to him. "You can have it. My stomach's a little queasy."

Lapping at her cone, he joked, "You're not pregnant, are you?" sure that it would get a reaction out of her. When she didn't so much as crack a smile, he stopped moving, but she kept walking. "Rylee?"

She backtracked to him. "What's wrong?"

"You're . . . not, right?"

Her brows furrowed. "Not what?"

"Pregnant," he whispered.

Rylee's eyes doubled in size. "*Pregnant?* What? No, I'm not pregnant. Why would you think I'm pregnant?"

"You said you were queasy. Then when I joked about you being pregnant, you didn't respond. I think I nearly blacked out," he said, dragging the back of his hand across his forehead.

For the first time since they'd left the ice cream shop, she smiled. "Don't worry, there's no way I can be pregnant, because I didn't say *Give it to me, big daddy.*"

Canten barked a laugh that drew Quade's, Lunden's, and Zachary's attention, who were all a good distance ahead of them.

"You two okay back there?" Lunden asked.

"Yes," they said in unison.

They started to move again.

"Do you want kids?" he asked, needing to pull her from this gloom that shadowed her.

"Yeah, I do. Several, actually. Four boys and a girl," she said.

Canten's head jerked. "That's specific."

"I want our daughter to feel protected the way Sebastian made me feel."

Our daughter? Had she just said *our daughter?*

Rylee stopped walking and touched his arm. "Oh God. I didn't mean *our* daughter, as in yours and mine. I meant *our* as in the man who fathers my children."

"I knew what you meant."

"Are you sure?" She laughed. "'Cause you're looking a little pale."

"Heat and too much sugar don't mix," he said, dropping both cones into the trash.

"*Hey.* What did you do that for? I wanted that cone," Rylee said.

Canten captured her hand, their fingers instinctively locking together. "Come on, we can go back to Lickety Split's to replace it."

Rylee rooted to the ground. "Oh, no. I've had enough of that place for one day." She tilted her head and narrowed her eyes at him. "I have a better idea." She called out to Lunden and Quade. "We'll meet up with you guys later."

Five minutes later, Canten sat on a cement bench in the park, Rylee on his lap, posing for a caricature artist. Something to commemorate their fake relationship, Rylee had said. Jacques-Pierre—otherwise known as Jack Perry when he wasn't pretending to be a famous artist from France—directed Rylee into a hundred different positions on Canten's lap. Canten breathed a sigh of relief when he finally settled on one. He wasn't sure how much more he could have taken of Rylee swiveling.

"*Le* light must strike you both perfectly so that I may capture the full interpretation of your energy," he said, in a horrible imitation of a French accent. "I draw what I see."

Le light? Full interpretation of our energy? The man was painting character art, not the damn *Mona Lisa*.

Jack—er, Jacques-Pierre—adjusted the fire-engine-red wool beret atop his head, then fiddled with the matching-color scarf tied around his neck. The plump man's deep-brown skin stood in stark contrast with his white shirt and pants.

Jacques-Pierre cracked his knuckles. "Shall we begin?"

"*Oui*," Rylee offered eagerly.

Canten focused more on trying not to get an erection than responding.

"What about you, Sheriff?"

He eyed her. "What about me, what?"

Jacques-Pierre snapped his fingers twice as if he were trying to get the attention of a disobedient puppy. "Eyes on me, please. Eyes on me."

Returning her gaze toward Jacques-Pierre, she said, "Do you want kids?"

At one point in his life there was nothing more he'd wanted than to be a father. Like Rylee, he'd wanted a big family. He'd grown up an only child but had wanted his kids to have siblings. Now he wasn't sure what he wanted. "I don't know," he said honestly.

"I think you'd be a great father," she said.

The conversation ended there.

"You were afraid," Canten said. "At the ice cream shop. It's understandable. There's no need to be ashamed."

Rylee's posture relaxed a little, and she turned her head to look at him. "I was afraid. But not for myself. I was afraid for *you*."

"Eyes to *me*."

Canten slammed his brows together. Had Jacques-Pierre just snapped at Rylee? When Canten sent a no-nonsense glare in his direction, Jacques-Pierre flashed a wobbly smile.

"*Please*," he said in a much softer tone. "Eyes on me, please."

That was better.

Rylee's lips curled a little, and then she returned her attention to Jacques-Pierre.

"My apologies, artist," she said.

"You don't have to worry about me." But he kinda liked the fact she had. It had been a long while since he'd had someone, other than Senior, fret over him.

Rylee had started to turn her head toward him again, but then she'd returned face forward as if she hadn't wanted to be reprimanded again. She didn't have to worry about that. He was sure Jacques-Pierre had gotten the message the first time.

"You ran headlong into danger. Yes, it was just a vehicle backfiring, but at the time, you didn't know that. You were in cargo shorts and a polo shirt. No bulletproof vest, no firearm of your own."

This time she did face him. Jacques-Pierre didn't utter a word.

"You were watching our backs, but there was no one watching yours," she said.

The concern in her gentle eyes was unmistakable. The worry she exhibited—and over *him*—tugged at his heartstrings. He shrugged. "That's the job, Rylee. Protecting you and everyone else in Honey Hill. And I did have someone watching my back." He pointed heavenward. "He's a pretty fierce guy. No one messes with him." This made her laugh.

"I'm just glad you're okay. I wouldn't want your death on my conscience too." She pinched her lids shut. "I shouldn't have said that. I'm sorry."

"What did you mean by that? That you wouldn't want my death on your conscience too?" Who else's death was on her conscience?

"Nothing," she said, facing Jacques-Pierre again.

"Ry—"

"Drop it, Canten. Please."

He would but just for now.

Over an hour later, Jacques-Pierre tossed his hat into the air, then cupped his hands under his double chin. "Finally. Oh, this has got to be one of my greatest pieces. *Your energy* . . . your energy is so intense. And I've captured it all, like a tub underneath a glorious waterfall, sparkling for the entire world to see." He pinched his fingers together, kissed them, then tossed them through the air. *"Magnifique."*

Canten swore he saw tears glistening in the man's eyes. And what was this energy he kept speaking of?

"Are you ready?" Jacques-Pierre asked.

"Yes," Rylee said, her face glowing.

Canten had to admit he was curious to see too. As long as it had taken, it had better be more than two stick figures with exaggerated features scribbled on the page.

Jacques-Pierre stood. "I present to you . . . *Énergie*."

Rylee gasped.

Canten blinked.

They were both speechless.

Canten absently ran a hand over his head. Clearly, this truly had been Jacques-Pierre's interpretation, because this wasn't the drawing they'd posed for. While he and Rylee had both trained their eyes on Jacques-Pierre—well, the majority of the time—this was not what he'd captured. His artwork depicted them staring into each other's eyes in a way he could only describe as loving. They were pictured in spectacularly vibrant color: blues, reds, greens, yellows. Were the rippling lines energy? If so, their *energy* flowed into one another in an ombré swirl; he couldn't decipher where Rylee began and where he ended.

"Wow," Rylee said.

Wow was right. Jacques-Pierre had said it best. The drawing was absolutely magnificent.

CHAPTER 15

Rylee loved owning her own business. What she didn't particularly care for was all the behind-the-scenes tasks that came along with it. Payroll, ordering supplies, and paying bills had kept her swamped most of the morning. Thankfully, she was finally done. Now she could return to what she truly loved: creating sinfully delicious treats.

Of course, the mention of sinfully delicious treats made her think of Canten. She eyed her watch. *Eleven forty-five? Already?* The delicious treats would have to wait because she had lunch plans with a delicious treat, her parents, and Senior.

Thinking about Canten made her lips curl, but a second later the corners of her mouth relaxed. The events of the past weekend and the incident at the ice cream shop trickled into her thoughts. When Canten had acted so nonchalant about his actions, she'd wanted to scold him for running headlong into perceived danger. But honestly, what could she have said? She had no right to dictate anything to him, because she had no stake in his life.

What if it really had been a gunman? The thought churned her stomach. She couldn't lose another person she cared about. And she did care about Canten. To her detriment, more and more each day. Her heart fluttered when she thought about the image Jacques-Pierre had drawn of them. He had stated he only drew what he saw. The couple on the canvas was unmistakably enthralled with one another.

"Knock, knock. Special delivery."

Rylee's gaze rose to Ezekiel, standing at her office door, his upper body hidden behind a lush floral arrangement that contained roses, hydrangeas, gerbera daisies, calla lilies, several types of greenery, and curly twigs. The flowers were in such abundance she wasn't sure how they'd all fit into the vase. The arrangement looked as if it weighed a ton, but Ezekiel didn't appear to have any trouble hauling it across the room. Probably because the man was a solid mass of muscle.

"What is this?" she asked.

Ezekiel placed the etched crystal vase on the small round table littered with papers. "My guess is it's the sheriff reminding you how special you are to him."

A good explanation but highly doubtful. However, Canten's name had been the first to pop into her head, but why would he send her flowers? Was today their imaginary anniversary? The thought made her chuckle. While flowers weren't really her thing, it didn't lessen her appreciation for the beautiful display. "Thank you, Ezekiel."

"You're welcome," he said, leaving the room.

Coming from behind the desk, she inhaled the fragrant blooms, then plucked the card attached to the plastic spike sticking from the vase. Before she could read it, Canten walked in. Rylee couldn't help but admire how damn spectacular he looked in his official uniform. Black pants, a crisp white shirt with patches on either arm and his badge pinned to the left side of his chest, a black tie with a golden pendant in the center, two *H*s for Honey Hill. His black hat was tucked under his arm.

"Hey, buttercup."

"Hi, dumplings."

They shared a laugh.

"Look at you. Enticing every woman in town," she said, taking him in from head to toe. *Mmm, mmm, mmm.*

"Every woman?" he asked with a smirk.

She shrugged. "Well, I guess there could possibly be one or two holdouts."

One side of his mouth lifted into a sexy smile that made her hyper-aware of just how fine this man was.

He nodded toward the flowers. "Nice."

"Yes, they are. Is it our fake anniversary?" she joked.

Canten flashed a confused expression.

"Wait, you didn't send these?" Rylee asked.

He shook his head.

"Huh," she said, tearing into the tiny envelope. Who would send her such an extravagant bouquet? Reading the message caused the smile to melt from her face. *Why won't he take the hint?*

"Who are they from?" Canten asked, moving closer to her.

"Leonard Jamison."

"Hmm," he hummed. "Guess he doesn't know you're not a flower person." A second later, he added, "You ready?"

Rylee tossed the card aside. "Yes, I'm starving." But her hunger wasn't necessarily for food. Her nipples tightened in her bra just from thinking about another night with Canten.

Fifteen minutes later they all sat at a table inside her mother's favorite Italian restaurant. The quaint eatery reminded Rylee of an establishment you'd find on a cobblestone street in Italy. Faux grapevines scaled the antique brick walls. Metal lantern-type lights dangled overhead, cascading a soft glow onto their table. Festive music played in the background.

Since Rylee planned to return to work, she declined a glass of wine with her mother. Observing the individuals at the table talking, laughing, and joking warmed her heart. She wished Sebastian had been there with them. That would have completed this blended family. *Faux blended,* she reminded herself.

This type of family outing was a first for her. Lucas hadn't been close with his family and hadn't cared for intimate gatherings of any sort, so they'd never dined with both sets of parents like this. Even though it was all pretend, she kind of liked it.

"Sweetheart, Canten, I had an interesting conversation about you two today," Mrs. Charles said.

Rylee shifted in her chair. "Conversation?"

"Yes. With Herbert Jamison."

Oh no. Don't panic. Take a deep breath. Don't stutter. "What did Mr. Herbert have to say about us?"

"Something about him hoping things work out better for you with Canten than they had with his granddaughter."

Canten closed his eyes and shook his head.

"I'm going to yank that fool's lying tongue slam out of his mouth and wrap it around his fat neck," Senior said. "That whole family is delusional. My son has never given that wacky granddaughter of Herbert's a sideways glance. He only has eyes for Rylee. Always has."

Rylee knew Senior didn't approve of what she and Canten were doing, but she was grateful he seemed committed to playing his part. *Always has. That was a nice addition.*

Canten reached for his glass, then chugged half the sweet tea inside.

"I told Dorsetta she shouldn't listen to nothing Herbert says," Mr. Charles said, claiming a piece of bread from the basket and looking bored with the current conversation. "The man has always loved causing discord. Thrives on it. Now can we talk about something else other than those Jamisons before I lose my appetite?"

Ignoring her husband as she sometimes did, Mrs. Charles said, "I don't get why he would think Canten had dated his granddaughter. Is he that delusional?"

"Canten drove Katrina home during a rainstorm once," Rylee said. *Rainstorm.* Something popped into Rylee's head. Something Canten had said to her once, that the only thing he felt during a storm was angst. Was this why? Filing that away for later, Rylee continued, "Katrina's been fascinated with him ever since." She eyed Canten. "I totally get why. I'm kind of captivated by him myself."

Canten brought her hand to his mouth and placed a lingering kiss to the back of it. He looked exhausted. Was it their fake relationship weighing on him? All the pretending had to be tiresome. Was it the Katrina thing? Or was it a combination of both?

"And to think I let Roberta talk me into . . ." Mrs. Charles's words dried up, and she waved her hand through the air. "Never mind that. I feel sorry for his granddaughter. Who would do such a thing? Lie about a relationship." Her mother looked disgusted. "I'm going to say a prayer for her. Clearly, she has a few screws loose. Faking a relationship," she said. "Just pitiful and a little sad."

Rylee experienced a moment of shame. What would her mother think about her if she knew she was doing the exact same thing?

❧

On Saturday morning, Canten met Quade and Sebastian at Lady Sunshine's shop. The only groomsman not in attendance was Quade's best friend and best man, Pryor, who wouldn't be able to come down until next week. Instead of utilizing Mr. Herbert, Quade had commissioned Lady Sunshine to make their suits because he'd wanted no dealings with the man. Turned out not only was Lady Sunshine a great dressmaker, but she could also tailor one hell of a suit.

Canten studied his profile in the corner-to-corner wall mirror. Not trying to toot his own horn, but he looked damn good in the cream-colored ensemble.

"I can take the pants out a little in the waist if you'd like," Lady Sunshine said. "Your measurements have changed slightly since last month." She gave him an accusatory look.

Quade and Sebastian laughed.

"I warned you Rylee's cooking would fatten you up," Sebastian said.

"That lotus flower's been feeding you well." Lady Sunshine flashed an approving smile, then disappeared to the back.

In the mirror, Canten scrutinized his midsection. *Dammit*. He'd known all of Rylee's good cooking would catch up with him.

Sebastian patted Canten's stomach. "You're getting pudgy, old man."

"Your sister isn't complaining," Canten said.

"Oooh," Quade said. "He got you with that one, Bass."

Canten and Sebastian tussled playfully, then ended their rough-housing with a brotherly hug.

"Love you, man," Sebastian said. He eyed them through the mirror. "We are three good-looking brothers, aren't we?" His gaze slid to Quade. "In one month, you'll be a married man. Are you *sure* you want to go through with this?"

"Brother, it would take fire and brimstone to keep me from marrying Lunden. I love that woman." Quade's expression turned serious. "It's crazy. I never knew I could love anyone the way I love her. I'm looking forward to calling her my wife, spending my life with her. Zachary too," he added. "That kid . . ." His words trailed. "He makes me feel like I'm the father of the year every single day."

"You need a tissue? You look like you're going to cry," Sebastian said.

"Kiss my ass," Quade said. "You'll understand one day."

Sebastian clapped Quade on the shoulder. "Love doesn't live here anymore," he said. "It's only one-night stands for me. No commitment and no expectations. Just how I like it."

Canten shook his head at his friend. He talked a big game, but he'd been head over heels in love once. Had even proposed. Then his ex had broken his heart. Two days before the wedding, she'd called it off and fled town. Rumor had it it was to be with the man she'd dated before Sebastian, but Canten couldn't confirm or deny that. Her betrayal had hardened Sebastian. In time, he would be all right. He just needed the right woman to come into his life and soften him.

"What about you, Sheriff?" Quade asked. "Would you ever walk down the aisle again?"

The question caught Canten off guard. "I think once was enough for me," he said. Canten caught Sebastian's eye in the mirror. A second later, Sebastian looked away.

"Tonight's the bachelorette party, right?" Sebastian asked.

Quade groaned. "I don't even want to think about that."

This only prompted Sebastian to say more. "They're going to have some big, burly, Mandingo-looking brother with a dick the size of a submarine grinding all over them, ball sweat flying everywhere."

"It's not that kind of party," Canten said. "Rylee told me it was going to be a quiet evening with her, Lunden, and Happi. That's how Lunden wanted it."

Both Quade and Sebastian burst into laughter.

"And you believed that?" Sebastian asked. "Man, you're gullible."

Now that he thought about it . . . Canten laughed at himself. He guessed he *had* been a little gullible. Of course there would be a stripper.

Sebastian's cell phone chimed. Retrieving it, he swiped the screen. A second later, he said, "Y'all up for a pickup game?"

"Heck yeah," Canten said because, thanks to Rylee, he needed the exercise.

A short time later, they arrived at the community basketball court. Had Canten known Leonard would be one of the men they would be playing against, he probably would have opted out. But he could play nice if Leonard could.

Canten wound up guarding Leonard. When the mouthy man received the ball, he attempted to psych Canten out. Leonard went up for the shot. Canten blocked it with what could have possibly been considered aggressive force. Leonard lost his footing and slammed to the ground.

That was for those damn flowers. "My bad," Canten said, offering his hand.

"Don't sweat it," Leonard said, accepting his assistance. "These things happen."

Later, another block from Canten sent Leonard crashing back to the ground. This time he swatted Canten's outstretched hand away, then walked off.

"Let's play some ball," Sebastian said, smacking Canten on the behind.

After a good three or four hours of balling, they called it quits. Canten was about to get into his vehicle when Leonard approached him.

"Good game, Sheriff."

"You too," Canten said.

Leonard smirked. "But I sensed a little hostility."

"The flowers were beautiful, but you probably shouldn't send Rylee any more." He was about to add, *Because she doesn't like flowers,* but Leonard cut him off.

"Flowers?"

A confused look spread across Leonard's face but faded a second later.

"Come on, Sheriff. You're not afraid of a little competition, are you?"

The man's smugness irritated him, but he kept his cool. Releasing a smooth chuckle, he said, "Competition? I have none. Not where Rylee is concerned. She's already mine, so who am I competing against, myself?"

"Well, Sheriff, you know what they say."

Canten folded his arms across his chest. "Actually, I don't."

"She's still a single woman until you put a ring on it."

At this moment, Canten regretted the fact he held himself to such a high standard. If not, he probably would have slugged this arrogant bastard. "Don't send any more flowers," he said. Sliding on his sunglasses, he added, "Enjoy the rest of your day." Behind the wheel, he cranked the engine and left Leonard standing there looking like a fool.

CHAPTER 16

Rylee should have known Happi had had something up her sleeve by the way she'd continuously checked her watch. That something had arrived at Rylee's place about twenty minutes ago in the form of a six-foot-four powerhouse of muscles with perfectly groomed dreads that hung to his waist, skin a perfect shade of deep brown, and a body that should be preserved for future study.

"Do you see that body?" Zeta whispered.

Zeta Deane, Honey Hill's no-nonsense town attorney, stared wide eyed across the room at Officer Delight—the name he'd offered—as if he were the eighth wonder of the world. Rylee could understand her captivation. It was hard to ignore those wide shoulders, sculpted abs, muscular thighs, sturdy-looking legs, and colossal feet. At least a size fourteen.

Officer Delight had arrived dressed in a policeman's uniform. Now he danced in front of them in nothing but skin-tight jeggings. Rylee tried not to stare at the imprint stretching the slinky fabric at the crotch, but it was hard not to focus on it. Was it real? The bulge made her *really* want Canten right now.

"Where did you find him, Happi?" Lunden asked.

Heaven would have been Rylee's guess, but the man wasn't an apparition. He was real as real could be.

"I know a woman who knows a woman," she said. "By the way, it's real, in case anyone was wondering," she added.

"Oh, I was wondering," Zeta said. "I was wondering."

Rylee felt sorry for the poor woman who experienced that punisher between his legs.

All four ladies tossed dollar bills Happi had given them. The man had crazy energy, even crazier moves, and insane flexibility. Officer Delight dropped to his knees and did a slow, sensual, predatory crawl toward Lunden. When he was within arm's length of her, he pounced to his feet. His body moved like rubber in front of her. Rules had been established beforehand, so he never touched her, except for removing his hat and placing it on Lunden's head.

A little after midnight, they said goodbye to Officer Delight, who'd given them one hell of a show. Shortly after one, Rylee stood on her porch, waving as the last car backed out of the driveway. As she turned to head back inside, she caught sight of the silhouette in Canten's living room window just as the room went dark.

He'd probably heard all the commotion of the ladies leaving. Inside, Rylee groaned at all the leftovers. What would she do with all this food? She popped her forehead. Of course—she knew what to do with it.

Lifting her cell phone from the counter, she texted Canten.

Rylee: Wyd?

The three little dots that indicated he was typing back were immediate.

Canten: Fell asleep on the couch. Woke up starving. Raiding the fridge. You?

Rylee gathered the food trays onto the counter, changed into something a little more comfortable, and grabbed her keys.

Canten: Did you fall asleep on me?

Oh, how she would love that. Instead of texting back, she headed over. Halfway across the street, she heard the distant rumble of thunder. She didn't recall the weatherman mentioning a storm. When Canten opened the door, shirtless, she nearly dropped the trays. He wore a pair of black plaid pajamas that were tied low on his hips. "A, um, little birdie told me you're starving. I brought you chest." *Oh God.* "Cheese. I brought you cheese and other stuff."

Canten chuckled softly. Taking the trays from her, he said, "Are you checking me out?"

"Yes. Yes, I am," she said.

Following him into the kitchen, her eyes fixed on his strong back. Blowing out a slow breath, she begged her body to behave. Canten popped the top off one of the trays, grabbed one of the sandwiches, chomped down on it, and moaned like it was the best thing he'd ever had.

"You really were starving, huh?"

"I skipped dinner."

Rylee's brows shot up. "*You* skipped a meal?"

"Well, someone has been cooking all these irresistible meals, and apparently, my waist size has increased. At least according to Lady Sunshine."

Rylee slapped a hand over her mouth to keep from laughing out loud.

"It's not funny. It's not funny," he said, claiming another sandwich.

"Sorry," she said. "If it makes you feel any better, I think you look great. With and without clothes."

He flashed a roguish grin. "Thank you. So tell me about your *quiet* bachelorette party."

The smirk on his face told her he knew it had been anything but quiet, but she played along. "Uneventful. Laughed a little. Talked a little. Wined a little."

Canten barked a laugh. "Was this before or after the stripper?"

Rylee leaned against the counter. "And how did you know there was a stripper?"

"I peeped through your window."

"What?"

"I'm just messing with you, but I did actually see him performing through your window. His reflection. He was doing this move."

Canten placed both hands behind his head and started rolling his hips. The way his body flexed filled Rylee with pure lust. He actually had some moves. If she'd had any dollar bills, she would have made it rain. "Take it off. Take it off," she chanted.

After gliding both hands down his chest in a way-too-arousing manner, he untied the drawstring of his pajamas and hooked his thumbs in the sides as if he were about to lower the pants.

"Yaaasss!" she cheered.

When Canten stopped, she groaned. "It was just getting good. Why did you stop?"

"You're not ready for all that."

Oh, she was ready. Ready, willing, and able. She looked on as he removed the top of the fruit-and-cheese tray. "For the record, you could give Officer Delight a run for his money."

"Officer Delight? That was his name?"

She nodded. The name was fitting, but of course, she didn't say that to Canten. "He was actually a surprise. Happi arranged his visit. At first I was a little perturbed that she would invite a complete stranger to my house, but he seemed okay."

Canten dipped a strawberry in chocolate. "Looks can be deceiving."

"Why are you trying to scare me?"

Canten stopped shy of biting the strawberry and flashed a look of remorse. "If you're afraid, you can always stay the night here."

Rylee took the strawberry from his hand. "I think I would like that," she said, then taking a bite of the fruit.

Canten's jaw muscles flexed several times. A beat later, his eyes lowered to her mouth. "You have chocolate on your lip."

Rylee lifted her hand to remove it, but Canten stopped her.

"Let me," he said in a near whisper.

Dipping his head forward, he dragged his tongue across her bottom lip. Pulsing with need, she sucked his tongue into her mouth. She kissed him with the hunger of a starved lover, and in a way, she was. Ever since their first night together, she'd longed to enjoy his mouth again.

He matched her energy with a starving need of his own. Their tongues tussled, teased, tasted. Searched, found, conquered. The sweetness from the strawberry and chocolate she'd savored reminded her of love and romance. This wasn't that. *Sex. Just sex.* And she was okay with that.

Canten broke his mouth away from Rylee's and hoisted her onto the counter. After removing her shirt and bra, he cupped both breasts in his hands and swiped his thumbs back and forth over her taut nipples, then leaned forward and wrapped his warm lips around one of them. She dropped her head back in pleasure as he suckled and teased it. He moved to her opposite nipple, giving it equal attention.

By the time Canten slid her off the counter and into his arms, her entire body was in full-arousal mode. She desperately needed, wanted him inside her. As he carried her to the bedroom, her legs circled around his waist, her arms around his neck. "Is this us needing each other again?"

"No," he said, pointedly. "This is us *wanting* each other. You do want me tonight, don't you?"

Tonight. Tomorrow. She stopped shy of thinking *forever*. "I can't put into words just how much I want you," she said.

"Good," he said, capturing her mouth again.

Inside his bedroom, Canten placed her on the mattress, removed her shoes, and tugged the black shorts from her body.

Canten froze, his eyes darting up to her. "You're not wearing underwear," he said.

She'd hoped she wouldn't need any. Coming up on her elbows, she said, "Is that going to be a problem?"

"Only for you," he said.

Tossing her shorts aside, he stood and removed his pants. His swollen manhood moved like a compass and pointed directly at her.

"You're beautiful," he said, staring at her from the edge of the bed.

"So are you." And she wasn't just saying that. Every inch of Canten's body was glorious. Every soft curve. Every hard line.

On the bed, Canten kissed his way up her leg until he was at her core. Rylee knew from previous experience how damn good Canten was with his tongue and that the odds of her lasting longer than a few minutes were slim to none. His skillful tongue twirled around her clit, sending volts of pleasure buzzing through her.

Her breathing grew ragged, blood whooshed in her ears, and her stomach muscles tightened at the onset of an orgasm. *Fight it,* she willed herself. *Fight it.* And she did, until Canten curled two long fingers inside and suckled her. Seconds later, she shattered into a thousand pieces. Her back arched off the bed, and she cried out his name.

Goose bumps prickled her skin as Canten kissed his way up her trembling body. He took a moment to enjoy her breasts again before continuing his trail of kisses to her mouth. Placing her hand behind his head, she brought his mouth to hers. They kissed long, hard, raw.

Rylee broke the kiss. "I want to feel you inside me," she said, staring into Canten's dark, hungry eyes. "I need to feel you inside me."

Canten studied her. "I want you, Rylee. Not just tonight. Until we end this thing, I want you in my bed. You said all I have to do is ask. I'm asking now. Will you give me what I desperately want?" He kissed her gently.

To say she was beyond stunned by his request would have been an understatement. The look in Canten's eyes told her he was dead serious. Not that she'd doubted that for a second. "Yes. You can have as much of me as you can handle," she said, then reached down and guided him inside her.

Rylee moaned, whimpered, cussed as Canten glided in and out of her with long, hard strokes. It felt so good. So damn good that her eyes misted. *No tears,* she warned herself. She couldn't risk Canten thinking something was wrong and stopping. Not now. Not when he had her on pleasure level infinity.

Canten kissed the delicate skin below her lobe and slowed his stroke. "You feel so good," he whispered into her ear. "Too damn good. I shouldn't be here," he said. "God, I shouldn't be here."

Rylee got the impression the last two sentences had been more for his benefit than hers. Instead of focusing on why he thought he shouldn't be here, she glided the tips of her fingers along his back. "You're exactly where you should be," she said, then turned her head to make contact with his mouth again.

Canten shivered. "Come for me, Rylee. I'm not sure how much longer I can last. You're going to break me, woman."

When Canten adjusted her legs, she swore he drove himself even deeper inside her. "Don't stop," she said over and over again until the onset of another orgasm snatched her voice. She couldn't make a sound, could barely grab enough air to fill her lungs. *I'm there.* She wasn't sure if she'd actually said the words aloud or just in her head. Either way, Canten would know soon. Rylee closed her eyes and welcomed the glorious pressure building inside her. Unable to hold it off another second, she exploded with pleasure.

Canten knew the very moment Rylee released, because her muscles contracted around his dick. That, coupled with the warm, wet feel of her, would surely do him in. A groan escaped his throat as a searing heat burned through his entire body. His heart pounded, and the room began to spin.

Seconds later, he burst with the force of a breached dam, filling Rylee with his hot seed. She still pulsed around him, helping to milk him dry. *Take it all.* The power strokes he'd applied earlier turned clumsy and puny. Still, he continued until he didn't have a single drop left to give.

They lay in each other's arms, nothing shattering the comfortable silence but the sounds of rumbling thunder outside the window. Instead of seeking the rest he needed, Canten stared at the ceiling, lost in his thoughts.

Rylee would be his undoing. He knew as sure as the night was long. Still, knowing this didn't prompt him to be more cautious. Instead, he'd done the very opposite and invited more conflict by asking her to entrust her body to him until their arrangement was over. *You are a selfish fool, Canten Barnes.* And he had no doubt he would pay dearly for his rapacity and stupidity. Being with Rylee intimately made the cost worth every penny.

A beam of common sense broke through a tiny crack in his head. Maybe he should make it clear to Rylee that he could never offer her anything beyond pleasure. Would that make him sound like a complete asshole for insinuating she even wanted more? He recalled what he'd said to her. *Until we end this thing.* The statement indicated there was a timeline and that this wouldn't be permanent.

"It's about to storm," Rylee said, her soft lips tickling his chest.

Canten held her a little tighter. "I thought you were asleep."

"No."

"I guess that means I didn't do my job."

She came up on her elbow to look at him. "You're awake too. Does that mean I didn't do my job?"

"Trust me, I have absolutely no complaints."

"Are you feeling any angst?"

Were they going to go through this every time they slept together? Canten flipped her onto her back. "No angst." He kissed her forehead. "No regret." Kissed the tip of her nose. "No anything." Kissed her lips. "I've been inside you enough now that we should be beyond any such negative feelings."

"I've never had any negative feelings about us and never will. I was actually referring to the storm. You said once that the only thing you feel during storms is angst."

Canten chuckled. "Oh." *Damn, this woman never forgets anything.* "I'm surprisingly okay. One might even say perfect." How could he not be with her in his arms?

"Katrina Sweeney?"

Katrina was the last person he wanted to talk about lying butt-ass naked in bed with Rylee. He planned to plant himself between Rylee's legs at least four more times and didn't need Katrina in his head, blocking his ability to get hard. "What about her?"

"Is that why you don't like storms? It triggers the memory of you driving her home and all the craziness that followed."

"Yes," he admitted.

"I guess we'll have to work on that by giving you something more desirable to recall when it storms."

He liked where this conversation was headed. "Any ideas?"

Rylee's lips curled into a half smile. "One or two." She pushed him onto his back, then dipped under the covers.

"Oh shit!" he moaned when she took him into her mouth. Yep, this would definitely do the trick.

CHAPTER 17

Rylee was in love.

Two-ounce glass jars filled with honey from the inn with a wooden honeycomb dipper attached with jute and adorned with a small brass honeybee. Yep, she was absolutely in love with Lunden's wedding favors. *Meant to Bee* was engraved on a small birchwood circle, along with Lunden's and Quade's names and their upcoming wedding date, July 24. A little over a month away.

Rylee couldn't wait until the big day, because it was sure to be the event of the season. Lunden and Quade had given her carte blanche in regard to the wedding cake, and she'd taken full advantage. The all-white, eight-tier buttercream wedding cake she'd designed for them required so many handmade sugar flowers she'd had to start making them last month. And she still had dozens left to craft. She couldn't wait until they saw it.

Rylee hadn't gotten the opportunity to experience her own wedding, so she found herself living vicariously through Lunden. While it seemed unlikely she'd ever walk down an aisle, on occasion, she found herself fantasizing about her own wedding like she had as a little girl. Doing so brought her both joy and sadness. Why hadn't she fought for what she'd wanted?

Boisterous laughter drew her from her thoughts. Since Lunden had extended a wedding invitation to almost the entirety of Honey Hill, they'd been forced to call in additional help to assist with the nearly three hundred favors they had to prepare. In addition to Rylee, Lunden, Happi, and Zeta, Ms. Jewel, the town matriarch, and the Chamber sisters, Harriet and Bonita, who operated the flower shop, had joined them at the inn to help.

No doubt this would be a fun afternoon because Ms. Harriet and Ms. Bonita brought excitement wherever they went. While the two ladies weren't twins, their kinship was undeniable. They both sported natural afros—which always looked freshly groomed. Both had the same smooth, chestnut-colored skin that gave them a more youthful appearance. Both had happy hazel eyes. Both were sassy, late sixties, and shameless. And like most of the elders in town, they loved to meddle. But like Ms. Jewel, they were the salt of the earth. Rylee cherished them dearly.

Rylee eyed the women, wondering what she'd missed. It didn't take her long to find out.

"Well, all I'm saying is the man spent five years in prison. Being the good citizen of Honey Hill that I am, I'm willing to spare some of my time, knowledge, and experience to reintegrate him back into society," Ms. Harriet said.

Ms. Bonita shook her head. "Sister, you are one of the horniest old women I know. That boy is young enough to be your grandchild, you mountain lion."

Ms. Harriet flashed an appalled look. "Who are you calling old?"

"I think the term is *cougar*, Auntie," Happi said from across the room.

"*Mountain lion* sounds more mature," Ms. Bonita countered.

The room rumbled with laughter.

"*Ezekiel, Ezekiel, Ezekiel*," Ms. Harriet said as if calling his name three times would cause him to appear. "Isn't that biblical? He can place those holy hands on me anytime."

"I'm telling Pastor," Ms. Bonita threatened.

"I'm not sure Pastor can keep his eyes open long enough to listen," Lunden said.

Rylee had missed last Sunday's service. She and Canten had lounged in bed most of the morning, talking, laughing, listening to the storm outside, and doing what they were becoming awfully great at . . . making love. Apparently, one minute Pastor White had been sitting in the pulpit, eyes closed, foot tapping to the sound of the choir. The next minute he'd fallen fast asleep, mouth wide open, snoring and all. The choir director had instructed the drummer to hit a hard note. Pastor White had bolted to his feet, singing a verse from a song two hymns prior. Rylee had nearly cracked a rib laughing as Lunden had told the story.

Ms. Harriet scowled at her sister. "You better not tell."

"Harriet, you better leave that child alone," Ms. Jewel said. "I told him he wouldn't be bothered here. Poor thing's been through enough without having to fend off a mountain lion."

More laughter erupted inside the room.

"Gram, I don't understand why you would invite a criminal to stay with you. It's dangerous, and I'm not happy about it," Zeta said to Ms. Jewel, her grandmother.

"Lawd, chile, he's not living with me. He's out back in the guest-house. Fixed it up real nice too. Plus, he's paid his debt to society. Everyone deserves a second chance."

"Mmm-hmm," Ms. Bonita and Ms. Harriet hummed in unison.

Rylee agreed.

"Well, unless he chopped someone up into tiny pieces, then ate them for breakfast," Ms. Harriet said. "Good Lord, he's not a cannibal, is he?" she asked.

"Quit talking silly, Harriet," Ms. Jewel said.

"What about a reformed serial killer?" Ms. Bonita asked.

Rylee wasn't sure there was such a thing.

"I am not entertaining any more of y'all's foolishness," Ms. Jewel said.

"What was he in for anyway?" Ms. Bonita asked.

Rylee fixed her mouth to respond but was cut off by Ms. Jewel.

"None of your beeswax. He's just trying to move forward with his life," Ms. Jewel said. "Let the child be. And don't go asking him his business," she added, "either of you. Or I might just have to tell a little of yours."

"Oh, hell," Ms. Harriet said. "You know too much of my business. My lips are sealed."

Ms. Bonita clammed up too.

Rylee knew with certainty Ms. Jewel would never spill anyone's business—that wasn't the type of person she was—but her threat had been enough to change the subject, so obviously, she knew some juicy dirt on the sisters.

Zeta's phone chimed. A few seconds later, she said, *"Gram!"* Eyeing Ms. Jewel, she said, "You fired the aide I sent to help you around the house?"

"Ezekiel has been helping me. That young man can fix anything. Plus, that girl you sent ain't never cleaned a thing a day in her life. Tried to clean my new microwave with furniture polish."

"Furniture polish?" they all said in unison, then burst with laughter.

"Grandchild, save your money. I'm just going to keep firing them anyway," Ms. Jewel said.

Zeta tossed her hands and sighed in exhaustion.

"Rylee, where is Dorsetta?" Ms. Jewel asked. "The woman should have been here an hour ago."

Rylee chuckled. "You know my mother. Always fashionably late."

"Is she bringing that handsome husband of hers?" Ms. Harriet asked.

"Now you're just trying to get cut, Harriet," Ms. Jewel said. "You know Dorsetta don't play when it comes to Gus."

No, her mother didn't.

"Lawd, I don't think I've ever seen that woman happier than when she talks about you and the sheriff."

"That sheriff," Ms. Harriet said. "Mmm-mmm. Another good looker. You girls are snatching up all the fine ones."

"Hands off, Ms. Harriet," Rylee said, causing yet more laughter.

Ms. Harriet flashed her palms in mock surrender.

Ms. Bonita beamed. "My sister and I predicted you two. Never seen anyone catch the sheriff's eye quite like you. I sorta suspected y'all were an item by the way Sheriff lit up when he saw you. You clearly make him happy. And you make a lovely couple."

"Thank you," Rylee said, guilt blossoming inside her. Not only was she lying to her mother, but she was lying to these women she highly respected.

"When will he be back?" Ms. Jewel asked. "This town doesn't run the same when he's away. Best doggone sheriff we ever had."

"Sho nuff better than that old one we had. Didn't do nothing all day but eat," Ms. Bonita said. "Arthur Grimley was in the diner so often, stuffing his chubby cheeks, he had a personal table."

"Tonight," Rylee said. And she couldn't wait. Both her body and her bed missed him tremendously.

Since they'd agreed to add an ongoing intimate dynamic to their relationship, they'd spent nearly every night in each other's arms. And every night, she ignored how hard it would be to let him go when the time came. Yet that fact hadn't stopped her from welcoming him into her bed, time and time again, though it probably should have.

"I see another wedding happening in Honey Hill, sister," Ms. Harriet said to Ms. Bonita. "We had better get our floral fingers ready."

Rylee released a nervous chuckle. "Nothing like that anytime soon," she said.

"How long did you say you two have been dating on the low down?" Ms. Harriet asked.

"*Down low*, Auntie," Happi said.

Uh-oh. Panic set in when Rylee couldn't recall the time frame Canten had given her parents. "H-how long?" she said, repeating the question in an effort to buy herself a little more time. *Dammit, I stuttered. Maybe Ms. Harriet didn't notice.*

Ms. Harriet did a slow nod, a curious look on her face.

She noticed. Think, Rylee, think. When her mother arrived, she was sure this would come up again, so it had to be accurate . . . "Um, we've—"

"Oh my God!" Lunden yelled out, bolting out of her seat and startling everyone.

"What is it, chile?" Ms. Jewel asked.

Lunden pointed at the window. "I just saw the biggest vulture swoop by. I thought for sure he would crash into the window."

When everyone's attention was fixed on the window, Lunden eyed Rylee and winked.

"Thank you," Rylee mouthed. Thank God for her best friend.

Luckily, the diversion prompted another discussion on something other than Rylee and Canten. Ms. Harriet and Ms. Bonita told a hilarious story about the bird that had stowed away in one of their floral shipments. They'd chased it around the shop with a shoe and flyswatter. Finally, it had flown out when a customer had entered the shop.

"We knocked over everything in the shop," Ms. Bonita said with a hard laugh. "Now we have the delivery guy check before he brings any flowers inside. I don't want to go through that fiasco again. Took us an hour to clean up all the bird shit."

After all the chortling stopped, Rylee said, "Speaking of flowers. If Leonard Jamison happens to stop by again, wanting to send me flowers, will you please deliver them to the hospital or the retirement home instead?"

"He sent you flowers?" Happi and Zeta said in unison.

"Lawd, bless his conniving little heart," Ms. Jewel said.

"So inappropriate," Lunden added.

Both Ms. Bonita and Ms. Harriet flashed confused expressions.

"That Jamison boy hasn't been to the shop in over a year. Last time he came in, he wanted a discount on an eight-dollar bouquet. Just plain ole cheap like his grandpappy," Ms. Bonita said, her face tightening into a ball of disgust.

Rylee thought about when Leonard had come into her shop for coffee and wanted an upgrade to a specialty beverage. Cheap was right.

A second later, her brows furrowed. "But I received a flower delivery from him maybe a week and a half ago."

"Oh, he didn't send those," Ms. Harriet said. "The girl did. His cousin. What's that child's name? The one at the diner with all that wild hair. Looking like one of those alpacas over at the Silverdale farm."

Ms. Jewel chuckled. "Hush your mouth, Harriet. You know God don't like ugly."

"Then he sure enough don't like her," Ms. Harriet said. "I'm not talking about looks. She's a decent-looking girl. I'm talking about her attitude. Just plain hideous."

The one at the diner? Was Ms. Harriet talking about . . . ? *"Katrina?"* Rylee asked.

"That's it," Ms. Harriet said. "I thought it was a little odd she was sending you such an extravagant floral arrangement, especially when you stole Canten right up from under her nose."

"Hmph," Ms. Jewel said. "Now how can you steal something that was never yours? That girl's been sniffing after the sheriff for the longest. Just pitiful."

"Exactly," Lunden said. She eyed Rylee with a smile. "Canten's with the woman he wants."

Why had it felt as if Lunden had placed hidden innuendo in her words?

Rylee's focus shifted to something else. Why the hell would Katrina send her flowers and say they were from Leonard? A beat later it hit her. Had she been trying to sabotage her "relationship" with Canten? Had she been hoping to make Canten jealous? Suspicious? Both? Was Katrina truly that desperate? *Obviously.* The scalawag would rejoice when she and Canten ended things.

Canten sat behind his desk, fiddling with the green crystal elephant he'd purchased on his recent trip to Charlotte. He'd held on to the trinket since his return a couple of days ago, debating whether to give it to Rylee. The woman had a fascination with elephants. His hesitation stemmed from the fact that giving her gifts might have suggested more than he intended it to. Then again, it could simply be construed as what it was, a friend giving another friend a gift. *A friend with exceptional benefits.* That part made it tricky.

When it came to Rylee, he could no longer decipher up from down. Like the Keith Sweat song, she had him twisted. The woman was making it real hard for him to decipher what in their make-believe relationship was the truth and what was the lie. His growing feelings for her confused him even more. What kind of black magic had she worked on him? Actually, he couldn't place the blame on her. He had himself twisted. In Charlotte, all he could think about was getting home to Honey Hill. But was it Honey Hill or Rylee he'd missed so much? Of course, he knew the answer but refused to acknowledge it. As if not doing so would change anything.

"Uh-oh. That's the look of a troubled man. Anything I can do to help?"

Canten glanced up to see his father entering his office. He insisted on going with Senior to his doctor appointments when possible so he could hear firsthand what the doctor had to say and not rely on his father's interpretation. With Senior's health issues, he wasn't taking any chances with miscommunication.

"Pop? I told you I would pick you up. You didn't have to walk here."

Senior eased into the chair on the opposite side of Canten's desk. "I was at the bakery. Figured I'd go 'head and walk over."

"What were you doing at the bakery?"

"Sampling the best doggone omelet I've ever put in my mouth. Turkey sausage, peppers, onions, mushrooms, cheese, and something else." His father pressed a finger to his chin.

"Dill," Canten said.

Senior snapped his fingers. "That's it. How'd you know?"

"Rylee made me one before I left for work this morning." Canten noticed the look on his father's face and added, "Wipe that smirk off your face, old man. I met her in the driveway." Oh, how the lies just kept right on coming. The truth was he woke up next to Rylee far more mornings than not.

"Mmm-hmm," Senior hummed. "That Rylee can throw down in the kitchen, son."

In the bedroom, too, but he kept that part to himself. She'd done this thing with her tongue that brought actual tears to his eyes, it had felt so good.

"You're a damn lucky man to have a woman like that," Senior said.

"Don't start, Pop. You know the deal."

"Did I misspeak? You do have her for now, right?"

Canten didn't argue, because he knew there was no need to counter. Plus, his father was right. "Just no more conversations with the Charleses about grandbabies, okay?"

Senior shrugged a shoulder but didn't commit. "Rylee said she hoped to add a few hot breakfast items to the menu soon. She also said you'd suggested it. Good call, son. That young fella she hired, Ezekiel, asked if I had any part-time work around the shop. Cleaning, organizing, that sort of thing. I don't, but I remember you mentioning something about needing someone to clean here at night since you had to let the other lady go. I didn't say anything to him, 'cause I wasn't sure how that worked with his record and all."

"I'll have a chat with him. I'm sure I can work something out."

"I know you did a background check on him. I'm assuming you didn't find anything too troubling."

"Why would I have done a background check?"

Senior tilted his head and gave him a *you know why* look.

Canten laughed. Yep, he had performed one. The second Rylee had told him she'd hired Ezekiel. "I looked into his case. I personally don't think he should have been charged with manslaughter, let alone convicted."

From the information Canten had read, Ezekiel had only been defending himself when his neighbor's intoxicated and high boyfriend had come after him with a knife because the man had believed Ezekiel had been sleeping with the girlfriend. The boyfriend just so happened to have been a relative of some influential businessman. Which meant someone had to pay. Sadly, Ezekiel had with five years of his life.

"What's that?" Senior said, pointing to the elephant.

"Oh, this? It's nothing. Just something I picked up in Charlotte." Canten placed it in the drawer alongside the letter he still hadn't shared with his father.

"An elephant. Rylee loves elephants. You should give it to her. She'll love it."

Canten knew Senior was being facetious. Undoubtedly, the man already knew Rylee had been the intended recipient. "I might," he said.

"You never said how your trip to Charlotte went. I imagine it was a little difficult being back there."

"It went well." His eyes lowered to the paper clip he twiddled between his fingers. "I drove by the house." His gaze rose to his father's. "You wouldn't recognize it. It's been completely remodeled. Neighborhood's changed too." *Too little, too late.*

"Let me guess, gentrification?"

Canten nodded.

"Is that the reason you went to Charlotte, son?" Senior asked, his expression showing concern.

"No." He reopened the drawer, fished out the letter, and passed it to his father. He would have had to tell him sooner or later. No time like the present. "This is why."

Canten watched his father intently as the man read, Senior's face revealing nothing. When Senior finished, he refolded the paper, stuffed it back in the envelope, and passed it to Canten.

"Bureau commander, huh?" Senior said. "So does this mean you're leaving us?"

Canten wondered what *us* Senior was referring to: Honey Hill or him and Rylee. "Nothing's been decided yet," he said, "but yeah, I'm considering taking the job if it's offered."

Senior nodded slowly. "Rylee know?"

"No." Canten wasn't sure she needed to. At least not now. "I want to keep it that way for now," he added. When Senior's eyes lowered, Canten said, "What's on your mind?"

"Just thinking about how proud of you I am. How proud your mother would be." Senior sighed. "I'm not going to lie: I'm going to hate to see you go, but I've always taught you to follow your heart wherever it leads you. Sounds like it's leading you back to Charlotte. Either way, I'm proud of you, son."

"Thanks, Pop."

Senior rubbed the side of his face as if he'd been slapped. "When will you know something?"

"August, probably."

"I see. Ideal timing for you, I suppose."

It was. Rylee's parents planned to return to Florida in August. He and Rylee would end their "relationship" in August. He could leave in August. The good thing about it: if he got the job, they had a solid explanation as to why they'd ended things. They could say Rylee didn't believe a long-distance relationship would work. Heck, it sounded a lot better than *We decided to be friends*. No one would believe two people with their level of chemistry would agree to just be friends.

Wait. What was he saying? They *were* just friends . . . with exceptional benefits.

When Senior stood and said, "Reckon we had better make a move," Canten took that as a sign that the conversation was over, so he stood too.

CHAPTER 18

Rylee had hoped the new additions to her menu would be received well, but she hadn't imagined there would be this kind of demand. At only nine in the morning, she'd run out of the hash brown casserole, twice. Ezekiel had just put the fifth batch of breakfast burritos in the warmer. The turkey-sausage omelet had been the superstar of the day, while the hot buttery croissants stuffed with Canadian bacon and cheesy eggs had come in a close second.

If she'd known the items would be such a hit, she'd have offered them a long time ago. Some residents she'd witnessed come through the line twice. Quade had been one of them. First for an omelet because both Canten and Senior had raved about it. The second time, he'd ordered the hash brown casserole. She'd thrown in a breakfast burrito.

Speaking of Canten . . . her eyes slid to the order-pickup area. Earlier, Canten had stopped by to support her new-menu-items celebration, and he'd wound up putting on an apron to help. She'd initially declined his assistance because it had been his day off. But he'd insisted. Plus, she'd needed the help.

Mmm, he sure looked good in an apron. Heck, he looked good in anything he wore. Looked even better when he wore nothing. *Stop it. Focus on work, not undressing him with your eyes.*

Rylee had intended to stop serving breakfast at eleven, but so many people were still arriving that she extended it until two. Honey Hill had shown her so much love; she wanted to make sure everyone got the opportunity to be served. By two thirty, the place had thinned out, and she was exhausted.

"That was insane," Ezekiel said, joining Rylee and Canten out front.

"Bonkers," Canten said. "But you guys operated like a well-oiled machine."

"Because my team rocks," Rylee said, giving everyone high fives. "And you rock too," she said to Canten, wrapping an arm around his waist. "Thank you for all your assistance and for helping to keep all the chaos under control. You ever want to retire from law enforcement, you have a place here."

"I'll keep that in mind, and you're welcome," Canten said.

Rylee popped him on the butt. "Now go home and get some rest. It's your day off, remember?"

"I will. I just need to holler at Ezekiel for a second." He eyed Ezekiel. "You have a minute to walk with me out?" Canten asked.

Ezekiel looked to Rylee for approval. She nodded. *What is that about?*

Canten removed his apron and handed it to Rylee. "I'll see you later."

He leaned forward and planted a kiss on her lips as if it were the most natural thing in the world to do. In fact, it had been so effortless she wasn't even sure he'd actually realized what he'd done. Who said they couldn't pull off being a fake couple? On occasion, it startled her just how real their fake felt.

"Today was a good day," she said, heading into the kitchen to work on the disarray the breakfast rush had created.

Later that evening—and just as Rylee left the bakery—her cell phone rang. She beamed at Canten's name on her screen. Making the call active, she said, "Hello?"

"Hey. I didn't catch you at a bad time, did I?"

There is never a bad time for you. Of course, she didn't say that aloud. "Not at all."

"Are you still at work?"

"Just locked up. Headed home for a much-needed long, hot shower. Do you mind if we postpone Taco Tuesday? I'm exhausted."

"Sure," he said. "But do you mind swinging by my place before you go home? I need your help with something. It'll be quick, I promise."

Well, the "quick" part ruled out sex. Canten always took his time pleasing her. Rylee was too beat to even ask why he needed her help. Despite how spent she was, there was no way she would have said no to him. Not after all he'd done for her. "Sure. I'll be there in five."

Rylee parked in her own driveway, then walked across the street. She reached for the doorbell, but the door opened before she could press it. Canten invited her in, then led her toward the kitchen.

"Something smells amazing." Her brow shot up. "Are you cooking?"

"Yes. Well, grilling, actually. It's nothing fancy. I just figured that after the day you had, you could use a hot meal that you didn't have to prepare."

Unpeeled potatoes and corn, waiting to be shucked, sat in the sink. Two juicy-looking steaks and shrimp kabobs sat in a dish on the countertop. "These steaks look amazing," she said.

"Well done, no pink, just like you like it," he said.

He knew her too well. "You did all of this for . . . *me?*"

"Why do you sound so surprised?"

Because no man had ever done anything like this for her before. Not even Lucas, who'd had an aversion to cooking and had often said she did it so well he didn't want to throw things off balance. Had she known how special it would make her feel, she would have encouraged him to at least try. But should she have even had to do that? "I don't know. I guess I am just a little bit surprised. Thank you, Canten. This is extremely thoughtful."

"I'm not quite finished. I know you wanted to take a shower, but I ran you a bath. I hope that's okay. While you're soaking, it'll give me an opportunity to make up for my lack of efficient time-management skills. I'd hoped to have all of this done by the time you arrived. But I fell asleep on the sofa. It threw me behind schedule."

He'd run her a bath?

Canten moved around the room doing this and that. "I put a towel and rag in the master bath. I also placed one of my shirts on the bed you can slip into once you're done. I should—"

He stopped abruptly, obviously noticing the way she was looking at him.

"What?" he asked.

What? He was making her entire night, that was what. "It was your day off. You didn't have to waste it on me."

Fine lines crawled across his forehead. "Doing something nice for a friend could never be a waste of my time. Now get, woman. I have stuff to do."

That was right. They were friends. Just friends.

After the most relaxing bath ever, Rylee slid into the red *Honey Hill's Finest* T-shirt Canten had left out for her and headed to the kitchen. A bowl of mashed potatoes, a tray of corn, and a salad sat on the table along with the steaks. A beer was placed at one setting, wine at the other.

"There you are. Did you enjoy your bath?" Canten asked, pulling fresh rolls from the oven.

"I feel amazing. I nearly fell asleep."

"I was worried you would. You look tired. Still beautiful, but tired."

"I am," she admitted, taking a seat at the table. But not necessarily in a *need for sleep* type of way. She was tired of lying to her parents, the town, herself. Tired of pretending to be okay with only being Canten's friend. Tired of being caged by her past.

She'd loved Lucas. Had been a good—no, great—wife. But it was time she stopped using his death as a jail cell. It was time she gave herself permission to live. She wanted Canten to be a part of her new existence. Which was why tonight she would risk it all and tell him how she felt about him and pray he'd be receptive.

"I borrowed a pair of your socks. I hope you don't mind." She modeled the black ankle garment.

"Not at all," he said.

"Wow," she said. "Everything looks so delicious. I can't wait to dig in. I'm starving."

"So am I," he said, joining her at the table.

As usual, their mealtime was filled with great conversation and plenty of laughter. If what they said was true—that laughter kept you young—having Canten would keep her youthful for an eternity.

"Music in the Square is this weekend. Should we go?" she asked. "Maybe invite my parents and Senior."

"Heck yeah," he said. "I love Music in the Square."

Things grew quiet for a second.

"I need to tell—"

"I have some—"

They laughed at themselves when they both tried to speak at once.

"You go first," Rylee said because she could use the time to build up some more nerve.

"I have some kind of exciting news," he said, dipping more mashed potatoes. "I may be taking a new position. In Charlotte," he added.

The air seized in Rylee's lungs. Had she heard Canten correctly? It sounded like he'd said he was leaving Honey Hill. Willing herself to breathe, she said, "What did you say?" a part of her afraid he would confirm it.

"There's a possibility I might be leaving Honey Hill," he said.

Yep, she'd heard him right. And he considered this exciting news? Rylee smiled, but she had trouble holding it in place. *The story of my life, men leaving me.* Obviously, Lunden's universe had had a change of heart about them. "Charlotte, huh." Her stomach quivered. "That's . . . that's great, Canten. Great. I'm so happy for you." And she truly was. There was nothing here holding him back. Of course he would jump at an opportunity like this. Who could blame him?

She'd been the foolish one to think that maybe, just maybe, they had something real. Somewhere between the rolls under the covers and Canten's nice gestures, she'd lost sight of the bigger picture, that anything and everything they shared was all based on a lie. *None of this is real.*

"Nothing is finalized yet. There's a lot of interest in the position. A lot of strong candidates."

"I have no doubt you're the best man for the job. They would be fools not to offer it to you," she said. "Does Lunden know?" Because her best friend hadn't said a single word to her about this.

"No. I plan to tell her soon because I don't want to blindside her. If I do get the job, I'll stipulate that I need some transition time. I don't want to leave the town in a bind. I should know something by August; then I'll submit a formal letter of resignation."

"Sounds like you have it all worked out." She offered another attempt at a smile.

Rylee gave the situation some thought. Maybe all wasn't lost. Charlotte was only a four-hour drive away. She could still tell him how she felt. If the feeling was mutual, they could try a long-distance relationship. People successfully managed them every day.

Canten continued, "If I do get the job, that will give us a flawless excuse for our 'breakup.'" He made air quotes. "The long-distance-relationship thing." He chuckled and sipped his beer. "Everyone knows those rarely work out."

So much for that. "Right," she said. "Your plan sounds perfect." She brought the wineglass to her lips and took a long swig. One minute she'd been ready to tell this man she wanted to be more than just friends; the next he was telling her he would likely be leaving town. Just once, she wanted to be the reason someone stayed.

"What were you going to say earlier?" he asked.

"Oh. I-I, um, just wanted to say that what you did for Ezekiel, offering him part-time work at the station, was nice. You're a good man, Canten Barnes. You're going to make someone in Charlotte an extremely lucky woman."

Canten flashed a half smile, then brought the beer bottle back to his lips and took a hard gulp.

Shaking off her emotions, Rylee stood, hiked her shirt, and straddled his lap. Maybe she couldn't have him exactly how she wanted him; she could, however, enjoy the time they had left together. "But until then, let's say you make me an extremely happy woman here in Honey Hill. August is right around the corner; we should make good use of the limited time we have remaining."

"Actually, I was thinking maybe we chill on the couch, watch a little television. I might even be willing to massage your feet," Canten said.

Was this his way of telling her their time had already come to an end? "Oh. Okay. Yeah, I mean, a movie could be nice, I guess." When she made an attempt to get out of his lap, he held her firmly in place.

"Where do you think you're going?" he asked.

"I thought . . . you said—"

Canten captured her words in a heady kiss. The unexpected action startled her, but it only took a millisecond to recover and fall right into the kiss. Anytime their lips touched, it never disappointed. But this time the kiss ripped through her entire body. It was packed with so much raw energy it made her head spin. What was he trying to prove?

She yelped when Canten stood and swept an arm across the table, causing dishes to crash together. Some breaking from the sounds of it. "What . . . ?"

He placed her atop the table. The next few moments were a blur, but things returned to crystal-clear focus when he drove himself inside her, deep and hard. His powerful strokes sent the table scraping across the floor. The sturdy wood creaked and groaned under the weight of their bodies but, luckily, held firm.

It wasn't long before they plummeted over the edge of pleasure together in the most glorious descent of her life. Canten collapsed forward, his upper body resting against hers, his heart pounding so hard she could feel it through his chest. Her hands caressed his warm, damp back.

While you will never know this, Canten Barnes, you've ruined me for other men.

Canten lay on his stomach across the bed, butt naked, head resting on his crossed arms, staring at Rylee, who stared back at him. They had been this way for the past ten minutes, neither speaking, just staring at each other in after-sex silence. This was what they did whenever they didn't fall asleep immediately after sex.

After he'd taken Rylee on the kitchen table, something he'd never done with any woman, they'd found their way into the bedroom, where he'd enjoyed her twice more. August, when her parents returned to Florida and they ended this charade, was right around the corner. He planned to get his fill of her before then. Hell, if that feat was even possible. Every time they had sex, it only made him want her more.

Typically, Rylee was the first to break the silence. She'd yet to make it past fifteen minutes. She loved to talk. He loved to listen to her talk. About anything. But this time, he was the first to penetrate the quiet.

"I've been wondering about something," he said, his voice croaky from his moans and groans of pleasure from being inside her.

"What's that?"

"That day in the square. You said something about not wanting my death on your conscience too." His brows furrowed. "What did that mean?"

Rylee's expression turned somber, and she rolled onto her back and stared at the ceiling. "Lucas," she said.

He'd been killed in action by insurgents. Why would his death be on her conscience? "I don't understand."

"He was in Afghanistan because of me."

Canten didn't know the specifics of how military life worked, but he was fairly certain Rylee had no say-so in where he'd been sent. "Wasn't he in Afghanistan because that's where he'd been assigned?"

When she turned her head to look at him, her eyes glistened with unshed tears. "He wouldn't have even reenlisted if it hadn't been for me, Canten. He was done. Those first two tours had been rough on him."

"Why did he reenlist?"

She returned her gaze to the ceiling. "My school loan debt had our heads barely above water. I worked two jobs to help get us ahead. I constantly stressed—no, nagged—about money. I just wanted us to be financially okay." She blinked several times. "One day, Lucas returned home and told me he'd reenlisted. He said it had been for the money, but a part of me believes he did it just to get away from me." A tear slid from the corner of her eye.

"Come on, Rylee, you don't really believe that, do you?"

She nodded. "I loved him. And I know he loved me. But I don't believe either of us had been happy for a while. The military had him away so much. We'd become strangers. I no longer knew my husband, but I wanted to get to know him again."

Canten swiped a thumb across her skin to remove the single tear that had escaped.

"When his previous tour had ended, I was thrilled because I finally had my husband back." She smiled as if recalling a good memory. A second later her expression morphed to sadness. "But he'd changed. Still, I was determined to get to know this new withdrawn, unfamiliar version of him, get our marriage back on track."

"And did you?" Canten asked.

"I never got the chance, because he was gone again. He'd reenlisted without even telling me he was considering doing so. I was livid. We argued. I said some things I can never take back. His first two weeks away, he never called me. Not once. I was insane with worry and fear that something had happened to him."

Canten was stunned. How could this man—who'd supposedly loved her—leave her wondering about his well-being like that? On the job back in Charlotte, he'd phoned Jayla multiple times a day just to let her know he had been all right. Canten couldn't imagine how helpless and hopeless Rylee had felt during this time.

When more tears fell, he wiped them away.

Rylee continued, "When Lucas did finally call, I was so cold to him because for two weeks he'd *intentionally* put me through hell worrying about him, so I wanted him to think I hadn't given a damn. Days later, a chaplain and two officers arrived at my door."

When she let out a sob, Canten wrapped her trembling body in his arms. "It's okay. It's okay," he repeated, holding her tight to him. Oddly, he wanted to ask had she been alone during this time, but he didn't. The idea she'd had to endure such devastating news without a familiar person to lean on bothered him.

"As these kind men delivered my husband's death notice, then extended their deepest condolences, all I remember is thinking I should have felt it. Why hadn't I felt it?"

"Felt what?"

"Lucas's death," she said. "My father is deathly allergic to bees. One day my mother and I were in the kitchen making lunch. My father was in the garden picking veggies. All of a sudden, my mother dropped her favorite serving dish and sprinted from the kitchen, calling my father's name. She knew. She knew he was in trouble. He'd been stung and hadn't had his EpiPen with him. My mother knew he needed her. Later, when I asked her, she simply said she could feel it." Rylee chuckled.

"Imagine that. Having such a deep connection to someone, being so in tune with them, you can feel when they're in distress."

Canten did imagine it. *What an amazing phenomenon.*

Things were quiet for a beat or two.

"Jayla's death is on my conscience too," Canten said, surprising himself that the words had slipped past his lips. Especially when he rarely talked about Jayla's death with anyone other than his father. And even then, he was usually limited in what and how much he offered. But Rylee got it. She understood how having someone you loved snatched away because of violence could affect you.

"Tell me," she said.

"I pushed her to participate in an urban renewal program called Friendly Neighbor. Where law enforcement can purchase a home at a steep discount in an inner city neighborhood that typically sees higher crime rates. I promised her we would be safe." His thoughts drifted to the discussion he'd had with Jayla, whose main concern hadn't been for her safety but for his. Thankfully, Rylee's voice pulled him from his thoughts before he descended too far down the rabbit hole of guilt. "I lied to her, Rylee."

"I'm sure you thought you both *would* be," Rylee offered.

"Not about that. To sway her, I looked her in her eyes and told her several more law enforcement families would be moving in, too, and that the city would be building a substation near the neighborhood." He massaged the back of his neck. "But I knew that wouldn't take place for at least another year, year and a half. I just needed her to say yes."

"You couldn't have known, Canten."

But he should have. He didn't deserve the compassion Rylee showed him, but he wanted it. "The police presence was supposed to give the residents a sense of safety. And it did for some. Others, my being there simply disrupted their unlawful activities. Our cars were egged. Home was TP'd. I should have moved us out, but with the program, we had to commit to thirty-six months. I could have taken the monetary loss,

Rylee, and I should have, but I was stubborn. I wasn't going to be intimidated by thugs. I paid the ultimate price for that stubbornness."

"You can't control the actions of others, Canten. Jayla's death wasn't your fault. How could you have known what would happen? It wasn't your fault."

Canten released her and sat forward, resting his elbows on his knees. "She was pregnant, Rylee. Carrying our first child."

She gasped. "Oh God, Canten. I'm so, so sorry."

Using the heels of his hands, he massaged his eyes. "Thank you," he said, his voice cracking with emotion. "I've never told anyone this, Rylee, not even Senior."

"Thank you for entrusting me with it," she said. "It's safe with me."

He'd known it would be. "I wanted to be a father. More than anything in this world."

Rylee didn't speak, didn't offer him a barrage of platitudes, didn't attempt to coddle him. She gave him exactly what he needed: comfort. Positioning herself behind him, she wrapped her arms around his waist and rested her head on his back. Her presence, her touch, had become like a blanket of comfort for him. He would miss it covering him.

A long time passed before either of them spoke again.

"I think the past is crippling us both," Rylee said, crushing the quiet.

He didn't dispute that.

"Let's make a pact."

"What kind of pact?"

"To forgive ourselves for whatever we believe we've done. I know it won't happen overnight, but let's make a conscious effort to work toward absolving ourselves. Let's choose to breathe again," she said.

When she offered him a hooked pinkie, Canten eyed it a second or two before curving his around it. "Let's choose to breathe again." But could he, when he'd sentenced himself to a life without happiness?

CHAPTER 19

Rylee couldn't believe how much fun she was having at the Music in the Square event. Then again, she could because she was there with all her favorite people. Her parents, Canten, Senior—who'd been on the dance floor for the past thirty minutes—Lunden, Quade, Sebastian, and Zachary. *Family,* she thought, scanning the happy faces she shared the oversize picnic blanket with.

Food was bountiful: fried chicken, potato salad, hand-chopped barbecue, slaw, rolls, salad, corn, and several more hearty dishes. Countless desserts accompanied all the other goodness. Everyone ate, talked, laughed, enjoyed the amazing music and each other.

"Oooh, I love this song," Mrs. Charles said, getting to her feet. "Which one of you young folks is dancing with me?" she asked.

"I'll cut a rug with you," Canten said. Before standing, he leaned in and kissed Rylee on the corner of her mouth. "I'll be back."

"I'll be here," she said, a grin on her face.

Rylee got such delight watching Canten and her mother dance to Kool & the Gang's "Hollywood Swinging." She loved how her mother had so much life still left in her. Rylee hoped to be half as spunky as her mother at that age. *Love keeps you young,* her mother had once said to her. Obviously, that was true.

"Hey, hey, hey," Rylee called out, along with the dozens of others singing along with the classic soul tune.

She eyed Senior on the dance floor, twisting and twirling Ms. Harriet. Those two looked awfully comfortable with each other. Continuing to scan the crowd, she relished all the happy, smiling faces. This was Honey Hill at its finest.

Rylee glanced over at her father, who sat next to her. Obviously, her mother had had him out all day shopping, because he looked a little tired. She threaded her arm through his and rested her head on his shoulder. "I'm so happy you and Mommy are here," she said.

Mr. Charles relaxed his head against his daughter's. "Me too, baby girl. I'm even happier to see how happy you and Canten are together. I can tell he absolutely adores you. That makes me the happiest." ·

Eyeing Canten, she said, "He's something special."

Once the song ended, Mrs. Charles waved Rylee over. "Take over for me, dear. Your mother doesn't have the spunk she used to," she said.

"I beg to differ," Canten said. "I could barely keep up with you."

"You're too sweet," Mrs. Charles said, hugging Canten and kissing his cheek. "Hold on to this one. He's a keeper," she said and moved away.

When the band began to perform the New Birth's "Wildflower," Canten spread his arms and Rylee walked into them.

"This has been the best night ever," she said. "I have all my favorite people in one place."

Rylee glanced toward the picnic blanket. Concern filled her when she saw her mother rest the back of her hand on her father's forehead, then cheek as if she were attempting to gauge whether he was running a fever. Now that she thought about it, he had felt a little warm. At the time, she'd just attributed it to the hot and humid evening.

"You think Senior and Ms. Harriet are creeping?" Canten said.

The question pulled Rylee's gaze away from her parents, who were now cuddled up and laughing. Her worry dissipated. "They do look awfully cozy, don't they. Looks like you could be getting a stepmother," she joked.

"I don't think Senior would ever remarry. He's always said my mother could never be replaced."

"Would you be okay if he did?"

Canten eyed her. "If he's happy, I'm happy."

"You're a great son. How does Senior feel about the fact you may be leaving?"

"I can tell he doesn't want me to, but he would never tell me to stay. Senior has always encouraged me to follow my heart."

"Good advice. Do you always follow your heart?"

"When it's feasible," he said.

They stared into each other's eyes like two star-crossed lovers. When the band performed Gladys Knight's "Neither One of Us," Rylee couldn't help but think how appropriate the song felt to her current situation. When the woman onstage bellowed about there being no happy ending, Rylee couldn't have agreed more.

"May I cut in?"

Rylee watched Canten's jaw muscles flex several times, and his expression hardened.

"I need to handle this," she whispered, then stepped out of his arms and into Leonard's.

"You look beautiful tonight," Leonard said, swaying her back and forth.

"Thank you." A second later, she said, "You have to stop, Leonard. I'm sure you're a great guy, but there will never be anything between us."

"I can take care of you, Rylee. Far better than the sheriff. I've got big money, big cars, and soon, a big house."

"One day, some woman will appreciate all you have to offer her. Just not me."

"None of that impresses you, huh?"

She shook her head.

He studied her a moment. "What does the sheriff have that I don't?"

Rylee didn't hesitate when she said, "A hold of my heart."

"Which means I have absolutely no chance, right?"

"Right. And I need for you to respect that."

"I hope he knows how lucky he is."

"I think he does. Thanks for the dance," she said and walked away.

Canten walked to the cash bar with Sebastian. A stiff drink was exactly what he needed to tamp down the irritation he experienced from seeing Rylee in Leonard's arms. The way he held her wasn't overly sensual, but still. Just the fact he held her, period, was enough to grind Canten raw.

Whatever Rylee had needed to handle, couldn't she have done it without Leonard touching her? He hated the idea of her being in the bastard's arms. Canten laughed at himself. *Damn.* What the hell was going on with him? He'd never been a jealous man. Yet here he was practically foaming at the mouth. *Rylee doesn't belong to you,* he reminded himself for the thousandth time. Eventually, that fact would stick, he hoped.

"Drinks are on me, man," Sebastian said. "Two cognacs."

"Make mine a double," Canten said. Sebastian whipped his head toward him. "What?" Canten asked, his tone a little too harsh.

Sebastian flashed his palms. "Damn. What's eating you?"

Canten clenched his jaw. "*Leonard Jamison.* Every time I turn around, that bastard's sniffing after Rylee. Sending her flowers. Asking her to dance."

Sebastian's brows furrowed.

"What's *that* look for?" Canten asked.

"But why are you upset?" Sebastian asked.

Why was he upset? What the hell did he mean, why was he upset? He was upset because Leonard's hands didn't belong on Rylee.

Lowering his voice, Sebastian added, "You and Rylee are just pretending, right?"

Canten ground his teeth, a little heated at Sebastian for even pointing that out. He didn't need a reminder that Rylee wasn't his. Actually, he did. "Right."

Sebastian clapped him on the back. "Jamison's just trying to get under your skin. He's not that dense to believe Rylee would give you up for him. She wouldn't give him the time of day, let alone anything else."

Anything else? The comment renewed Canten's strife.

Sebastian pushed the cup toward him. "Here, drink your drink. You'll feel better."

"There you two are," Rylee said, joining them. Sebastian held open his arms, and Rylee walked into them.

Dammit. Canten hated the fact Rylee could smooth his ruffled feathers with just the sound of her voice.

Rylee claimed Sebastian's cup and took a sip. *"Yuck!"*

"That's a big boy's drink, little sis. You—" Sebastian stopped abruptly, his look of elation vanishing. *"Oh shit."*

"What?" Rylee asked, concern etched into her face.

Canten followed Sebastian's gaze over his shoulder to see Leonard headed in their direction. *You have got to be kidding me.* This disrespectful bastard just couldn't take a hint.

"You cool, Big C?" Sebastian asked, pointing to the crushed cup in Canten's hand.

When had that happened? Probably the second he'd seen Leonard. Canten tossed the mangled plastic in the receptacle. "I'm good," he said.

Rylee looked confused as if trying to figure out what was going on.

To Canten's surprise, Leonard offered his hand. Canten studied it with a crinkled brow. What the hell was Leonard up to? Did he plan to throw a sucker punch once he had Canten's hand clasped in his?

"I want to apologize for any disrespect," Leonard said.

Canten's head jerked in surprise, and then his gaze slid to Rylee. Clearly, she had handled something. What the hell had she said to Leonard? Canten reluctantly shook his hand, but he still didn't trust the man any further than he could toss him. Without another word, Leonard walked off.

"That was interesting," Sebastian said. A beat later, he excused himself.

Canten folded his arms across his chest. "What in the world did you say to Leonard?"

"I told him the truth. That one day a woman would appreciate all he had to offer but that that woman would never be me."

Damn. That had been direct.

CHAPTER 20

Today was the big day, and Rylee was thrilled. She'd gotten up at four that morning to add a few last-minute touches to Lunden and Quade's cake. She couldn't wait for them to see it. With the help of Ezekiel, she'd delivered the massive dessert to the inn in one piece. It had only required minor touch-up work, which she'd mostly masked with the dozens of sugar flowers that had taken them close to two hours to intricately place.

By midmorning, the inn buzzed with excitement. Florists, caterers, photographers, videographers, lighting technicians, rental companies. The list went on and on. Lunden's fabulous wedding coordinator, Ashanti Bellevue, kept all the chaos under control.

The smell of bacon made Rylee's stomach growl. Quade; his best friend, Pryor; Canten; and Sebastian had all spent the night at the inn. Lunden had arranged a catered breakfast for them. Unfortunately, Rylee hadn't seen any of them yet. Obviously, they'd had a long night.

Rylee checked her watch. She was still good on time. Earlier, she'd promised Lunden she'd be at her house no later than one. While she could have allowed Ezekiel to handle the remaining setup of the cake, she just couldn't relinquish control. She'd needed to make sure every single aspect was as perfect as it could be.

"*Whoa.*"

Rylee turned to see Quade standing at the door, hands resting on top of his head, eyes wide. "Good morning. I hope that's a good *whoa*," she said, placing another fresh rose around the base of the bottom tier.

"It's amazing." Closing the distance between them, he scrutinized the cake from every angle. "I can't . . . how did . . . ? Lunden was right— your hands are gifted."

The compliment swelled her with pride. She loved what she did. Loved even more when she received these kinds of reactions to her work. It always kept her motivated.

"Silly question. How are you going to get it from in here to out there," he said, referring to the large tent set up to accommodate the reception. "This cake is enormous."

Rylee lifted the satin tablecloth. "It's on wheels. Since the frosting is made of all butter, heat is my nemesis." While she could have opted to do a butter-and-shortening combination, in her opinion, all butter tasted so much better. "It'll stay in this temperature-controlled room until the reception." The tent was air-conditioned, but she didn't trust it to hold a consistent temperature with so much in and out. "Don't worry, I have so many wooden dowels in this thing, it's not going anywhere."

"Have you talked to my bride?" he asked.

"About thirty times," Rylee said.

"Is she nervous?"

"Not at all. She's excited. When you see her, you're going to fall in love with her all over again."

"I fall in love with her all over again with the changing of the day."

"I am insanely happy for you two."

"Thank you," he said, giving her a hug.

When Quade released her, she said, "Where are the rest of the fellas? Lunden's arranged breakfast for you guys."

"I love that woman," he said. "Does breakfast happen to be one of your omelets? Or possibly a breakfast burrito?"

"Your fiancée forbade me to take on another task for the wedding."
She paused. "But of course, I didn't listen. Ezekiel is setting everything
up now. In addition, the caterer provided bacon, sausage, and country
ham. And a few more items, I believe."

"As long as I can score an omelet, I'm good." He hugged her again.
"Thank you again for everything. Lunden's lucky to have a friend like
you."

"I'm the lucky one," she said.

Hours later, Rylee stared at Lunden, tears in her eyes. She'd never
seen a more beautiful bride. The gown looked even more exquisite on
her now than it had in Lady Sunshine's shop. "You look absolutely
amazing," Rylee said.

"Thank you." Lunden stared into the full-length mirror. "I'm getting married. I'm getting married," she repeated.

Rylee adjusted her veil. "Yes, you are. Now, let's get this show on
the road."

Ten minutes later, the coordinator lined them up in the order they
would walk down the aisle. Lunden had chosen to have all the men
come out with Pastor White and Quade. She'd wanted the ceremony
to be as short as possible.

The pianist and cellist began to play Pachelbel's Canon. The white
drapery opened, and Zeta walked out. The curvy woman stunned in a
one-shoulder, rose-gold, asymmetrical chiffon dress. Happi followed,
looking equally gorgeous in a sleeveless A-line scoop-neck dress, also in
rose gold. Happi looked as if she should have been on a runway in Paris.
God, she and Sebastian would make a beautiful couple.

"I just want to tell you again how fabulous you look," Rylee said to
Lunden before making her own way down the aisle. She felt like royalty
in the shimmering off-the-shoulder dress that hugged her curves like
a second skin.

The grounds of the inn had been transformed into a scene right out
of a fairy tale. The guests sat in beautiful solid-wood chairs with white

rose pomanders attached to each chairback. A path of fresh rosebuds led to the altar.

On her walk down, Rylee marveled at the altar, draped in white fabric and adorned with what looked like hundreds of roses in white, mauve, and soft pink. Clusters of roses in the same shades hung from the large sycamore tree.

When her gaze locked with Canten's, he mouthed, "Beautiful." Sebastian whispered something to him, and he nodded, but his eyes never left her. What had her brother said that Canten had agreed with?

With Rylee in place, everyone waited for the woman of the hour. Once the flower girl and ring bearer made their way to their designated spots, the draping closed. Seconds later, a trio of violinists began to play a beautiful melody. When the curtains opened again, Lunden appeared, looking like an angel who'd just descended from heaven.

"My God," Quade said, eyeing his future wife with adoring eyes.

There were gasps, oohs, aahs, and other sounds of fascination from the audience. And rightfully so.

Lunden began her slow march toward the altar. The gown sparkled with every step she took, bouncing brilliant bursts of colorful light off the onlookers.

"Here she comes," Quade said, seemingly more to himself than to anyone else. His eyes never left his bride. "She's gorgeous. My God, she's gorgeous." Quade rubbed at his eyes.

Tears. Just as Rylee had expected.

Once Lunden stood in place, Rylee accepted her bouquet—a lush arrangement filled with roses to match the altar and greenery. Each bridesmaid carried similar ones, only smaller. Ms. Bonita and Ms. Harriet had outdone themselves . . . again. Making sure the detachable train was picture ready, Rylee returned to her spot.

Lunden and Quade—both emotional at this point—recited their vows to one another. Tears streamed down Rylee's face too. Using her hand, she wiped them away. When she felt eyes on her, her gaze drifted to Canten. A concerned look distorted his handsome face. She smiled to let him know these were happy tears.

When Quade made a loving vow to Zachary and presented him with a watch, the back engraved with *To my son*, Rylee wasn't sure there was a dry eye in the place.

When the newlyweds were pronounced husband and wife, thunderous applause erupted. Had she ever seen two happier people in her life? When it didn't appear Lunden and Quade would ever end the kiss, Pastor White joked that they might want to come up for air. Everyone laughed.

Lunden and Quade faced the audience and were presented as Mr. and Mrs. Quade Augustus Cannon of Honey Hill. Cheers and woot woots sounded as they walked down the aisle hand in hand.

After a barrage of photos, the wedding party joined the other guests in the huge tent. White fabric draped the ceiling of the large structure. Alternating short and tall flower arrangements sat on each of the nearly fifty round tables. Uplighting washed the walls of the tent in soft pink light. Overhead lighting projected a large *C* on the wooden dance floor.

Lunden and Quade shared their first dance to John Tesh and James Ingram's "Give Me Forever." Rylee didn't flinch a muscle when Canten's arms wrapped around her from the back and he started to sway from side to side with her. Closing her eyes, she reclined her head back and enjoyed the warm, hard feel of him. The man deserved an award for the performance he'd given over the past few months.

"I thought it was bad etiquette for the maid of honor to upstage the bride," he whispered into her ear.

She smiled.

"You look absolutely amazing in that dress. Promise me I can take it off of you later," Canten said.

She loved the fact that he couldn't seem to get enough of her. Unfortunately, he wouldn't get many pieces of her this week. "I would love to make you that promise, but did you forget I'm watching Zachary until Lunden and Quade return from their honeymoon?"

"I'm willing to sneak through your bedroom window. Role play. It could be fun. Cat burglar and unsuspecting homeowner," he said.

Rylee laughed.

Lendell Pruette, the town's unofficial historian and amateur photographer and videographer, stood in front of them. "Looks like we'll be celebrating another wedding before long," he said. "Smile for the camera."

The man snapped like a dozen pictures of them before finally moving on.

"How many more times do you think we're going to hear that tonight?" Canten asked.

"Countless. We're going to hear it countless times," she said.

After a delicious buffet-style meal, guests poured onto the dance floor. The talented DJ, who didn't look to be much older than sixteen, curated a mix of old-school soul and new-school R&B. His energy kept the crowd moving.

When a slow jam came on, Rylee's parents hit the dance floor. She marveled over just how much in love those two still were after all these years. *To be so lucky.*

"You outdid yourself with that cake, Ry," Lunden said, walking up behind Rylee.

"You really like it?" Rylee asked.

"Like it? I absolutely *love* it." Lunden pulled Rylee into a tight hug. "Thank you so much for everything. You're the best best friend a girl could ever ask for. I love you so much."

"Stop it. You're going to make me cry again," Rylee said.

Lunden flashed a sly grin. "I saw you and Canten hugged up earlier. You looked awfully comfortable in his arms."

She had been. "All for show," Rylee said.

"If you say so." Lunden winked and moved away to greet more of her guests.

Working her way around the room, Rylee delighted in all the positive energy flowing. Even the contentious Herbert Jamison appeared to be enjoying himself—and the shrimp display. Leonard was in attendance. Relief washed over Rylee when she saw him hugged up with some woman she didn't recognize. Two people who hadn't attended, and all for the best, were Hilary and Katrina. Rylee had been sure they would come just to be nosy.

"Hi, sweetheart."

Rylee faced her mother. "Hi, Mom. Do you or Dad need anything?"

"No, no. We're perfect."

"I saw you two on the dance floor," Rylee said. "I want what you two have one day."

Her mother threaded her arm through hers. "I believe you already have it, dear."

If she only knew the truth.

"What a lovely ceremony," Mrs. Charles said.

"Yes, it was. I don't think I've ever seen Lunden happier."

"I don't think I've ever seen *you* happier," her mother said. "I've been asked ten times already when the two of you plan to tie the knot."

"Oh, Mom. I hope you didn't lead anyone to believe Canten and I are close to marriage. We're not even really—" She stopped shy of blurting out *dating*. Thankfully, she'd caught herself. That would have been a disaster. "That serious," she said instead.

Mrs. Charles laughed. "Dear, I would say the two of you are leagues past serious. That man is crazy about you. And he should be because you're an amazing young woman. He should be damn proud to call you his."

"Thank you, Mom."

Exhausted from answering the same question over and over again—when would she and Canten be tying the knot—Rylee needed fresh air.

She'd started off deflecting the question but had ended providing the same open-ended response to anyone who asked: *Who knows.*

Slipping out of the tent, she walked down to the creek that ran in back of the inn. Listening to the flow of the water soothed her. Folding her arms across her chest, she closed her eyes, inhaled a deep breath, and released it slowly.

The moment the atmosphere shifted, without looking, Rylee knew Canten was near. Giddy with anticipation, she readied herself for the second Canten would wrap his protective arms around her from the back and her body would press against his. She'd grown accustomed to his touch, craved it. Unfortunately, it never came.

🐝

Canten didn't want to disturb Rylee, because she looked so peaceful by the creek. So instead, he observed her from a distance. The purples, pinks, and oranges of dusk's descent on them provided the perfect backdrop for her curvy silhouette. He'd always said her body was a work of art. The picture before him proved it.

He'd lost count of the number of times he'd been asked when he planned to propose to her. In an imaginary world—where a chance of a proposal might have existed—did they really think he would have given them the details of when? To appease them, he'd provided the same response over and over again: *Well, you never know.* Noncommittal and intriguing. At least, he'd thought so.

What stories would these same people, who'd made comments about how he and Rylee made such a lovely couple, craft about them once they ended things? He could guess a few. He'd cheated. She'd cheated. They had been unhappy, unfulfilled. The gossip would burn around town like a wildfire, fueled by countless ridiculous rumors.

At one point he'd actually found himself fantasizing about their fake wedding day, specifically how Rylee would look in her dream wedding gown. *Far from generic,* he thought, recalling how Rylee had used the word to describe herself when she'd talked about her courthouse wedding.

He'd spare no expense giving her the day she'd always dreamed of. He'd encourage Rylee to change into at least three wedding dresses that night, just to make up for the one she hadn't gotten to wear during her first marriage.

Canten imagined them standing at the altar, staring into each other's eyes, the entire room packed with people but it feeling like they were the only two there. Similar to how it was looking into her eyes in real life. And their vows . . .

Without prompting, his brain processed all the words he'd say to her. Her smile would touch her ears because he'd tell her just how grateful he was to have her. There would be tears, his and hers. Especially when he shared with her how she'd changed his life. But there would also be laughter when he reminded her their forever included his lame jokes. Yeah, that would get a good chuckle from her.

His fantasy continued with their wedding night. Whatever destination they traveled to, he wasn't sure how much of it they'd actually see. If given the choice, he would never leave their bed.

And kids. Selfishly, he'd suggest they wait at least two years, though, before having them. He'd want Rylee all to himself for a while. But when their first child arrived, he'd be over the moon. A vision of standing in the delivery room, cradling their son in his arms, rocked him. Scattering the thought, he scolded himself for allowing any of this into his head.

You have a plan. It doesn't include love. It doesn't include marriage. And it damn sure doesn't include Rylee.

The scenes of them had come so easily. *Too damn easily.* What was in his head had played out more like a premonition than a daydream.

"I know you're there," Rylee said.

Canten's head jerked. How could she have known he was here? He hadn't made a sound. All this time he'd believed women only grew eyes in the backs of their heads when they became mothers. Advancing toward her, he said, "Yeah, but I bet you didn't know it was me." She flashed him a smile that suggested otherwise.

"I needed some fresh air," she said as if reading Canten's thoughts.

He almost let it slip that he'd seen her sneak out. But then she'd know he'd been watching her. "Me too. I saw you standing out here, but you looked so tranquil I didn't want to intrude." *Instead, I ogled you from afar like a stalker in the brush.*

"It's peaceful here," she said.

"I can leave you alone if—"

"I want you here," she said.

Good, because he wanted to be here.

The sun continued its descent into the horizon. And in that moment, he realized he'd never watched a sunset. It was a sight to behold.

"Are you ready for next week?" she asked, penetrating the silence that had fallen around them.

"I am."

Things grew quiet again.

"You're going to do great, and you're going to get this job," she said. "I can feel it."

"Thank you for the vote of confidence."

"What kind of friend would I be if I didn't support you," she said.

Friend? Maybe that was how they'd started out, but now . . . now they felt like so much more.

CHAPTER 21

Rylee wasn't sure this could get any more intense. If ever there was a time she needed to show her poker face, it was now. There was too much at stake. She couldn't falter like the last ten times she'd tried to do this.

She eyed him.

He eyed her.

They battled with their gazes.

Challenged with their stares.

He'd made the last move, declared his position. Now it was her turn. Just as she was about to risk it all, a second of hesitation crept in. *What if . . . no!* There were no what-ifs. It was go time. The moment of truth. She'd already waited for too long to say it. Rylee took a deep breath to prepare herself. *You've got this.*

She eyed him.

He eyed her.

She made her move.

Finally, she parted her lips and said it . . . *"Connect Four! Boom!* In yo' face. I win. You lose. *Woot woot."*

Zachary tossed his hands into the air, slapped his forehead, and sighed. *"Finally."*

Okay, maybe she was being a little dramatic over a game of Connect Four, but the kid had beaten her ten times.

"I don't want to play anymore, Aunt Rylee."

"Afraid you'll lose?"

"Uh-huh," he said with a fast nod and grin.

She sent a narrow-eyed gaze in his direction. Something told her he just didn't want to play with *her* anymore. "Fine."

Zachary collected the pieces and returned them to the box. "Do you think my mom and dad are having fun on their honeymoon?"

"Yes. But I bet they would have even more fun if you were there," she said.

"I know. But moms and dads need alone time during their honeymoon to whoopee."

Rylee's head snapped back. "Um, to . . . whoopee?"

"Yeah. That's what my friend Johnathan said. I think it means to watch movies together. I don't know what kind, but when I asked Alexa, a lady with dreads came up, and she acted in a lot of funny movies. So probably those kind."

It was all she could do to not laugh, because she was sure he was talking about Whoopi Goldberg. "You're exactly right," she said. "Have I ever told you how smart you are?"

"Yes, ma'am. A lot of times. But you can keep telling me. It builds carrier."

Rylee snickered. Should she tell him he'd pronounced *character* wrong? Nah. "Okay, so what do you want to do next?"

"Hmm." He pressed his finger into his chin. "Eat pizza?"

"Perfect idea. Now, I have a very important question for you. Are you ready for it?"

He nodded and rubbed his hands together as if waiting to hear some devious plan. "Yeah, yeah, yeah."

"Do we order it, or do we make it ourselves?"

"Make it ourselves," he said, sending his arms straight up into the air.

"I was hoping you'd say that. We have to make a run to the market to get what we need."

"Okay. I'll put on my shoes."

Fifteen minutes later, they strolled the pasta aisle in search of ready-made pizza crust. While she could have easily whipped one up, it was quicker this way. Plus, she was starving.

"Aunt Rylee?"

Rylee glanced down at Zachary. "What's up, kiddo?"

"You're going to make the bestest mom when you and Sheriff Canten have the baby."

The baby? Rylee laughed because it sounded like he thought she was already pregnant. "You think?"

"Yep." He swung their joined hands back and forth. "Aunt Rylee?"

"Uh-huh?"

"Do you love Sheriff Canten?"

She stopped moving and eyed him. "Why do you ask?"

"Because when he left to go to Charlotte this morning, you looked like you were going to cry. One time when my friend Johnathan's dad left to be a soldier, his mom cried a lot. Johnathan said she loves him a whole bunch. So do you love Sheriff Canten a whole bunch too?"

She glanced around to make sure no one else was within earshot, then lowered her voice and whispered, "Yes. I love him a whole bunch." Lowering her voice even more, she said, "But don't tell anyone, okay?" A second later, she regretted answering the way she had. What had she been thinking? Though she loved him to pieces, Zachary couldn't hold water.

Zachary shrugged. "But why? Johnathan's mom tells his dad all the time. It makes him really happy. Shouldn't we always tell people things that will make them really happy?"

This kid. "Yes, we should, but—"

Rylee stopped speaking when someone cleared their throat behind them. Glancing over her shoulder, she groaned when she saw half of HIKE. Normally, she would have rolled her eyes and walked off. But wanting to set a good example for Zachary, she plastered on a fake smile and spoke to Hilary and Katrina. "Good afternoon, ladies. Lovely day we're having."

Hilary wiggled her manicured fingers in a wave. Katrina *smeered*—half smiled, half sneered.

"I hear the sheriff will be taking a new job in Charlotte. You must be devastated by his departure," Hilary said.

How the hell did Hilary know this? Anyone who didn't know the devious woman would have been convinced the sympathetic look Hilary flashed was genuine. Rylee knew better.

"Especially since he didn't ask you to go with him," Katrina said. She shrugged. "Guess he's just not that into you," she added.

Rylee saw right through Katrina's wordplay. She'd wanted to get a reaction out of her. *Nope. Not falling for that game.* Rylee channeled her inner Michelle Obama. *When they go low, we go high.* "Maybe not every day, but he does get pretty *deep* into me quite often," Rylee said. *Okay, that was petty AF.* Her inner Michelle definitely needed some work.

Katrina's face tightened.

"Is it true he has a shrine of his dead wife in his house?" Hilary asked.

Rylee's brows slammed together, but she caught herself before lashing out. *If you're easily agitated, you're easily manipulated,* her mother used to say. So she relaxed. But before she could address the asinine question, her cell phone rang. "I have to take this. It's been a . . ." Her words trailed. "Gosh, I was about to say *pleasure,* but we all know that would have been a lie." Well, she'd tried.

"And my aunt Rylee doesn't lie," Zachary said.

"Say bye, Zachary," Rylee said.

"Bye, Zachary," he said, then stuck out his tongue at Hilary and Katrina. They both scowled and scurried off.

Rylee gave Zachary a high five. "Don't tell your mother," she said. She'd set a better example next time. "Hello?" Rylee said into the phone.

"Rylee?"

Rylee froze, instantly sensing something was wrong. She could hear it in her mother's trembling voice. Fear consumed her. Rylee pressed her hand flat against her stomach in hopes of stopping the quiver inside. "What is it, Mom? What's wrong?"

"It's your father."

Standing at the window of his hotel, Canten stared out at the Queen City skyline. While not as rousing as a Honey Hill sunset, it was beautiful in its own right. God, this place used to bring him so much joy. But since his arrival several hours ago, all he'd felt was homesick for Honey Hill. For Rylee, too, if he was being honest.

A smile touched his lips when he thought about how she'd stood on her porch that morning and waved to him until he'd driven out of sight. The corners of his mouth curved upward even more when he recalled how she'd made him promise to call her as soon as he'd made it safely to the hotel.

However, about thirty minutes into the drive to Charlotte, he'd needed to hear her voice, so he'd called her. She'd answered in half a ring. *Well, it's about time you called,* she'd said with a sweet laugh. They'd talked the entire drive. How was that even possible? To hold a conversation with a person for almost four hours without ever experiencing a dull moment?

An urge to call her came over him, so he walked across the room and lifted his cell phone off the nightstand. The phone vibrated in his hand, indicating an incoming call. *Pop* showed on the screen. "What's up, old man, you miss me already?" Because he sure as hell missed him. Leaving Honey Hill would be one hell of a transition. He would be leaving the three people he cared about most in the world.

"Hey, son," Senior said.

Canten stilled. "What's wrong?" he asked, noting the tiredness in his father's voice. "You okay? You've been checking your blood sugar, right?"

"Of course. And I'm fine. It's Gus. They rushed him to the hospital a little while ago. Apparently, he blacked out. We don't know much more than that yet. They're running tests."

Damn. "How's Rylee?" Not that he really needed to ask. Rylee was a daddy's girl, and if something was wrong with him, she wasn't all right.

Senior sighed. "She didn't want me to call you. Didn't want you to be all stressed before your big interview tomorrow. But I knew you would want to know."

Canten ran a hand over his head. "But how is she, Pop?"

"Z-man is here, so she's putting up a good front for him. But I can tell she's really worried, son. I'll make sure she and Dorsetta have any and everything they need. Sebastian should be here within the hour. I gotta get this coffee back to Dorsetta, but I'll keep you posted."

"Thanks for letting me know, Pop," he said.

Immediately after ending the call with his father, Canten made another, snatched up his keys, and hurried out the room.

A little less than an hour later, Canten rushed through the electronic doors of Honey Hill Hospital's emergency department. He hated hospitals with a passion. The constant beeps of machinery. Overhead announcements that usually alerted of incoming traumas. The smell of disinfectant. Even the fluorescent lighting that highlighted the grief on loved ones' faces. While this wasn't where Jayla had died, still, being here briefly triggered memories of that fateful night he'd lost her.

The first person he spotted was his father, topping off a Styrofoam cup with coffee. "Pop?" he said.

Senior whipped toward him. "Son? What are you doing here? And how the hell did you get here so quick?"

"I chartered a helicopter," he said. "Where's Rylee?" he asked, scanning the waiting area.

"Chartered a helicopter? Holy smokes."

"Pop. Rylee?"

"She's in a private family waiting room around the corner. Come on, I'll take you there. She'll be glad to see you."

Canten fell in step with Senior. When they entered the room, all eyes landed on them. Probably believing they were a doctor with an update.

Rylee gasped. She stood but didn't move toward him. Her eyes narrowed on him as if she weren't 100 percent convinced he was really there. *"Canten?"*

The sight of her red-rimmed eyes told him she'd been crying. It broke his heart. Closing the distance between them, he wrapped her in a tight embrace. She clung to him, her body trembling in his arms. "I got you," he said.

"What are you doing here?" she asked.

"Where else would I be?" he said, tightening his hold on her.

"Thank you," she said. "Thank you."

Once they finally released each other, Canten showed Mrs. Charles and Sebastian some love too.

"Thanks for being here, brother," Sebastian said, the two men embracing.

"Family," Canten said.

Canten settled into one of the blue leather-covered love seats next to Rylee and put his arm around her shoulders. Her body relaxed against his. "Do you need anything? Are you hungry? I can grab you something from the cafeteria."

"No, I'm good. Senior has taken great care of us."

Thanks, Pop. "Just let me know if you need anything," he said.

"Okay." She was quiet for a moment. "What about your interview?"

"I'll fly back after we know what's going on with Pop Charles. The helicopter is on standby."

Her head rose. "Helicopter? You took a helicopter from Charlotte?"

"Driving would have taken too long," he said with a wink.

Rylee stared at him for a long, hard moment, then rested her head back against him.

A little after midnight, they were finally given an update. Mr. Charles had suffered something called a transient ischemic attack or TIA, sometimes referred to as a ministroke. Luckily, there wasn't any permanent damage, but they were told a TIA could be a warning sign of a future stroke. And since Mr. Charles suffered from both high blood pressure and high cholesterol and was an older African American man with a family history of strokes, he was at a much greater risk.

Canten remained in the waiting room with a sleeping Zachary when Mrs. Charles, Rylee, and Sebastian were allowed to go back and visit Mr. Charles, who was being kept overnight for observation. Amid his father's protests, Canten had urged him to go home about an hour earlier to get some rest, with a promise to phone if anything changed with his good friend.

A little after two in the morning, Canten drove Rylee and Zachary back to her place, while Sebastian took their mother to his house to stay the night. After getting Zachary settled in bed, Canten joined Rylee in her bedroom. Still fully clothed, she lay stretched out across the bed. She didn't protest or resist when he began to undress her, removing everything except her panties. Kicking out of his shoes, he climbed in bed with her and pulled her into his arms.

"Get some sleep," he said.

"What if my dad—"

He cut her off. "Don't do that. He's fine. He'll be fine. We'll make sure he's fine."

"I couldn't handle if something happened to my daddy."

"You can handle anything, Rylee. You're one of the strongest women I know. Plus, you wouldn't be handling anything alone. But you won't have to because Pop Charles is going to be a-okay."

"Canten . . ." Her words trailed. "I, um, I just want you to know how much I appreciate you. How much I . . . think you're the best," she said.

He held her a little tighter. "I think you're the best too."

CHAPTER 22

When Rylee woke that morning, Canten was gone, but he'd left her a note on the pillow. *Good morning, beautiful. Didn't want to wake you. I'm cutting my trip short. I plan to return to Honey Hill after my interview. If all goes as planned, I should see you around four.*

"No," Rylee said. *You can't cut your trip short. Not for me.*

Canten had intended to spend the remainder of the week in Charlotte, catching up with old friends. She didn't want to be the reason he altered his plans. He'd done enough simply by showing up at the hospital. She still couldn't believe he'd chartered a helicopter just to get to Honey Hill to support her. The man was truly one of a kind.

Rylee eyed the clock. It was only eight fifteen. Canten's interview wasn't until ten. Retrieving her cell phone off the nightstand, she dialed his number but regretted making the call the second he answered. By his groggy, croaky voice, she'd woken him up. She hadn't even considered the fact he was probably exhausted.

"I'm sorry. I didn't mean to wake you," she said.

"You didn't."

Yep, she'd expected him to say that. "Liar," she said, with a soft chuckle. "I won't keep you long. I just wanted to tell you that under no circumstances do you cancel your plans. Hang out with your buddies. Catch up. Have fun. We're good here. And just in case you forgot, you're on vacation, remember? Something you don't seem to do very well, I've noticed."

"What can I say? I can't sit still."

"Sure you can. You just refuse to," she said.

"You're taking care of your parents, taking care of Zachary, and running a bakery. You're going to run yourself ragged. Let me help."

"If I said no, would it matter?"

"No."

She laughed. "I kind of figured that. I guess I'll see you later. Good luck this morning. But you won't need it. You're going to knock their socks off."

"I had a dream about you last night," he said.

Rylee sat up and rested her back against the headboard. *Dream?* "What was the dream about?"

Canten chuckled a sexy laugh into the phone that made her keenly aware of how much she missed him next to her. Her head turned toward the space he'd occupied hours earlier.

"We were in, like, a private room in a restaurant. There was a lot of fresh fruit. A lot of toppings: whipped cream, fudge, honey."

"Mmm. I love fresh fruit. Go on," she said.

"I fed you strawberries, grapes, cantaloupe. When it came time for you to feed me, you undressed in the middle of this room, climbed on one of the tables, and sprayed your body with whipped cream."

This dream was getting better and better by the second.

Canten continued, "You told me to choose the fruit I had a taste for and place it anywhere on your body I wanted."

Her nipples beaded. "And where did you put it?"

He chuckled again. "I'll tell you later. I have to take a shower," he said.

"No fair."

"I'll see you later this afternoon," he said.

"I'll see you later."

Rylee ended the call and dialed her mother's cell phone to check on her father. After receiving a good report, she headed to the kitchen. Zachary usually popped up at the crack of dawn and was probably starving. When she entered the living room, Zachary, still in his *Black Panther* pajamas, sat in front of the television, watching cartoons. "Good morning."

"Morning, Aunt Rylee," he said, never pulling his attention from *Tom and Jerry*.

Kids and cartoons. Tom and Jerry had been one of her favorites too. "Sorry I overslept. Bacon and eggs?"

"I'm not hungry," he said. "Sheriff Canten made us cheese sandwiches before he left this morning and said not to wake you unless it was an emergency, because you needed to rest. The cheese sandwiches were delicious. He's a good cook."

Cheese sandwiches? She usually prepared bacon, eggs, grits, buttered toast with jelly. And he was excited over cheese sandwiches? *How little it takes to impress a child*. If Canten had made Zachary breakfast, that meant he hadn't left to return to Charlotte until sometime after five that morning. Now she felt even worse about waking him. He was running on fumes. "Well, since you've already eaten, I'm going to take my shower. Once your cartoon goes off, get dressed, please, so we can swing by the hospital to see Papa Charles."

Zachary jumped up. "I'll get dressed now," he said, darting toward his room.

Rylee had enjoyed having Zachary with her these past few days. If she ever had kids of her own—and that was looking less and less likely—she hoped they were as sweet, polite, and thoughtful as Zachary. She recalled how he'd wrapped his tiny arms around her at the hospital and told her everything would be okay. It had brought a smile to her face then and did now.

Rylee phoned the bakery just to make sure everything had gone smoothly. Thank God for Ezekiel and Sweet Sadie. Neither had hesitated a second when she'd asked if they could open the bakery that morning. A raise was in both their futures because they truly held her down. She had the best crew ever. Happy to hear things had gone off without a hitch, she headed into the bathroom.

An hour later, Rylee and Zachary arrived at her father's hospital room. Sebastian was knocked out in one of the chairs. He looked so uncomfortable. He'd brought their mother here first thing that morning. It had taken them both to convince her not to stay overnight at the hospital, because she wouldn't have gotten any sleep with the constant in and out of nurses and keeping a watchful eye over their father. According to Sebastian, she hadn't gotten much sleep anyway.

Rylee hugged her mother, then moved to her father's bedside. "How are you feeling, Dad?" she asked, placing a kiss onto his forehead.

"Like a brand-new penny," he said. "Ready to get out of here."

"The nurse said he'll be discharged in a few hours," Mrs. Charles said.

Rylee breathed a sigh of relief. Hearing that they wouldn't need to keep him an additional night made her happy.

"I made you something, Papa Charles," Zachary said.

Mr. Charles accepted the picture Zachary presented to him. The drawing was of a boat with Zachary, her father, Sebastian, Canten, and Senior fishing. Colorful fish jumped from the water all around them. Everyone had the hugest smiles on their faces—and really big heads. Her father responded as if it was the best thing he'd ever received in his life, which made Zachary grin from ear to ear.

Around noon—knowing she wouldn't get much work done at the bakery anyway, because her mind would be on her father—Rylee informed Ezekiel and Sadie she wouldn't be in and to close early if things became too overwhelming. They assured her there wouldn't be any problems, which set her mind at ease. One less thing she had to worry about.

Now there was just one more thing she needed to address. This one was with her parents. However, it wasn't the appropriate time to broach the conversation.

Canten had intended to leave Charlotte immediately after his interview, which had gone great, in his opinion, but he'd run into an old colleague, who'd invited him to lunch. Detective David Pollock had been his partner. They'd lost touch when Canten had returned to Honey Hill. More honestly, Canten had avoided him. Too many memories. He and Jayla had spent a lot of time with David and his wife, Reva.

The six-five, no-nonsense man still looked just as Canten remembered: deep-brown skin, black hair (now peppered with gray), goatee (sparkled with gray, as well), stone faced, and unapproachable looking. And probably still scared the hell out of criminals. However, to know him was to like him.

"I heard you were in town for an interview. Bureau commander. Jayla's dream. She'd be proud."

"Both mine and Jayla's dream," he corrected.

David nodded. "Word on the street is you have a good chance of getting it. I can't think of a better man for the job. Besides me, of course."

Curious, Canten said, "Why didn't you throw your hat in the ring?" They'd both had ambitions of holding the position one day. Canten knew had David been in the running, none of them would have stood a chance. The man was an exceptional law enforcement officer with numerous awards under his belt. He could be a little hotheaded and reckless at times but, still, a damn good detective.

David's eyes lowered to his sweet-tea glass. "Too much going on." His gaze settled on Canten again. "Reva and I are going through a divorce."

"What?" How was this even possible? Back in the day, David and Reva had been the poster children for what love looked like. What had changed? Canten felt bad for not keeping in touch with him. Not that doing so would have saved his marriage, but at least David would have had another someone to talk to. "What happened?"

David gave a humorless laugh. "A bunch of shitty decisions on my part. I stepped out on her. Worst decision of my life."

Damn. In a million years, David would have been the last person Canten would have guessed would have had an affair. He'd always cherished Reva.

"Too many drinks. Too little thinking. It only happened once. But once is all it takes, right?" The man massaged his forehead. "We'd been going through some things. But that's no excuse," he said more to himself than to Canten.

Canten was unsure what to say next, so he asked, "Any chance of reconciling?"

"Man, she won't even speak to me. I can't blame her. I hurt her, Barnes. Deeply. I could see it in her eyes. I would give anything to take it back. I miss her. She was a good wife, a damn good woman, who probably deserved much better than me. She loved me even when I had nothing."

David looked to be mulling over things in his head, because he stared off. He wore a hard but sad expression on his face. Canten felt bad for him. But if he still loved Reva, and it was obvious he did, he needed to fight for her.

"You're a good brother," Canten said. "You just made a bad decision."

"Good brothers don't cheat on their wives, but I appreciate you for trying to make me feel better."

"It'll all work out how it's supposed to," Canten offered, but then he regretted the comment when he thought about the fact that David might never get Reva back.

"Enough about me and my depressing-ass life. What's up with you? I would ask if there is anyone special in your life, but I know better."

"Actually, there is someone," he said, unsure why. Maybe it was the way David had made it sound as if he hadn't been able to move on after Jayla's death, even though that had felt like the case for a very long while.

David's head snapped back. "Really? Damn. I never thought I'd see the day. She must be something special."

"She is," Canten said, an image of Rylee filtering into his head. "She really is."

CHAPTER 23

It poured as Rylee made her way home. After pulling into the driveway, she sat there several minutes, hoping the downpour would subside. She hadn't bothered grabbing her umbrella that morning, because the weather report hadn't said anything about rain. And of course, the one she usually kept in her vehicle was only God knew where.

When she saw a flash of lightning, she got out of the vehicle and sprinted across the yard to the front door. She didn't need to use her key to get inside, because the door was already unlocked. As she entered, her nose crinkled at the charred smell. Something was burning.

Rylee followed the ruckus of banging pots and pans to the kitchen and gasped. "What . . . ?"

Both Canten's and Zachary's gazes snapped toward her, both showing stunned expressions. Flour speckled their faces and covered their clothing. Their hands looked as if they'd been making Play-Doh. Every dish she owned appeared to be either in the kitchen sink or on the flour-dusted counter, including her favorite casserole pan, the inside of it black as asphalt.

Zachary jabbed a finger in Canten's direction. "It was him," he said.

"Traitor," Canten said.

Zachary shrugged with a laugh.

"You're home early," Canten said.

"I missed you guys. Um, what's happening here?" Rylee asked, fanning a hand across the disarray in her kitchen.

"We're cooking you dinner," Zachary said. He scratched his forehead, leaving a clump of dough behind. "It's not going very well."

Canten eyed Zachary. "It's fine." Then eyed Rylee. "It's fine, really. We just need to regroup. I'd planned to grill, but it started to rain."

"Sheriff Canten, are you better at grilling than you are at cooking in the kitchen?" Zachary asked.

Rylee covered her mouth with her hand to keep her laughter in.

"As a matter of fact, I am," Canten said, smearing flour on the tip of Zachary's nose.

"Hey," Zachary said in protest and through laughter.

Noting the ingredients scattered about—eggs, milk, butter—Rylee asked, "What were you two making?"

"We were making you a happy cake, Aunt Rylee. But it caught fire."

Rylee's eyes widened. *Caught f—*" She looked at Canten. *"What?"*

"It didn't catch fire," Canten said, then looked at Zachary. "It didn't catch fire."

"There was smoke," Zachary said. "And my mom said where there's smoke, there's fire."

Canten pinched his thumb and forefinger together. "There was a little smoke. Just a little."

"We couldn't see in the kitchen at all." Zachary swept his arms around the room. "Smoke was everywhere."

Canten rested his hands on his waist and dropped his head. Rylee couldn't help but laugh. By now, he should have known there was no altering an eight-year-old's version of the events.

"You both get an A for effort. How about the two of you go get cleaned up, and I'll handle this mess and cook," Rylee said, her head swimming from the disarray in her usually spotless kitchen.

"No," Canten said. "We'll clean up here. You relax. Take a hot bath. A *long*, hot bath. I'll handle dinner."

Zachary slapped a hand against his forehead. "Oh no. We're never going to eat."

Entering her bedroom, Rylee closed the door behind her and opened a window so the rancid smell could escape. She sat in her reading chair, grabbed her book, and read as she waited for the storm to pass.

From the bedroom, she could hear the clink and clank of pots and pans. At least she hadn't heard anything shatter. *And I spoke too soon.* She fought the urge to rush from the room to see which of her favorite dishes had met its demise.

Once she no longer saw the flash of lightning outside her window, Rylee headed into the bathroom. Instead of a bath, she took a long, hot shower. Afterward, she took her time moisturizing and getting dressed. In a generic purple T-shirt and jean capri pants, she made her way back to the kitchen.

"Oh, wow," she said. The space no longer looked as if a flour bomb had detonated.

"How does it look, Aunt Rylee?"

"Just perfect," she said, hugging Zachary to her. "Did you do all of this by yourself?"

"Sheriff Canten helped a little," he said with a grin.

"Hey, don't be taking all the credit," Canten said.

They all laughed.

Rylee sniffed several times like a dog who'd caught a whiff of something delicious. "Something smells good."

"Come with me," Zachary said, taking her hand and pulling her into the formal dining room.

Canten trailed them.

A bounty of food covered the tabletop. Steak, chicken, ribs, green beans, fried okra, mashed potatoes, rolls. Lemonade filled three wineglasses. They'd gotten fancy. "Where did all of this come from?"

"Grubhub," Zachary blurted.

Canten tossed his arms into the air. "We were supposed to tell her we cooked it," he said.

"Aunt Rylee loves us. And my mom said when people love you, they sometimes believe anything you say." Zachary rolled his eyes to the ceiling. "But I don't think Aunt Rylee would believe that story."

Aunt Rylee loves us. God, she'd known that day in the market would come back to haunt her. When Rylee glanced at Canten, he stared at her, a quizzical expression on his face. "Um, everything looks fantastic. I'm starving. Let's eat."

Zachary pulled out one of the wooden chairs. "Sit, Aunt Rylee." Once she had, he attempted to push it in. "*Uh. Uh,*" he said, putting all his roughly sixty pounds into trying to move the chair forward.

Rylee used her feet to help the chair glide across the wood floor.

"There," Zachary said.

"Thank you." She tapped the tip of his nose. "Such a gentleman. And so strong," she said.

"I know. I move heavy stuff all the time."

Rylee wasn't sure if she should have been amused or insulted.

"Let's eat," Canten said.

Rylee looked on in amazement as Zachary polished off a small chicken breast, half of a rib eye, and three rib bones. Where did he put it all? The kid wasn't big as nothing, yet he ate like a grown man.

Zachary wiped his mouth. "Johnathan said—"

"Oh Lord," Rylee and Canten said in unison.

Zachary's brows slammed together. "What?" he asked, looking back and forth between them.

Rylee snickered. "Nothing. Go on. What did Johnathan say?" Something told her she would regret asking.

Zachary's perplexed expression relaxed. "He said the way to a heart is by cooking it delicious food."

If love was as simple as that, Canten was certainly head over heels for her because she'd prepared some fantastic feasts over the past couple of months. And according to Lady Sunshine, he had the increased waistline to prove it, though she couldn't tell. His body was picture perfect. At least in her eyes.

Rylee's eyes slid to Canten. The way he studied her made her cheeks warm. What raced through that head of his as he stared at her?

"Sheriff Canten, you must have cooked Aunt Rylee a lot of cheese sandwiches. Definitely not cake. But you make the best cheese sandwiches. Don't tell my mom I said that, though, okay?"

"Your secret's safe with me," Canten said.

Canten eyed her again. This time, he looked as if he was attempting to figure something out. No doubt whatever gears turned in his head had something to do with what Zachary had just said. She needed to change the subject before Zachary said more.

"That's a mighty big appetite you have there," she said to Zachary.

"Yeah. My dad said I'm a growing boy. May I have more mashed potatoes, please?"

"People who love my cheese sandwiches can have anything they want," Canten said, dipping him more.

What about people who love you? What could they have? Rylee thought but didn't dare say.

🐝

Canten wasn't sure what Zachary had meant by the cheese-sandwich comment, but it had made Rylee nervous. She'd attempted to hide the fact, but he'd noticed. Plus, she'd changed the subject real quick. What had she thought Zachary would say next?

He thought back to Zachary's delicious-food comment. Was this why Rylee was so lodged in his heart? The woman definitely could cook. *Nah.* In this case, food had nothing to do with what he felt for Rylee.

"Since you two went through all this trouble, the least I can do is clean up," Rylee said, standing. "Zachary, why don't you challenge the sheriff in Connect Four?"

"Sheriff Canten, do you know how to play Connect Four?"

"Do I know how to play? I'm the *king* of Connect Four."

Rylee snickered. Clearly, she doubted his claim.

An hour later, Zachary had Canten reevaluating his life. Who got beaten back-to-back-to-back by an eight-year-old in a game based on strategy? Strategy was his thing. He'd been hustled by a kid.

"I'm pretty good at Connect Four," Zachary said. "Don't feel bad. I beat Aunt Rylee a bunch of times too."

As if on cue, Rylee entered the room. "So how many games did you win, *king*?"

Canten chuckled. "You could have warned me that this kid was some kind of Connect Four genius."

Zachary was all teeth at the compliment.

"You'll get better with practice," Zachary said.

Rylee washed a hand over Zachary's head. "It's bath time."

"Aww, man. Do I have to?"

"Yes. I made it extra bubbly for you."

Canten enjoyed watching Rylee with Zachary. She was so good with him. Zachary had been right—she would be a great mother. Patient, loving, beautiful. The last had nothing to do with motherhood; he'd simply thrown it in because it had been the next thing that came to mind.

"Sheriff Canten, will you be here when I get out of the tub?"

Canten stood from the floor where he and Zachary had sat to play. Could that have been the problem? Next time he'd play the kid on the table. That would give him a better viewpoint. "Probably not, little man. It's getting late. I need to get home to get my beauty sleep."

Zachary bent over in laughter as if Canten had told a great joke. "You're funny," Zachary said. "I'll see you tomorrow."

"You can count on it," Canten said.

Zachary darted down the hall, came to a screeching halt, ran back to Canten, and hugged him. "Thank you for playing with me. And thank you for all the fun today while Aunt Rylee was at work."

"Anytime, kid."

A second later, he sprinted away again.

"Before you go," Rylee said, pointing over her shoulder, "can you take a look at something in my bedroom? I think it's broken."

The last place he wanted to be was in Rylee's bedroom. They hadn't had sex since Zachary had come to stay. He'd gone through withdrawal these past few days. It was hard weaning himself off a drug like Rylee. Unfortunately, he'd gotten a taste of what it would be like if he got the job in Charlotte. He didn't much like the flavor. "Sure."

The amount of willpower it took not to pull her into his arms the second they entered the room nearly crippled him. He turned at the sound of the door clicking shut. Rylee stood shirtless, her back against the closed door. One side of his mouth lifted into a smile. She summoned him closer with her index finger.

Pressing his ready body against hers, he said, "I thought something was broken."

"It is. *Me*," she said, unfastening her pants. "Can you fix me?"

"I'll damn sure try," he said, capturing her mouth in a greedy kiss.

The second their mouths touched, his entire body reacted. The joy he experienced from simply kissing Rylee revealed just how deep he'd fallen for her. *This wasn't supposed to happen,* he said to himself, deepening the kiss. He needed her. So damn bad. "What about Zachary?" he said against their joined mouths.

"Make it quick," she said.

The way his body ached for her, quick wouldn't be a problem. Unfortunately, his speedy performance wouldn't be by choice. With all the pent-up longing he held for her, she'd be lucky to get ten minutes. And even that would be a stretch.

Shaky hands caused Canten to fumble with his belt buckle. Luckily, Rylee took over, unhooking it effortlessly. Unfastening his jeans, she pushed them, along with his underwear, off his hips. Hoisting her into his arms, he wasted no time entering her.

Rylee cried out.

"*Shh*," he whispered, kissing her neck.

With her back against the door, Rylee worked her lower torso in an up, down, circular motion. It felt so good he went cross-eyed. Clearly, she wanted to do him in. "You feel so good," he said. "Damn, I've missed being inside you."

"Harder, Canten," she said. "Harder."

He gripped her ass. "You want it harder?"

"*Yes!* Oh God, *yes.*"

Then he would give it to her harder. Moving from the door to the bed, Canten placed Rylee on her feet, spun her around, bent her over, and drove so deep and hard into her they both nearly toppled over.

The sound of flesh smacking flesh reverberated off the wall. Rylee buried her face in one of the decorative pillows that sat on her bed. Canten did his damnedest to hold in his grunts and groans. Rylee's muffled scream, along with the feel of her muscles pulsing around his dick, told him she'd come. A stroke or two later, he exploded so hard his legs buckled. Yeah, he would miss this.

CHAPTER 24

Days after her father's episode, Rylee sat on the back porch of the lake house with her mother, while her father, Canten, Senior, Sebastian, and Zachary fished on the lake. Rylee was thrilled her father had bounced back so fast, but her concern still lingered.

"Mom, there's something I need to say. Something I need to talk to you about."

Fine lines crawled across Mrs. Charles's forehead. "You sound so serious. What is it, dear?"

Rylee took a deep breath, then released it slowly. "I want you and Dad to move back to Honey Hill. So that I can keep an eye on you two," she added.

Mrs. Charles chuckled. "Dear, you have your own life. You don't have time to supervise two old fogies. We'll be fine. Besides, before long you'll have your own family," her mother added with a smile.

This nearly prompted Rylee to tell her mother that this was all a lie. There was no relationship, which meant there would be no family, which also meant she had plenty of time to watch over them. But she and Canten were too close to the finish line to blow things up now. Plus, her mother had already been through enough this week. In fact, Rylee considered asking Canten if they could push the breakup from next month to September. Just to give her parents time to adjust to their new normal, without having to worry about her.

Rylee's father's new diet of more fruits and veggies and less sodium, accompanied by increased exercise and limited alcohol, would be an adjustment, especially for a true southerner accustomed to consuming soul food. Rylee had seemingly convinced him it was necessary. But if they were in Honey Hill, she could ensure he did everything he needed to do. Plus, focusing on them would keep her mind off Canten.

"You're always worried about everyone around you. You don't have to worry about us. I'm going to make sure your father adheres to this lifestyle change. He knows I need him here with me for as long as possible."

Rylee saw something on her mother's face she rarely witnessed. Fear. The idea of losing the love of her life had put her mother in this state. "If you and Dad were here, I could help him stay on track. We all could go for walks, explore new healthy meal options, have sleepovers."

The last garnered a laugh from her mother. "We're fine in Florida, sweetheart. You just focus on that handsome man of yours."

Canten wouldn't be hers to focus on much longer. While there were still several more candidates in the running, by the sound of it, Canten was a strong front-runner for the position.

Rylee decided to start laying the groundwork for her and Canten's breakup now. "Canten might be leaving Honey Hill," she said. "For Charlotte. He's been interviewing for a position he's wanted for a very long time. Bureau commander," she added as if it mattered.

"Sounds . . . important," her mother said. "What will this mean for the two of you?"

Rylee shrugged. "He'll be there. I'll be here."

"Have you asked him to stay?"

"No." Because she had no right to do so. "I would never do that. I would never keep him from his dream. He'd only resent me later."

The impact of Canten's leaving hit her differently now than it had in the past. Maybe because she'd said it aloud to someone else. There would be no more daily visits from him at the bakery. *Just to say hey,* he would say. No more 4:00 a.m. well-being drive-bys that he probably didn't think she knew about. No more hour-long talks. At least not face to face. No more Canten in her bed.

A reel of them and all the moments they'd spent together recently played in her head in quick snapshots. The scenes were almost unbearable. He hadn't even left yet, and she already felt a deep loss. Until now, his departure hadn't felt real. Canten was leaving, and he would take a chunk of her heart with him.

"Oh, sweetheart, don't cry," Mrs. Charles said, passing her a napkin.

Don't cry? Rylee's brow furrowed as she touched a hand to her cheek, pulled it away, and studied her wet fingertips. Where had these tears come from?

"That man spent nearly two thousand dollars to charter a helicopter just to get to you. Do you really think he's going to allow distance or time to keep you apart?"

"Two thousand dollars?" Rylee asked. She'd been shocked when Canten had told her how he'd gotten to Honey Hill, but she'd never imagined he'd paid that much to get there. To get to her. "How do you know he spent that much?"

Her mother flashed a sheepish expression. "I may have *overheard* him and Sebastian talking. Sebastian wanted to help cover the cost, but Canten wouldn't hear of it. Said he would have paid double that amount to get there."

Mrs. Charles's brows knit, and she looked as if she were trying to figure something out.

"What is it, Mom?"

"Your brother said the strangest thing to Canten. Something about when the lie becomes the truth. Any idea what that meant?"

Rylee's heart skipped a beat as panic set in. "N-no," she said. "Did he, um, say anything else?"

"No." Her mother stared off, looking as if she were trying to figure out this piece of the puzzle. A beat later her expression relaxed, and she chuckled. "Who knows. Immediately after that they started play boxing like two oversize kids."

Rylee inhaled a deep breath, then blew it out slowly. What if Sebastian had said more? She had to remind him to be more careful.

Things fell quiet between them for several minutes. Rylee eyed the pontoon boat in the distance, bobbing in the water. Before her father and the others had headed out, her mother had made him promise they'd stay within sight of the lake house. *Just as a precaution,* she'd said. And as always, Gus Charles did whatever it took to make his wife happy.

"I liked Lucas, sweetheart."

Rylee eyed her mother. *Where did that come from?*

Mrs. Charles continued, "But I never felt he had been the right one for you. I don't mean to speak ill of the dead. Like I said before, I liked Lucas. I truly did. But you shone with such a blinding light before you met him. Over time, I watched that light dim."

Rylee looked away, embarrassed by her mother's observation. Mostly because she'd been right. A darkness had crept inside Rylee and had smothered the part of her that had once beamed. Something her mother used to say to her and Sebastian as kids played in her head. *You're both stars that are meant to shine. Don't ever let anyone dull you.* Had her mother been disappointed in her for forgetting this?

"My heart blossoms every time I look at you and Canten. Do you know why?"

Rylee could think of one or two reasons but shook her head instead.

"Because you shine again," Mrs. Charles said. "Not just shine, you sparkle."

Shine? Sparkle? Her mother made her sound like glitter. Apparently, Mrs. Charles witnessed the confusion on her daughter's face.

"Sweetheart, Canten recharged you. And I don't know if I've ever seen you glow brighter."

She hated when her mother was right.

"Do you love him?" Mrs. Charles asked.

Rylee nodded. Which would make saying goodbye so much more difficult.

🐝

Since Canten had cut his vacation short, he'd gone into the office as opposed to sitting at home doing nothing. He welcomed a ride-along with him on his daily trot around town. Zachary had talked nonstop since they'd mounted Ellington nearly an hour ago. Canten wasn't sure how he'd done it, but the kid had plowed through at least twenty topics in just as many minutes.

"Sheriff Canten?"

Canten had told the kid a hundred times he could drop the *Sheriff* and just call him Canten, but clearly, he liked tacking on *Sheriff*. "Mmm-hmm."

"Are you going to miss Honey Hill?"

How did Zachary know he might be leaving? He'd purposely not mentioned it to Lunden, deciding it would be best to wait until after their honeymoon. And Rylee wouldn't have told him. "How do you know I'm leaving?" he asked.

"Ms. Hilary told Aunt Rylee she heard you were taking a job in Charlotte."

Hilary? How the hell did Hilary know his business?

"Ms. Katrina said you didn't ask Aunt Rylee to go with you, so that meant you weren't into her."

Anger seeped in from what Zachary told him. How dare Katrina say something like that to Rylee. She knew shit about shit.

"Aunt Rylee told her you get deep into her a lot. I don't know what that means, though, but I don't think Ms. Katrina liked it, because her face got all ugly and scary."

Way to go, Aunt Rylee.

"I bet Aunt Rylee cries a lot when you leave. My friend Johnathan's mom cries when Johnathan's dad sometimes leaves to be a soldier. She loves him a whole lot. That's why she cries. When Aunt Rylee starts to cry, I'll hold her hand. But I can only hold it for a few days. Not like a week or anything. I might have stuff to do."

Canten laughed. This kid was something else. "I don't think you have to worry about that. Rylee won't cry."

Zachary nodded fast. "Yes, she will, because she loves you. A whole lot. She said so. I'm not supposed to tell anyone, though. I told you because it will make you happy. We should tell people things that will make them happy."

Canten's brows furrowed. "Rylee told you she loves me?"

"Yep. In the grocery store. On the pasta aisle. That's where we saw Ms. Hilary and Ms. Katrina. They are *mean*. I stuck my tongue out at them. Don't tell my mom or dad, okay?"

"I won't," he said absently. His thoughts were all over the place. *Rylee told Zachary she loves me?* Giving more thought to what Zachary had said, he chuckled at himself. Why the hell was he believing an eight-year-old? Surely Zachary had misinterpreted what Rylee had said. She'd probably meant she loved him as a friend.

"Sheriff Canten?"

"Yes?"

"Do you love my aunt Rylee? I bet you do, because you like hugging her. Johnathan said—"

"Your friend Johnathan says a lot, huh?"

"Yeah. His mom said he talks way too much," Zachary said. "Johnathan said his dad hugs his mom a lot because that's how he says *I love you* because he's not mushy."

"Oooh, did you see that?" Canten said in an attempt to distract Zachary from the current conversation.

"See what?" he asked, his head whipping from left to right.

"It was a huge purple rabbit," Canten said.

Zachary laughed loudly. "Nah-ah. Rabbits don't come in purple."

"Are you sure?"

"*Yes.*" Zachary laughed some more. "You're going to be a good dad because you know how to make kids laugh. And you teach them how to ride horses. And you're a policeman and will protect them from bad guys. And girls. You should protect them from Ms. Hilary and Ms. Katrina."

"I agree with you," he said. At least about keeping kids from those two. Those two witches would probably cook them.

Zachary got quiet; however, the silence didn't last long.

"If you move to Charlotte, how will you and Aunt Rylee have a baby?"

Man, the questions from the eight-person panel in Charlotte had been easier to answer than Zachary's. Well, at least he'd forgotten about the love question. Or more likely, he'd probably only postponed the inquiry. "We, um . . ." How the hell was he supposed to answer this? "Hmm . . ." Canten sighed. "You know what, I'm going to have to get back to you on that one."

"You should probably stay here in Honey Hill until you figure that out."

Canten chuckled. "I'll consider that."

Things went quiet again. *The quiet before the storm.* Canten was convinced when Zachary went silent like this he was simply thinking up some other way to put him on the hot seat. But what else could the kid ask? He'd covered everything. Wait. He hadn't asked anything about him and Rylee getting married.

"Sheriff Canten?"

And here we go. "Yes."

"What's a shren?"

Canten pushed his brows together. "A *what*?"

"A shren. When we were in the market, Ms. Hilary asked Aunt Rylee if you still had a shren of your dead wife at your house. Is it like a picture or something?"

Bertha Harlowe, Canten said to himself. She was the only way Hilary could know so much of his business. Bertha had been the night-time cleaner at the station. He'd hired her once or twice to do a deep clean of his place. He'd recently had to let her go from the station when one of his deputies had caught her snooping through desk drawers. Obviously, she'd read the letter he'd stashed in his drawer. Clearly, she'd snooped through his house as well.

CHAPTER 25

Rylee sat with Lunden on one of the cement benches in the square. She did her best to be present as Lunden told her all about her honeymoon in the Mediterranean. While Rylee smiled, laughed, and gasped where appropriate, her attention wasn't 100 percent on this conversation. It was on Canten, as it had been a lot recently.

Her thoughts drifted. She couldn't put her finger on it, but something felt off with them. For the past several days, when they were together, he seemed distracted. And when she asked what was wrong, he'd say, *Nothing*. Every single time. She wished she knew what was going on in his head.

"I'm moving to Greece and becoming an olive farmer," Lunden said.

"You'd be good at that," Rylee said, absently. "Olives are delicious."

"Rylee?"

Maybe he's busy getting things in order. Even though he hadn't gotten an official word about the job, Rylee could feel in her gut that it was coming.

"*Rylee!*"

Rylee jolted back to reality. "What's wrong? What is it?" she asked, her eyes sweeping from left to right.

"What's up with you?" Lunden asked. "You're a thousand miles away." She pointed to her hand. "And you haven't touched your hot dog."

Rylee eyed her friend. "I love him. I love Canten."

Lunden squealed. "*Finally!* Even though I've known all along because I'm your best friend and I know things. I'm glad you finally admitted it aloud. Now all you have to do is tell Canten."

Why had Lunden made it sound so easy? Rylee shook her head. "I can't. I don't want to put him in a position to have to choose between me and Charlotte. I can't do that to him. I won't." Why had she assumed it would be a choice at all? She loved Canten, but that didn't mean he loved her too.

"Why?"

"Because he might decide to stay in Honey Hill?"

Lunden's brows knit. "I'm confused. Isn't that what you want?"

"Yes. But I don't want him to one day resent me for holding him back."

Lunden laughed. "Canten could never resent you. In fact, he's probably waiting for you to give him a reason to stay. But resent you? That would never happen."

"It did with Lucas."

Lunden's smile melted, and concern spread across her face.

Rylee slid her gaze away and stared at nothing in particular. "Before Lucas reenlisted this last time, he'd told me he wanted to open a custom car shop." She remembered the conversation and smiled. "God, he was so happy talking about all the ideas he'd had. How he'd become the most sought-after designer on the East Coast. I have no doubt that he would have been." Rylee frowned. "I crushed his dream."

"What does that mean?"

Rylee explained how instead of supporting Lucas as he'd always done her, she'd reminded him of how far in the hole they had been. How she'd reminded him that she was trying to get out of debt, not accumulate more. How she'd asked—even demanded—him to wait until their heads were further above water. And how she would never forget that look in his eyes moments before he'd walked out of their home and had stayed gone all night. *"Resentment."*

"Canten and Lucas are two totally different people, Ry. Don't base your present off past experiences. If you love Canten, truly love him, you have to tell him how you feel. Give him that much. And what he does with the information is up to him."

Rylee considered Lunden's words. "Maybe you're right." Maybe she should tell Canten exactly how she felt and allow the cards to fall where they may. But not today. Probably not tomorrow. Soon.

"Of course I am. I'm the mayor. Everyone knows the mayor is always right."

They shared a laugh.

"Okay, okay, okay, enough about me. Finish telling me about this amazing honeymoon," Rylee said, giving Lunden her full attention.

"I'm pretty sure my husband tried to impregnate me. We spent a great deal of our time in bed."

"Um, TMI," Rylee said with a laugh.

Lunden went all starry eyed. "My husband. God, I love saying that. And speaking of kids, Zachary keeps going on and on about how much fun he had with you and Canten."

"I just love that kid," Rylee said. "And we did have a blast. He's a beast at Connect Four. I felt bad that he'd had to be at the hospital with me."

"What's this I hear about Canten chartering a helicopter from Charlotte to get to you?" Lunden must have seen the quizzical expression on Rylee's face, because she said, "Mama Charles told me when Quade and I went to visit them. You have another sibling, by the way. She adopted Quade."

"That's fine. He's like a brother anyway."

"Now about this helicopter," Lunden said.

"I admit it. It kind of touched me."

Lunden's brow arched. "Just kind of?"

Rylee tried to bite back her smile. "Okay, it completely swelled my heart, and I think I fell in love with him even more. He was my rock, Lu. That night, when he brought me home from the hospital, he held me so tight. I didn't even have to ask. He knew exactly what I needed. I felt so cherished, so protected. And when Dad was discharged, he was there every single day checking on him and my mother."

"Is that the kind of man you want to let slip away?"

No, it wasn't. But she wasn't sure she had a say in the matter.

That night, Rylee found herself in what had become her favorite place. Canten's arms. Earlier that evening, she'd brought over a cheesy chicken-broccoli-and-rice casserole. Her intent had been to deliver it and return home, especially since it had looked as if he'd been busy, by the several empty storage boxes that had sat in the living room. She'd assumed the boxes had been in preparation for his potential move but hadn't asked.

However, Canten had needed to talk to her. To her surprise, he'd apologized for if he'd seemed distracted lately and explained how he'd had a lot going on. He hadn't delved into details about what, but again, she'd assumed it had something to do with Charlotte.

He'd certainly given her his undivided attention when he'd carried her into his bedroom and stripped off her clothes. Her body still tingled from the things he'd done to it.

Obviously, he'd been dead tired, because she had never heard him snore before tonight. It wasn't a loud, nerve-racking sound, just a low rumble. He didn't budge when she slunk out of his arms and into the bathroom. Afterward, she headed to the kitchen for water. On her way back to the bedroom, the light radiating from underneath the bed-room door Canten always kept closed—the one she'd dubbed Canten's naughty room—caught her eye.

Rylee's first instinct was to ignore it since it was behind a closed door, but she decided, What would be the harm of entering simply to switch off the light? When she opened the door, she wished she'd gone with her first instinct and let it be, because she hadn't been ready for the scene before her.

As she entered, her curious eyes swept the room. The question Hilary had asked her at the market played in her head and didn't seem so asinine now.

Pictures of Canten and Jayla sat all around the room. A wedding album sat open on the bed. Rylee flipped through page after page, greeted with smiling, visibly happy faces. Jayla made a beautiful bride in the all-white princess gown. Canten was handsome in a black tux.

Something on the nightstand caught her eye. Rings. A platinum band encrusted with diamonds, alongside an etched platinum band. Side by side, touching. Next to the jewelry, a digital image. She reached for the ultrasound, pulled back, then reached for it again. Holding it between her fingers, she stared at it, the developing fetus no bigger than a kidney bean.

Gently replacing the printout, she allowed herself to take in the whole of the room once more before backing out, switching off the light as she closed the door. On the opposite side, she stood a moment to catch her breath.

How could he have kept something this important from her? They'd talked at length about their spouses. How could he not mention this room? She recalled how Lucas had done the same regarding his enlistment. Obviously, she hadn't been important enough to either of them.

Rylee wanted to kick herself. Over the past couple of months, she'd foolishly allowed herself to become too comfortable in a relationship that had been nothing more than a theatrical performance. *How could I have been so stupid?* Despite how authentic things had felt, seeing this room, Canten's tribute to Jayla, she knew better.

Obviously, he wasn't over the loss of Jayla, because he'd preserved their life together. Regardless of how potent Rylee's feelings were for Canten, what they'd shared couldn't hold a candle to the very real and clearly lasting love Canten shared with Jayla, and she damn sure couldn't compete with a dead woman.

Something was up with Rylee, but Canten couldn't decipher what. The past week and a half she hadn't been herself. Instead of being the feisty, always optimistic woman he was used to, Rylee hadn't given him a full-wattage smile in days. Even telling one of his lame jokes hadn't been able to get a laugh out of her. And that was rare.

Initially, he'd assumed the shift was because her parents would be returning to Florida soon, and she and Sebastian hadn't been able to convince them to move back to Honey Hill or at least extend their stay. But now he was thinking that maybe it had something to do with him, especially since the past several times he'd initiated intimacy, she'd pulled away.

"Rylee, do you want to talk about something?" he asked.

"Something like what?" she said, never looking up from the zucchini she sliced.

"Well, we can start with why you're being so distant with me. Did I do something?"

She eyed him, then shrieked. *"Shit! Shit, shit, shit!"*

"What's wrong?" It only took him a second to notice the blood trickling from her finger. "You cut yourself." Ushering her to the sink, he turned on the water and placed her hand under the stream. "Stay here. I'll get the first aid kit."

Moments later, he led her over to the table and tended her wound.

"Luckily, you won't lose the finger," he said. He expected at least a chuckle. Nothing.

"Thank you," she said.

When she attempted to stand, he blocked the move. "Want to tell me what's going on? Obviously, I've done something. Just tell me what so I can fix it. I don't like seeing you like this. I don't ever like seeing you unhappy."

Rylee's gaze lowered to her fresh bandage. Her mouth opened, then closed as if she'd reconsidered saying whatever lingered on her tongue.

"You have to talk to me, Rylee. Please."

When her gaze rose, the unshed tears he saw glistening in her eyes concerned him.

"Canten—" Her words trailed. Swallowing, she started again. "When we make love, who are you making love to?"

His brows slammed together, stunned. "I don't think I understand the question," he said.

"It's a simple question. When you're inside me, who are you making love to?" Her tone grew louder, words terser. "When you're looking into my face, who do you see? When you're holding me in your arms, is it me you feel there? Or Jayla?"

Where in the hell was this coming from? "Rylee—" He paused. "Why would you even ask me that?"

"The other day in the market, Hilary asked if you still had a shrine for your dead wife in your house."

Agitated, he said, "You're listening to Hilary now? Come on, Rylee. You—"

"I saw the room, Canten," she said. "I wasn't snooping. The light was left on. I cracked open the door to switch it off. I saw all the pictures, the open album on the bed, the frozen video on the computer screen, rings, and the—"

"And instead of coming to me, you came to your own conclusion that I was, what, using you as some kind of substitute for Jayla?" He hated how stern his words had sounded.

Rylee pushed to her feet. "Canten . . ." She paced back and forth, her arms folded across her chest. A beat later, she stopped and looked at him. With a shrug, she said, "What am I supposed to think?"

Canten stood. "Anytime I'm with you, Rylee, I'm with *you*. A *hundred* percent. When I touch you"—he was about to place his hand on her neck but reconsidered, allowing his arm to fall to his side—"I touch *you*. When I kiss you, I kiss *you*. And when I look at you . . . you're all I see." This time he shrugged. "But hey, what are you supposed to think, right? You saw a few pictures and a photo album, so I must be obsessed with my dead wife, right?"

"You're putting words in my mouth," she said.

"Am I?"

"Yes."

He chuckled. "So you get to come to conclusions, but I don't?"

"Why wouldn't you tell me about the room? We're friends."

"I'm entitled to some privacy, Rylee." It sounded better than confessing it felt as if he'd been juggling two relationships: a fake one with her that was becoming extremely real and one that had been real but no longer existed in any other way than memories.

Rylee looked away. "Yes, you are."

Canten shook his head. They were having a lovers' spat and weren't even lovers. It would have been cute had he not been so upset. How could Rylee have ever believed she'd been a stand-in? "I'll see you later," he said, leaving the room without giving her an opportunity to say anything else.

CHAPTER 26

For the past several hours, Rylee had gone through a range of emotions. Currently, she was snuggled firmly in anger. And her weighted blanket did little to help her to feel all warm and cozy. *Okay, I get he's upset.* She'd seen that on his face. But to walk out on her?

Okay, so he hadn't actually walked out on her. He'd excused himself cordially, skipping the delicious meal she'd been preparing. He never passed up an opportunity to eat her cooking. Had she been so wrong to question him? Why hadn't he been able to see things from her viewpoint?

How did he expect me to act after seeing that room? Obviously, he'd never intended for her to see it. In hindsight, she wished she'd simply kept on walking right past the closed door. It was Canten's electricity bill, not hers.

Grabbing the remote, she increased the volume of the radio to drown out the thoughts in her head. Closing her eyes, she crafted a love story based on the song playing on the radio. Luther Vandross's "If This World Were Mine" filled her room and her thoughts.

Rylee imagined two people at the altar. The groom, placing all that he owned at his bride's feet in a show of his commitment to her. The bride, crowning her groom a king. They gave each other the moon and the stars.

Several more songs played, each receiving their own happily ever after. The DJ's voice replaced the soulful baritone of Barry White in "The Secret Garden." Man, she loved that song.

"Lovers near and far," he said, "we have a dedication. This one a little cryptic and goes out to 'you' from 'me.'"

That is cryptic.

The DJ continued, "Don't you love the mystery? 'You,' whoever and wherever you are, this one's for you. I hope you enjoy."

Patti LaBelle's "If Only You Knew" poured through the speaker. Obviously, she wasn't the only one unable to tell someone how she felt. Rylee didn't have to craft a tale to this one, because she was living it. Closing her eyes, she listened to the lyrics of the song and wondered how many women tuned in now fantasized about being the infamous "you" the song had been dedicated to.

The following morning, Rylee was awakened by someone screaming, *"Good morning."* She jolted forward, her eyes sweeping the room. It took her several seconds to realize it had come from the morning-show host on the radio. Her heart banged out of her chest. Clearly, the auto-shutoff feature on the radio hadn't engaged the night before.

Pulling herself together, she showered and headed out the door. Backing out of her driveway, she tossed a glance toward Canten's place. Guilt riddled her for how she'd reacted the night before. It wasn't his fault she'd lost sight of things and made their situation more than it truly was.

When Rylee arrived at the bakery, she prepped for the day. At 4:25 a.m., she moved to the front window and waited in the shadows. At exactly 4:35 a.m., headlights lit up Main Street. A second later, Canten's SUV came into view.

The vehicle slowed in front of her shop. Canten surveyed the area, then continued on. A sentimental feeling washed over her. Even upset with her, he still went out of his way to make her safety a priority of his.

All morning long, Rylee found herself eyeing the door every time someone entered, hoping one of them would be Canten. It never was. After the morning rush, she packed up two boxes of goodies and informed her crew she'd return later. Parking outside the sheriff's department, she grabbed the baker's boxes and went inside. Canten had been a great friend to her. She didn't want to lose that. Which meant she needed to apologize.

"Rylee? Nice to see you, especially with boxes in your hand."

"Hey, Fallon," Rylee said to Deputy Clarke, who manned the front desk. She passed the woman one of the boxes. "Enjoy. Is he in?"

"He asked not to be disturbed, but I'm sure that doesn't apply to you."

Today, it probably did. "Thanks," she said.

Rylee tapped twice on Canten's door.

"Come in," came from the opposite side.

When she entered, Canten's attention was focused on his computer screen. "I hope it's important," he said.

"It is."

His head whipped toward her. "Rylee?"

"Hey. I know you're busy. I won't stay long. I just wanted to drop these off." She placed the box filled with all his favorites on the small round conference table. "And apologize."

He stood and rounded his desk. Sitting on the edge, he said, "After tossing and turning half the night, I get how you could have come to such a conclusion. I should be the one apologizing. For the way I left."

"Don't apologize. You had the right to be upset."

"I wasn't upset, Rylee. I was hurt." He paused a second. "Hurt by the fact you would think I could use you like that. I would have thought you knew me better than that."

As if she hadn't felt bad enough. "I do. I just . . . the room . . ."

"Things aren't always how they seem, Rylee," he said.

Well, it sure had seemed like he was still clutching to his dead wife. Of course she kept that to herself. She waited for him to offer more, but he didn't. Instead of more words, they stared at each other for a long while. The heat generating between them threatened to ignite the entire station. While Canten might have been shackled to the past, their connection, chemistry, attraction to one another was undeniable. Something paralyzing lingered between them.

When her body couldn't handle Canten's form of hands-free eye foreplay a minute longer, Rylee snapped out of the trance. "I should let you get back to work." With her heart racing, she made an attempt at escape. Canten's words stopped her at the door. She just needed to get through the next few weeks.

"No hard feelings?" he said.

She turned to face him. "No hard feelings." Not that she could have ever harbored any toward him.

"How's the finger, by the way?"

Rylee held up her hand, showing a fresh bandage. "Like new."

Three fast taps sounded at the door before it swung open. Unfortunately, Rylee hadn't been fast enough to move out of the way. At the odd angle she stood, the doorknob hit her in the stomach. In a blink, Canten dashed across the room.

"You okay?" he said, resting a hand on her lower back.

God, how she'd missed his touch.

"*Crap.* I'm sorry, Rylee, I didn't know you were there. I'm really sorry," the young deputy said, his freckled face turning beet red. "Sorry, Sheriff."

Rylee held up her hand. "It's okay. It was an accident." She would definitely have a bruise tomorrow.

Canten's words were tight when he spoke. "What do you need, Deputy Kemp?"

"There's a problem downtown," Deputy Kemp said.

There was always a problem downtown. Instead of being called Main Street, it should have been called Drama Drive or Problem Plaza or Rapture Road. Okay, Rapture Road was probably a bit much.

"Are you sure you're all right, Rylee?" Deputy Kemp asked.

Rylee flashed a smile. "Yes, I'm fine. Stop worrying."

"What's the problem, Deputy Kemp?" Canten asked.

"Mr. Patterson and Mr. Herbert are having a disagreement about Presto. Mr. Herbert's threatening to shear him."

Rylee's brows furrowed. *Can you shear a peacock?*

Deputy Kemp continued, "Mr. Patterson told Mr. Herbert if he came near any of his bevy, he'd strangle him with one of those raggedy suits he sells. I hear that escalated things."

"Jesus," Canten said. "And why do they need me on the scene?"

Obviously, Canten was trying to get out of whatever foolishness awaited him on Main Street. A clear effort to protect his sanity. She bet he couldn't get away from here fast enough. In Charlotte, he definitely wouldn't have these types of small-town problems.

"Apparently, you were specifically requested," Deputy Kemp said.

Canten gave a heavy sigh. "Let them know I'll be on the scene shortly."

"Ten-four," Deputy Kemp said and backed out of the room.

The second the door clicked closed, Canten knelt and lifted the hem of Rylee's shirt. For a delusional moment, she thought she'd get to feel his lips on her. But hope died when he pressed his fingers into her stomach.

"Does this hurt?" he asked.

Staring down at him, she laughed and said, "No. I'm okay, Canten, really. I got hit in the belly with a doorknob. It happens to people all the time."

He chuckled. "I've never seen it happen. Ever."

"Huh. Well, I guess that makes me special."

"That part was never up for debate."

Why did he do this? Why did he continuously make her feel so special? Rylee guided him back to a full stand. "I have no internal injuries. I'm fine. If I were pregnant, then you could worry." Her eyes widened when she realized what had just slipped past her lips.

"And if that were the case, you'd be on your way to the ER," he said. "No questions asked."

Now he was just making it plain impossible for her not to keep falling deeper and harder for him. She had to find a way to shut off her feelings for him. But how, when they revved to life anytime they were together? Some fine mess she'd gotten herself into. "I should let you get going."

"Ride with me. Afterward, we can have lunch. My treat."

Like he'd ever let her pay for anything anyway. Why did she get the feeling he didn't want to experience whatever ridiculousness he was headed into alone? Well, she had a few minutes. She nodded. "Okay."

When Canten had said to ride with him, Rylee had assumed he'd meant in a vehicle, not on a horse. But with her arms wrapped tightly around him, her body pressed against his, she wasn't complaining.

"You okay back there?" Canten asked over his shoulder.

She couldn't have been better. "Perfect."

Canten had to admit he would miss the daily antics of Honey Hill residents. But what he would miss most was the woman currently clinging to him, her head resting on his back. He'd been so damn happy to see her standing at his office door this morning that he'd nearly darted over and hugged her.

All night long, he'd tossed and turned, regretting how he'd handled things the night before. After hours of replaying the scene in his head, he'd come to his own conclusion. He'd acted hastily by leaving. That night he'd wanted to call Rylee to talk but that damn male pride. What he had done instead was dedicate a song to her. *To you, from me.*

He'd recalled her saying she listened to the station every night. He hoped she'd been listening last night. Not that she would have known he'd dedicated the song to her. Had she made up a story as she'd listened to Patti LaBelle say the things he hadn't built up the courage to say?

He didn't get it. He'd never been a fearful man a day in his life. So why the hell was he so afraid of his feelings for Rylee? *Because they shouldn't exist.* To be with Rylee, he would have to release the hold he had on the past. For so long, the memories had been a life preserver, the one thing keeping his head above water. Then had come Rylee, who made him feel as if he were floating without any kind of apparatus other than her presence.

When they arrived on the scene, a small crowd had amassed outside the menswear shop.

"What the hell is that on Mr. Herbert's head?" Rylee asked.

Canten squinted toward the man. "I don't know. A ferret, maybe?" he said.

Two of Canten's deputies stood between Old Man Patterson and Mr. Herbert. On second thought, he might not miss any of this at all.

Mr. Herbert folded his arms across his chest. "*Sher-reef Cun-tone,* this is official business. I need your full attention to this matter. What is your ladylove doing here?"

Canten dismounted. "I'm conducting a ride-along." He eyed Rylee, still sitting high on Ellington. "For educational purposes. Now, what seems to be the problem here?"

"And what exactly are you teaching?" Mr. Herbert asked.

"Conflict resolution. Now, what is the problem?"

The next thing out Mr. Herbert's mouth was how he disapproved of mixing business with pleasure and fraternizing on the clock. His opinion didn't matter, because Canten didn't need his approval.

"This imbecile's always trying to run everything. The only thing he's good at is running his big mouth," Old Man Patterson said. "And I'm about to stuff that ugly tie he's wearing in it."

"Bring it on," Mr. Herbert said. "Don't let this classy seersucker suit fool you."

Canten's deputies continued to hold each boisterous man back from the other. With Old Man Patterson's arthritic knees from years of farming and Mr. Herbert's bad hip from a fall he'd taken on the ice a few years back, neither man was in any condition to wage war on a fly, let alone each other.

Canten flashed his palms. "Let's just all calm down. What's the problem?" he asked a third time.

"That dang peacock of his chased me into my store," Mr. Herbert said.

Canten found that odd. Despite peacocks being territorial, Presto was one of the most mild-mannered creatures he'd ever come across.

Old Man Patterson jabbed a finger toward Mr. Herbert. "He probably had a flashback of when you and your crazy wife tried to steal one of his plumes."

"Don't you bad-mouth my Roberta," Mr. Herbert said. "And you better be glad that beast didn't get to me."

"I wish he had. Maybe he would have plucked that mockery of a toupee off your head."

Snickers came from the onlookers.

Mr. Herbert flashed a look of utter affront. "*Toupee?* I'll have you know this is all my hair."

All his hair? Canten wanted to know what type of hair-growth regimen Mr. Herbert had used that had produced a full head of dark locks overnight. Just yesterday the man had been practically bald.

"*Sher-reef Cun-tone,* here it comes again. Here it comes again," Mr. Herbert yelled, shielding himself with one of the deputies.

Canten eyed Presto, the fancy peacock who graced the streets of Honey Hill. Someone whistled, and Presto fanned his feathers in a showy display of colors—green, blue, orange—then spun as if modeling for the crowd. Everyone—except Mr. Herbert, of course—clapped and cheered for the majestic creature. After an encore spin, Presto strutted on to his next destination, not giving a second thought to Mr. Herbert.

"Herbert tossed a rock at Presto. Saw it with my own two eyes. That's why Presto came after him," came from an onlooker.

"Lies," Mr. Herbert said. "All lies."

Canten shook his head. Guilt was written all over Mr. Herbert's face.

"Why, you old scoundrel," Old Man Patterson said. "I'll teach you to toss rocks at my Presto."

"Bring it, you rickety-kneed heathen," Mr. Herbert shot back.

Lord, it's too dang hot for these shenanigans. With his patience wearing thin, Canten held up his hands. "Enough. I'll give you three options. Number one, the two of you go your separate ways. Number two, I have my men haul you both down to the station to cool off for a few hours. Number three, you duke it out right here and get it over with. In fact, that sounds like the best option since you're so determined to get at each other anyway."

Both men whipped their heads toward Canten. In unison, they said, "You want us to fight?"

"No. I want you to shake and go on about your business, but you two seem determined to brawl, so I'm going to allow you." Canten waved his men away, giving Old Man Patterson and Mr. Herbert free rein over each other. "You have ten minutes," he added.

"I-I don't really have on the right shoes," Mr. Herbert said.

"Yeah, and I-I don't want to scuff up a man's shoes," Old Man Patterson said.

"Your shoes will be fine, Mr. Herbert. And don't you worry, Mr. Patterson. If you scuff them up, I'll shine them myself. Now, let's get this thing started."

The hesitant men squared up, both holding their fists like neither had ever thrown a punch a day in their lives. Canten needed to prove his theory that they both were all talk and no jab. If it panned out how he suspected it would, he wouldn't have to worry about these two again.

"Um, are you sure about this, Sheriff?" one of his men asked.

Canten folded his arms across his chest. "Yep."

"They're kind of old. What if they have a heart attack or something?" the other deputy whispered.

"We call EMS," Canten said. He clapped his hands. "Okay, gentlemen, your time starts now."

Both men started shuffling their feet.

"Here it comes, Herbert. You better watch out. It's gonna strike like a lightning bolt," Old Man Patterson said.

"Take your best shot, Patterson." Mr. Herbert performed two mini punches that came nowhere near reaching his opponent.

The two men circled each other—verbally threatening to strike but not doing so—for the next five minutes. Canten had to bite back his laughter. This was the funniest thing he'd seen all month. And that was saying a lot for Honey Hill. Both men looked as if they needed to take breaks. Deciding to put them out of their misery, Canten intervened.

"I'll tell you what, gentlemen," Canten said. "Since you both handled yourselves so well, how about you shake like they do in the professionals and walk away."

Some of the chatter from the thinning crowd nearly made Canten laugh aloud, but he held it together, just barely.

Surprisingly, Mr. Herbert offered his hand first. "You were a fitting opponent, Patterson."

"You too, Herbert," Old Man Patterson said, gripping his hand.

"Great. Now that that's all settled, you gentlemen carry on with your day. No more rock throwing," Canten said, eyeing Mr. Herbert.

Mr. Herbert grumbled something under his breath, then scurried back into his shop.

"He better be glad you called it early," Old Man Patterson said. "I was about to really let him have it." A second later, the man hobbled off.

Canten returned to a waiting Rylee and remounted Ellington. He gave a yank of the reins, and they trotted off.

"That was hilarious," she said. "And impressive. The way you handled the situation."

"Thanks," he said. "Both men are all bark and no bite."

"Out of curiosity, what would you have done had one of them actually thrown a punch?"

"No chance of that happening," he said.

"How could you be so sure?"

Canten chuckled. "For one, Old Man Patterson has horrible range of motion after all those years working his fields. For two, Mr. Herbert probably couldn't even see Old Man Patterson. His eyesight is terrible, but he won't wear his glasses, because he says they make him look old."

"That's what makes you such a great sheriff. You know and care about the people of Honey Hill."

Yes, he did. And he cared about some far more than he should.

CHAPTER 27

When Canten had asked Rylee what she wanted to eat for lunch, she'd said pizza in the square. They'd swung by Jolly's Pizzeria, then found a shaded spot under a massive oak tree that had occupied the space long before the square was the square. Because of the plushness of the grass, they hadn't even needed a picnic blanket.

Crystal-clear skies, gentle breeze, perfect location, Canten. Rylee couldn't have asked for more. She took a bite of the pepperoni-supreme pizza with double cheese and moaned a sound of satisfaction. "Oh my God, that's good," she said.

"It sounds like it," Canten said, taking a bite from his own slice. "Damn, that *is* good."

Rylee hadn't been sure about Jolly's since it had changed ownership several months back. Surprisingly, the New York–style, thin-crust pizza tasted even better than it had in the past.

"So how long do you think it'll be before Mr. Herbert makes a call to Lunden to complain about our ride-along?"

Canten chuckled. "He already has. I got a message from Lunden when we were picking up the pizza."

"Oh no. Did I get you in trouble by riding with you?"

"No. The sheriff's department actually does have a Ride Along with the Sheriff program, so I wasn't breaking any protocols. Plus, Lunden implemented it. As a community-engagement initiative. I'm not sure many people know about it, though, because I've only had two people take advantage of it. You and Zachary."

Rylee laughed. "Zachary couldn't stop talking about his day with the sheriff. You really have a fan in that kid. Don't be surprised if he comes to work for you one day. Well, I guess I should say comes to work for Honey Hill Sheriff's Department since you're leaving to be a Charlotte big shot."

Her mouth curved upward into a smile, but she didn't truly feel the joy it symbolized. In a perfect world, Canten would stay in Honey Hill, she'd express her feelings for him, he would reciprocate, and they would live happily ever after. But this wasn't one of her romance novels. And nothing in life was perfect. More importantly, there could never be anything permanent between her and Canten when he was in a relationship with a ghost.

"I haven't been offered the job yet. There are several other candidates equally as qualified," Canten said. "I might not get it."

"You will. You have dedication, drive, a passion for serving. Those panelists saw all of those things in you, I'm sure. They know you'd be the perfect man for the job."

"Thank you."

Things were quiet for a moment.

"I'm going to miss you, Sheriff Canten."

"Charlotte's only a short drive away," he said. "You can come up anytime."

"Nah. I'd only be in the way. You'll have a new life. New people in your life. New places. New things."

Canten's expression turned serious. "We're friends, Rylee. We'll always be friends. That won't change if I move away. That won't change ever. You know that, right?"

Why couldn't he see that it would? What happened when he moved to Charlotte, eventually decided to give love another try, and met someone, started a new relationship? Did he think his new love would approve of them being friends? And could she bear seeing him with someone else, knowing that individual got to enjoy the pleasure of him? *We'll always be friends.* He was such an optimist. Instead of dampening his flawed vision, she said, "Right."

"And it's not like I won't ever return to Honey Hill. Senior wouldn't have that. Plus, you'll be back on the market soon. Some man's definitely going to snatch you up. He'd be a fool not to. Hopefully, you'll invite me to the wedding."

Deciding to play along, she said, "I promise yours will be the first invitation I send. You can even bring a plus-one."

A corner of Canten's mouth lifted but fell quickly.

Canten had believed he could handle this hypothetical conversation with Rylee. He couldn't. The second she'd said something about sending him a wedding invitation, a knot had yanked tight in his stomach. Served him right for bringing up anything about a wedding, especially hers. Like he'd ever be able to stand witness to Rylee meeting another man at the altar. The RSVP he returned would definitely be a *regretfully unable to attend* reply.

Selfishly, he'd wanted to hear her say a relationship was the furthest thing from her mind. She hadn't. And it affected him more than it should have. Charlotte would be the right move for him. With time, his feelings for Rylee would fade.

"We need music," Rylee said, pulling him from his thoughts.

Rylee fished her cell phone from her pocket and tapped an icon on the screen. The female crooner coming through the phone sang about needing to know how it felt to be loved. When she mentioned jealousy getting the best of her, Canten could relate because that was exactly what had gotten the best of him. The idea of another man occupying any of Rylee's time, even an imaginary one, had caused the negative emotion to root inside him.

Canten's eyes returned to Rylee when she started to sing along. A line about having no peace until getting clarity and needing to hear and see if she mattered at all. When Sebastian had once told him Rylee was like a songbird without a song, he'd thought he'd meant it figuratively to explain how he'd viewed her in her marriage.

Canten swore the birds in the trees stopped singing just to listen to her. At the conclusion of the song, Rylee's eyes fluttered open. A sheepish expression spread across her face.

"Sorry. I got lost for a second."

"Don't apologize. You sounded great. I didn't know you could sing like that."

"I don't," she said. "Not anymore."

Why did he get the feeling this, too, had something to do with her late husband? "I think you should start again," he said. "All the time. Any moment the feeling hits you. In fact, I want to amend our agreement to include a daily serenade."

Rylee pushed him playfully. "You wish."

Finishing his fourth slice of pizza, Canten stretched out on the carpet-soft grass. Rylee had picked the perfect spot. Locking his fingers behind his head, he closed his eyes.

"If you fall asleep, I'm leaving you here," she said.

He cracked a lid. "That's cold. Besides, who could sleep with all this noise?"

Rylee's brows knit. "What noise? All I hear are birds chirping."

"Exactly. They went quiet when you were singing. Maybe you should start again."

"I'll sing for you on your birthday."

Canten repositioned himself onto one elbow. "That's next March."

"Which means I'll have plenty of time to practice."

Rylee pulled her knees to her chest, rested her cheek against them, and stared at him. These moments, the ones when all they did was gaze into each other's eyes, brought him unexplainable peace.

"I stopped singing because of Lucas," she said.

I knew it.

"He had PTSD. At least, I suspected he did. All the signs were there. Behavioral changes, mood swings, insomnia, nightmares, when he actually slept. Repetitive noises caused him anxiety, including singing."

Her voice had had the opposite effect on him, but he didn't suffer from a debilitating disorder. Canten didn't doubt Rylee had been happy in her marriage, but it seemed as if she'd sacrificed a lot emotionally in the name of love. Was this why she hadn't dated in so long? Was she afraid to allow anyone to get too close? Afraid she'd be forced to sacrifice even more of herself? "Living like that had to be rough."

"I'm not sure how much living I did. Sometimes it felt as if I merely existed and nothing more. Some days I was so . . ." Her words dried up. "It must sound as if my marriage was horrible. It wasn't. Lucas and I had some really good times together that far outnumbered the not so good."

"Marriage is not always easy," he said. "But it's those difficult times that make it stronger. Two people determined to love each other through the trials and tribulations, that's love."

"You get it," she said.

"I do." He sat forward and rested his arms on his bent knees. "I was stuck for a long time after Jayla's death. I thought leaving Charlotte would help. It did a little. I thought filling a room with memories of our life together would help. It did a little. The room isn't a shrine, Rylee. But it was my oxygen for a long time. It had been a while since I'd gone inside." He glanced away briefly. "I was embarrassed, Rylee. That's why I didn't tell you about the room."

Worry etched her beautiful features. "Embarrassed, why?"

"Jayla's death was hard on me. Much harder than I'd admitted to anyone. The loss. The guilt. The idea that it had all been my fault. In my head, holding on to her memories would somehow absolve me."

"And now?" she asked.

"I'm letting go. I no longer need it to breathe. The light was on because I'd gone inside to pack the room up, but I got sidetracked. You showed up at my door, holding a cheesy chicken-broccoli-and-rice casserole," he said. "I couldn't turn away your casserole."

"If memory serves me right, we never actually got around to eating that night."

"I ate that night," he said. "Just not the casserole."

"Stop it," she said with a laugh.

He loved the sound of her laughter. Loved seeing her smile. Loved making her happy. "I need your help," he said.

"Sure. Wait, with what?"

"Painting the room. When I left your place last night, I went home and packed the room up. It was long overdue."

"Of course I'll help you." She chuckled. "You know, the last time we painted a room together, we wound up in a fake relationship. What do you think will happen this time?"

That was a good question.

CHAPTER 28

The bright lights, chimes, dings, screams, laughter took Rylee back to her childhood. And walking around the carnival—a large bag of cotton candy in her hand—had her feeling like a kid again. Had it not been for Zachary insisting she and Canten come along, Rylee would have missed out on all this fun.

Lunden, Zachary, and Quade had headed over to kiddie land while Rylee and Canten had explored. She eyed Canten, who carried a half-eaten corn dog in one hand and an oversize elephant he'd won for her in the other. The amount of money he'd spent on the dart game, he'd have come out cheaper simply offering the man fifty dollars to purchase the stuffed animal, but he'd been determined to score it for her.

Rylee pulled a chunk of the sugary confection off and held it out to Canten. "Want some? My hands are clean."

"I know. You've sanitized them like fifty times in the last thirty minutes."

When his soft, warm lips closed around her fingers, it sent a shiver up her spine. They hadn't had sex since the whole shrine thing, nearly a week ago. Her body craved his, but he no longer seemed interested in her sexually.

"Delicious," he said.

Crashing back to reality, she said, "It's a raspberry-blueberry mix."

"I wasn't referring to the cotton candy, though it was tasty too." He winked. "I'd almost forgotten how scrumptious your skin tastes."

"It seems as if you're no longer interested in my particular flavor."

Canten released a sexy chuckle. "I can see how you could have come to that conclusion." He stared straight ahead. "What you said bothered me, Rylee. Still bothers me." He looked at her. "But that didn't keep me from wanting you like crazy. I just needed you to come to me. I told myself that when—or if—you did, I would know you were convinced that it's *you* I see. No one else."

Wow. Had Canten thought the same thing she had? Had he questioned if she was still interested in him? "I wanted to come to you," Rylee said. "But I was afraid."

"Afraid? Of what?"

"Afraid you'd reject me."

Canten stopped walking and turned his entire body toward her. "Reject you?" He laughed. "Woman . . ." He shook his head. "How could you ever think that?"

"You no longer seemed interested. I know how it feels not to be wanted by someone who you—" She stopped abruptly. "I *never* want to feel that way again."

"Do you remember telling me I can have as much of you as I can handle?"

She nodded. "Yes."

"I'm nowhere near reaching my limit."

A smile lifted one corner of her mouth. They started to move again. Every so often, someone stopped them to tell Canten they'd heard he'd be leaving soon and how sad they were to see him go. Continuously, he had to repeat the same line: the decision hadn't been made. No one seemed convinced of that. Probably because they all had her same thought: the Charlotte-Mecklenburg Police Department would be fools not to want him on their roster.

As for herself, she winced every time someone commented about knowing how much she would miss him. None of them could possibly know. What Rylee found odd was the fact no one had asked if she'd be relocating with him. Not one single person. Had they held doubt about their relationship from the start?

"Let's go on the Ferris wheel," Canten said, yanking Rylee from her thoughts. "I need a reprieve from all the premature good wishes."

So did she.

Rylee's eyes swept the sky. At the top, she could see all of Honey Hill. Even from up there, it was still the most beautiful place on earth. Why would anyone ever want to leave? "It's so beautiful up here," she said.

"Yes, it is."

When she looked at Canten, his eyes weren't on the town; they were on her. "So after we're done here, would you like to come back to my place for a nightcap?" she asked. By *nightcap*, she meant an entire night of hot, unbridled lovemaking. They needed to make up for lost time.

Canten's eyes lowered to her mouth. "I would prefer dessert," he said. His gaze rose slowly. "Something . . . sinfully delicious."

"I think I have one or two things that will satisfy your sweet tooth."

Rylee and Canten met back up with Lunden, Quade, and Zachary a little after nine. When Lunden invited them over to their place for drinks, Rylee promptly declined, citing a slight headache. "Too much sugar," she said. The truth: she needed to be fu—

"Funnel cakes," Zachary said. "*Funnel cakes, funnel cakes, funnel cakes,*" he repeated, bouncing up and down and pointing to a food truck plastered with images of the fried dough.

Lunden ran a hand over her son's head. "Oh, I think you've had enough sugar for one night."

"*Please, please, please,*" he said, cupping his fingers under his chin like he was praying. "I won't eat the whole thing. Cross my heart."

Zachary made a huge X on his chest. Appropriate since his heart was gigantic.

"*Okay, okay, okay.* But just a small piece," Lunden said.

Zachary pumped a tiny fist in the air. "Yes. Are you coming, Aunt Rylee?"

Rylee knelt to Zachary's level. "No, sweetie. I'm going to head home. But I am so happy you invited me. I had loads of fun."

"You're welcome. I like spending time with you and Sheriff Canten. You're my second-favorite people. My mom and dad are my first." Zachary looked around. "Hey, where's my dad?"

Rylee glanced over her shoulder, spotting Canten and Quade off to the side, talking. They looked to be in deep conversation. Canten stood with his arms crossed over his chest and appeared to be listening intently.

When Canten massaged the side of his neck, Rylee's brows furrowed. What were they talking about? A second later, both men glanced in her direction. She turned away quickly as if she'd been caught peeping through the keyhole of a door.

After hugs and goodbyes, Rylee and Canten headed to her place. The second they entered, Canten pinned her back against the closed door and kissed her as if her lips were the only things keeping him alive. Obviously, he'd missed her mouth as much as she'd missed his.

Traces of sweetness still lingered on his tongue from the cotton candy he'd eaten on the drive home. When Canten rested his hands on either side of her neck and deepened the kiss, she whimpered in pleasure.

In a swift motion, Canten scooped her into his arms. Instead of locking lips again, they held each other's gazes in an intense and silent journey toward her bedroom. She'd stared into his eyes a hundred times before, but she saw something different in them tonight. Something so tender and sweet it made her heart flutter.

Inside the bedroom, they wasted no time stripping down and climbing into bed. Canten peppered kisses on her inner thigh before claiming her sex. Damn, she'd missed his mouth on her. Her toes curled when he hooked two fingers inside her and worked them slowly in and out. His skillful tongue circled her clit in a slow, deliberate manner. When he gently suckled her between his lips, she lost control as a powerful orgasm took hold of her.

Rylee held Canten's head in place as she cried out his name. The room spun around her, forcing her to close her eyes. Blood whooshed in her ears. Her heart pounded in her chest. Legs shook. Teeth chattered. Canten kissed a trail up her body and pulled one of her taut nipples into his mouth, teasing it with his tongue. The action electrified her even more. Kissing his way to the opposite breast, he lavished it with equal attention, then made his way to her mouth.

Against her lips, he said, "I want you so bad I'm not sure how long I can keep it together. Don't hold it against me if I don't last too long."

"Give me what you got," she said, hungrily claiming his mouth.

Canten pushed inside her. More a gentle glide than a powerful thrust. "Damn, I've missed being inside you," he said against her lips. "I don't know how I'm going to . . ." His words dried up. "I feel you everywhere."

Rylee wanted to admit she felt him everywhere, too, but she couldn't speak, could hardly think straight. A tingling sensation bloomed between her legs. The muscles in her stomach tightened. Her heart rate ticked up. With the impending release gripping her body, she held on by threads. Canten's unhurried strokes clipped them, one by one, catapulting her over the edge and into another powerful orgasm.

Canten tore his mouth from hers and buried his face in the crook of her neck. *"Rylee—"* A beat later, he grunted as if he'd been punched in the stomach with an iron fist.

The feel of Canten throbbing inside her supercharged the currents sparking through her, and she came again. How was that even possible? What had this man done to her body? She'd never reached these sexual heights before.

Canten's body collapsed down onto hers as if every joule of his energy had released at the same time he had. Their chests rose and fell in sync and hearts thudded in harmonious rhythm.

"I can't move," he said.

Finding her voice, she said, "I don't want you to. I want you to stay." Her arms tightened around him. "Stay here with me."

While Rylee knew Canten had been referring to not being able to move from his current position, she'd been talking about something else entirely. Not only did she want him to stay as he was now, but she also wanted him to stay in Honey Hill. But that wasn't possible without him having to defer his plan.

Canten was convinced his day couldn't get any more chaotic. It just wasn't possible after the morning he'd had. At seven, he'd gotten a call from an irate goat farmer, complaining that their local aerial crop duster had intentionally buzzed his goats, causing them all to faint.

At eight thirty, when someone had come into the station to report their neighbor for painting his own horse lime green and Canten had stated there was nothing he could do about it, he'd been subjected to a near hour-long lecture on animal cruelty.

It hadn't stopped there. At ten, Ms. Paulina Benderhyme had arrived to report her dog, Francisco, had run away from home. When one of his deputies had suggested that maybe Francisco had no longer liked living there, the woman had cried for twenty minutes. He'd signed the deputy up for sensitivity training on principle.

And it got better. Canten's favorite of the day, thus far, had been around noon, when Ms. Ruda Tolbert had actually walked into the station with her head held high and lodged a grievance about Deacon Dewberry for not properly seasoning the chicken at the recent church picnic. He'd had to tell her assault on the taste buds wasn't a chargeable offense.

When Canten had started the job as the sheriff, he'd made it his mission to be a sheriff of the people, not just to sit behind a closed door all day, as it had been rumored his predecessor had done. Fast-forward to present day—maybe he should have placed some stipulations on his availability.

"Pardon me, Sheriff," came from his speakerphone.

Canten dropped his head on his desk. *No more.* "Yes, Fallon."

"Um, your ride-along is here."

Shit. Canten eyed his desk calendar. *Is that today?* Had he remembered, he would have definitely canceled. For some reason, there had been renewed interest in the program. He guessed he should have been thrilled that the townsfolk wanted to hang out with him. And any other day he probably would have been. But today, he'd had just about all the excitement he could handle.

It's only thirty minutes. You can do half an hour. A quick circle around town, a stop at Rylee's bakery for the Ride Along with the Sheriff complimentary cupcake, a picture or two for social media, and he'd be done. The idea of seeing Rylee made it less daunting. Plus, he wanted to check on her. These past couple of days, she hadn't been herself. He knew it had to do with the fact her parents would be leaving soon.

"Sheriff, you there?"

"Yes. Please put them in the conference room and make sure they sign the necessary forms." Zeta, the town attorney, had insisted individuals wanting to take part in the program sign a waiver releasing the town from any liability claims. Smart move. "Will you also make sure the utility vehicle is gassed up and ready to go?"

"Will do, Sheriff." Fallon's voice dropped to a whisper. "Um, Sheriff?"

"Uh-huh?"

A pause.

"Never mind," she said, then clicked off the line.

Yep, this day is getting weirder and weirder.

After giving Fallon enough time to complete her tasks, Canten stood, rounded the desk, and headed to the conference room. Stopping at the front desk, he queried Fallon on the names of the individuals he'd be taking out. He liked making his interactions as personal as possible.

"There's only one person," she said. "It's, um, Katrina Sweeney."

Convinced he'd misheard the name Fallon had given, he said, "Who?"

Fallon massaged the side of her neck in what he took to be a nervous tic.

"Katrina Sweeney. I didn't schedule her," she said.

Dammit, he'd heard her correctly. What had he done to piss the universe off? Keeping things professional, he nodded. "Thanks, Fallon." He cussed all the way to the conference room. When he entered the room, it felt twenty degrees colder than usual. An icy chill shot up his spine.

Canten kept things as generic and professional as possible with Katrina. Addressed her as Ms. Sweeney. Shook her hand as he would have anyone else. Laid out the game plan. His skin crawled at the way her hungry eyes raked over him. This would be the longest damn half hour of his life.

"I thought the ride-along was on a horse," Katrina said as they approached the utility vehicle.

"It's a liability thing," he said.

"But I signed a waiver."

"For the utility vehicle."

"Then where's the waiver for the horse? I'll sign it."

Canten slid behind the wheel and cranked the engine. "There isn't one. Utility vehicle only."

"I guess you have to be a snot-nosed kid or sleeping with the sheriff," she said just loudly enough for him to hear.

Slipping on his sunglasses, Canten grumbled under his breath, then punched the gas. As if being here with Katrina weren't bad enough, she pulled out her cell phone and went live on social media.

"Hi, my sweets. Have I got a treat for you. I'm doing a ride-along. Yep, you heard that right. Just like Kevin Hart. Your girl K. K. Sweeney is gallivanting around town with the one, the only, Sheriff Canten Barnes."

K. K. Sweeney?

"Say hello to my followers, Sheriff Barnes."

"Hey," he said dryly, never taking his eyes off the road. *Note to self: have Zeta put in a clause banning live videos.*

"Let's read some comments. Marlo715, yes, he is handsome. That's right, BlackOnyx24, you should make a trip to Honey Hill for a ride-along too. Well, I don't know, MahoganyBrown, let's ask."

Canten tensed when Katrina turned the camera toward him again.

"Sheriff Barnes, MahoganyBrown would like to know if you work out regularly, because your arms are ripped."

He gave a single laugh but didn't respond beyond that.

"Oooh, that's a good question, Tandi007. Yes, he's single, so—"

"Actually, I'm not," Canten said. "I'm seeing the beautiful goddess who owns and operates Pastries on Main here in Honey Hill. She ships nationwide. Check her out at www—"

"Well, you know what they say," Katrina said, reclaiming the spotlight. "You're still single until there's a ring on it." She panned to his hand. "Nothing there. Okay, sweeties, that's it for now. I will see you all soon. Keep it sexy."

Katrina ended the recording, then eyed him with a scowl.

"What the hell was that?" she asked. "Why are you shouting out businesses on my video? I don't give free advertisement. And why did you say you were seeing someone? Everyone knows you have one foot out the door."

Canten slammed on the brakes. Katrina's phone flew one direction, and she bounced the other.

"Are you insane?" she asked, retrieving her phone from the floor.

"This conversation is long overdue," he said. "The night I drove you home, I was simply being cordial. There was absolutely no romantic intent. The fact you turned it into something more than it was isn't cool. I'm not, nor have I ever been, nor will I ever be, into you in that way."

Canten hadn't wanted to sound cruel, but he knew you had to be direct with people like Katrina, who bordered on being crazy as hell. Being straightforward in a similar situation with Leonard had worked for Rylee. He hoped it would for this particular member of the Jamison clan.

"Then why did you hold the umbrella over my head, walk me to the door, wait until I was safe in the house?"

Jesus. Was she serious right now? "I held the umbrella because it was raining." That should have been obvious. "I walked you to your porch because it was my umbrella." He loved that umbrella and didn't want to risk never getting it back. "The reason I waited until you were safely inside . . ." He shrugged. "I was raised to be a gentleman." She would have to blame Senior for that.

Katrina shifted away from him. "You're one of the few," she mumbled, her eyes lowering to the phone in her hand. "I'm not really *that* into you either," she said. "But I was a little. What woman wouldn't be?" She sighed heavily. "Hilary convinced me I had a chance with you. Now I'm realizing she probably only said it to mess with Rylee. She has something against her and Lunden."

He got why Hilary would want to mess with Lunden, because of Quade—who Hilary had once had her sights on—but what did she gain from agitating Rylee? Then it occurred to him. Guilty by association. Hilary had wanted to get to Lunden through Rylee.

"So we're on the same page now, right?" he said.

"And you're sure there's no chance that we—"

"Katrina . . ."

She laughed. "Just making sure. Yes, we're on the same page."

Finally.

"You really love her, huh?"

The question caught him off guard, but his brain immediately processed the answer; however, he didn't allow it to fly out his mouth. He wouldn't dare trust Katrina with such sensitive information, especially since he hadn't even told Rylee how he felt. At this point, he wasn't sure he ever would.

CHAPTER 29

With a few minutes to spare before Lunden arrived, Rylee opened her personal email and sighed at the fifty-plus notifications she found there. Usually, she checked it every night, but Canten had kept her so busy—getting busy—she'd skipped a day or three. The man was insatiable.

Sorting by sender, she did a batch delete of all the junk emails, which made her inbox dwindle by half. She flagged the promotional ones offering discounts to her favorite stores. The email from her online pharmacy provider made her roll her eyes at the screen. Had her physician's office failed to renew her birth control prescription again? The way Canten had practically lived inside her these past few days, she couldn't risk a lapse in protection.

The urgent subject line caught her eye. RECALL was typed in all caps, followed by the drug name. *This can't be good.* She swallowed hard and clicked the message to open it. Red bold letters at the top read: IMMEDIATE ACTION REQUIRED! As she browsed the body text, her heart rate increased and the room grew scorching hot.

Nationwide voluntary recall. Packaging error. Increased possibility of unintended pregnancy. Placebo. Stop use immediately. Rylee's head swam. "*No, no, no.* This can't be happening." Her heart banged against her rib cage. How could they have sent out a bad lot of birth control pills? Weren't there safeguards to protect against this kind of thing before they ever left the plant?

Rylee's breathing became ragged, and she was sure she was about to hyperventilate. Closing her eyes, she focused on steadying her breath. Resting a hand against her clammy forehead, she reread the email. Maybe her pills weren't a part of the defective batch.

She laughed at herself. As usual, she'd overreacted. Besides, she knew her body and would know if she were pregnant. Right? With a tremble in her hands, she phoned Lunden.

"I'm on my way, I promise," Lunden said in lieu of a customary greeting.

"I need a huge favor," Rylee said.

Fifteen minutes later, someone burst through Rylee's front door, dressed in black from head to toe. She screamed and grabbed the closest thing to her to use as a weapon—a jar candle—and drew back to hurl it toward the intruder.

"Don't throw that. It's me."

Rylee's brows banged together. "Lunden?"

Lunden removed her sunglasses and the hood of the sweatshirt she wore. "Yes."

"Why are you dressed like a damn ninja? You scared the hell out of me. And why are you whispering?"

"I didn't want anyone to recognize me at the drugstore, especially purchasing a pregnancy test. And the door is open. I don't want anyone to hear me." She passed Rylee the plastic bag. "I think I nearly blacked out at the counter. It felt like I was trying to cross the border with a trunk full of illegal narcotics and the *Federales* were closing in. I grabbed the first box I saw and got out of there."

With her nerves frayed, Rylee still laughed at Lunden's use of the term *Federales*, from one of Rylee's favorite Martin Lawrence movies.

"I don't know why *I* was so nervous. I'm not the one who's pregnant."

"Lu!" Rylee said. "Why are you jinxing me?"

"Sorry. Sorry," she repeated. "How late are you?" Lunden asked.

"I don't know that I am. I'm irregular. Sometimes my cycle skips a month, even two." Rylee wouldn't have even considered being pregnant had it not been for that damn email.

"Take the test already. I need to know if I'm going to be an auntie." Lunden clapped like an excited toddler at Christmas.

"This is not a happy occasion. What if I'm pregnant? I'm not prepared to be a single mother." Yes, she knew women had been raising children alone since the beginning of time. But this was not how she'd envisioned welcoming her first child into the world. She in one city, the father in another. Designing calendars that determined who got them on which holiday. She didn't want that for her child.

Lunden guided her toward the bathroom. "Let's discuss this *after* you take the test."

"Okay. Okay. Yeah, you're right. I could be getting worked up for nothing," Rylee said.

Inside the bathroom, Rylee tore into the box. She didn't bother reading the instructions, because she'd done this a thousand times when she and Lucas had first been married. While Lucas had wanted to start a family immediately, she'd wanted to wait a couple of years to get the full experience of being newlyweds. Ultimately, she'd given in to what he'd wanted.

Rylee sat on the commode and put the stick in place. Nothing came. Which was odd because minutes ago it had felt as if she'd consumed ten gallons of water. *Relax.*

As she waited for her bladder to cooperate, her mind wandered. Had that been the start of her and Lucas's marital problems? Her trouble with conceiving? They'd tried and tried with no success. Instead of beating herself up, she'd chalked it up to something that would happen when it was meant to happen. It never had.

Finally, she thought, wetting the plastic.

Lunden banged on the door. "Are you done yet? What's taking so long?"

"*Shit,*" Rylee said.

"What's wrong?" Lunden asked, her voice laced with concern. "You okay? Is it positive?"

"You scared me. I dropped the test in the toilet."

Lunden laughed.

"It's not funny. It's not funny," she repeated, laughing a little.

After three bottles of water and a prayer, Rylee felt the urge to go again. She retrieved another test from the multiple-count box. This time she successfully completed the task. After placing it on the counter and washing her hands, she joined Lunden out front. Hugging her BFF, she said, "Thank you for always having my back. I love you."

"Always. And I love you right back." Lunden held her at arm's length. "You do know if you are pregnant that you're not alone, right?"

Rylee nodded, fighting the tears threatening to fall.

Moments later, Rylee paced in one direction, Lunden in the other. Rylee's thoughts were all over the place. Eyeing her trembling hand, she wished Canten were there to wrap his protective arms around her. That would make her feel so much better. Oh God. What was she saying? Here was the last place Canten needed to be. What would she do if he walked through the door right now? The possibility catapulted her onto another level of panic.

How would she tell him she was carrying his child? Rylee shook her hands as if slinging off water. *Stop getting ahead of yourself. You're not pregnant, silly woman. The universe is looking out for you. You got a good batch of pills. There's no baby in your belly and no need to worry. You would know. Right?*

"*Stupid, stupid, stupid,*" Rylee said more to herself than Lunden. "I should have insisted Canten wore a rubber. I was reckless. We're not even in a committed relationship."

"Stop beating yourself up. What's done is done," Lunden said.

Rylee hugged her arms around her body. "He's going to hate me, Lu. He's going to think I got pregnant to trap him here. I didn't."

"Canten knows you'd never do that," Lunden said.

She hoped so.

When the timer sounded, both Rylee and Lunden yelped, then stared at each other as if an intruder had entered and neither knew which direction to run. Snapping out of it, Rylee rushed into the bathroom, Lunden on her heels.

Snatching the test from the counter, Rylee studied it. A beat later, her legs turned to noodles at the sight of the two pink lines. The plastic stick fell from her fingers as she dropped onto the closed toilet seat. "This can't be happening," she said. "It's wrong. I have to take another one."

Four positive tests later, Rylee rested a hand on her stomach. *I'm going to be a mother.* She almost smiled because, at one point, there had been nothing she'd wanted more. And she still wanted it. *Just not like this.*

"What am I going to do, Lu?" Rylee asked.

"Get out of this bathtub, for starters?" Lunden said.

"I'm never getting out."

After the last test, instead of returning to the living room, Rylee had taken up residence in the empty bathtub. Lunden had joined her, occupying the opposite end. Rylee had gone through nearly all the stages of grief in the roughly twenty minutes they'd been in the waterless basin. However, she struggled with acceptance. Her inability to embrace her reality didn't alter the fact her life would forever be changed.

"I'm suing," Rylee said. "I'm suing the drugmaker. I'm suing the pharmacy. I'm suing the post office for delivering the worthless contraception."

"I know it's a shock now, but you're going to be a mother, Ry. You're bringing life into the world." Lunden reached over and collected what remained of the box of pregnancy tests from the floor and pointed to the smiling baby gracing the front. "Look at that adorable face. One of these will be staring up at you every single day."

Rylee smiled a little, then squinted. Seconds later, she snatched the box from Lunden. A second after that, she reached over and retrieved the trash can holding the discarded tests. *Purple. All purple.* "*Lunden Cannon!*"

Lunden jolted forward. "What?"

"These aren't pregnancy tests. I've been taking ovulation tests."

Lunden reclaimed the box. *"Ovulation tests?"* She studied the front. "Look how tiny that writing is. Oh my God. I'm sorry, Ry. Like I said, I grabbed the first box I saw. I thought they were pregnancy tests. Who places ovulation tests alongside pregnancy tests? *I love you.* And we'll laugh about this one day." She gave a nervous chuckle. She pointed to a corner of the box. "The good news is it says right here there's one pregnancy test included. It's the one with the blue writing."

Rylee smiled so wide it felt as if the corners of her mouth would crack. An included pregnancy test wasn't the good news. The truly good news was the fact that if she was ovulating, she couldn't be pregnant. Both relief and a little disappointment swirled inside her. For as much as she hadn't wanted to be pregnant, a part of her had because a baby meant she would never be alone again.

Canten had almost gotten through his day without any commotion. But when he heard what sounded like a collision outside his office window, he knew his quiet streak had come to an end. Dreading it, he peered through the slats of his blinds. An intense glare temporarily robbed him of sight. Squinting, he drew back from the window and readjusted his focus. Instead of waiting to be summoned, he rushed from his office to see what had transpired outside his window.

He rounded the corner of the brick building that housed the sheriff's department. "What the . . . ?"

Cantaloupe, corn, squash, watermelon, and zucchini littered the road. Canten recognized the banged-up teal-colored 1954 Ford F100 as belonging to the Whitman farm. A tall, brown-skinned older man fumbled out of the vehicle. *Sam Whitman.* Patriarch of the Whitman clan. Thankfully, he appeared to be okay but was visibly shaken.

"Are you hurt, Mr. Whitman?" Canten asked.

"No. But look at Delloreese," he said, fanning his hand the length of his vehicle. "She's ruined."

Canten didn't have to ask to know the truck had been named after the late actress Della Reese. Everyone in town knew how much Sam Whitman had loved the talented woman. "What happened?"

Mr. Whitman pointed to the 1975 AMC Pacer—painted a reflective metallic silver—pulled off on the side of the road. *Oh shit,* Canten said to himself when he saw who Deputy Kemp chatted with. *Roberta Jamison. This family is going to be the death of me.*

Roberta Jamison, Honey Hill's mayor before Lunden, was a little over five feet in both directions with deep-brown skin and a head full of unruly blonde curls. Like most of the elders in town, she, too, was outspoken, feisty, frisky, and eccentric.

"That damn-gone monstrosity is what happened. Blinded me while I was coming down the road. Made me wrap Delloreese round this pole."

Canten wouldn't exactly call it wrapped around, but Mr. Whitman would definitely need some extensive bodywork. Why in the hell was Mrs. Jamison driving a mirror on wheels?

"Hang tight, Mr. Whitman. EMS will be here soon to check you out." Just as the words escaped, Canten heard the sirens. "I'll be right back."

Canten squinted as he approached Deputy Kemp and Mrs. Jamison. "Afternoon, Mrs. Jamison," he said.

"Oh, Sheriff. I'm so glad you're here. I feel safer already."

When Mrs. Jamison wrapped her arms around Canten in a tight hug, it caught him off guard. He slid a glance in Deputy Kemp's direction that screamed, *Help me.* The only assistance Deputy Kemp offered was a shrug.

"Sheriff, have you been working out? You're so firm," Mrs. Jamison said.

"*Sher-reef Cun-tone*, you remove your hands from my Roberta this instant."

What hands? Canten wanted to ask Mr. Herbert since Canten's were in the air as if someone held a gun to his back. He should have been instructing his wife to remove *her* hands since they were the offending ones.

Mrs. Jamison released Canten. "Oh, hush up, Herbert. You're so jealous," she said with a wide, adoring smile. Apparently, she liked being fussed over.

Mr. Herbert pulled his wife closer to him in a possessive manner. "I assume you will be charging Sam for nearly causing my Roberta to crash her brand-new giddyap."

Don't ask. Don't you dare ask. "Giddyap?" Canten asked. Obviously, he was a glutton for punishment; however, he needed to make sure they were on the same page.

Mr. Herbert beamed almost as bright as the Pacer. "Our grandson gave my Roberta this fine automobile a few days ago. Said the second he saw it, he thought of her." He ran his hand over the exterior of the car, then snatched it away and shook it as if it were on fire.

Canten eyed the automobile. "It's . . . something special, indeed," he said.

Deputy Kemp snickered but cleared his throat and sobered immediately when they all looked at him.

Canten continued, "I do, however, have concerns about the reflective nature of the paint."

"What kind of concerns?" Mrs. Jamison asked.

Mr. Herbert rested a hand on his hip. "Yeah, what kind of concerns?" he echoed.

"For starters, it blinded Mr. Whitman and caused him to hit a telephone pole."

Mr. Herbert shrilled, "Nonsense. His homemade scuppernong wine is probably what caused him to hit that pole, not my Roberta's giddyap. I demand you make Sam take a Breathalyzer."

Mr. Herbert and his demands.

"It's okay, Honey Bear. It's okay," Mrs. Jamison said, patting Mr. Herbert on the chest.

Honey Bear? With a name like that, you'd have expected the holder to be sweet. Mr. Herbert definitely gravitated more toward the bear aspect of the name.

"You don't need to get worked up. It messes with your testosterone," Mrs. Jamison added. "We need it for later."

Canten gagged a little. *Shoot me now.*

A half hour later, Canten headed back into the station. On his way inside, he was stopped by the mail carrier to sign for an envelope addressed to him. Scribbling his name on the electronic board, Canten accepted the large envelope. Noting the sender, he froze. *Charlotte-Mecklenburg Police Department.* A letter instead of a phone call? Did that mean bad news?

Hurrying into his office, Canten closed the door behind him, tore into the envelope, removed the pages inside, and read. Finishing the last page, he blew a heavy breath and smiled. It hadn't been bad news at all. He'd been offered the position as bureau commander and at a salary almost double what he received as sheriff of Honey Hill. *The job's mine.* So why wasn't he as thrilled about it as he should have been?

Later that evening, Canten arrived at Senior's place for a celebratory dinner. While his father had prepared some of his favorites—smothered cube steak, homemade mashed potatoes, sautéed green beans—Canten didn't have much of an appetite.

"Son, you sure don't look like a man who just landed the job of his dreams," Senior said, cutting into Canten's thoughts.

Canten's gaze rose. "Hmm?"

Senior chuckled. "What's going on with you, son? You've been as quiet as a church mouse since you arrived."

"Sorry. Just thinking about everything I need to get done. I scheduled an appointment with the Realtor to put the house on the market. Looked online at apartments in Charlotte. The prices aren't how I remember them. I guess I need to schedule the movers."

"You sure are doing a lot for someone who hasn't officially accepted the offer yet," Senior said, forking a piece of meat into his mouth. "I would have thought you'd have given them a call as soon as you read the letter."

"I have a couple of weeks to accept the terms. No rush," Canten said.

"Definitely don't want to rush into anything," Senior said.

Canten got the impression his father's words held a hidden message.

"Have you shared the good news with Rylee?"

Canten rotated the half-full beer bottle against the table. "Not yet. I think I'll wait until after her parents leave this weekend. I know Rylee. She'll want to have a dinner party or something." The fact her parents were leaving would be taxing enough on her.

Senior did that squinting-one-eye thing he did when there was something he wanted to say, right before deciding it was none of his business and clamming up. Usually, Canten would urge it out of him. *Not tonight.* He wasn't sure he could handle anything heavy.

Silence descended on them.

"I sure am proud of you, son. You've wanted this opportunity for a long while. Now you have it."

Yes, he did. Canten recalled the numerous conversations he and Jayla had once had about this very moment. They'd fantasized about the large house they would purchase with his increased salary and one day fill with kids. Jayla had told him exactly how each room in the house would be decorated. All the possibilities had made her beam. Had made them both beam. So why wasn't he just as elated now? Their dream had come true. "Thanks, Pop."

"And that salary. Whew."

"It's nice," Canten said. But the money didn't motivate him. He'd survived the past several years on much less. With the low cost of living in Honey Hill, his current salary could be considered a fortune.

Senior stirred his mashed potatoes. "With money like that, you'll be able to afford any place you want."

Canten pushed his green beans around on the plate. "Yep." He hoped he could find a place that brought him as much comfort and joy as his current home here in Honey Hill had all these years. He didn't need anything huge since it would only be himself occupying the space. *Just me.*

"And that title. *Bureau commander.* You're sure to garner a lot of respect with a powerful label like that. My son, the *bureau commander.*"

Senior shook his head, a proud smile on his face. But the glow didn't mask the sadness Canten saw in his eyes. Watching him leave would be hard on Senior. Just as hard as it would be for Canten to say goodbye. But it wasn't like he was moving to another planet. *I'll visit. All the time.* Well, maybe not all the time. By the way the panelists had made it sound, this job would keep him busy. *I'll visit as often as possible.*

"You're probably right," Canten said. But he doubted it would give him the same feel as being a small-town sheriff. Here, he got to see how he'd helped someone. Whether it was chasing fleeing alpacas, coaxing peacocks from trees, or simply walking one of the elders home.

"Strange," Senior said.

Floating back to reality, Canten said, "What's that?"

"Such a bounty of blessings would have most men beaming from ear to ear. You haven't cracked a smile." Senior's brows creased with lines of concern. "You having second thoughts, son?"

Canten gave a jittery laugh. "No. No," he repeated. He sighed. "It's just that . . ." His words trailed.

"Just that what, son?"

Canten glanced away briefly. "It's just that I never intended on falling in love with Rylee."

The corners of Senior's lips twitched slightly but didn't blossom into the smile Canten could tell he was concealing. The news undoubtedly made Senior ecstatic. The man hadn't exactly hidden the fact he favored Rylee.

Senior sat a little straighter in his chair. "Well, that certainly complicates things, doesn't it?"

Canten downed the rest of his beer. *It damn sure does.*

CHAPTER 30

Several days had passed since Rylee's ovulation-test incident, and she still hadn't fully recovered. This week had been exhausting. First, a pregnancy scare. Thanks to a best friend who apparently couldn't read when nervous. Then chaos at the bakery. The *Honey Hill Herald* had run the incorrect cookie coupon in the paper. It should have read: *Buy one, get one free*. They'd left off the *Buy one*, and everyone had rushed in to get their free cookie.

Honoring the misprint, she'd had to bake cookies nonstop to accommodate everyone. People she hadn't recognized as locals had come to collect too. Ever since Canten had shouted out her shop during his ride-along with Katrina (and yes, she'd been a little jealous Katrina had gotten some of his time), new faces were in the shop regularly.

Katrina's followers had been so moved by Canten's support of Rylee that they'd rallied Katrina to do a live from the bakery. Rylee could only imagine how off putting it must have been for Katrina to have to come to her for help. Of course, Rylee had agreed. No sense in turning down free advertising.

And if all these events hadn't been enough for one week, now she had to deal with this, her parents' departure. Since their arrival three months ago, she'd dreaded this day. While they'd stayed in Honey Hill a week longer than originally planned, it still hadn't made their departure any easier on her.

As Rylee stood in her kitchen and packed her parents' sandwiches for the road, it took everything inside her to hold the tears in. Her mother and father were perfectly capable of taking care of themselves. They'd done so long before she'd ever been a thought. But their years of experience didn't stop her from worrying about them, especially when her mother had confessed that her father had been struggling with his blood pressure months prior to their arrival in Honey Hill.

Rylee had known her mother had been hiding something when they'd first arrived. Now she knew it had been her father's health issues. Maybe she should pack up and move to Florida. She laughed at herself. Honey Hill was the only place that had ever felt like home. She'd never leave. *Pull yourself together.*

Did her overly emotional state have something to do with the fact her parents' departure signaled the end of her and Canten's charade? They'd agreed to not dissolve their relationship until next month, because doing so now would seem far too abrupt. Still, it felt as if she were losing him this second.

Her eyes landed on Canten across the room, entertaining her parents. They loved him so much. Rylee prayed that wouldn't change once she told them they were no longer an item. Another wave of emotion hit her, causing her eyes to mist. As if her mother sensed her turmoil, she glanced in Rylee's direction. Rylee averted her tear-filled gaze and hoped her mother wouldn't join her in the kitchen.

Hormones, she told herself. *It's hormones.* She blew a heavy breath. Between her current stress level and cramps, she was surprised she hadn't gone delirious. *Give it time.*

Just as suspected, Mrs. Charles made her way to her daughter. First, she pretended to need some water, despite having an unopened bottle on the counter. Next, she cited wanting to help Rylee. Finally, she flat-out confessed her reason for being there. "I saw the tears in your eyes.

You have to at least tell him how you feel about his leaving. If you don't, it's going to eat you up inside," Mrs. Charles whispered.

Rylee turned her back to her father and Canten. In an equally muted tone, she said, "If you must know, these tears are for you and Daddy. I don't want you guys to leave."

"Something tells me our staying would not do a thing for the sadness I see in your eyes."

"We can test it out to confirm."

Mrs. Charles sighed. "Sweetheart, what's really going on?"

Rylee rested her backside against the counter and blinked rapidly to keep the tears stinging her eyes from falling. "I'm losing everyone I love. Sebastian's rarely in town. You and Daddy are leaving."

"And Canten may be headed to Charlotte," Mrs. Charles said, rubbing Rylee's back.

Rylee nodded.

"Sweetheart, you're not *losing* any of us. Regardless of where we are in the world, we're always with you." Mrs. Charles placed a hand over her daughter's heart. "Until those times when we can physically be together, you can find each one of us here."

"Everything okay?"

Though gentle, the sound of Canten's voice startled Rylee. She shifted away from him to swipe her tears.

"I think your *buttercup* needs a hug," Mrs. Charles said, rubbing a hand up and down Rylee's arm before leaving them alone.

"Just tired," Rylee said.

Canten didn't hesitate to envelop her in his strong arms and hold her snugly to his chest. She pulled in a lungful of his delicious scent. His smell, the feel of his solid frame, the warmth of his body, only made her even more emotional.

"They'll be okay," Canten whispered into her ear.

Pushing out of his hold, Rylee said, "I know," then washed her hands and returned to making sandwiches.

"Mr. and Mrs. Charles, how about Rylee and I drive you two to Florida?" Canten said. "We can catch a flight back tomorrow."

What? Rylee eyed Canten, taken aback by his offer. He wanted to drive her parents to Florida? Had he suggested this to give her more time with them? When he winked at her, she knew he had.

"Thank you for the offer," Mr. Charles said, wrapping an arm around Mrs. Charles, "but I must decline. Mother and I are looking forward to the drive back. Just the two of us." He stared longingly into his wife's eyes. "Who knows, we might even take a detour or two."

"Oh, I love your detours," Mrs. Charles said.

Why did she get the impression her mother hadn't been referring to a destination?

As hard as Rylee tried, she couldn't keep the tears from falling as her parents backed out of her driveway. Canten stood in the yard with her and hugged her from behind. One last performance for the benefit of her parents.

Kissing the back of her head, he said, "Please stop crying. You're killing me here. We'll drive to Florida soon to see them if you want."

Rylee forced her way out of his arms, then turned to face him. "No, we won't, because soon, you'll probably be gone too." A beat later, she closed her eyes and rested a hand on her forehead. "I'm sorry. I'm sorry. I didn't mean to snap at you. It's been a rough week. And these cramps . . ."

Canten captured her hand and led her inside the house, then to her bedroom. "Lay down. I'll be right back."

"I don't have time to take a nap," Rylee said. "I have to clean the kitchen." Keeping busy kept her mind off everything.

"Woman, do not leave that bed," he said. "I'll be right back," he repeated.

"Fine," she said with an eye roll.

Rylee twiddled her thumbs as she waited for Canten to return. She eyed the door. *What is taking him so long?* When the microwave dinged, her brows furrowed. *Oh no. Is he trying to cook again?* Surely he couldn't go wrong using the microwave. Rylee came up on her elbows. *What's he doing?*

Canten reappeared carrying a bottled water, ibuprofen, and a . . . *steaming towel?*

"Hold out your hand."

When she did, he dumped two pills into it, then passed her the water. Once she'd swallowed, he directed her flat on the bed, lifted her shirt to expose her stomach, shook the towel a couple of times, then spread the warm fabric in place.

She flinched from the feel of the warmth as her brain processed hot. But in actuality, it was comfortable to the touch. "That feels good," she said, closing her eyes in satisfaction.

"This is supposed to help with the cramps," he said. "I'll go and let you get some rest."

Rylee's eyes popped open. "No," came out a little too urgently. "Stay. Please."

"You sure?"

Rylee nodded.

Kicking out of his shoes, Canten climbed into bed and stretched out beside her. They both lay silent for a while. The heated towel on her stomach brought Rylee almost instant comfort.

"Thank you for this. And for what you did earlier. Offering to drive my parents to Florida."

"I think it would have been a nice drive," he said.

So did she.

"Were your parents talking about sex when they said something about detours?"

"Pretty sure they were. They act like horny teenagers instead of two people who should be somewhere playing bingo."

Canten laughed. "Your parents don't strike me as bingo players. I think it's great they clearly still enjoy each other after all these years.

Marriages like theirs are rare nowadays. Folks are lucky if they make it two years."

"My mom is my dad's *entire* world. And vice versa. They are definitely hashtag relationship goals," she said.

"They remind me of Senior and my mom before she died."

If Rylee remembered correctly, Canten's mother had died of heart disease. She rarely heard him talk about his mother. Clearly, her death was still very much a soft spot for him, so she didn't ask any questions. Just enjoyed the feel of him nestled beside her and considered how much she'd miss this when he was gone.

Instead of viewing the glass as half-empty, maybe she should see it as half-full. A possibility Canten wouldn't get the job still remained. Which meant he would remain in Honey Hill. Her gut told her it was a slim chance—but a chance, nonetheless.

Good upbringing taught her never to wish for another's misfortune, but in this case, Rylee ignored her parents' teachings and prayed, hoped, wished the job would go to someone else. But a second later, her conscience set in, and she took it all back. If anyone deserved a blessing, Canten did.

"You're hogging all the body pillow," Canten said.

"It's my favorite."

"You could share?"

"If I shared my pillow with you, I'd also be sharing my hopes and dreams, too, because I speak them into it every night."

"Let me hear."

When Rylee pushed a part of the pillow toward him, he rested his ear against it. She laughed at the animated faces he made.

"I knew it," he said.

"You knew what?" she asked with alarm as if the pillow had actually spoken to him.

"I can't tell you. It's a secret."

Since he was selling the house, Canten deemed it a good idea *not* to burn it down, so he hadn't tried his hand at baking another happy cake, as Zachary had called it. Instead, he'd gotten Ezekiel to bake him one on the low. Red velvet with vanilla-bean-cream-cheese frosting. Rylee's favorite.

Rylee's eyes widened when he slid the delectable dessert in front of her. "Who baked this?" Her gaze narrowed. "Are you cheating on me with another baker?"

"What do you mean, who baked this? *I* baked this."

She pursed her lips. "Number one, I didn't smell smoke when I arrived. Number two, the last time you 'baked a cake'"—she made air quotes—"I spent two hours scrubbing my oven."

Canten laughed. "Man, you are hard on a brother. Okay, I didn't bake it. I hired Ezekiel to do it."

She folded her arms across her chest, the move causing her breasts to rise. Canten tried to ignore it, but his body wouldn't cooperate. It had been far too long since her ample cleavage had spilled from his hands, his eager tongue had teased her nipples, their hungry mouths had explored each other. Far too long since he'd found his peace inside her.

Canten performed a quick calculation in his head. Her parents had been gone two days. He'd slept at his own place another two days. She'd had a headache one day. Five days. Ones that had felt like an eternity. As desperately as he wanted her, he hadn't pushed.

"So you *are* cheating on me. And with my associate. Shame on you."

He loved her quirky sense of humor. Chuckling, he said, "I couldn't have you bake your own cake, could I?"

"My cake?"

"Yes."

"Why did you get me a cake? And why does it say *thank you*?"

"Because I wanted to tell you how much I appreciate all you've done for me these past few months."

Rylee's brow arched. "All I've done for you? Canten, I should be the one giving *you* a cake. Heck, the whole bakery. You altered your entire life for me. And without a single second of hesitation. Well, maybe two or three seconds of hesitation."

They laughed.

"But seriously," she continued, "what I've done for you—prepared you a few meals—pales in comparison to what you've done for me. I'll never be able to repay you."

While she might have stuffed his belly, she'd also filled his heart, nourished his soul, fed his spirit. But how did he tell her something like that without making things weird? *I don't.* What would be the purpose? Things had simmered between them this long. Why stir the pot now? Especially when he'd be leaving soon.

Long-distance relationships rarely worked. And it wasn't like he could ask her to uproot and follow him to Charlotte on the hopes of their relationship working out. Sure, their fake relationship was perfect, but the real thing was always more complicated. Canten thought about David and Reva. They had been two of the most in-love people he'd known. If they hadn't made it, did anyone else really stand a chance?

Besides, what gave him the right to even ask such a thing of Rylee? Her business was here. Her family (Sebastian) was here. Her friends were here. In Charlotte, she'd be starting over from scratch. Her life here in Honey Hill was already well established. He couldn't ask her to give it all up for him. She couldn't go, and he couldn't stay.

"Your friendship is payment enough. And to be honest, the past few months have been . . . nice."

A low-wattage smile touched Rylee's lips. "I agree."

"So I have good news," he said.

"Katrina asked you to marry her?" Rylee said with a snicker.

"You've got jokes." Since the ride-along, Katrina had no longer been the nuisance she'd once been. When they saw each other, they spoke and kept it moving. The woman no longer attempted to hold meaningless conversations or make feeble attempts to get him to notice her. He liked this new dynamic.

"I'm just messing. What's your good news?"

"I've officially been offered the bureau commander position," Canten said. "Just like you said I would," he added for no particular reason other than it sounded good.

Rylee's body went stiff, and the joyful expression she'd worn minutes earlier faded. She stared at him, her face unreadable. Seconds later, her head jerked as if she'd been snatched back to reality.

"*Wow.* That's great. Congratulations. That's really great. I'm so happy for you. You deserve this. *Wow.* This is . . . great. Amazing news." Her glow dimmed a little. "Really great. When do you leave?"

"I'm not sure yet. A few weeks, maybe? I've spoken to a Realtor about putting the house on the market." Canten wasn't sure why he kept saying that. He'd said the same to Senior. As if selling his home would give the offer more legitimacy.

"I see," she said.

Rylee flashed a look he couldn't quite name. Her lips parted as if she wanted to say something, closed, parted, then closed again. She twiddled with her fingers the way she did when nervous. Clearly, there was something she wanted or needed to say. What? And why was she holding it back?

Whatever thoughts bounced around in her head she obviously dismissed, because her body finally relaxed and the corners of her mouth quirked upward. However, she wasn't quite selling the cheerful look on her face.

"This is certainly good news. Not just good, great." She clapped her hands together. "Let's have cake to celebrate. We should also do something this weekend. A cookout, maybe? You, me, Lunden, Quade, Senior. Sebastian, if he's in town. It'll be fun."

"We'll see," he said. Which meant no. He didn't want a hoopla over him.

Canten wholeheartedly believed Rylee was genuinely happy for him. But while he couldn't quite put his finger on what, something told him Rylee wasn't as gung ho over the news as she would have him believe. Maybe it was all the babbling she'd done. Going with the flow, he echoed her words: "Let's have cake."

He cut a single slice, forked up a bite, and brought it to Rylee's mouth. When she attempted to eat it, he pulled it away. After his second time doing this, she said, "Really? You're playing keep-away with the cake?" She released an exasperated sigh, stood, and walked off.

Canten's head jerked in surprise. *What the hell just happened?* Placing the fork down, he trailed her into the living room. "What's wrong? What was that all about?"

"I just wanted cake."

His brows furrowed. "Wait. Are you seriously upset?"

"You can't just go around teasing a person with delicious cake, get their mouth watering for it, and then just snatch it away. People have feelings for cake. Strong feelings."

Damn, had he known tasting the cake meant that much to her, he would have immediately let her have it. "Rylee, it's really not that serious. I was just playing around. Come back to the table. You can have all the cake you want. Hell, the whole cake if you want it. It's yours."

"It's not mine. That's the problem."

Convinced cake couldn't cause such discord, he said, "What's really going on here?"

Rylee rested a hand on her forehead. "Nothing. I'm just . . ."

"Tired," he said, finishing her sentence. "You use that excuse a lot. I've figured out it's when you're trying to mask what you truly feel or really want to say. If you have something to say, Rylee, just say it."

"I should go," she said, then turned and headed for the door.

"Say something, Rylee. Do you think I'm making a mistake? Do you think I should stay in Honey Hill? Say something. Anything. Just stop hiding from me."

She whipped around. "Yes! Yes, I think you are making a mistake. Yes, I think you should stay in Honey Hill. But I only think these things because *I* want you to stay."

"Why?"

A look of surprise spread across her face. "Why?"

"Yes, Rylee. Why? Why do you want me to stay?"

"Because I . . ." Her gaze left him briefly. "Because I like having you around." She attempted a smile that wobbled, then fell flat. Her shoulders slumped, and she seemed to deflate a bit. "I'm just being selfish."

That's it? She likes having me around? The fact that he sounded like nothing more than a puppy to her annoyed him until he considered how silly he was being. The past few months had been nothing more than a stage performance. He couldn't fault her for being better at remembering that than he had been. "You're just being honest," he said.

"Right." She closed the distance between them. "This is your moment, Sheriff Barnes. Charlotte is damn lucky to get you. And I'm going to be your biggest cheerleader."

Rylee cradled his face between her hands and pressed a single delicate kiss to his lips that replenished his soul. She pulled away and stared at him for several long seconds. He'd read once that the eyes said what mouths failed to say. If that were the case, he was revealing a whole lot at this moment. Hers weren't so quiet either.

"You better write," she said.

Canten laughed.

"Good night, Canten. Sweet dreams."

"Good night, Rylee. Sweet dreams to you."

Canten watched as Rylee made her way safely inside her house. She flicked the porch light twice. Another way they had of saying good night. After cleaning the kitchen, rereading the offer letter twice, tossing it aside, and taking a hot shower, he climbed into bed. The silence was deafening, so he activated the music subscription on his phone.

Sam Cooke's "Nothing Can Change This Love" poured through the speaker, scattering his thoughts. The first line made him think of Rylee and when she'd joked about him writing. He smiled, claimed his phone, dialed the radio station, and made a request.

Removing the letter from the dresser again, he reread it for the third time that night. The words hadn't changed. Yet it felt as if something inside him had changed. "Am I getting cold feet?" he asked himself. He tossed the pages back onto the nightstand. "It'll pass." The night before his and Jayla's wedding, he'd gotten ice-cold feet and briefly questioned if he'd been making a mistake. This felt like that. Luckily, it had passed, and he'd experienced some of the happiest years of his life. *The same will hold true for Charlotte,* he told himself.

His cell phone rang, slicing into his thoughts. *David Pollock* flashed across his screen. What was the man doing calling him at close to ten at night? He hoped everything was okay. "Hello?"

"Congratulations, man," David said, slurring his words. "You're going to make one hell of a bureau commander."

"Thank you," Canten said. "It's late. Everything okay?"

"Yeah, yeah, everything's fine. I meant to call you earlier, but I forgot."

"You been drinking, Detective Pollock?"

David chuckled. "Always on the job. Just one or two beers, Sheriff Barnes," he said. "Maybe three. Don't worry. I'm not stupid enough to drive."

Tequila shots had been David's poison. Canten wagered the man had consumed a few.

David continued, "I'm just . . ." His words trailed. *"Shit. Shit."*

"You with me, Pollock?"

"Jayla would have been proud of you, man," David said out of the blue. "She'd wanted you to have that title more than you wanted it. She had your future all planned out. First bureau commander, then deputy chief, finally, chief of police. She had big dreams for you. I remember when all you had wanted was to be a small-town sheriff like your grandfather. Remember how she laughed at that?"

The memory was like a slap in the face to Canten. He recalled how he'd felt that night at the dinner table. As if his simple dream hadn't been valid. "Maybe you should get some—"

"Her dream for you has finally come true. Too bad she's not here to appreciate it," David said. "But I know she's looking down from heaven."

"Our dream," Canten said. He wasn't sure if it was more for David or himself. "Our dream," he repeated.

"Nah," David said.

Nah? What the hell did that mean? Remembering the man was drunk and talking out the side of his neck doused some of the frustration swelling inside Canten.

"You're lucky, Barnes. Always have been. You have someone special in your life. Promise me you won't blow it and wind up alone. Just like me."

When the man's voice cracked, Canten hoped David wouldn't start to cry.

"And maybe you should stay true to *your* dream. Jayla was ambitious, but I think she had this one all wrong. Shit. I gotta go, Barnes. My popcorn's burning. I'll call you soon."

The line disconnected.

Canten leaned forward and rested his elbows on his thighs. David's words haunted him. The man had brought back some long-abandoned memories. There had been a time in his life when his one and only dream had been to hold the job he currently held. *Cold feet,* he told himself a second later. *Just cold feet.* It would pass.

CHAPTER 31

Rylee wished she could stop thinking about what Canten had told her a couple of days ago, especially when she should have been relaxing and enjoying this amazing massage. But she couldn't. His words continued to ring in her ears like annoying cowbells, determined to drive her deaf and insane.

When she recalled how she'd blown up at him over the cake, she groaned from embarrassment. The cake had had nothing to do with it. She'd used it as an analogy because she hadn't had the guts to say what she'd wanted to say.

The news shouldn't have come as a shock. She'd known the chances of him being offered the job had been great. So why had it rattled her? Because until now, there had been a small window of hope to peep through. Unfortunately, said window had been slammed shut on her fingers and the curtains snatched closed.

Rylee cleared her mind of all things Canten and focused on the calming scent of lavender and the strong hands kneading into her muscles.

"I needed this," Lunden said on the massage table next to Rylee's.

"So did I," Rylee said. Stress had her shoulders in knots.

"Are you okay? You've been awfully quiet," Lunden said.

"Are you saying I usually talk too much?" Rylee asked.

Lunden laughed. "Of course not."

"I'm good. Just tired." The *just tired* made her recall what Canten had said. That she used the words to mask what she really felt or wanted to say. He'd been right. She hated that he knew her so well. "The bakery has been insanely busy with online orders. Who knew Katrina had such a dedicated following or that she would *ever* tell them to patronize my shop?"

Canten had mentioned to Rylee the conversation he'd had with Katrina. The one where she'd told him Hilary had influenced her behavior. While that might have been true, Rylee knew Katrina's interest in Canten had been real. However, the handsome man she'd seen Katrina strolling down the sidewalk with earlier in the week suggested Katrina had her hooks into someone else. *Poor fellow.*

"Stranger things have happened," Lunden said.

After an hour of being chopped, squeezed, and rubbed, Rylee and Lunden made their way to Happi Curls. Usually, Rylee would have protested when Lunden insisted they walk, but today she didn't. The sun wasn't beating down on them. The temperature was a comfortable eighty-two degrees with a gentle breeze. An overcast grayed the sky as if Mother Nature wasn't sure whether she should allow it to rain, but according to meteorologist Cannon, it wouldn't. Rylee hoped not because she would be pissed if she got her hair done and then got caught in a downpour.

As usual, laughter could be heard spilling from the shop. Entering, Rylee and Lunden spoke to the other women occupying the space.

"You two are just in time. We're trying to figure out who's 'to you from me,'" Happi said.

Lunden flashed a confused expression. "What?"

"On the radio," Happi clarified. "The person who keeps anonymously dedicating songs."

"Ah," Lunden said, easing into Happi's chair. "It's romantic. But do you think it's someone in Honey Hill? The station broadcasts over three counties."

Rylee took a seat at the empty chair next to Happi's workstation and thought about the last tune that had been dedicated. "It has to be someone mature, right? Both songs were clearly chosen by someone with quality taste in music. Patti LaBelle. Sam Cooke. Classics. No youngster would have chosen either of those."

The room agreed.

"Do you think it's a man or a woman?" Happi asked Rylee.

"Hard to say. Initially, I would have said a woman because of the Patti song, but then they followed up with Sam Cooke."

"I bet Lady Sunshine knows," Lunden said.

"No, she doesn't," Happi said. "She was the first person I asked. It's even a mystery to her, and that's saying something."

A puzzle Lady Sunshine couldn't piece together? Times were changing in Honey Hill. Rylee, Lunden, and Happi spent the time it took Happi to work her magic on their hair ruling out half the town for one reason or another. By the time Rylee and Lunden said goodbye, they were no closer to solving the mystery than they had been when they'd arrived.

"Zachary keeps asking me if he can go on another ride-along with Canten," Lunden said out of the blue. "I think he got a kick out of his friends seeing him riding around town with the sheriff. They all thought it was 'so cool,' as he put it."

"I'm taking Canten out to celebrate tonight." While Canten hadn't wanted a shindig, he hadn't objected to her taking him to dinner. Though she would probably have to fight him to pay the bill. "I'll let him know. Hopefully, he can arrange something before he leaves." *Before he leaves.* A knot tightened in Rylee's stomach at the thought.

"You haven't said much about that," Lunden said. "Canten's leaving," she clarified. "Want to talk about it?"

Rylee wasn't sure she could without tears. "No."

"Okay," Lunden said delicately. "Want to go for ice cream?"

At the mention of ice cream, Rylee couldn't help but think about what had happened the last time they'd visited the ice cream shop. "I live my life in fear, Lu," Rylee said.

"What? That's ridiculous. You're one of the most fearless women I know. A warrior."

"I put up a good front. At one point in my marriage, I thought Lucas was having an affair," she said.

Lunden flashed a look of concern. "You never told me that. Was he?"

Rylee shrugged. "I don't know. I was too afraid to ask the question because I feared the answer. I went on with life smiling like everything was perfect when it was far from it." Rylee batted away tears and continued, "I loved my place in Goldsboro, but after the online-dating incident, I was too afraid to stay. Instead of telling my mother I was happily single, I chose to lie about being in a relationship because I feared she would think I was incapable of moving forward."

"Oh, Ry."

"And worst of all, I had the opportunity to tell Canten I've fallen head over heels in love with him, but I blew it." Scared to leave her comfort zone. Afraid of what he might have said. Terrified by the fact he might not have felt the same. Petrified that he did but would still choose to leave her behind.

Lunden stopped and faced Rylee. "You are so much fiercer than you know."

Rylee rolled her eyes heavenward. "Coming from my best friend."

"Coming from a strong woman who knows strong women. It took courage to move forward after Lucas's death. It took bravery to start your business from the ground up. You didn't let that bastard who'd tried to violate you break you. That's fortitude. And it takes heart to love someone, especially when doing so scares the hell out of you. How could you not see how mighty you are?"

Rylee swallowed hard to force down the lump of emotion lodged in her throat. "Well, when you put it like that."

They laughed.

Starting to move again, Lunden said, "You know, there's still time to tell Canten how you feel. From what I understand, he still hasn't accepted the job offer. Seems kind of strange it's taking him so long to do so. Maybe he's waiting for a special baker to give him a reason to stay."

If he cared about her, wouldn't he already have a reason?

Later that evening, Rylee put the finishing touches on her outfit, then moved to the full-length mirror and performed a turn. "Perfect," she said, admiring herself in the deep-purple sequin tube top and silky fitted capris. The black, sparkly heels paired well with the outfit. She would definitely turn heads in this. Not that it had been her goal when she'd decided on her attire.

Canten proved as punctual as usual when he rang her bell at exactly six forty-five. Their reservations weren't until seven thirty, so they had a little time to kill before they had to leave. *No sex,* she reminded herself.

After the whole false-pregnancy ordeal—*dammit, Lunden*—she'd decided to no longer carry on a sexual relationship with Canten. Her body hadn't liked the decision, but her sanity had approved. Every time their bodies had joined, she'd felt even more attached to him. She needed to sever those strings.

With so much going on in Canten's life, he was clearly too occupied to think about sex, because he hadn't so much as brushed up against her. Which usually led them to the bedroom. Or maybe he, too, needed to break their connection. Either way, she'd convinced herself it was for the best.

After giving herself one last perusal, she headed to the front to let him in. Rylee opened the door and actually moaned at the sight of Canten in the black-on-black getup. *Damn.* Black button-down shirt—the top few buttons unfastened—a black suit, and black shoes.

How the hell was she supposed to wean herself off him when he'd shown up at her door looking like a chicken dinner with all the fixings? And boy, was she famished.

"Hey," she said, stepping aside to welcome him in.

"Hey."

Usually, Canten's eyes gobbled her up whole. Right now, they barely nibbled. Obviously, her outfit wasn't as jaw dropping as she'd thought. No, that wasn't it. Something felt off with him.

Her body shuddered at how delicious he smelled as he passed by. She inhaled deeply to get another fix of him. Pushing the door closed, she took a moment to pull herself together. "Is everything okay?" she said, turning to face him.

In the blink of an eye, Canten had her against the door, her arms pinned above her head. His mouth crashed down onto hers, and he kissed her as if he harbored a grudge against her lips. The kiss was everything. Urgent. Thorough. Raw. Fulfilling. Wanted. God, it was wanted. Far more than Rylee felt comfortable admitting.

They kissed long and hard for what felt like an eternity. When Canten finally broke their mouths apart, their connection left her breathless. Her chest heaved up and down in rapid succession. He'd kissed her with fervor plenty of times before but not like this. Not in this desperate, needy manner.

Canten rested his forehead against hers. "I know you've been pulling away from me, and I've respected that. I've never wanted you to feel obligated to lay with me," he said. "But I need you tonight, Rylee. More than I've ever needed anyone or anything in my life."

How the hell was she supposed to respond to that? Seeing the pure desperation in his eyes snatched her breath away.

"Tomorrow, we can hit the reset button, but tonight, I need you. I need you," he repeated.

Rylee had never witnessed him so vulnerable. What had happened to put him in such peril? It didn't matter. All that mattered was that she held the key that would free him. Cradling his face between her hands, she whispered, "Then take me."

Canten could barely control himself. Kissing Rylee had awakened a caged and starving beast inside him. The second she'd offered herself to him had unleashed it. He hoisted her into his arms and kissed her the entire walk to her bedroom.

Clothes flew in every direction until they both stood naked. Every action from that point forward became a blur. Him tasting every inch of her, her reciprocating. However, time stood still the moment he slid inside her wet heat. They cried out in unison.

She felt better than he remembered. If that was even possible. Not wanting the moment to end prematurely, Canten glided in and out of her with slow, steady strokes. Still, even that was proving too much for him to handle. He kissed along her shoulder, neck, and jawline and to her ear. "You're my peace," he whispered. "Being inside you—" His words were clipped by the clench of an impending orgasm.

Canten slowed his movements even more to ward off the release. He fought to ignore how good Rylee felt. Prayed for more strength. In the end, none of it worked. He exploded with the force of an angry volcano. He growled in both pleasure and pain. The latter caused by Rylee's nails digging into his flesh. But that, too, brought him a level of delight.

When Rylee came seconds after him, he couldn't help but think how in tune their bodies were to each other. The blood whooshing in his ears muffled her sounds of satisfaction.

Canten's body trembled, heart raced, lungs burned. Still, he continued to rock in and out of Rylee with clumsy strokes until he had zero left to give. Collapsing onto his back, he pulled Rylee to him. They lay in blissful silence for a long time. When he'd arrived at her door, he'd had the weight of the world on his shoulders. Now, he felt as light as air.

"The man who showed up at my door tonight is not a man I'm used to seeing. Do you want to take a late-night stroll and tell me what's wrong?"

Late-night stroll? Hell, after what his body had just gone through, he was lucky he could still talk. Walking was definitely out of the question.

"I'm fine. *Just tired*," he said. Rylee pinched his nipple. *"Ouch."* He kissed her fingertips. "What's this late-night stroll you speak of?"

"When I have a lot on my mind, I walk to the square, sit in the gazebo, and quiet my thoughts. It helps."

"Don't tell me that, Rylee. I don't want to think about you walking the streets at night alone." And since he doubted she would listen to him if he told her to stop, he made a mental note to adjust the nightly patrols to include multiple passes of the gazebo.

"Sheriff Barnes, Honey Hill is one of the safest places in America to live because of you. The way you've dedicated your attention to the town and its residents has given us all a sense of comfort. I'm never afraid to walk down the streets here. Day or night. Thanks to you, I know I'm safe."

"You're giving me too much credit. I haven't done anything spectacular here, Rylee."

Rylee's head rose to eye him. "I really think Mrs. Rogers would disagree," she said.

Last summer he'd given Mrs. Rogers CPR when she'd collapsed at the church picnic. Doc Vickers had said if it hadn't been for Canten's quick actions, the woman would have died. "I was just doing my job," he said.

Rylee continued, "And what about Ida Davidson? It wasn't your job to handle her yard work while her husband recovered."

Mr. Davidson had fallen down the stairs after a bout of vertigo and broken his leg. Figuring Mrs. Ida could have used one less thing to worry about, he'd done the neighborly thing and seen to the upkeep of their yard. "Can you imagine that sixty-year-old woman trying to cut grass?" he said.

Rylee laughed. "What about the ramp you built for Mr. Davidson?"

"I didn't do that alone. Sebastian and a few other guys helped."

"Yes, but Sebastian said it had been your idea. Face it—you've been a lot of things to Honey Hill and its residents, not just its sheriff. It's one of the reasons you'll be missed so much."

Just following in his grandfather's shoes. He'd seen the man's love for Honey Hill firsthand. Giving food to the hungry, leaving money in people's mailboxes when they didn't have enough to pay their mortgage. Clothing the near naked. The man had made an impact here. One of Canten's goals when he'd first accepted his current position had been to continue the work his grandfather had started. Was he truly finished?

CHAPTER 32

Rylee rarely stayed at the bakery this late, but it was nearing ten, and she was still here cranking away, finishing the full-size sheet cake she'd started earlier, along with a few other tasks. Canten would probably freak if he knew she was here alone at this late hour. But since he'd gone out of town on unexpected business, she guessed he wouldn't find out. Before going home, she'd need to take a trip to the gazebo. A lot plagued her thoughts these days.

Rylee thought about their weekend together. Three days later, and her body still tingled. So much for weaning herself off him. What the hell was it about Canten that made her so damn weak?

Everything.

It wasn't just one single huge thing that drew her to Canten but a million small ones. The way he prioritized Honey Hill. The love he showed Senior. The concern he showed her. His selflessness. The way he touched her, teased her, made her feel so special. Both in and out of bed.

Rylee sighed. She had it bad for him. And as soon as he returned, she planned to tell him. Maybe. Possibly. Yes, she would. Not that she expected him to alter his plans. In fact, that was the last thing she wanted him to do. But she wanted him to know. Simple as that. She wanted Sheriff Canten Barnes to know she loved him.

There hadn't been a dedication the past several nights, so every time the DJ came over the radio, Rylee's ears perked. "Okay, ladies and gents, our mystery caller has a special dedication tonight. Many of you have wondered about the infamous 'to you from me' caller. Well, you might get the opportunity to find out. Stay tuned after this song by the incomparable Otis Redding for a special message. 'You,' wherever you are, I hope you're listening." A beat later, "That's How Strong My Love Is" poured through the speakers.

Rylee's phone rang, startling her. Lunden's name flashed across her screen. Removing her gloves, she made the call active. "Hello."

"Oh my God. Are you listening to the radio?" Lunden asked.

"Yes. Do you think they're going to reveal names?"

"I hope so. We've been kept in suspense for far too long. I love this song, but Big O needs to sing just a little faster. What is this, the extended version?"

Rylee laughed. A minute or so later, the song faded, and the DJ's voice returned.

"We're back, lovers. And as promised, a special message. 'Take a late-night stroll, and meet me at the place where you go to clear your mind.'"

Rylee froze. "Wh-what did he say?"

"Something about meeting for a late-night stroll." Lunden sighed. "I guess we'll have to keep wondering."

"Lu, I'll call you back, okay?"

"Is everything—"

Rylee ended the call before Lunden could respond. Removing her apron, she left the kitchen and slowly made her way to the front of the bakery. Stopping momentarily, she took a deep breath, then continued. Once outside, she sent a glance toward the square. A second later, she gasped, then slapped a hand over her mouth.

Canten.

Rylee's heart pounded in her chest, and she trembled from excitement. All this time, Canten had been the mystery caller "me." And she'd been the famous "you." Elation filled her, but instead of sprinting toward him like they did in the movies, she darted back into the bakery.

※

From the gazebo, Canten watched Rylee exit, send a glance toward the square, slap her hand over her mouth, then dart back inside the bakery. This was not how he'd seen the events play out in his head.

In his version, Rylee had come out to see him standing at the gazebo, squealed loudly enough to startle wildlife for miles, dashed toward the square, and flung herself into his arms. In turn, he'd spun her around again and again, kissed as if their lips hadn't touched in several lifetimes, then confessed their undying love for one another. Like they did in the movies. Unfortunately, real life wasn't so well scripted.

Moments later, Canten entered the bakery to see Rylee pacing back and forth, her arms wrapped tightly around her body. "Honestly, that's not quite how I'd imagined you would respond," he said.

Rylee continued to move. "I . . . I don't . . ." She stopped abruptly and faced him, concern etching her beautiful face. "What are you doing, Canten?"

"Reclaiming *my* dream."

Rylee's brows furrowed. "What does that mean?"

"It took a late-night phone call from an inebriated man to make me realize something important."

"Which is?"

"That I'm not finished."

Confusion spread across Rylee's face. "Again, what does that mean?"

"I'm not finished with my grandfather's work here. I'm not finished living *my* dream. No one else's. *Mine.* And I'm damn sure not finished loving you."

Rylee gasped, her trembling hand coming to rest over her heart. "W-what did you say?"

Canten closed the distance between them. "The past few months we've pretended to be something we're not. But I think we are, Rylee. We're everything we masqueraded to be. I love you, Rylee Harris. And I have for a very long time. There is something special about you, woman. Magical, even. You freed me, and I didn't even know I was caged."

Rylee rapidly batted her glistening eyes, then studied him long and hard. "I . . ." She blew a hard breath and shook her head. "There's no way we can work, Canten. You said it yourself: long-distance relationships rarely work."

"I'm not asking you to be in a long-distance relationship."

A troubled look spread across Rylee's face. "I can't leave Honey Hill, if that's what you're asking," she said. "I'm sorry, but I can't."

"That's perfect because neither can I."

"I don't get it."

"I drove to Charlotte to tell them face to face that I won't be accepting the bureau commander position," he said.

"*What!* You can't do this, Canten. You can't turn down this amazing opportunity. Not for me. I'd never forgive myself if you gave up your dream for me. And in the long run, you would never forgive me either. I've been here before. I don't want you to resent me. It's best if—"

Canten cradled her face between his hands. "*Shh.* Take a breath."

Rylee drew in a stream of air.

"Yes, you influenced my decision, Rylee. I won't lie and say you didn't. But ultimately, I didn't do this for you. I did it for me."

"But . . . why? This is what you've always wanted. I don't understand why you would let it slip away."

"You're right, buttercup—this is what I've always wanted. And I damn sure don't intend to let you slip away." He chuckled. "Oh, wait, you're talking about the job."

Rylee grinned, feeling so damn special that it felt as if she floated. "Yes."

"My dream, before I allowed it to become overly complex, had always been to do *exactly* what I'm doing now. Be the best lawman I can be for the small town I love."

"You are that without question," she said.

"Somewhere along the way, I lost sight of what *I* truly wanted and settled for what others wanted for me."

"Jayla?" she asked softly.

Canten nodded. "I don't fault her for wanting to push me toward my full potential. But the man I was then is not the same man I am now. Back then I chose to believe my simple dream wasn't big enough. I don't think that any longer."

"What happened to change your mind?"

"*You* happened, Rylee Harris. The other night in bed, you pointed out that I am far more to Honey Hill than just its sheriff. In that moment, you made me realize just how colossal a simple dream can be. You showed me that I've been dreaming big all along. I love so many things about you, Rylee. But what I love most is the way you breathe life into me, the way you make me feel."

Rylee's lips curled into a teeny smile. "How do I make you feel?"

"Like a king on the throne."

"Because you are," she said.

"Be my queen."

Rylee rested a hand against her forehead. "This is—"

"How it was always supposed to be," he said, completing her thought. "I don't need your mouth to tell me what your touch, your eyes, your body, your heart have already told me, Rylee. But I really want to hear you say it," he said.

"Hear me say what? That you are absolutely insane? Fine. Canten Barnes, you are absolutely insane." She regarded him with loving eyes.

"Or do you want to hear me say I am head over heels, undeniably, deliriously in love with you?"

"That part," he said.

"*Fine.* Sheriff Canten Barnes, I am head over heels, undeniably, deliriously in love with you. And I have been for a very long time. You have no idea how long I've wanted to say this to you. Thank you for giving me the courage to say it now."

"Why didn't you just say it before?"

"Because you had a plan and I didn't see where I fit into it."

"Then I should probably show you." He covered her mouth with his. They kissed in a slow, sensual manner, laminating their new normal. Pulling away, he stared into her eyes. "I love you, Rylee Harris."

"I love you, Sheriff Barnes. Wholly." She grinned.

"What?"

"I'm so glad we don't have to tell my parents anything."

"*Actually*, buttercup, we do. We need to make this right," he said. "That means telling them everything."

"*But—*"

Before Rylee could finish, the bakery door banged open. Rylee screamed, causing Lunden to do the same. They both looked spooked.

"What's wrong?" Rylee asked with urgency.

She clung to Canten for apparent safety. She knew he would protect her from anything.

"Nothing. You ended our call so abruptly I thought something was wrong with you. I came to make sure you were okay." A smile replaced Lunden's horrified expression. "I see that you are. Hey, Sheriff."

"Mayor."

A second later Quade and Zachary pushed through the door. Clearly, Quade hadn't allowed Lunden to venture here alone. He totally understood the desire to protect the woman you loved.

"I tried to tell my wife you were fine," Quade said, draping an arm around Lunden's shoulders. "But she had to see for herself."

"Hey, Sheriff," Zachary said, wearing airplane pajamas. Obviously, he'd been plucked out of bed. He grinned, revealing a missing lower tooth. "Aunt Rylee, are you having an orgasma?"

All eyes darted toward Zachary.

An orgasma?

Wide eyed, Lunden said, "*Zachary!* Where did you hear that word?"

"I heard you and Aunt Rylee talking on the porch. Aunt Rylee said she gets an orgasma every time Sheriff Canten touches her. I bet it means you get really happy, because Aunt Rylee is smiling really big right now."

"It means you get really, *really* happy, son," Quade said, making them all laugh.

Lunden pinched Quade. What was with these Honey Hill women and pinching?

"I knew it. So are you, Aunt Rylee?" Zachary asked with eyes round with excitement. "Are you having an orgasma?"

Rylee eyed Canten. "Yes, I am. And something tells me it's never going to end."

Damn right.

EPILOGUE

A month later . . .

Rylee's horoscope had lied. It had said her day would be filled with marvelous surprises. There had been nothing marvelous about having to tell her parents she'd lied to them. It had been even less marvelous when her mother had told her she'd already known about her and Canten.

Rylee had been so worried about everyone else spilling the beans, but she'd inadvertently been the one who'd let the cat out of the bag. A week after returning to Florida, her mother had received a call from Lady Sunshine with the most peculiar question: Why were Rylee and the sheriff faking their relationship?

Apparently, the day of Lunden's dress fitting, Rylee had been recorded on the in-store camera *boasting*—as her mother had put it—about how good she and Canten were at faking a relationship.

Surprisingly, Lady Sunshine had urged her mother to remain quiet. Why? Because, apparently, Lady Sunshine had seen Rylee and Canten's future. According to Lady Sunshine, their journey would begin with an elephant wearing a lotus flower. That part still made Rylee laugh. How ridiculous. Who knew Lady Sunshine could actually keep a secret?

Luckily, her mother had claimed to understand why Rylee had gone to such lengths. But she'd chastised her for dragging Canten into her mess. In their eyes, he'd done nothing wrong, simply been a great friend to a friend in need. They loved their Canten. Her mother had promised to butt out of both her and Sebastian's love lives.

Unfortunately, Rylee hadn't believed for one second she planned to butt out of Sebastian's love life, especially when her mother had asked a hundred questions about Happi before ending their call. Happi and Sebastian were a connection Rylee approved of. But it would take a miracle to bring together two people who shunned love.

Rylee eyed the bed inside Canten's guest room, where the portrait Jacques-Pierre had drawn of them rested. Canten had been adamant about wanting it to grace the most prominent wall in the room. Her gaze slid to the framed image of Jayla sitting on the nightstand. When Canten had asked why she'd placed it there, she'd told him Jayla was a part of their story. Canten reentered the room, put his hand behind her neck, and pulled her mouth to his.

"Hmm," she moaned from the sweet kiss.

Pulling away, he said, "Did you miss me?"

"Always. You okay? It took you an awfully long time in the bathroom."

"I'm perfect, buttercup," he said with a wink.

While Rylee wouldn't tell him this, she loved when he called her that. Actually, she guessed the horoscope hadn't been all wrong. Staring at Canten in a white T-shirt and paint-splattered jeans did bring about marvelous sensations. They'd finally gotten around to painting his spare bedroom.

"You know what happens when you look at me with those hungry eyes," Canten said.

"Feed me," she said.

"Oh, I plan to. After we finish this wall," he said.

She laughed. "Killjoy."

Rylee thought about the last time they'd painted a wall, and smiled. It had started them on one hell of a journey. "Babe?"

"Buttercup?"

"Aren't you forgetting something?"

Canten flashed a confused look.

"My water," she said.

"Damn. I knew I was forgetting something. I left it on the table. Let me wipe my hands, and I'll grab it."

"I got it," she said, placing her paintbrush down.

"You're just trying to get out of painting."

Rylee winked and headed out the room but stopped at the door and backtracked. "Funny story. A few weeks back, I got a correspondence from my pharmacy. A recall on my birth control pills. A possible mix-up—"

Canten whipped toward her. "Rylee, are we pregnant?"

"What? No." She gave a nervous laugh.

"Oh," he said.

"Why do you look so disappointed?"

He shrugged. "I guess I just got a little excited at the idea of being a daddy. I think I'd make a good father. Zachary seems to think so."

"And so do I," she said. "I actually thought I was pregnant. I took like six pregnancy tests, and they all came out positive." She briefly recalled that crazy day.

Canten flashed a look of confusion. "Wait." His brows knit. "If they all came out positive, doesn't that mean you *are* pregnant? All six pregnancy tests can't be wrong, right?"

"They weren't pregnancy tests."

"Okay, I'm officially confused."

"Apparently, the only thing that can rattle our fearless mayor is purchasing pregnancy tests, which she did for me. The BFF thing and all. But instead of grabbing pregnancy tests"—Rylee snickered—"she mistakenly got *ovulation* tests. Neither one of us noticed."

Canten burst into laughter.

Rylee rested her hands on her hips. Why did this feel so much like déjà vu? "Sheriff Barnes, do you recall what happened the last time you laughed at me while we painted a room?"

"In my defense," he said, through laughter, "you did start with the words *funny story*. And it is." He laughed harder.

She pouted playfully, folded her arms across her chest, and stuck out her bottom lip for effect.

"Aw, come here, buttercup. Let me touch you and give you an *orgasma*." He wrapped his arms around her and kissed her gently. "Does this make you feel really, really happy?"

"I don't think anything in this world could make me feel happier."

Canten kissed her again, then popped her on the behind. "Grab me a water too."

Rylee rounded the corner to the kitchen and froze. Her eyes spread wide, her heart rate kicked up, and the room grew a little unsteady. For several seconds, all she could do was blink dumbly. On the table, next to her water bottle, sat the most beautiful green crystal elephant. Adorning its trunk, a ring encrusted with diamonds.

Finally, her heavy feet trudged forward. She reached for the ring, pulled back, then reached for it again, retrieving the platinum-colored piece from the trunk. A shaky hand covered her mouth when she realized the top of the ring resembled a . . . *lotus flower*. The conversation she'd had with her mother instantly popped into her head. *Our journey begins with an elephant wearing a lotus flower.* Rylee's heart thudded against her rib cage.

Large sparkling petals acted as a bed for the large round center diamond. More diamonds covered both sides of the ring. It was . . . *gorgeous*.

Before she could process anything beyond the obvious, music began to play from the small speaker also on the table. Al Green's "Let's Stay Together."

"I . . . I'm so in love with you," Canten sang behind her.

Rylee whipped around so fast she nearly stumbled over her own feet.

Continuing to sing, he reached over and removed the ring from her trembling fingers. A second later, he went down on one knee in front of her. "I can't promise you riches. I can't promise you every day will be sunshine and roses. But what I can promise you is that I'll love you on your best days. I'll love you even harder on your worst. And I'll love you all the days in between. I promise you I'll do my damnedest to love you like you've never been loved before."

Tears streamed down Rylee's face, but she didn't bother wiping them away.

"I know you've been here before, and I get that you might be afraid. Don't be, because you haven't been here with me. I know you might be thinking to yourself this is too soon, but . . ." He shrugged. "When you know, you know. So, Rylee Athena Harris, will you marry me?"

Rylee dropped to her knees in front of him. With no hesitation, no second-guessing, and absolutely no fear, she said, "*Yes! Yes! Yes!* I'll marry you. Because I know. I know," she repeated.

When Canten slid the ring on her finger, she threw her arms around his neck with so much force they toppled over.

Once their laughter subsided, Rylee lay on her back, lifted her left hand into the air, and stared at her newly clad ring finger, then Canten. "You are chock full of surprises, Sheriff Barnes."

"Well, soon-to-be Mrs. Sheriff Barnes, you ain't seen nothing yet." He brushed a stray hair from her face. "I want to give you everything, Rylee. The moon. The stars. Love, laughter, a lifetime of happiness. And the wedding of your dreams. Your fairy-tale day. The one you dreamed of as a little girl. Whatever the cost."

Rylee rested a hand on his cheek, tears clouding her eyes. "I love you so much. *You* are my fairy tale, Sheriff Barnes. As long as you're waiting for me at the altar—and I don't care if it's in the middle of a pasture—it'll be my dream wedding because you're there."

"And I always will be."

Yep, her heart would be safe with the sheriff.

ABOUT THE AUTHOR

By day, Joy Avery works as a customer service assistant. By night, the North Carolina native travels to imaginary worlds—creating characters whose romantic journeys invariably end in happily ever after.

Since she was a young girl growing up in Garner, Joy knew she wanted to write. Stumbling onto romance novels, she discovered her passion for love stories; instantly, she knew these were the kinds of stories she wanted to pen. Real characters, real journeys, and real good love are what you'll find in a Joy Avery romance.

Joy is married with one child. When she's not writing, she enjoys reading, cake decorating, pretending to expertly play the piano, and driving her husband insane.

Joy is a member of Romance Writers of America and Heart of Carolina Romance Writers. Find her books and sign up for her Wings of Love newsletter at www.joyavery.com. Connect with her on Facebook, Twitter, and Pinterest (@authorjoyavery), or email her at authorjoyavery@gmail.com.